The
Man
Who
Loved
Birds

The
Man
Who
Loved
Birds

A Novel

FENTON JOHNSON

UNIVERSITY PRESS OF KENTUCKY

Published by The University Press of Kentucky

Scholarly publisher for the Commonwealth,
serving Bellarmine University, Berea College, Centre College of Kentucky,
Eastern Kentucky University, The Filson Historical Society, Georgetown
College, Kentucky Historical Society, Kentucky State University, Morehead
State University, Murray State University, Northern Kentucky University,
Transylvania University, University of Kentucky, University of Louisville,
and Western Kentucky University.
All rights reserved.

Editorial and Sales Offices: The University Press of Kentucky
663 South Limestone Street, Lexington, Kentucky 40508-4008
www.kentuckypress.com

Library of Congress Cataloging-in-Publication Data

Johnson, Fenton.
  The man who loved birds : a novel / Fenton Johnson.
    pages ; cm. — (Kentucky voices)
  ISBN 978-0-8131-6659-9 (hardcover : acid-free paper) —
  ISBN 978-0-8131-6661-2 (pdf) — ISBN 978-0-8131-6660-5 (epub)
  1. City and town life—Kentucky—Fiction. 2. Interpersonal relations—
Fiction. I. Title.
  PS3560.O3766M36 2016
  813'.54—dc23   201503417

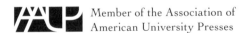

For Dr. Darril Hudson
scholar, patron, friend
and for all teachers and learners

Part One

The Earthly Paradise

. . . this scripture must be fulfilled in me: And he was counted among the lawless.

—*Luke 22:37*

Chapter 1

Brother Flavian was not entirely certain what brought him, a Trappist monk soon to celebrate his seventeenth year in the monastery, to be standing in the Miracle Inn with a draft beer in one hand and a pool cue in the other. That afternoon he had set off to deliver the remnants of last year's fruitcakes to the diocesan soup kitchen in the city, where they would be sliced and used in . . . well, he didn't really know how they would be used and didn't much care. The errand was an excuse to go *over the wall*, a term Flavian took some grim satisfaction in knowing was used by both monks and prison inmates to mean the same thing, except that at the end of the day the monks usually came back.

The day had been warm, fox spring, with the promise of summer in the bright sun but with many idyllic days to come before the big heat clamped down. For miles he drove along country lanes where nameless birds soared up from the fencerows and the sky was a great bowl of blue. Then he was negotiating crowded city streets with parallel parkers and confusing intersections and children darting from who knows where bent on self-destruction.

Flavian triumphed over these obstacles and performed his task dutifully and was heading back down the road in time to make Vespers at 5:30, when at the fork where he ought to have continued straight he turned left, toward the tavern in the town. He would stop in the tavern and order a beer. His pulse raced at the thought—he was thirty-eight years old and had never paid for a beer at a bar, he'd been just shy of legal age when he'd entered the monastery. He fished in his pocket—a few dollars and change left over from the allotment he'd been given for lunch and gas. He promised himself he'd find a way to pay it back. No one need know he was a monk—he was wearing jeans and a plain white shirt, clothes any farmer might wear for a trip to town, and in any case he had made a lifetime practice of anonymity.

He was thin, slant-shouldered, with thin lips, sharp features, and a nose that drew into something startlingly like a beak. The effect was so remarkable that his eyes, a pale, watery blue magnified by thick eyeglasses, stood out as a kind of genetic conjuring trick. As he'd grown older his features softened—the saddlebag spread that transformed his fellow brothers into overstuffed feed sacks served to fill Flavian out, making him look a little less like a heron and a little more like a bespectacled owl. Even so, his was not a face that drew attention. He'd order a beer and stand in the corner and breathe in the smell of freedom and vice, cigarettes and stale beer, and then he'd leave. With any luck he'd be inside the enclosure wall in time for Compline.

The bar was long and slim and smoky and dark, lit only by the fluorescent wings of a duck flying eternally over a Miller Lite waterfall and a single bulb covered with a green glass conical shade hanging above the pool table. Flavian hung back in the shadowy corners, watching how the men propped their feet on the bar rail and ordered, and after he felt he had the routine down he closed his eyes and steeled his will and delivered himself an ultimatum: *You will cross the room and do this thing before that duck makes one more trip across that falling water,* and on the third try his feet moved and the rest of him followed, six long bony feet of elbows and knees. "I'd like a beer, please," he said to the bartender, as thin and angular as Flavian but sporting a drooping handlebar mustache and a goatee of black flecked with silver.

"Draft or bottle?"

Even so simple a question caused Flavian's heart to leap but going this far he figured he might as well choose the unknown over the safe. The bartender nodded and pulled a frosty glass from the freezer and a few moments later Flavian stood taking comfort in the sting of the ice-cold mug against his palms. He took a sip—how could something be both bitter and bland? He was on the verge of setting it down and leaving when he found himself face-to-face with a ruddy-cheeked ham of a man with a huge paw of a hand-shake. "Benny Joe," the man said, "but most folks call me Little."

"Uh, Tom," Flavian said.

"You don't look like no Tom I ever met. Who's your daddy?"

And then there was another voice, this one from the shadows beyond the cone of light over the pool table. "He means what's your last name."

"Aquinas, Tom Aquinas," Flavian said and then felt a little smug about how he'd pulled that rabbit so easily from the hat.

Little (Flavian secretly named him Ham) laughed. "No Aquin-*asses* around here."

"It's Italian," Flavian said, even as he thought, *Lord, Lord, what lies we weave.*

"They play pool in Italy?"

The voice from the shadows spoke. "He's looking to shoot a game."

"Sorry," Flavian said. "I've never played."

"First time for everything," this from the voice in the shadows. "Let this be a lesson," and that was when the cue stick came sailing into the light, and only because he hadn't seen it coming Flavian caught it with his free hand like this was the most natural thing a man could do when in fact before this particular moment he'd never caught a flying object in his life.

"Hope you can find a better teacher than that sorry-assed son of a bitch," said Little.

"Watch your tongue," said the voice from the shadows, "this one's got manners." A quarter flipped onto the baize.

Little put the quarter in the slot and the balls thunked from some secret place into some less secret place and each falling ball drove a nail into Flavian's racing heart. Little gathered them up into the triangle and rearranged them, his hands moving in a complicated little dance (an education, to see such big hands perform such a delicate maneuver) and then he removed the rack gentle as squeezing a peach and there they were, a pristine triangle of colors with a spot of black at their heart. "Break?" Little asked.

"I think I will, if you don't mind," Flavian said, and went to the bathroom. Then he returned to palpable impatience and realized he had been given a request, that this had been a question of some sort and so he guessed the obvious and said, "No, you go first."

And so they played. Little sank a stripe on the break and emitted a little grunt of pleasure. He clutched at his crotch and said, "I got the big balls," and then proceeded to knock them down one by one while Flavian watched until he finally missed a shot— deliberately, or so it seemed to Flavian, leaving the cue ball lined up with a shot that any child could make. Flavian muffed it, striking the cue ball so hard it jumped off the table.

"Easy, easy," and the voice from the shadows stepped partly into the light. "Let me show you a thing or two," and he had his arms wrapped around Flavian and his hands on Flavian's hands, and Flavian, who had never in memory been held by a living soul, was spoons with a stranger. The Voice (for that was how Flavian thought of him) guided his hands onto the cue stick. "Think about when you're jerking off," the Voice said. "Do you pump your pecker fast and hard or slow and easy?" To this question Brother Flavian could summon no response.

Little sucked on his cigarette and then rested it on the pool table's edge so that the burning ember stuck out, then took a shot with his eyes closed. The ball did not drop into a pocket but Flavian got the message: Little was the cat and his job was to be the compliant mouse.

But now the cue stick rested more easily in his hands and on his next turn Flavian knocked a solid into a pocket—not the pocket he'd been aiming for but still he glowed as if it were Christmas, until he realized that Little was waiting and he guessed that he was being allowed a second turn. Once again his teacher draped his body around Flavian's and nearing the bottom of his beer Flavian relaxed into it, let himself be guided by the Voice. "Check the angles. It's all about angles, angles and English and power," the Voice said as he lined up Flavian's cue stick. "Take a breath, always a deep breath and let it out easy, easy, the power comes natural, it's already there, it's always been there, you don't got to make it happen, what you got to do is to learn how to use it," and then Flavian was free to take the shot. But once freed from the guiding hand of the Voice he was too rattled to stay focused and again hit the cue ball too hard. It caromed around the table, dangerously close to the black ball, which, even in his ignorance of the game, Flavian understood was a fate to be avoided.

They played three games. The Voice stepped in from time to time and offered help and Little seemed not to object until they were into the third beer and the third game and some part of what the Voice was showing him clicked for Flavian and his body took over the job at hand. He had a vision of the cue stick as an extension of himself—he stopped thinking of the stick and the balls as objects, as nouns, and began seeing the whole picture, he and the stick and the balls and the table as a process outside of time, as one big verb. And then he ran three in a row and the Voice said, "Hot damn!" and Little said, "Beginner's luck," and when Flavian finally missed a shot he took as great a pleasure as he had ever known from seeing the newfound seriousness with which Little took up his stick.

Then they played neck and neck, ball for ball, and it came down to this, the white ball and the black ball on the grassy green field in the smoky cone of light and the Voice with his arms crossed over his taut white t-shirt and his full lower lip stuck out and no longer offering help or even so much as a word of advice. Then Flavian muffed a gimme and left Little set up and Little, as close to a pro as came in these parts, sank the eight ball with a smooth quick stroke and a smack of his lips and it was over.

Flavian turned to the Voice. "Thanks, teacher."

"Your favor to return."

"I'd buy you a beer but I have to go," Flavian said, uncomfortably aware that he was too late to make Compline.

"Suit yourself, Brother Tom."

"How did you—" and then Flavian caught himself and turned to the door and then he was crossing the parking lot to the monastery minivan and wondering if he'd said or done something to give away that he was a monk, or maybe the Voice called everybody *brother* at the end of an evening of pool and beer? Flavian was in the driver's seat and had the van started when the Voice appeared at the window.

"Hey, listen. You're one of the brothers at the monastery, right?"

Flavian considered denying the fact—after all, the apostle Peter had denied Jesus himself—but in the end he resolved to play it straight. "How did you know?"

The Voice shrugged. "It's in the walk."

"The walk?" Flavian set aside this cryptic comment for later consideration. "Anyway, I was just stopping by . . ." His voice trailed off into the certainty that any excuse he gave was only going to dig his grave deeper, besides which he had none. Why had he "just stopped by"?

The Voice stuck a stuffed, oversized manila envelope through the window and dropped it in Flavian's lap. "I put this together for the abbot but hadn't found the chance to get it over to him. Much obliged for the favor," he said and vanished.

"Hey!" Flavian turned off the van and jumped out but the Voice was nowhere to be seen. Flavian walked over and peered in the bar windows—the bartender was wiping down the bar top, where Little's broad beam was tossing down one last draft. Flavian looked up and down the street, around the corner of the building—nothing, no one.

Flavian sighed, climbed back into the minivan, tossed the manila envelope on the passenger seat, and put the van in gear. He rolled his window down—the night held the chill of winter and the cold clean air rushed over him but he could still smell beer and smoke, the sweet smell of possibility and of sin. He drove under a high bright full moon and as he moved under the early spring sky he spoke aloud the prayers of Compline, the day's last office he'd long since missed. After seventeen years he was indifferent to the ritual—in this world of television and cars and planes, what was the point of all that hocus-pocus? But some childish part of him still took comfort in saying the *Salve Regina*.

> Hail, Holy Queen, Mother of Mercy, hail, our life, our
>   sweetness and our hope
> To you we cry, poor banished children of Eve
> To you we send up our sighs, mourning and weeping in this
>   vale of tears.
> Turn then, most gracious advocate, thine eyes of mercy
>   upon us,
> and after this our exile
> Show us the fruit of thy womb, Jesus. O clement, o
>   precious,
> o sweet Virgin Mary.

Flavian pulled into the monastery drive—all was dark. He unlocked the wide metal gate to the enclosure. It swung open with a screech that would wake the dead—how had that rusting hinge escaped his notice? All the same, he doubted anyone would wake. If anybody asked he would make a clean breast of everything he'd done. Maybe. He would deal with that tomorrow.

He extinguished the headlights and used the light of the

moon to pull the van into its parking spot. He studied the battered manila envelope, bequeathed by the Voice, riding shotgun. It had no address, no markings at all—it might have been salvaged from someone's garbage. Flavian served as the abbot's personal secretary and would be responsible for opening it in any case but he considered tossing it right here, right now. He'd had what for him passed as a wild and crazy evening. With luck it would be a long time before the demon seized him again and in any case opportunities were few and far between. He'd made no commitment to delivering the envelope. He was entirely within his rights, legal and moral, in pitching it in the can.

He considered this dilemma carefully. The stranger had bought him two beers and taught him a bit about shooting pool, and brief as the evening had been, it had held the bond of companionship. The Voice had asked a small enough favor in return. All the same, discretion required that Flavian open the envelope in the privacy of his own counsel to see what sort of business his teacher and unwitting partner in crime might have with, of all people, the abbot.

Flavian turned on the van's dome light, undid the clasp on the envelope, and looked inside, to find it stuffed with cash.

When the talk came to cars or guns Johnny Faye went outside for a smoke and didn't return until the conversation came back to a subject he knew something about—growing knock-your-socks-off marijuana, say, or breaking the law and getting away with it. He was relieved when his flashlight revealed that this particular backhoe had only a button for a starter. He jumped in the seat and got to his business.

The construction site was remote, adjacent to a stretch of woods that Johnny Faye's mother owned where fully mature black walnuts grew straight to the sky, each worth several thousand dollars. More than once Johnny Faye had suspected that in choosing the location for his golf course subdivision the county attorney had his eye on those walnuts, that some plan was afoot involving his mother's land. The site favored the making of mischief exactly because it was so far from anybody who would be listening or looking in the bright light of a full moon night.

Blu-ue mo-on of Kentucky, keep on a-shinin' . . .

Johnny Faye tested the levers while he sang. He glanced at the moon in all its splendor, well above the dark line of woods to the south. He lowered the bucket until he felt, through the roaring, jaw-rattling machine, the bite of its steel lip against the earth.

He was nearly one with his moonshadow by the time he had the hole dug as big as he planned but the second half of the job would go faster. Filling in was always faster than taking out. By the time his shadow began to lengthen the hole was finished. He parked the backhoe to one side, then switched it off. The roar faded from his ears. He took a swig from a flask of bourbon he carried in his back pocket, then lit a joint and took a couple of hits slowly enough that by the time he was buzzed a nearby whippoorwill felt comfortable enough to raise its after-midnight voice.

He studied the golf cart, to be struck by a moment of panic— when he arrived he hadn't thought to check to see if it required a key. But then he saw the key right in the ignition where the county attorney left it because this was his county and he thought himself immune to anybody wreaking mischief with anything that belonged to him.

Johnny Faye drove the cart down the little earthen ramp and into the hole, its little grave for a little while. He was pleased to see that even with only the full moon to light his work he'd dug the hole as big as it needed to be. Only a couple of inches of dirt would separate its bright orange pennant RIDGEVIEW POINTE from daylight and discovery.

For the second time on that soft spring night he lit his joint, but as he was taking a hit he was struck by an avalanche of dirt from the pile beside the golf cart's grave. "*Jeee*-sus!" he cried. The falling dirt knocked him sideways into the cart frame and buried him to his knees.

Gently he leveraged himself sideways and crawled up the pile to the grave's lip. A quick sign of the cross—"Jesus, Mary, Joseph," he breathed and inspected the damage. His shirt was ripped down its side and his skin burned raw. He reached to pull his flask from his back pocket and felt the real damage—the stab of pain made him yelp. Gently he reached for his back pocket with his other hand. He unscrewed the top of the flask, gritted his teeth, splashed some whiskey on the bloody raw wound, and took a swig.

Now, though the ache in his side grew into a throbbing wracking diamond star of pain, he smoked while he worked—time was getting short, the last thing he needed was the contractor's men deciding to get a little work done in the early dawn light and coming across him smoking pot astride one of their backhoes. He pushed dirt into the golf cart's grave until the cart was covered.

By the time he finished smoothing out the dirt the woods were giving a horizon to the brightening light and he could see the lines on his hand when he smoked the last of the roach. The flame was a puny child of the rising sun but he had finished the job before dawn as he had figured he must do. A backhoe alone on the site where before there'd been a golf cart to keep it company and no trace of the latter and no one the wiser.

The sun broke free of the trees' tangle of limbs and leaves. Johnny Faye took up his walking stick—before setting out on this expedition he'd considered leaving it at home, but it turned out to be a necessity, his third leg as he limped across the field and vanished into the brush as if he were a whitetail deer or the whippoor-will whose night of courtship he'd so rudely troubled.

The government agency that assigned Dr. Meena Chatterjee to this poor rural county had warned her that men were more reluctant than women to visit a doctor, the more so if the doctor was a dark-skinned woman from a country they'd never heard of whose Bengali-accented English they found hard to understand. After two weeks of seeing women she received her first male patient— a farmer, she guessed, from his coarse, ruddy complexion—complaining of chest pains.

Dr. Chatterjee held out a clipboard and a medical history form and pointed him toward the second of her two examination rooms. "Please provide the basic information. I shall be with you in a moment."

He raised his cane and waved aside her clipboard. "My mamma told me never to put down on paper nothing you don't want nobody to read. And I'm in the habit of obeying my mamma. I just need you to take a look at my side."

"The paperwork is not for you, Mr.—"

He took her hand and gave it a vigorous shake. "Johnny Faye. Pleased to meet you."

She extracted her hand from his grip. "A pleasure to meet you, Mr. Faye. Now, if you would—"

"No Mister to it, nor Faye neither. Just Johnny Faye."

"You must have a last name."

"I got a belly button, if that's what you mean." He gave her a broad wink.

"Mr. Johnny Faye. Please restrict yourself to the subject at hand."

He furrowed his brow in contrition. "I never made the acquaintance of my daddy. Which is just as well, according to my mamma."

"Whom you are in the habit of obeying."

"That's right."

"Surely your mother would tell you to complete this form."

"I'm sure she'd never tell me to do no such thing. Besides, you aint my mamma, and if that aint the best news you'll hear all day I want you to tell me better."

"I have no intention of being anyone's *mamma*, thank you,

.ne world has quite enough people without my contribution." She
waved him into the tiny hallway that led to the examination rooms.
"Let me take a look and we'll proceed from there."

When she entered the examination room he was shirtless and
standing. She pointed at the table. "If you would, please, take your
seat, Mr.—Johnny Faye."

"Thank you, ma'am, but I'm more comfortable on my feet. A
man can run faster with his pants up than a woman can with hers
down."

She tightened her lips into a puckered line. "You will please
keep personal comments to yourself." Then she noticed his right
side, where a yellow-blue bruise blossomed amid a broad scrape of
clotted blood. "A nasty scrape. You have most likely cracked a rib.
When did you injure yourself?"

"This morning, ma'am. Or last night, depending on how you
look at it."

She pressed the stethoscope to his chest. "Take a slow, deep
breath, please."

He breathed in. "I aint going to be taking any *fast* breaths,
that's for certain."

She removed the stethoscope from his chest. "You have not
punctured a lung. Most likely the rib is cracked, not broken."
She pressed her stethoscope to his back. "The ribs are encased in
muscle, which expands and contracts the chest with each breath."
She pressed the stethoscope to his sides, then again to his chest.
"When you breathe deeply, you're moving that cracked rib, which
is letting you know that it's cracked. You should obtain an X-ray
to be certain you have no jagged edges and unless you have had
a tetanus booster recently you should renew that. You do not
want a punctured lung and you do not want tetanus. Then you
would have—" she paused, searching for an Americanism "—*real
trouble.*"

"I been in *real trouble* most of my life. My mamma tells me it's
my natural state. Considering the alternatives I kind of come to

like it. Ever noticed how much trouble people go to, to get into a little real trouble? From my point of view I'm performing a community service. Which I would be happy to perform for you."

She took up her pen and clipboard. "You will do me the courtesy of not taking me for a fool. Please tell me how this happened."

He gave her a sly, conspiratorial glance. "Promise not to tell a soul."

"As your doctor I am sworn to confidentiality."

He cupped his hand at her ear and whispered, "I was burying a golf cart."

She felt as if she were interrogating a child. "And what were the circumstances that led to your burying a golf cart?"

He grinned, showing big horse teeth with a wide gap. The front center tooth was chipped, making him look a little crazed. "It's a good one but this time you got to cross your heart."

"Mr. Faye. You may be certain—"

"*Johnny* Faye. Go on, do it."

She pantomimed a cross over her heart—a gesture she had last performed late in her one year at the Loretine Sisters boarding school in Calcutta, where an English classmate with ruddy cheeks and flaxen hair had decided to teach the heathen how to keep their word.

He told her then how he had decided to play a little joke on Harry Vetch, the county attorney, to get back at him for building his mess of a subdivision right next to Johnny Faye's mother's woods. "No great harm done," he said, since he had taken care to bury the cart so that once dug up it would have suffered only a few permanent stains on its green-and-white striped upholstery—"a little reminder, might teach him a lesson, not likely but anything is possible, right? But I guess it was the teacher that got taught." He pointed to the scrape down his side.

She bent to look more closely. "Unless you object, I had best provide your tetanus booster now." She removed a vial from a small refrigerator, swabbed its top, stuck in the hypodermic and withdrew its contents. She swabbed his arm with disinfectant. "This will sting." She thrust in the needle.

"*Ow! Damn!*"

"I am so *very* sorry."

"I aint. I'm glad to see you get riled up. That's a good sign."

"Sign of what?" She pulled out the needle and swabbed the bright drop of blood, then picked up his right thumb and pressed it over the ball of cotton.

"How much you'd enjoy a little walk in the woods. I built this little shack where I go when I want to keep myself out of *real trouble*. Sort of a blind except I don't use it for hunting, just for watching birds and such. Not too far from here, neither, over by the monastery."

"There is a monastery nearby?" She applied a Band-Aid and gave it a pat.

"Sure, a big one. Well, used to be big. A lot of the monks are gone now, to the grave or married or whatever. I'm surprised you hadn't heard of it. That's what usually brings strangers to these parts."

"I must say I know very little about *these parts*."

"I could show it to you sometime. The blind, that is, not the monastery, even if the blind's on monastery land so I guess it *is* the monastery, sort of, but it's outside the wall so women can go there, no problem. A afternoon walk before it gets too hot."

"I do not socialize with patients."

"And I do not go to the doctor."

"Well, then, there we have it." She handed him his shirt.

"Anyways I'm not your patient."

"For the last fifteen minutes you have been sitting in my office."

"Show me the paperwork. If it aint been writ down it aint happened."

"Which is why you must now complete this form." She handed him the clipboard and form and opened the examination room door. "There is really nothing you can do about a cracked rib except to return home and suffer. I could write you a prescription for something stronger than aspirin—"

"I don't take nothing stronger than aspirin except whiskey and a certain not-so-secret little vice. Matter of fact I don't take aspirin."

"Then I am at a loss as to why you paid me a visit." She moved to the door and made a pointed gesture of holding it open. "Ring me or ring *somebody* immediately if that scrape gets red or swollen. I assume you have a family member whom you may ring up to drive you home?"

"We got no need for a chaperone."

She placed her hands on her hips. "You bring to mind a phrase I learned from a medical school colleague but that I never thought would have professional application. *When hell freezes over.*"

He stood but paused in the doorway, pensive. "Just try and stop the light from changing."

She handed him his stick. "You may find your cane useful."

"I aint telling a living soul about burying that golf cart, not even my mamma. Better for her to be ignorant. So I'd appreciate it if you'd keep that story to yourself. Though I do understand how a good story wants to be told. Later," he said, and he was gone.

He would leave without paying, that was why he dodged the paperwork, she understood that, but that was why she sent him into the front room, so as to get rid of him. The singsong rhythm of an old and familiar prayer, learned from her grandmother, came to mind.

Cows in the cowshed and
Corn in the storehouse
Vermilion between the parting of my hair
Every year a son and
May not a single one die and
Never may a teardrop fall from my eye

"One hundred two weeks remaining," she muttered. She heard the front door open and shut. In the waiting room she found the blank form, with five twenty-dollar bills clipped to its top.

Chapter 2

On her first afternoon in her assigned post, delivered to her new office and home by the county judge executive, Dr. Chatterjee had to acknowledge that hers was not an auspicious beginning. The judge executive (so very American his title, with its seamless blend of government corruption and corporate inefficiency) had dropped her here, mumbled something about an appointment with the garbage collection agency, and vanished. In their one phone conversation before her arrival he'd told her only that, since the town had gone many years without a doctor, its men's clubs (Optimists, Knights of Columbus, Fish & Game) had joined forces to acquire and refurbish "a former commercial site" into a medical office and living apartment. In the transparent light of a spring afternoon she could not escape the thought that she had risen to the bait in a trap.

In its first incarnation her office had been a gas station. The pipes and valves that had once serviced fuel pumps still protruded from the cement apron, a troubling sight, though she rather liked the weathered sign of the winged horse hanging from rusting hinges that creaked with every breeze. In the tiny waiting room with its speckled Formica countertop sat a telephone, a desk, and an oak office chair scarred with pocketknife carvings and cigarette burns. At the building's other end: A small apartment cluttered with mismatched furniture. Here she would live for the two years of her term of service as specified in the contract under which she had retrained in an American medical school. As she distributed her meager belongings around the rooms, she recalled the words Krishna spoke to Arjuna as he and his companions were banished from their forest home: *Profit from exile.*

She carried with her a hole in her heart. She would not describe it as a longing to return to the land of her birth—on this point she could not be more clear. Once, though, she had been whole and round—for better and worse she had belonged to a particular place, her family's village situated on one of the many branching arms of the delta of the great mother Ganges. She lived in the assumption that the whole world resonated with her landscape of memory. Everyone knew and dreaded the brutal heat just before the monsoons came on; everyone knew the longing for rain and the joy of dancing in its first drops; everyone knew how tiresome it became, how troublesome to be confined in the village by flooded roads and turbulent rivers. Everyone knew the heart's leap of anticipation at the news of guests and the crushing disappointment when some obstacle prevented their arrival.

She had not known then and could not have understood that in leaving she was cutting herself off from any possibility of knowing that kind of belonging. Now she was a wanderer, a planet, an exile, and as such one place was as good as another, though her experiences of cold and snow had persuaded her that she would trouble her wound less by living someplace warm.

On darker days she lived in envy. She did not envy them their big shiny cars or their brick houses or their television sets or even their plumbing—no. She envied their casual assumption of place. They walked on the land as if they knew the wide world in all its grandeur and heartache from these lumpy hills and snakey valleys. Having known no other place, they assumed—as she had once assumed—that all places were like their place. It was their unknowing that she envied—she who had grown up with the distant, palpable presence of the Himalayas presiding with calm majesty above the fertile plain; she who had walked the paths of the living, breathing jungle, and had seen that same green labyrinth of shadow and light burst into flame, while jets screamed overhead and she stared, unable even to run, transfixed in awe and learning that this was the way the world is, the only way it could be because it was the only way she had ever known. A neighbor's child, whom she'd been charged with watching while her mother worked the fields, was struck by flying, burning debris and fell to the earth. In that moment Meena felt herself chosen to seek a life in medicine.

Among her first local patients was a young, garrulous woman whose face was already creased from a lifetime of smoking. "You must feel mighty lucky to have got yourself here," the woman said.

"Of course I am very fortunate."

"Aint this the most beautiful spot on earth? You've been all over, you tell me."

Dr. Chatterjee acknowledged that this place was very beautiful indeed.

"'Course, it's getting ruined, but I guess that's probably true of every place. People, they see we got a good thing here and they want to get in. Oh, I don't mean you—you're bringing us something important, but all those others—I don't blame 'em, mind, I'd do the same, but even so. Every bird protects its territory."

To go through life without a place—she who had been raised in a family whose roots reached deeper than the mountains. Compared to her people, the mountains were young—that was how she'd once thought of herself and her family. And here she was, placeless on the land.

On long slow Sunday afternoons the bright spring weather called Meena to take her first steps toward becoming American: she took to the road. During her retraining she learned to drive and had acquired a monstrous, rusting Buick Electra from the graduate student whose apartment she had taken. Recalling her conversation with the wild man with the cracked ribs, she set out to find the monastery.

A lightly traveled country road led to its ornate, rusting gate—Meena slowed to a crawl and craned her neck but she could see little more than the abbey steeple poking through greening trees rising above a nubbled cement block wall with a rusting metal sign WOMEN NOT PERMITTED INSIDE ENCLOSURE. Not far down the road, she encountered a small graveled parking lot with a sign TO THE STATUES, from which she deduced that these, at least, were available to visitors.

At this time of year—high spring—the path made its way through delicately branching dogwoods and redbuds that lifted clouds of white and lavender against a budding spring green, with the last of the bright yellow daffodils underfoot. Along the way the monks had scattered fragments of a century of outmoded religious statuary—a grinning gargoyle peered from behind forsythia, a Virgin and Child poked from a clump of bleeding heart.

Meena climbed a small knoll to a copse of Virginia pines. In their midst a small glen sheltered a tableau in black stone—the apostles Peter, James, and John reclining in granite sleep, while a few steps up the path Jesus knelt in agony, hands clasped to his face.

Some years back a large pine had fallen near the sleeping Peter and the remains of its trunk bridged a protected hollow. The monks had placed a bench at the edge of the statues' clearing, but Meena chose to sit on the trunk of the fallen pine—by edging sideways she could dangle her short legs above the sheltered hollow underneath. She kicked off her squat black pumps and warmed her feet in the spring sun and closed her eyes. Here and only here, she decided, would she permit herself nostalgia for the watery green countryside of her childhood.

As a result she visited the statues at every opportunity, until an evening came when she sat on the pine and edged sideways and kicked off her shoes only to see them land in the midst of a coiling mass of snakes, impossible to count how many because where one left off another began, twisting and rising and falling. She screamed, a high-pitched fright.

"I'll be damned. I heard of such a thing but I never seen it."

Meena looked up to see Johnny Faye, gravedigger for golf carts and one-time patient, looking on. She composed herself. "And what sort of thing might that be."

"In winter a rattlesnake'll hibernate—the young know their mother's smell and they'll follow it back to the den where they was born. Then they coil up together to sit out the winter and don't much move til spring. You give them one more warm night and a hot day and they'll be scattered far and wide. But I'd wait a day or two before I come back."

He took his walking stick and thrust it gently into the coiling mass. "Greetings, brother snakes. Summer is coming but not here yet. Welcome, sister snakes. You'll need another day of sun before you're ready to rumble." Using the stick he lifted the longest and thickest of the snakes, almost as thick as his bony wrist and a good deal longer than his arm. It twisted in the evening light, its dark diamonds beads against its brighter brown hide. "A good walking stick comes in handy. That must have been one powerful prayer you was saying. I'd like to learn that one someday if you'd be so kind." He bowed from the waist and pointed with his homemade caduceus. "I'd walk back in that direction if I was you. And I'd think about wearing jeans if you're taking your religion outdoors, especially in these woods." He replaced the snake among its relatives. With the tip of the walking stick he plucked one of her shoes from the pit and extended it to her.

She hesitated, then slipped it on, followed by its mate. She scooted from the pine. Once a safe distance from the pit she drew herself up. "Mr. Johnny Faye. I am a woman of reason and a doctor who has had quite enough experience of religion and its wars. If I am religious you may be assured it is in my own way, which demands peace and quiet and solitude." She paused for effect. "May I make myself clear. *Peace* and *quiet* and above all *solitude*."

"Is that a fact." He laughed, not mocking but conspiratorial. Then he disappeared into the woods.

On these spring nights—the window of his cell propped open for the first time in months—Brother Flavian woke aching with emptiness and desire, but experience had taught him that he could wait his longing out. Reading Thomas Aquinas was an especially effective soporific, and when Flavian woke in the morning's bright light all that longing had vanished like a bad dream. The lambent days passed in a flurry of busyness, undertaken less as a way of avoiding what one of the older, less embittered brothers called *the challenge of the dick* than as a way of dodging looming terror. Here he was thirty-eight years old and had never done so many things, most things, most everything—he had never touched another person in lust or in love, had never held a child of his flesh and blood, had made no money, had not seen God despite a couple of years right after his final vows when he had worked at it pretty hard and come up empty-handed. He had searched for God, all right, and had come up with only silence.

A day came when the afternoon stretched out empty as a hand, the devil's playground. Seventeen years earlier, on his second day at the monastery Flavian had found the statues in their pine grove and he returned to them often, seeking solace. He set out to visit them now, but on this particular day the statues offered only silent witness to his crisis and so he continued walking, to the far reaches of the abbey property, where he encountered a steep, north-facing slope, unfamiliar to him even after his years of exploring the abbey acreage.

He bushwhacked down the hill until he found a path that deer had worn on their ways to some source of food or water. The path led him through a dense prickly wall of cedars to the lip of a small creek. The stream was broad and shallow and carried enough water to enable the bordering water maples and sycamores to grow to great heights—they came together overhead to form a

pantheon of green. In their center a bright oculus of sunlight illuminated a looping oxbow of the creek that cradled a small patch of
bottomland. The broad shaft of light struck the creek bottom as if
it were a stage.

Flavian climbed down the bank to find at the oxbow's outer
edge a sycamore with three great limbs that branched out low to
the ground to form a hollow large enough for sitting, and the limbs
were like arms, each with a branch where a monk might rest his
elbows. He climbed into the tree and sat. He was in the habit of
taking long walks to sit and think over troublesome conundrums,
and on this day what he thought about was what to do with his
desire, and with that damned manila envelope full of money. To
give it to the abbot would require explaining how he came by it,
a conversation Flavian did not care even to imagine, partly from
embarrassment but partly because he had found the adventure he
sought and was not ready to let it go.

As if catalyzed by his thoughts the Voice came climbing down
the creek bank carrying a sack with long handles poking out, a big
slobbery dog at his side. It took Flavian a moment to realize that he
hadn't conjured an apparition, that in fact the Voice—who had so
monopolized his thoughts for days—was standing before his eyes.
"What are *you* doing here?" Flavian asked.

The Voice shrugged. "You got your secrets, I got mine. The
left hand washes the right." He threw down the knapsack and set
about laying out his tools—several varieties of hoes, a spade, a
pick. He vanished back into the woods.

Flavian and the dog studied each other. He was a big lumber-
ing galoot of a dog, a little too much in touch with his wolfish roots
for Flavian's taste—in his glittering agate eyes Flavian saw a dog's
heart and a wolf's temper.

The Voice reemerged, this time carrying a plastic bag that he
threw down and that spilled forth what looked like green, unshelled
walnuts. "JC." Flavian had no idea what the Voice meant, until he
shrugged a shoulder in the direction of the dog. "Where he goes I

go and vice-a versa. JC," he said again, and Flavian understood that he was being introduced.

"Hello, JC." Flavian jumped down from his sycamore throne to pat the dog's head.

The Voice nodded at the bag. "Watch where you put your feet. Bittersweet's contribution."

"Bittersweet?"

"My horse. We're a little farming collective around here, everybody does his part. Nothing better for fertilizer than a nice aged horse apple dropped in the hole right before you stick in the set."

"Oh. Of course."

The Voice took up the hoe and began turning up the small patch of creek bottom. In the focused energy with which he set about the task Flavian understood that this was the first step of a process that had been some time in the planning. The hoe rose and fell, turning over the soft moist earth. The creek gurgled past.

"Um—you mind if I ask what you're up to?"

"Not at all. I'm getting this plot dug up before the weeds take over. Two weeks from now it'll be nothing but smartweed and sassafras saplings unless I get it turned up and planted first. Which I'm intending to do."

"Hey—I mean, this is the monastery. Monastery land."

"That's why I give you that money. I'm leasing your land for my crop."

"But I'm the abbot's secretary. If he'd signed a lease on land out here I'd have seen a copy of it. Besides, we don't lease small parcels."

"Don't I know it." The Voice swung the hoe in intervals steady as a heartbeat—a few minutes into his digging and he'd found his rhythm. "You monks are leasing land to every rich farmer in the county but hey, you're the church, your job is to help the rich feel good about robbing the poor but I figure no harm in a poor buck like me getting in on the deal so long as I meet the terms. Thus like they say the envelope. Or maybe you're complaining about the terms."

"No, you were very generous. I mean not that I counted it or anything. The good news is that now I've found you and I can give it back."

"Didn't your mamma teach you no manners? You caint give back a present, especially when it aint your present in the first place. It's lease money for the abbot, to do with whatever he wants."

"Look, I can't go taking envelopes full of money from any stranger I happen to meet."

"Why not? Aint that pretty much what you guys do ever Sunday in church?"

"We don't take up a collection, we're not that kind of place."

"Because somebody else is taking up a collection and passing it on to you."

"Whatever you want to think. But you let me know where I can meet you and I'll give you that money back and then you can give it to the abbot yourself if you're so hot to get rid of it."

"I expect Sundays are as good a day as any. Show up any Sunday you'll most likely find me here. But you tell the abbot I said to pass along that money to some deserving soul and be done with it. Like maybe to that pretty new doctor. You been in her office? She don't hardly have a pot to piss in. Better her than another dress for his majesty the pope. You tell the abbot I said that and then you give him that money and save your worrying for something you can do something about. Like turning this little bit of creek bottom into a nice little vegetable garden."

"*Vegetables?* Here?"

"You mind helping out a little? How 'bout you take the easy job." The Voice picked up another hoe and tossed it to Flavian and for the second time in Flavian's life he caught a flying object. "Here, break up the big clods, that's all I want you to do for right now. Once we have the heavy work done I'll bring down this little hand plow I have and make it sweet. Rows for planting corn and everything else in between."

"Why would you mix vegetables with corn? The corn will shade them from the sun."

"You're the labor. You let me worry about management. You talk, I'll listen. It makes the work pass."

Flavian took up the hoe and began hacking away at the dirt. "I don't really have much to say."

"Everybody knows something about something. Or somebody."

"Well, what I know about is God. At least, that's what I was looking for when I came here."

"You thought about looking under the table? OK, sorry, go on. I could stand to learn something about God."

"What I know you don't want to learn."

"Try me."

Flavian considered this. Surely the point was to teach, both Jesus and St. Paul said as much. "Well, to start with, there's no gray-bearded guy in the sky."

The Voice made a noise of disgust. "Everybody knows that. At least, everybody who's bothered to look. I know what there's *not*—Nam taught me that. I want you to teach me what there *is*."

Flavian found himself suddenly shy. "Look, I come from a school of thought that says you shouldn't talk about God, that to talk about Him is to diminish Him because we have no language adequate to the conversation."

"He invented the words. You think he would have left hisself out?"

"I see your point but I don't know how to teach somebody about God without making reference to Him and I'm not comfortable talking about Him. Maybe it's just the word."

"So find some other word."

"Some other word isn't God."

"From the way I look at it, everything is God."

Brother Flavian heaved a great sigh. "I tell you what. I'll find some books or sermons on the subject and arrange to have them and that envelope left at any place you name."

"I don't got time to read. Besides I'd just as soon hear it from you."

"To be honest I'm not the best person to be talking about God. I'm not much of a monk. I showed up at the monastery because it was that or be drafted for Vietnam."

"Then you're a smarter man than me. They called, I went. At least I come back alive, which is more than some guys around here can say."

The Voice turned back to his work, which was fine with Flavian—anything was better than being quizzed on the subject that for too many months now had bedeviled his thoughts and dreams.

For a while they worked in silence. When Flavian had first arrived at the monastery, the community still honored the traditional division between the choir monks, many of whom were priests and had college degrees and held down the desk jobs, and the lay monks, who dirtied their hands in the fields. Flavian had graduated from college but had no formal theological training and so he had entered as a lay monk and been assigned manual labor. He'd hated it—hated the endless work and especially hated the dairy herd that furnished milk to make the monastery cheese. Many times the herd gave him reason to contemplate the phrase "dumb animal," so often had the cows tried his patience to the point of wishing them all turned into hamburger.

But he enjoyed the camaraderie of the lay monks and took solace in the fact that, however miserable the labor in summer's high heat or on winter nights so cold the snot froze in his nose, he shared the work with his brothers. Their community motto was *Ora et Labora*, Prayer and Work. They'd scrabbled for their livelihoods and depended on the yield from their gardens to pull them through the winter—potatoes and carrots and pears and apples buried in straw and brought forth in February, with each vegetable and fruit a distillation in miniature of the summer past. They heated with logs cut from their woods, sawed into chunks then hauled to feed their hungry furnace. They had been bound together in the fraternity of sweat.

Then the abbey sold off the draft horses and bought tractors and then it did away with the farm altogether, leasing its bottom lands to distant corporations and working only at the business of making and selling fruitcakes and cheese. The vegetable gardens gave way to trucked-in deliveries of canned and frozen foods. The monastery installed oil furnaces, gas ovens, air-conditioning. On all their acres of field and forest they kept only the dairy herd, and even it was endangered. At the end of the previous summer the abbey had been visited by salesmen from large dairy conglomerates who brought colored charts and graphs and demonstrated that the monastery would save a great deal of money by trucking in milk from afar.

Flavian had been all in favor of decommissioning the cows—he had been the first to use the word, in a memo to the abbot. They were not farmers but monks, he had argued, their lives dedicated to the business of silence. Over the next several months there had been a flurry of correspondence—Flavian had opened and read it—competing offers and counter offers from agribusiness corporations. The abbot played coquettish suitor to salesmen in distant cities. Rumors were rife that the dairy herd was slated for the slaughterhouse, even though without the cows not a domesticated animal would remain on all the abbey acreage except Origen the cat—not a single animal to disturb their silence.

In short order the hoe blistered Flavian's amateur hands. He stopped—it was close on to Vespers, reason enough to quit. The sun had slipped down to the line of woods but it still gave forth enough heat that the Voice dripped with sweat. He wore a singlet of thin white cotton, sweat-stained and now soaked through so that it stuck to his back and outlined the bands of muscle fanning outward from his knobby backbone. When he raised the hoe his upper back took the form of a wine glass, with his muscles as its vessel and his backbone as its stem. He had shoulder-length hair that shone slick with grease but was streaked with sunlight even this early in the spring. A sprinkling of moles scattered across his broad shoulders—a negative of the Milky Way, a constellation in

melanin, the cosmos in miniature. He swung the hoe with grace—
Flavian marveled at his smooth, even repetition of the task, trans-
forming it into a kind of litany of labor, the same formula repeated
until it lost meaning and became an unconscious prayer.

The Voice stopped and turned the hoe upside down and
propped its handle against a rock and rested his buttocks against
its wide iron head. "My right side is killing me."

"Your right side?"

"A long story. Stay away from golf carts is my advice if you
want the lesson without the pain, though I aint yet come by a lesson that got learnt without a little pain. Speaking of pain, you
need to take a leak?" The Voice pulled down his zipper and pulled
it out. Flavian looked away. "Go ahead, do it here if you got any
need to. Anywhere right here in the bottom will do but around
the edges is best. Once I get the plants in I'll spray some wolf piss
around."

"Wolf piss?"

"Sure, you buy it in a bottle at the Big Store, best thing for
keeping deer away. I'd sure like to see how they get a wolf to pee
in a bottle. However they make it happen the deer know what it
is and they don't like it. But you know people piss does almost as
good. I don't know why they don't bottle and sell that. That's how
the old lady knows it's spring—I set out a milk jug next to the
toilet."

In fact Flavian did need to pee. He kept his back turned and
his head bowed, only to look up from zipping up his jeans to see
The Voice had his hand stuck out practically in Flavian's face.
"Thanks for your help, Brother Tom."

Flavian winced at this casual reference to his first lie in what
was becoming a swamp of deception. "Any time. But I have to go.
I have to make Vespers."

The Voice studied the sky. "Aint no clock time here. That's
why I come here. That and planting my babes."

"Yes, well, you tell that to the abbot." Flavian took the Voice's hand. A warm grip of leathered horn—*he* would have no blisters. "You know, I never caught your name."

"That's because I never mentioned it." The Voice grinned. "Fools' names and fools' faces are often seen in public places. That's the last nun I had talking. Sister Mary Immaculata Schmuck. Fourth grade, I think she might have been. 'Mind of your own,' she told me, 'but bad attitude.' After her I was out of there for good. Come to find out she got me exactly right. Johnny Faye."

"Johnny Faye what?"

"No what to it. Just Johnny Faye. Thanks for the help."

And then Flavian climbed out of the creek and pushed through the wall of cedars to walk over the hill and down the lane, stepping smartly so as to reach the abbey in time for Vespers. As he jogged along he realized that now he could put a name to the Voice and that was something, on top of which he had figured out a plan to get rid of the manila envelope.

Chapter 3

Flavian sat in the monastery minivan, studying the doctor's office. When he last visited this building it had been a gas station with a garage door that rolled up to reveal a hydraulic lift for raising cars and trucks. Now he tried imagining that bay furnished with medical equipment. What came to mind instead was the thought of corpulent Brother Bede, being elevated for inspection.

Crammed into the glove compartment of the monastery minivan: the manila envelope left by Johnny Faye, on which Flavian had written in large block letters DR CHATTERJEE—DONATION TO THE DESERVING. He had decided to take Johnny Faye's suggestion—he would locate the doctor's mail slot, drop the cash-stuffed envelope through it, and make tracks.

But as he was cramming the envelope into the slot, the door opened a crack. "May I be of assistance?"

Flavian was charmed by her accent, not quite British, not quite anything but itself, and mortified by the hint of suspicion in her voice. He told her he was a monk right off—it seemed the surest way to keep her from looking inside the envelope, on which, after all, he had written her name.

His identifying himself seemed to put her at ease. She opened the door. "Won't you come in for a cup of tea? In my country it is what one does when monks come to the door. That or give alms. But here you have brought *me* a gift."

Flavian grinned weakly. He knew he should decline—a monk, outside the enclosure after Compline, delivering money that for all he knew was contraband, only to accept an invitation to sit alone with a woman? Was there any rule he wasn't breaking? "Sure," he said, and in his flat, cheerful inflection of that word, he who had never traveled abroad understood for the first time that he was American.

Inside Flavian sat on the worn vinyl couch, sweating through his shirt. From his seat he watched her move efficiently about her cubbyhole of a kitchen. He had always thought of the monastery kitchen as cramped; suddenly it seemed as vast as America. It occurred to him that she lived in space in a very different way than he—given a burner, a sink, and a few square feet, this woman could prepare a meal for twenty.

"Do you have a preference among teas?"

"Iced," he said, and when this was followed by silence, "Unsweetened. But if you've already put in the sugar that's all right, too."

After a few minutes she brought in a tray furnished with teacups, a sugar bowl, a bowl filled with ice, and a saucer with four thin cookies placed in the form of a cross. "Please tell me about your monastery," she said, and Flavian, who thought he would have little to say on the subject, talked through the pot of tea—of the long and checkered history of the order, begun by enthusiastic reformers who through hard work had transformed Europe from swamps and forests into fertile fields; how they grew wealthy and corrupt until a new reform arose; how these monks fled France during her revolutions and came to America to begin anew. As he spoke he felt some small glow of pride—despite their great sins, and there had been many, they had made their mark as a community of men.

The evening light faded from the windows. The envelope sat on the coffee table, its inscription face down—the doctor had not mentioned it, probably waiting for him to offer it in formal presentation, which he was not about to do, but standing to leave would prompt the question of what it contained. The tea was having its effect but he did not dare visit the bathroom from fear that in his absence she would pick up the envelope and turn it over and read the note. Then she would open it and there would be questions, and above all he wanted to avoid questions. He crossed his legs.

"I am pleased to meet a monk," she was saying. "So much of this country is so foreign to me. In medical school one had time only for study and work, and now I find myself for the first time, really, out and about in the real America, and whom should I encounter but a monk? You have some quality of being a monk that I recognize. I believe I might have recognized you as a monk even had you not told me." Flavian shifted in his seat. He uncrossed and recrossed his legs. "More tea?" she asked. He declined. "I can see that you are American even before being a monk. That particular quality of self-assurance, I know it from your movies. I ask myself if someone from a small, obscure country might ever acquire it."

Do not think of water, Flavian told himself sternly. Immediately there came to mind the duck flying over the tavern's Miller Lite waterfall. *If only she would excuse herself to another room, even briefly. If only—*

A knock at the door. "If you will excuse me," Dr. Chatterjee said.

A tall thin woman stood outside, carrying a young boy who was clawing and biting the air and making terrible, strangled, gasping sounds and the woman's face was a study in terror and then the child stiffened in her arms and Flavian could see, anyone could see that he was fighting for breath.

"Doctor—I'm sorry, asthma—" and in that moment the world of ordinary life fell through a hole and everything became immediate and important and necessary.

"Bring him in," Dr. Chatterjee said. "Follow me." The doctor opened the door into her medical office. As the woman passed Flavian caught a glimpse of the boy's face, his eyes wide and alert with terror, and then his small body seized up and he gave a stran-gled, choking moan. "Lay him there," Flavian overheard the doctor say, even as to his lifelong shame he picked up the manila envelope, unbuttoned his shirt, and stuffed it between his shirt and his chest.

"Brother Flavian," Dr. Chatterjee called from the examina-tion room. "Telephone the ambulance and tell them to come imme-diately. The telephone and the number are both on the counter. Please tell me what happened," this last she spoke to the woman.

Flavian rebuttoned his shirt as he made the call. *Ambulance, now, emergency, Dr. Chatterjee's office, boy can't breathe, cause?—asthma, come now, come right away.*

The boy was lying on the table, gasping. "He was playing with this knife," the mother said. "I don't know how he got the knife, I told him a thousand times if I told him once that if I caught him with a knife that would be the end of—"

"Yes, yes." Dr. Chatterjee took a stethoscope from a hook on the wall. "And then what happened."

"Well, I don't rightly know, I wasn't looking or I'd of seen the knife, you know, and I'd of taken it away. All I know is that I come out in the yard to get the clothes and then I saw him there and the knife on the ground and him choking."

One side of the boy's shirt had a blossom of red, blood from some kind of wound but no great amount—evidence of a cut or a scrape but not the blood of a life. Then Dr. Chatterjee flicked on the overhead fluorescent and in its glare Flavian saw the boy's twisted neck and something wrong that he couldn't name except that he knew some order known to the body was terribly out of place. "Mother of Mercy," the mother whispered. "Please do some-thing, please help."

Dr. Chatterjee motioned to Flavian. "There's a pair of scis-sors in that side table. Bring those, I need to cut away his shirt."

The mother started forward. "Oh, no, ma'am, I don't think—"

"I will buy him a new shirt if it comes to that," Dr. Chatter-jee said. She took the scissors and sheared down the back of the shirt in one smooth motion. The boy's mother held back, her head bent. The shirt fell away and Flavian, who was leaning in to hold the flailing child by his arms, saw first what Dr. Chatterjee saw next: Across the boy's skinny back were four welts, three horizontal bands and one at an angle and all four so precise as to insist that they existed not by accident but by design.

Flavian looked away.

A moment of silence.

"I see." Dr. Chatterjee looked closely at the welts, then turned from the child to pull open various drawers. "Lay him on his back. One at either end. We cannot wait for the ambulance. You are—?"

"I'm Officer Smith's wife. The state policeman. We live across the road."

"Yes." Dr. Chatterjee pulled an envelope from the drawer and tore it open and drew out a pair of latex gloves. She took them by their wrists and pulled them on, then laid their plastic wrapper flat on the table next to the boy. "Mrs. Smith, take his feet. Brother Flavian, stand at his head. Hold his arms, lift them above his head, pin them to your sides. Do not let him move. Hold his legs, Mrs. Smith, no, not like that, he must *not* be able to move, climb onto the table and sit between his feet and put your weight on his calves, yes, like that." Dr. Chatterjee scrabbled in the drawer and took from it a silver-handled knife and another plastic envelope and tore it open and removed a thin sharp blade and snapped it onto the knife and placed the scalpel on its flattened plastic envelope. She crossed to a closet and opened a door. "No proper chest tube, no proper chest tube, we will use this," and she returned with another envelope and a bottle the color of dried blood. "Keep him still." She opened the bottle, spilled a bit of its contents onto a tissue, wiped the blunted scissor clamps, peeled open the envelope, and then used the scissors to lift a plastic tube from inside. Dr. Chatterjee took up the scalpel and pinched off a bit of tubing, which she left lying on the square of opened plastic. "Brother Flavian, talk softly at his ear. Keep him still." Flavian clamped the child's arms at his sides as the mother spoke *Hail, Holy Queen, Mother of Mercy, hail, our life, our sweetness and our hope.* Dr. Chatterjee bent to the child's side and felt along his rib cage, and when her finger reached a certain place she made a small noise of satisfaction. "Still, still, my lad," and the doctor dropped her voice and spoke at the boy's ear in a slow, smooth murmur in a language Flavian had never heard while he responded to Mrs. Smith *To thee we cry poor banished children of Eve* even as Dr. Chatterjee continued her murmur, she might have been speaking in tongues as she wiped the boy's chest with the tissue, a swath of ochre on his white skin. *Mourning and weeping in this vale of tears,* Flavian spoke as he pulled back, the boy was so strong and fighting, twisting, the tendons in his neck taut with labor as he struggled for air, and Flavian braced his feet, grateful for his clodhopping farm boots. Now Dr. Chatterjee was laying the scalpel to the boy's chest and cutting with a quick, deep stroke, the strength of her shoulders leaning into the blade as the strength of her arms and hands held it back, and then something inside the boy gave way and Dr. Chatterjee made another small noise of satisfaction. With one hand holding the scalpel in place she took the scissor clamps in the other and inserted them into the wound. "Do *not* let him move, hold him still but yes, keep his arms pinned back, link his hands and hold them together yes, not much longer now," and with one hand she removed the scalpel and laid it on the square of plastic and then turned back to the boy and gave the clamps a half-turn and spread their handles wide so that the wound opened and it was as if she had punctured a tire, air and blood spattering out, blood sprinkling Flavian's shirt, and then the boy took a deep gasping breath and another and another and the color returned to his lips and face. "Now hold this hemostat exactly where it is and do *not* let it move," and Flavian leaned forward to hold the hemostat in place. Using a second set of clamps Dr. Chatterjee took up the piece of tubing and inserted it into the open wound. "Use this hemostat to hold the tube," and she removed the first hemostat and laid it aside as she was turning to take another small plastic envelope from the drawer. She peeled it open and took out a curved needle trailing a long black silken thread. The boy had stopped struggling now and his breathing was calming—his eyes still stared up at Flavian's but the terror in them had been replaced by ordinary fear. Dr. Chatterjee bent to the tube and inserted the needle into the boy's flesh on one side of the incision, then pulled the thread with a deft tug and looped it around the tubing and inserted the needle again and pulled with another tug, she might be sewing a button on a shirt, but at the end of the gesture Flavian could feel the tubing held in place now by the sutures, and after several more passes with the needle Dr. Chatterjee straightened her back and dropped her shoulders and exhaled a small sigh, and Flavian understood that it was over, that she had done what she set out to do. She cut and knotted the thread, then placed her hands gently on Flavian's hand and released the clamps of the hemostat and the tubing stayed in place, making a little bubbly sound each time the boy breathed. She turned to the desk and removed a length of gauze and another envelope of gloves.

The boy's lips and skin continued to brighten. The mother slipped from the table to her knees like a dropped stone. She took the boy's feet and pressed them to her forehead. On a table to one side Dr. Chatterjee was preparing a compress of gauze and adhesive tape. Flavian moved his hands from the boy's shoulders to cradle his head. The pitiless fluorescent blue.

Dr. Chatterjee bent again to the boy's ear. "His name is—"

The mother did not raise her head. "Matthew Mark."

"Matthew Mark. Do you know where you are? Do you know who I am?"

The boy looked up at Dr. Chatterjee and the monk. "Yes, ma'am. You're Doctor Chatterbox."

"Very good. And could you tell me what day today is?"

"Um—Thursday."

"And could you tell me the name of the president of the States?"

"Yes, ma'am. President Ronald Reagan."

"Very good, Matthew Mark. You are a brave boy, and smart, I see. I am very sorry that we had to treat you so roughly, but you know that you could not breathe and we had to make it possible for you to breathe, and now you can breathe, yes? Very good. Now you may close your eyes. Everything is going to be fine, but we shall take you on a short ride in the ambulance so you may have a story to tell your friends."

"And will you tell me a story on the way?"

"You're a young man now, you may go by yourself, though I'm sure you will have attendants. Perhaps they can tell you a story. Now turn on one side, so I can listen to your breathing."

"Promise you'll tell me a story."

Dr. Chatterjee smiled. "If you will turn on your side, I will tell you a story. For now we will want to take a look at your back."

At this the mother lifted her head. "Oh, I don't think you need to do that, no, ma'am. You can see for yourself, he's doing fine now. His color. I don't know how I can thank, what I can do to thank—"

"Mrs. Smith. If you could just help me give him a turn—"

The mother stood. "Oh, no, he'll be just fine, I don't think we need—"

His eyes focused on the boy's sun-streaked hair, Flavian took the boy by his shoulders and gently turned him on his side.

Dr. Chatterjee examined the welts. "The skin is not broken— that is good—I see no visible evidence of internal trauma, but an X-ray will be required. Evidently there was enough trauma to induce pneumothorax." She spoke calmly and to no one in particular. "If a trauma causes a gap, even a small tear to open between the chest cavity and the exterior, each breath pulls in air and that serves to collapse the lung, making it impossible to breathe. Asthma is a complicating factor but only rarely is it the proximate cause. We have equalized the pressure so that the boy can breathe, and as a result he is in no immediate danger, but we will need X-rays to determine if he requires further treatment." For a moment she held her silence, then she motioned the woman into a chair and sat next to her and took her hand. The woman pulled away. Dr. Chatterjee gently took her hand again. "Mrs. Smith. Can you tell me again how this happened? Bear in mind that your son's health depends on my knowing precisely what took place."

At that moment Flavian heard the ambulance wail—it had been a half hour since his phone call, the time it took a driver breaking the limit to reach their small town from the hospital thirty country miles distant. The mother said nothing. The boy's eyes were closed—asleep? or possum? The wail enlarged itself. Those welts striped across that small back. Flavian turned away and did not look at the boy again until Dr. Chatterjee had wrapped the torn shirt around his shoulders and the paramedics were wrestling a stretcher into the room.

Chapter 4

The priest and the policeman were fishing. They had become friends because, as Father Poppelreiter pointed out, they shared a mutual interest in the law, whether that of God, in his case, or of man, in the case of Officer Smith. They became fishing buddies because they each took Mondays off. Father Poppelreiter recovered from a day of saying mass in five different parishes scattered across two counties. Officer Smith recovered from a weekend of checking IDs on underage kids or seething under the threats and pleas of speeders (they might as well save their breath, he always wrote the ticket, no exceptions, tell it to the judge). Smith was young, with a weak chin and small narrow black eyes and eyebrows so thin and faint and the folds beneath his eyes so dewlapped that he gave the impression of having always been old. He was young but not naive—he knew perfectly well that the old priest spent their first hours on the lake in an agony of desire. Smith could see it in the priest's eyes, darting to the cooler under the middle seat, he could read it in the priest's ruddy face, where the intricate branchings of broken capillaries bore witness to a lifetime of longing. Smith knew those signs since before memory—his earliest recollections were of the smell of whiskey on his father's breath.

Smith stalled the small motor and let his boat drift in the middle of the lake. "No respect," he said. He pulled out a cigarette, tapped it on a gunwale, took it between his lips, and cupped a hand to shield his match from the slight breeze. "I get no respect. Not from the sheriff, not from my wife, not from the kid, not from the lawyers, and God knows not from the judges."

"At least you carry a gun," Father Poppelreiter said. "Imagine enforcing the law without it. I have thought on many occasions that my interests as well as those of the Church would be best served by small arms. And when you reach retirement age they'll let you ride into the sunset instead of keeping you in the traces til you drop."

"Pull up that minnow cage, would you." The priest retrieved the cage, let the water drain into the lake, and handed it over. The officer pawed among the flipping and flapping minnows. He scooped one out, stuck it on a hook, and tossed his line and the cage into the murky water.

After a moment the priest retrieved the cage, baited his own line, and threw it into the lake on the opposite side of the boat. "You have to *command* respect," Father Poppelreiter said.

"I do my job, I do it good. You got other suggestions, I'm listening."

"That's your problem," Father Poppelreiter said. "You think doing a good job is the way to earn respect. You take it from me. Your sheriff is the same as my bishop. You're not going to get respect from him unless you give him some reason to be afraid of you."

"So how do I get them to be afraid of me? I'm just a cop. It's their job to beat up on me. It's my job to take it."

"How about killing somebody? That will get their attention." The priest cleared his throat. "That was a joke."

They sat staring at the flat green water, with its two red-and-white bobbers.

"Kind of warm out here," Father Poppelreiter said.

"You might wear something other than black. Jesus."

The only sound was the quiet lap of water against the boat.

"I didn't mean to whip him so bad," Officer Smith said quietly. "But he wouldn't obey, he was just sassing me because he could get away with it—he gets those ideas from his mother—he sure as hell didn't get them from me. Somebody has got to set him straight, right? Toughen him up for the world. Better now than later, right?"

The old priest sighed deeply and turned his back.

"I'll catch him a mess of perch, that's his favorite," Smith said. "Nothing better than a pile of those little perch dipped in cornmeal with a little salt and pepper and a egg to make it stick and then fried. He does love his perch."

The lake had been dug as a raw red hole in the earth and only junk saplings lined its banks. Though it was still spring, at midday the sun made its heat known. The aluminum seats grew hot.

Officer Smith's red-and-white float bobbed. He flipped the butt of his cigarette into the lake and raised his line—a perch flopped at its end, shattering with silver droplets the lake's green mirror. The officer raised the pole too quickly. He grabbed for the line, but it sailed out of reach and the hooked fish smacked the priest's cheek. On the second try Smith brought the fish into the boat. He worked the hook from the perch's mouth, then skewered it on a stringer, dropped it into the minnow bucket's cage, and lowered the cage into the lake.

The old priest held his silence, even through the indignity of being slapped by a fish—he was a silent black pillar of longing. Finally Smith relented. "Calls for a little celebration, wouldn't you say?" he said. The priest held his tongue. From under the middle bench Smith pulled out his cooler and extracted two beaded longnecks and slipped them into cup holders. "Keep 'em low," he said. "I've known a nosy game warden too big for his britches who'd like nothing more than to come across me drinking in the park." He reached under the bench again and pulled out his flask. "A little whiskey for a chaser?"

"It would be impolite to refuse." The priest poured the whiskey into the flask's screw top, then tossed it down.

They drank their beers in silence. Neither floater budged. The priest finished his beer first. The officer took his time, but in the end he was as interested as the priest in getting a buzz on and they had a second round.

The sun was nearing the treetops when they heard the first of many cars. The gravel road that served the lake continued past it to dead-end at a run-down house, lost now amid the greening trees of spring. Every few minutes a car whizzed around the lake, vanished into the trees, then came to an audible halt at the door of the shack. A few minutes later the car reappeared, whizzing back to the highway. The cars arrived exactly on the quarter hour—Smith timed their coming and going. "They say the guy who owns that auto parts lot across from the bank is into it big time," Smith said. "You never see a customer in there. And the parts—"

"Not what we'd—"

"Strange."

"You'd think he was building formula racecars. But nobody here—"

"Weird."

"What is his name?"

"Foreign parts."

"Sends his kids to the public school. Parochial school not good enough for them."

"Or maybe he's afraid his kids might talk about what they see at home. Benny Joe—that's it. Big guy—they call him Little. I'm guessing the auto parts are a cover."

A squeal of tires in the distance. A black van streaked by. "You don't want to turn 'em in," Smith said. "We're the only people back here on Mondays. They'd know who did it right away." He took out the flask and took a swig, keeping his eyes on the old priest, who no longer troubled to hide his interest. "And it's not just from below," Smith said. "Now the big guys from Washington are coming in with helicopters and fancy X-ray machines. Like I couldn't tell them the location of every patch of pot in the county, not that they'll ask. It's no problem finding it. The problem is getting a jury to convict a guy who's their first cousin, or their cousin's cousin, or their aunt, or their bastard son. Do you know what I get paid? These guys make my monthly salary in a single sale. The temptation, Father. Take Little. He comes to me offering—"

"Offering what?"

"Naw, never mind. Johnny Faye's the ringleader. His trial's next month. Third time he's up for growing. The guy is guilty as a Nashville hooker and I'll bet you a nickel the jury lets him off scot-free."

"I'll double that," the priest said, reaching for the flask.

The officer moved it out of his reach. "Scare us up a few bites first. I don't know that I've seen a slower day. Maybe they hadn't stocked it yet. Maybe we're too early in the year."

The priest looked at his outstretched hand, then turned it palm down and extended it over the water. "'Put out into the deep water and let down your nets for a catch,'" he said. He pulled up his line—empty—some turtle or fish had nibbled away the bait. He gave up, laying his pole in the boat.

"I get a fish, you get a drink," Smith said.

At that moment the lake swallowed his floater whole, dragging the line after it. Officer Smith tightened his grip on his pole, barely saving it from following the line. "Jesus!" he cried. "Must be a fucking whale!" Under cover of the excitement the priest took a sip from the flask, then a second, while the officer struggled with the pole, bent almost to breaking. The line moved in a frantic zigzag. "I didn't know this puddle grew 'em this big," Smith said. He wrapped the line around one fist and dropped the pole, then began taking the line in hand over hand, past the floater, until he pulled up a slime-covered gray-green creature as long as and thicker than a burly man's arm. "Holy shit," Smith said. "What the fuck is that?"

"Call it a miracle." The priest surveyed the fish. "Around here people call them mudcats, though where I grew up we called them hellbenders. They're bottom feeders—they don't usually move more than a few feet in their very long lives. No good for eating—you can't get the mud out of the meat. You don't want to let your hand near its mouth—they've got a nasty temper and sharp teeth. The question is, how did it get into this lake? My father told me that on wet nights they can crawl across land but I never believed it before now. Either that or it's been here since before the dinosaurs."

"Ugly motherfucker."

"Officer Smith. Please."

The officer pulled the gun from his holster. Taking the barrel in his fist, he slammed the butt down on the creature's head. A trickle of blood flowed from its mouth, but the long muscle of a body still struggled and flapped and the fish glared up at them with baleful eyes. "Die, you fucker," Smith muttered and pounded it until the boat rocked.

"Why do you have to do that?" the priest asked.

"It's our God-given duty to rid the earth of vermin and I'd say this piece of shit qualifies. You said yourself, don't get your hand near its mouth. Anyway, it's dead," and in fact the creature lay unmoving, a thick remnant of a time before time, blood oozing from its mouth. "Might as well save the hook." Smith took up a pair of pliers and bent to the task. He was prying the hook free when the fish convulsed with a last twitching heave and clamped its bony jaws on the officer's fingers. "Jesus fucking Christ!" Smith cried. He grabbed up his buck knife and cut the line and tossed the creature into the water, where it turned over and floated, white belly to the sky. He seized the flask and upended it over his bleeding hand, but under cover of the struggle the priest had drained the contents and only a few drops trickled out. The officer threw the flask into the bottom of the boat, pulled out his gun, and fired a round at the fish. The report echoed from the surrounding trees. The fish floated idly, untouched.

Smith sat to the motor and started it with a savage pull to the cord. "Last time I ask you to bless the waters."

"Be careful what you pray for," the priest said.

Officer Smith sucked on his wounded hand. "I'd just as soon be shut of the sermon, if you don't mind."

The priest sighed. "Let me give you some advice. It's too late to do me any good but somebody might learn something from my life even if I haven't. The world is filled with trouble. You sit where I sit and you hear and see it all the time, and you live long enough and it will come to you. I can't get away from it, it follows me to the ends of the earth, even to this godforsaken little pond in the middle of nowhere trouble follows. So I say, next time it comes to you to bring more trouble into the world, think about how much there is already. Mercy is by definition a virtue reserved for the powerful, a fact I learned from having no power and so never having the luxury of exercising it. So next time life presents you with an opportunity to exercise your power, think about how maybe you can bring a little less trouble into this weeping world."

By the time they reached the bank the trees were a line of jagged black teeth against a sullen gray sky and the air was chill. The officer emptied the minnow bucket into the lake and held up the stringer, with its single flapping perch now glistening, now dull in the slanting sun. "No pleasure in a single perch," he said. He bent to the water, unclipped the stringer, slid the fish from its tine and released it into the lake, where it floated on its side, bleeding and dazed.

Chapter 5

The Smiths lived in a brick shoebox of a house across the highway from Dr. Chatterjee's office. Two small double windows, their curtains always drawn, framed a white door. Mangy grass struggled to get a purchase in the yard, rocky and uneven from the digging of the foundation. A yellowing boxwood hedge grew under one of the windows. In the center of the yard, a dogwood sapling with two or three blossoms was staked to the ragged dirt. Dr. Chatterjee searched for the doorbell but found only wires, wrapped in black tape, dangling from a hole. She knocked once, then again. Officer Smith's wife opened the door. Dr. Chatterjee held out her hand. "I have come to inquire after your son. I stopped by his room at the hospital to discover he had been discharged."

The door opened to the width of Mrs. Smith's thin shoulders. "That's awfully nice of you, ma'am. He's doing just fine. And you got no need to worry about the bill—"

"I am not concerned with the bill but I feel his situation is unresolved and as his admitting doctor I am responsible. Perhaps we could sit and talk for a moment?"

Mrs. Smith's hand strayed to her hair. "Oh, ma'am, that's so very sweet of you to trouble yourself but I'm in the middle of spring cleaning and the place aint fit for a pig. You just let me know how much we owe and I'll see to it that my husband—"

Dr. Chatterjee took her hand. "Please, dear Mrs. Smith, I am not concerned with the bill. Your husband's insurance will cover all but the most incidental expenses, and those we can attend to in due time." She brought forth a package she had concealed at her side. "I had promised you a fresh shirt."

Mrs. Smith drew back. "Oh, no, ma'am, we couldn't, my husband would never accept charity, not after you've already done so much, it wouldn't be right. We should be buying a present for you."

The afternoon sun streamed into the front room. Dr. Chatterjee caught a glimpse of quick movement behind Mrs. Smith's back. She thrust the package into Mrs. Smith's hand. "It was so very little, a pleasure, you will allow me, please, it may be too big but they assured me you could exchange it."

"I thank you very much, better to buy too big, by the time you wash it for the first time he'll already have outgrown it, I'm much obliged, I'm sure he'll like it just fine. I'll be sure to let you see him wearing it." She was closing the door.

"Do stop over for a visit any time you would like to discuss the matter further," Dr. Chatterjee said, but the door was closed.

As she turned to go the officer drove up in his police cruiser. She lifted her hand in greeting. He did not glance in her direction but continued to the rear of the house. Her grandmother, half a world distant and long dead, spoke at Dr. Chatterjee's ear. *Some day you will have to go to your father-in-law's house. You must learn to be a good wife or you will be disgraced.*

Crossing the highway to her office Dr. Chatterjee was a roiling mass of emotions dominated by a fierce anger. She bent to the street's graveled edge and picked up a stone to throw it at . . . whom? The stone fit perfectly in her hand, gray and round and smooth, and gave at least that satisfaction. She stuck it in the pocket of her suit.

Chapter 6

The county attorney, Harry Vetch, had a smooth oval face with pink cheeks and eyes that changed color depending on the time of day—in full sun they were palely and innocently blue but in shadow or at night they were some complex shifting color closer to green. In bright light they twinkled—the result of overactive tear ducts—but they gave him an earnest air, the look of someone who needed mothering. His hair was fast disappearing but he could still claim to be blond. He was as tall as he needed to be but slight of build—in high school he had played football mostly to be popular, though on the field he had been doggedly, foolishly fearless.

He was a churchgoer and a believer—not in the window dressing of doctrine or dogma but in the institution, the great edifice of the Church. As an attorney he understood that the Church was less about principle than about precedent. Precedent translated into continuity, continuity enabled stability, stability enabled civilization, civilization enabled prosperity. "People want strong leaders," he said to Maria Goretti as she helped her daughter into her pajamas. "People want to be led."

"And you want to lead them."

"I think that is what I have been called to do." He swirled the last of his drink before downing it in a gulp. "Does that sound too, I don't know. Grandiose?"

"Well, *called*. How about just saying, 'I'm ambitious'? That's OK with me—I like ambitious."

"How about *dedicated?* Dedicated to public service. It's not easy taking on responsibility. People envy the power and the perks—"

"—and the money."

He sighed. "I could make a lot more money moving to a big city and going to work for a corporation. You know that."

"Where everything would be a lot more expensive and you'd be one of fifty lawyers working in cubicles."

"I'm just pointing out the burdens of elective office. Dealing with every crackpot telephone call. Trying to help people bring some order into their messy lives."

"I want a story, Mom," her daughter said. "You *always* read me a story."

Maria Goretti scooped her up. "I always read you a story except for tonight, Baby Doll. You're old enough to know that *always* always comes with some exceptions. Mamma needs to spend some time with her guest." She lifted the little girl onto her shoulder. "Say night-night. You want to give Mister Harry a goodnight kiss?"

Vetch held out his arms. Baby Doll buried her head in her mother's shoulder and he laughed. "That's OK. Next time I come *I'll* read you a story, how about that."

Baby Doll raised her head and let out a long wail. Maria hastened her down the hall and for the next fifteen minutes he heard her wails and whimpers until Maria Goretti returned, shut the door and flopped on the couch next to him. "Jesus. I don't know what's got into that kid, she's usually so sweet. That jealous phase, they all go through it around her age but that doesn't make it any easier to put up with. You want a refill?"

"Sure, why not."

He spoke to her over the comforting noises—the suck of the freezer door opening, the slam of its close, the clink of ice against glass. "I like that. You stood firm and that was the right thing to do. Kids want discipline, just like grownups. We think we're so different from kids when the fact is we're pretty much the same, only bigger."

She returned with his drink and sat. "You're right so far as you go but you forgot the other half of the picture."

"That being?"

She snuggled closer. "Kids need love too."

He took a careful sip. "Well, sure. So talk to me about the new doctor. You've met her at the hospital?"

"Sure, of course, the director brought her around and introduced her to the lab staff. I'd say we're lucky to have her, much as you can tell from a ten-second introduction. She's very—*serious*."

"India is a pretty exotic place to come from for somebody who ends up just past the middle of nowhere."

"Well, if by *exotic* you mean dark-complected, she is that. Olive-skinned, with that beautiful coal black hair they always have—at least the ones I've seen on TV. Short. All business. A little—not *fat*, no, not at all fat, but let's say *full-figured*. She wears her hair pulled back so tight you'd think it'd give her a headache. She has these dark eyebrows that almost meet in the middle—they make her eyes big and dark and round, but it's not off-putting, just—different. Attractive. She's not your bleached-blonde homecoming queen, if that's what you mean, but I'd call her—well, pretty. In her way."

"Has she said anything about her office? A converted gas station. What were they thinking? I would have tried to talk a private provider into coming here."

"She hasn't said a word to me but if she uses my name she'll be the first doctor to remember it. Doctors only remember the names of other doctors. She can be awfully—I don't know. Cold. She'd be a hard woman to love."

"Maybe she needs somebody to take the lead."

Maria sat back and folded her arms. "Harry. You can be such a pill."

"That was a joke, Maria." He leaned over and kissed her forehead.

"Every joke contains a grain of truth, is what my mother told me." She laid a hand on his arm. "Your chance to prove my mother wrong."

He took a sip and set down his glass. "Really, I have to be going. I've got a big trial coming up. We're trying Johnny Faye for growing pot. Again. It should be an open and shut case except the officers didn't do their job right, on top of which it's Johnny Faye and between his cousins on the jury and who knows what threats and promises he's laid down I'll be lucky to get him fined, forget about doing time. And then I have meetings with some potential Ridgeview Pointe investors. And *then* I'm going to talk to some folks about raising money to furnish that gas station. Doctor's office. Can you imagine a doctor in that place in the summer? She'll roast."

Maria ran her hand up his arm and onto his shoulder. "I was hoping you'd stick around to play some piano."

"Air piano?" He struck a chord with his hands.

"I was thinking of a different kind of piano."

"Look. Uh, Maria." He took another sip. "You know I'm an honest man."

"You're afraid you're leading me on. And you don't want my feelings to get hurt."

"Well—yes, something like that. I don't really have the time to talk about this right now. I just don't want you to get the wrong idea. I hate to have to remind you, but this was your idea. You've been very understanding, but I've been clear from the first about where this wasn't going."

"Harry, I'm not understanding, I'm smart. I am *touched* that you'd be so considerate of my feelings, but my feelings are my business, not yours. Now. Can we fuck?"

"Not tonight. Next time."

"Harry. You're always saying that. Meanwhile I've lost track of the last time we actually did the deed."

"A couple of weeks. OK, three. Anyway, you're old enough to know that *always* always comes with exceptions." He downed his drink. "This will be the third time I've tried Johnny Faye and I'm going to go home and come up with a new approach. I'm going to appeal to, I don't know. That's what I'm going home to think about." He gave her another kiss and stood.

"Suit yourself." She stood and opened the door with a bow. "Maybe think about how sex might be something other than a weapon."

He grinned. "To the warrior everything is a weapon."

On the drive home he thought not of Johnny Faye but of Maria Goretti. She had the complexion of a woman not a day over thirty except for the fine lines at the corners of her lips. She was smart and full-breasted and full of fire without being annoying, a tough act for an older woman. He did not know who had fathered her child and had never asked—knowledge of a detail so intimate opened the path to responsibilities and he was not interested in responsibilities, not with a hospital lab tech with an illegitimate daughter, but they were reaching that point where responsibility was hard to avoid. He had always been up front with her, but he had stayed too long at the dance.

Of course he could let this thing with Maria Goretti continue and nobody would ask questions. "But that's just the point," he said out loud. "They won't ask questions, they won't say a word, they'll smile and shake my hand and they might even give money and then once they're in the voting booth they vote for the guy whose life is just like theirs." He had been given a mission, he understood this, he had felt it from his earliest consciousness—the guiding hand, the summoning voice, in service to which one must make sacrifices. This affair with Maria Goretti was dallying by the wayside, dodging his destiny.

And now there was a stranger in town—a doctor, who could have imagined that coming to pass, and *well, pretty, in her way.* New to town and a stranger . . . it might not be a bad idea to make her acquaintance.

Chapter 7

Judge Drummond was a Presbyterian running a Catholic county and it was not an easy job. On bright and sunny days (today was not one of them) he thought the combination felicitous. He kept the Catholics in line with his Presbyterian rigor and upright tone, while their inclination to place having a good time above all other considerations—well, he was sure it served some good end, the Lord worked in mysterious ways and it was not his place to question, only to bow his neck to the yoke.

Two centuries earlier his ancestors had come from one rocky, hilly land to another and made it theirs—they had settled this county earlier than the Catholics, only twenty years earlier but first come, first served, even though the Catholics had multiplied as was their wont and now outnumbered the Presbyterians four to one. The judge was well aware that he lived in a democracy and that his job depended on the Catholic vote, but he had gotten this far by trusting the judgment of the voters to distinguish selfless public service from greed for power, and that was where he placed his faith, which for a fifth-generation Scots Presbyterian in the South meant to administer impartially within the bounds of good judgment and to impose some kind of civilization on the congenitally unruly and to relax into a couple of highballs in the late afternoon to take the edge off all that responsibility.

On this particular morning Ginny Rae had not poured his

second cup of coffee before he started on the antacids, whose chalky taste he associated with turning seventy and, more recently, with the rise of the pot growers. Two days earlier his secretary had conveyed the message that a team of federal attorneys would be pleased to meet with him and appointing—not requesting—a date and time in Harry Vetch's private offices.

Why the county attorney's private offices rather than the courthouse? Why not the judge's private offices? In the end the judge made silk of that particular sow's ear by arranging to be conveyed the two blocks to Vetch's office by two state troopers, Officers Smith and Jones, and on their arrival he invited them to accompany him to the meeting. He took pleasure in the unhappiness evident in Vetch's features when they entered. Without the cops the count was 3–1; with them it was 3–3 and his men were in uniform. The guns stayed.

The federal attorneys had filled the county attorney's office with placards using pie charts and bar graphs to prove a contention that one phone call to him, the judge, would have established in ten seconds: The marijuana business was big and getting bigger and in this part of the nation it was centered here, among the first hills south of the cities of the Midwest. Years ago the hillbillies made moonshine, one of the attorneys said, and now they were growing pot. The second attorney chimed in, noting that one of the biggest sources of the problem was the leniency of judges, who often looked the other way and sometimes had their hands in the till. "Which is why we chose you to meet with. You have a reputation for probity and we knew we could count on you to back us up."

"But I have no role in the courts, you know that. I'm only an administrator."

"And among the most respected and influential." Vetch was speaking now. "You don't conduct trials but people look to you for leadership."

The judge made a little accordion with his fingers, touching their tips and flexing them in and out. "Not so very long ago we had a case where Miss Lucia Beene, resident poetess and somewhere on the full side of seventy, was convicted of growing pot on her sister's sun porch and selling it through her Christian bookstore. Now it's not six months later and you're telling me you're going to throw Miss Beene into the federal pen for fifteen years without possibility of parole."

"Twenty years, and we can confiscate her sister's property whether or not her sister was aware of the crop." This from the second attorney. "We put out the message of take-no-prisoners, slash-and-burn, mandatory sentences and people will get the point. This is a new ball game with new rules. We've got a federal forfeiture fund now. We confiscate a couple of farms of those guys who don't know what's going on, or who claim they don't know, and we put fear in people's hearts. And when we confiscate land people will figure out that we mean business. That's what we want. We want the people down here to understand that this is the law that's at stake. We flat-out take some property, break a few bones, and we'll see who's growing a year from now. Fear is the best means to power and surprise is the attacker's most powerful weapon. We don't *want* to give them warning, and we have no legal obligation to give them warning."

The judge rolled his eyes to the ceiling. "The next step from what you're proposing is imprisonment without habeas corpus."

"Oh, please, Judge." Vetch's passion brought him forward in his seat. "There's no point in using that kind of language. You're an attorney. This is the United States. We don't hold people in prison without probable cause. Habeas corpus is a constitutional right. If you could only hear yourself. You sound like an old man hanging on to old ways."

"That's because I *am* an old man," the judge said. He took another antacid.

And now the feds and their placards were gone back to the city and the officers dismissed. The judge faced Vetch across an expanse of glass-topped desk empty except for a telephone and a computer.

Behind the desk stood a brand-new grandfather clock, its pendulum chamber backed with a mirror. The clock was placed so that a client—sitting in the chair where the judge sat now—saw his own reflection, in a way that was profoundly discomfiting, as the eye invariably sought itself out while Vetch, his back to the mirror, talked on.

The judge stood, shoved the chair a few inches to the right, and sat again. In the mirror the light caught the shine in Harry Vetch's thinning blond thatch. The judge had thick, waving, silver hair. *Come*, he thought, *let us dance.*

Vetch pulled a sheaf of papers from a drawer and slid them across the desk. "I don't know if you're aware of the implications of the new property confiscation regulations."

The judge ignored the papers. "I was certain that I could depend on you to bring them to my attention."

"Under these regulations the federal government has the right to confiscate and sell the property of those growing marijuana and their collaborators as well as those who have the crop on their property, regardless of whether they are aware of its presence."

"I understood Mr. Reagan to have committed himself to the lessening of big government's intrusions into our small lives. I gather I have been mistaken."

Vetch indicated the papers. "Our friends neglected to single out two key words which I'm drawing to your attention. Those being *and sell*. What is confiscated is sold. What is sold brings income. At the enforcement agency's request the government returns most of the income received from the sale of confiscated properties to the enforcement agencies. The idea being that the criminals finance their own arrest and trial and jail time."

"The idea being, as best I can tell, that the enforcement agency has been provided an almost irresistible incentive to confiscate the property of almost anybody who has the misfortune to come under its surveillance, that is, everyone in its jurisdiction."

Vetch hunched forward, narrowing his eyes. The judge held up his hand. "I hope you will not take offense, but speaking as an older attorney to a respected but younger colleague, you must master the art of the blank countenance. I see your point. With not much labor on either of our parts we could have, oh, to offer one example drawn from many, the three hundred acres located adjacent to your golf course development and owned by Johnny Faye—to be more precise, owned by his mother, but this is a technicality that the new regulations are designed to circumvent—we could have this land confiscated and sold to finance two new policemen, or a helicopter for the county sheriff and a pilot to fly it. With the added bonus of Johnny Faye in prison."

Vetch looked stricken. "Judge. I readily acknowledge that I'm committed to putting Johnny Faye in prison and so far as I'm concerned they can throw away the key. But the future of his land—his mother's land—had not crossed my mind, not once. I don't think in those terms and I object to any implication that I do."

The clock struck eleven. The judge stood. "Well. You are the enforcer of the law, as you know. I'm just the administrator."

Vetch stood and leaned forward, hands flat on the green baize of his desk blotter. "We can take him down. For the sake of our children—"

"*My* children. Or have you fathered a child while I was looking elsewhere?"

"—we *have* to take him down. The Administration has given us the means to that end and I intend to use those means. And bankrupting and imprisoning a lifelong criminal is a small and necessary price to pay. We can use those funds to hire more policemen—"

"Who can justify their salaries by making more arrests and confiscating more land."

"With due respect, Judge, I don't think you grasp the seriousness of what's happening here. There is a great struggle between good and evil and there's no room for wafflers. If anyone causes these little ones to sin, it would be better for him to have a millstone hung around his neck and to be drowned in the sea."

"It's been a long while since I've heard Scripture quoted in an office of the law."

"You're about to see a lot that you're not used to. There's a sea change happening in this country and I'm inviting you to get on board the ship before it leaves."

"Look. Harry. First philosophy, then politics. Am I concerned about the pot growers? You bet I am. But these guys only know one way to put food on the table and that involves sticking something in the ground and making it grow. You are not going to change human nature by throwing them in jail, you're just going to get a lot of people in jail and at the considerable expense of the taxpayers, not to mention the Constitution. Meanwhile I don't have the budget to equip the doctor's office or to build a softball field where those kids might spend their nights doing something other than smoking pot."

"You don't have to convince the people of this county that we're doing the right thing in throwing the pot growers in jail." Vetch shook his finger in emphasis. "All you have to do is to sit back and cooperate with *our* government in making it happen. As for the future of his mother's land—we will cross that bridge if we come to it. Which, I will not deny, I hope we do, because that will mean we have him in the pen."

The judge pushed Vetch's pointed finger to the side. "And now we get to politics. As you know, I am judge by honorific only—I have no power to do what you ask, except in the matter of placing a bid on confiscated lands. And I am relieved to hear you're not thinking about that, since it absolves me of the need to lecture on the inappropriateness and potential illegality of such thinking."

"I beg your pardon, Judge," Vetch said in a low intense voice, "but I love these people. I love them more than they love themselves. It drives me crazy to see them put themselves down. I want to give them a chance at a real job, making real money." Here Vetch pushed himself up from the baize and turned his back. The clock ticked off the seconds. In the mirror of the pendulum compartment the judge could see him clenching and unclenching his jaw. Finally Vetch turned around. "There's power and there's power," he said evenly. "I have the power of the law. You have the power of . . ."

Another long pause. "Funny," the judge said, "how that clock seems to tick louder at some times than at others. I'm sure it's all in my head. I imagine that if I could somehow keep track of that, I'd have some clue to my own thinking." He stood and replaced his chair in its original location. "On second thought, I'd rather not have a clue to my own thinking. Everybody is better off that way, especially me. I will take my leave, and I will be interested, very interested, in the proceedings from here, but I am especially interested in how you complete that last sentence. Oh, and a parting bit of unsolicited advice which I offer from my commitment to the political party that I have loyally served, one of whose rising stars, or so I am led to believe, is you. Marry that Shaklett girl, what's her first name, sounds like a pizza parlor. Maria Goretti."

"I don't know what you're talking about. *You* don't know what you're talking about."

The judge sighed. "You think everybody in this county isn't following every detail of your colorful personal life?"

"You can leap to conclusions but that doesn't make them right."

The judge made a great show of pulling down one corner of his mouth, rolling his eyes upward and studying the ceiling.

"For God's sake, Judge, she's a lab tech."

"And what is wrong with marrying a lab tech? I'll save that question for the next time you need a blood test in short order."

"Look, Judge, I'll be honest. I'm looking for a wife who's prominent. Visible. Somebody who shares my vision. Somebody—"

"—as ambitious as you are. Sounds like a recipe for disaster but whatever, marry some girl, any girl sooner rather than later and preferably shorter or at least no taller than you—this will look better when you're together on stage. If I may presume on your ambitions, as a bachelor you have no political future in this state.

You may philander all you want, but you have got to have a wife so that when you're caught, and you will be, she can extricate you from the mess of your making. Now try to enjoy spring before it turns hot."

The judge lived in a sprawling old home near the county attorney's office, and on these spring afternoons he enjoyed seeing the town—his town—leaf out. Anything seemed possible, even prosperity, for a place that had steadfastly resisted it for so long. Leadership, which he had once so eagerly sought, seemed a struggle and a burden, as young men did what they must do and snapped at his heels, and as the manners that had once governed the process vanished. "Sir," "ma'am," grace before meals, dances on Saturday evenings with Paul and His Privates on the bandstand, every band member a decorated veteran and the music with a syncopated beat to steps you had to learn and practice; Benediction for the Catholics on Sunday afternoons, and though his Presbyterian soul had nothing but disdain for all that smoke and mirrors, it kept their idle hands occupied—better smoking incense than smoking pot.

The day was somber and gray to match his thoughts. On the two-block walk to his house he found himself reconsidering the notion of a new home. Maybe he *should* buy a lot in Ridgeview Pointe as a peace offering to Harry Vetch. And who knew, maybe in a couple of years he'd build a nice little low-maintenance one-level ranchette with a guest room for the kids when they came to visit. He would miss their old house but the time had come—was past, really—to leave. The water pressure was lousy, the bathroom was downstairs and the bedrooms were upstairs, Ginny Rae's knees were going, and sometimes—he'd never told her this—he had to pause on the landing to catch his breath. A nice new house all on one level and with a golf course at hand—yes, that was the thing, and he would have the pleasure of knowing that he had left his mark on the place—left the town more civilized than when he'd been born.

But then his heart grew hot, he wished he were young again

at the thought of federal attorneys, who knew everything about the ever-changing law and next to nothing about the enduring heart, come to tell *him* what to do, how to run *his* county—and at the thought of the county attorney, *his* county attorney, collaborating instead of closing ranks.

Chapter 8

On certain days in early summer some last gasp of winter sneaked down from the vast north we call Canada and the air was clear and dry. At night the stars were close enough to pluck from their blue-black velvet case while on earth every hollow and ravine pulsed with the yellow lamps of an infinitude of fireflies. During the day the town was a palette of every shade of green, from the gray-green of the sycamores lining the creeks and rivers to the chartreuse of the locust trees dripping long cones of honey-scented white blossoms to the emerald maples with their whirligig seeds to the green-black magnolias, whose glossy leaves and creamy white flowers recalled to Dr. Chatterjee the jungles of her childhood.

The building that housed the doctor's offices formed a shallow U—its wings embraced a cement pad where mechanics had serviced vehicles too large for the interior bay. Someone had painted the slab lime green and supplied it with second-hand patio furniture, and in the evenings the doctor enjoyed a moment outdoors between the day's work of seeing patients and the night's paperwork. On such an evening, sitting with a cup of bitter American tea, the doctor received her first social call from her most locally famous patient.

Matthew Mark was a thin little boy with great dark circles under his eyes, a full and pouting lower lip, and a high rose blush in his pale cheeks that emphasized his delicacy while making him seem older than his years. He had approached as a small waif peering around the corner, wearing the shirt Dr. Chatterjee had left with his mother, his eyes larger and darker in the evening light. He edged forward to some invisible line perhaps twenty feet distant, then halted and stood, tentative in his boldness. "Thank you for the shirt. But now you owe me a story. You said so, I heard you tell my mamma."

She waved at a chair. "Would you care to be seated?"

He nodded and climbed into the chair. His legs, thin sticks ending in oversized shoes, dangled above the cement. She went inside and took some biscuits from a tin and arranged them on a chipped china plate that she found in a cabinet and that bore a stencil of a floppy-eared rabbit wearing a threadbare vest.

Matthew Mark took one biscuit. "Someone has taught you manners," the doctor said.

He pointed to the figure on the decorative saucer. "I'm too old for Br'er Rabbit."

"Of course you are, but I don't know the story of Mr. Rabbit and I brought him out so that perhaps you could tell it."

"I know lots of Brer Rabbit stories," he said, taking a second biscuit.

"Then tell me your favorite."

At this he paused and twisted his lips, thinking. "No, not Brer Rabbit," he said. "I have a better favorite. But you have to go first."

"Dear boy, stories are like tropical flowers—bring them to a new and foreign place and they wither and die. I have left my stories on the far side of the world, where they are at home."

"That's not true."

She frowned. "I beg your pardon?"

"I hear stories from places I never been all the time. They're my favorites. You come from some place I never been." He gave her an accusing look. "You *promised*."

"And I promised myself that I would leave all that behind."

Silence, born of stalemate. He spoke first. "You *saved my life,*" he said. "That's exactly what my mamma said to my daddy. 'She saved his life.' So now you have to do what *I* tell you to do. I read it in a story."

Dr. Chatterjee knitted her brows and pursed her lips. "Someday, little man, you will be a great barrister. Very well, one story only. This is the story of the goddess Durga, who was the patron of my country as the Virgin Mary is the patron of yours. Durga was married off at a tender age, just like Mary, except that she married Shiva, Lord of Destruction. Like so many boys Shiva was not ready to grow up—he would never grow up, not in ten million *skandas.*"

"*I'm* ready to grow up. I can't wait to grow up. What's a *skanda?*"

"A very, very long time. Shiva grew his hair long and spent his days drinking and his nights smoking *ganja*—"

"You mean, like Johnny Faye."

The doctor tucked down her chin and looked carefully at the boy. "How do you know about Johnny—Mr. Faye?"

Matthew Mark waved a hand dismissively. "Everybody knows about Johnny Faye. He's a character. Least, that's what my mother calls him. I'm not allowed to say what my father calls him."

"And what does your mother mean when she says, 'he's a character'?"

"Well, you know. A *character.* Somebody everybody talks about."

"Then yes, I think you could say Shiva was a *character.* Exactly like Johnny Faye. Shiva hung out at the burning pyres— in my country we do not bury the dead but we burn their bodies on big stacks of wood—"

"That's creepy."

"I beg your pardon?"

"*Creepy.* You know. The feeling you get when you're wading in the creek when it's muddy and something skitters under your feet and you can't see what it is."

"Ah, yes, *creepy*, exactly so. Well, for most of the year Durga stayed home, waiting patiently for Shiva's drunken returns, preparing his meals and raising their children. But once each year Durga returned to her homeland, to the villages and to the great city of Bengal, to Calcutta, her city, and oh, what rejoicing among her blood kin, the familiar places, the foods of her childhood!

"But the year came when her return was barred by the evil demon Durgo, who was running rampant, destroying the world. The gods had thrown all their might against him to no avail because Durgo was invincible to any man. But the goddess Durga was not a man and so she came astride her rampant lion, her ten arms brandishing ten weapons, her loyal children at her side. The demon Durgo took many forms. First he tried to trick her, then, once things started going badly, he tried to escape. But she won every battle until she ended his life by piercing the water buffalo—the last form he took—to his blue demon's heart.

"And every year to celebrate her victory there is a great festival. The priests of each village and neighborhood of Bengal select one girl from among all Brahmin girls according to rules set forth in instructions handed down from the gods. She must be flat-footed, thin-lipped, possessing enough curvature of the spine to be graceful but not so much as to be sensuous. You see?" Dr. Chatterjee stood to demonstrate. "Durga, virgin daughter of the Himalayas, chooses one girl as her incarnation for that particular year. And I was that girl—chosen from the girls in my dance class as one destined to lead an extraordinary life. In the same way as she has chosen you."

"She chose *me?*"

"Yes, of course. You have died and come back to life. Nothing could be more extraordinary than that."

"I like that story," Matthew Mark said. "Can I keep it for my own?"

"Of course, but you must learn the magic words that end it."

He sat up straight, serious. "OK."

She recited then the incantation with which her father ended all his stories and that she recalled as effortlessly as a prayer.

Thus my story endeth,
The Natiya thorn withereth,
"Why, O Natiya thorn, dost wither?"
"Why does the cow on me browse?"
"Why, O cow, dost thou browse?"
"Why dost the neat-herd not tend me?"
"Why, O neat-herd, dost not tend the cow?"
"Why dost thy daughter-in-law not give me rice?"
"Why, O daughter-in-law, dost not give rice?"
"Why does my child cry?"
"Why, O child, dost thou cry?"
"Why does the ant bite me?"
"Why, O ant, dost thou bite?"
Koot! Koot! Koot!

This formula Matthew Mark found especially thrilling, and he asked her to repeat it several times. "That story might be my new favorite," he said.

"Oh, and what did you like about it?"

"I am the mighty Durga!" he cried, jumping from his chair. He lifted his shirt and pointed to the bright splotch of scar on his skinny stomach. "And this is from my battles with the evil demon."

"Matthew Mark, it's an hour past your bedtime." Dr. Chatterjee looked up to see Mrs. Smith peering around the corner. "More'n an hour."

"Please forgive me, Mrs. Smith. I didn't realize it was so late and here I have been filling his head with stories."

"Oh, ma'am, you should call me Rosalee, like everybody else."

"A lovely name. But then you must call me Meena."

Rosalee took her son by the hand. "I'm sorry if he's been bothering you."

"He is quite the barrister. He tugged a story from me by charm and eloquence."

"Better you than me. That boy done memorized every story I know to tell and all the ones from the books at school." Rosalee pointed Matthew Mark across the road. "Go on, now, you've had your story for the night. I'll be back there in ten minutes and I want to see you with the covers pulled up and the lights out and the sink still wet from where you brushed your teeth."

Matthew Mark stood and jumped off the concrete pad, shouting as he flew through the air, *"Koot! Koot! Koot!"*

Then they were alone, the doctor and the mother, and the silence prolonged itself until finally Rosalee spoke. "You done your best and I have thanked you already and if you don't raise another finger I'll be thanking you ever time I lay eyes on that boy. He is smart as a whip, you can see that. Fearful smart. I caint keep up with him and the teachers at the school don't like to admit it but they caint keep up with him neither. I half think my husband is so hard on him out of plain jealousy.

"And I don't know what the Lord wants me to do. A few days after I got him home from the hospital I saw him playing in the yard—I was inside, making custard on the stove and before I could so much as knock on the window he had picked up a switch and was whaling away at this little girl, Paddlefoot Medley's girl that had come over to play, you know Paddlefoot, rings the bell at church, sets out the chairs, a good heart but none too bright but that's the Medley in him, they's all good farmers, those Medleys, could turn thistles into gold but they was slower than me in school and that tells you something. I left my custard to curdle and went outside and put a stop to that, let me tell you. I gave Matthew Mark a good dressing down, but I aint been able to put a stop to where he learned it. And I don't know what to do. But then you come halfway around the world, scared the living daylights out of me at first but now it seems to me like you are the answer to my prayers, somebody to tell me what to do. Somebody to help my boy."

Rosalee stood unmoving, her head bowed. After a moment Meena said, "Long ago I decided to place my faith in human action, the gods having been of little assistance. Of course I will help in whatever way I may. Let me give the matter some thought. Shall I speak to your husband's superiors?"

"Oh, no, ma'am, not that, please, no, anything but that. I didn't mean to ask—"

"Speaking with discretion, I assure you. I am aware of the delicacy of your situation."

"I trust you, ma'am. But not that, please, dear Mother in heaven. It's just—my husband—" Her hands opened, then closed. She clutched her arms to herself. "I guess what has to happen is what has to happen."

Meena followed her to the cement step to watch her cross the road.

Chapter 9

Sunday afternoons were an agony of solitude, a long stretch of time with a million things to do and no energy to do them. Meena found herself on the road, a small woman in a large car driving to the monastery, walking to the statues to watch the light that changed so rapidly at this latitude—even now, with the sun slowing to the peak of its solstice, in every wood on every day there was a different green. By way of proving to herself that she was dauntless she sat on the Virginia pine above the hollow where she'd been startled by the snakes. The jungle surrounding her childhood village had sheltered more lethal creatures, after all, the lithe leopards invisible against the jungle's striping of light and shadow, the kraits and cobras coiled amid tree roots, and yet she sought out that jungle as a source of consolation and strength much as she sought out the grove where she now sat, a clearing in a forest in a country where she had no relatives or friends.

Since Johnny Faye had rescued her from above the pit of writhing snakes, she was conscious that she was no longer alone. The quality of being watched—how to name this feeling? *Creepy.* She never saw him watching but her skin felt his eyes as surely as sunlight. A certain thrill in knowing she held his attention— she who had never been courted or allowed to court. An annoyance in the extreme that even in this new world she could not take a walk without a man thrusting himself upon her. The memory of his forearms presented itself against her will.

At first she sat with her back to where she presumed he must be, but the day came when she turned her head to peek and before long she was facing head-on the thicket from which he'd emerged on that day when she had perched above the snakes. She saw no one. She knew he was there.

Until an evening came when she discerned him sitting at some distance—fifty yards or more, far enough that she had to squint to be certain it was he. He sat so still and was so nearly invisible against the forest that the thought came to her that he had always been there but was only now allowing himself to be seen. He gave no sign of seeing her.

Now the midday heat enforced evening visits, but each time she sat on the fallen log she saw him, always accompanied by a shaggy mongrel of a dog. He never moved closer and never acknowledged her until an evening came when he stood and took a deliberate stretch, unfolding his lanky frame and turning his head to the sky in a gesture that conveyed as clearly as a handshake that he knew she was there and that he knew that she knew he was there. Her pulse quickened, her skin grew warm. He took something from his pocket and bent to tap it on a stone, then stood and struck a match. Sweet-scented smoke drifted through the still evening air. He sat again to stillness.

In this way they kept company, each aware of the other, until the first hot evening of summer, the air as close and breathless as the last evenings before monsoon. She stood and strode across the clearing. He was staring into the trees.

"Mr. Faye."

"Now you hush up."

"I understand that anyone may visit—"

"I said *hush up.*"

"Sir, I will not *hush up.* I am well aware that anyone may visit this place of meditation but I must express my extreme discomfort at being watched. As if you are a spy and I am your quarry."

He turned to face her. "I'll be damned. You don't think I been watching *you*."

"That is precisely what I think."

"Now why in the hell would I go and do a dumbass thing like that."

She drew herself up. "Because you are ignorant of the proper ways of courtship and this is the best you can do."

"Is that a fact." He looked down at the ground, dug a little hole with the toe of his boot, covered it back. His shoulders shook, a secret little laugh.

"Mister Johnny Faye. Please." She was annoyed with herself, she a doctor. *His* doctor.

Johnny Faye pointed at the ground a few paces distant. "Here. You come here. Now dammit, I aint going to lay a finger on you, I just want to teach you something. Come over here. Stand here. Right here. Now you *hush up*, like I asked, *hush up, pretty please*, a little sugar for the medicine if that makes it go down better, *Doctor* Chatterjee. Come on, it aint going to break your stiff neck and you just might see something that's worth looking at instead of plain old me."

She glared at him. He grinned. He turned to look east, away from the setting sun. He turned his broad shoulders to her—the phrase *broad shoulders* came to her of its own accord, unbidden and unwanted. She was turning away to walk to her car when his hand began to rise, deliberate as sunset. She followed his pointing finger.

At first she saw only a curtain of green trembling in an evening breeze. He kept pointing. She looked until her eyes tired. Then she saw a shiver of leaves, then a flying drop of scarlet so red against the evening's deepening blue that she caught her breath.

"He's been up there for almost a month now, don't know why he's taking so long. Maybe he was *ignorant of the proper ways of court-*

ship like yours truly. Anyways he finally got hisself a mate and they been at it for a couple of weeks, I'm expecting to see the young any day, at least if I'm lucky and I pay close enough attention. Scarlet tanager, is what the specs call him but we always called 'em redbirds, not the same as a cardinal, no, this guy is special, not that a cardinal aint special but I always had some trouble with a bird named after a man of the cloth, it aint his fault, of course, but I'm partial to the redbird, maybe because he don't like asphalt, he aint civilized, he hangs out in the high places in the deep woods." He turned to face her. "Like somebody else I know."

She recovered herself.

"Thank you for pointing it out. All the same I would be most grateful if I could have your assurance that you are here only to watch birds."

"The only way to come at 'em is slow and gentle. You got to shut up and pay attention. You got to test the edges of what you see. You caint come with your questions ready to ask. You got to let the place and the time and the bird tell you what to ask."

"Nonsense. Birds sing for a reason. To attract a mate, or signal each other that food and water is to be found, or for some other reason. Because we do not yet understand all the reasons does not mean those reasons do not exist. Enough time and intelligence applied to the task and we could find them out. We will find them out."

He made a great show of looking upward. "Oh, for certain sure. Only birds."

"Thank you. And now if you don't mind—"

"Don't mind at all." He took her arm. "I hear you saved the life of Rosalee's boy."

She withdrew her arm. "And where did you hear that?"

"I got my sources. Good ones, too, but I'd rather hear the story from the horse's mouth."

"He came in manifesting acute pneumothorax—"

"Sorry, I aint so good with the big words. You mean the good officer beat him to a pulp."

"No, not *beaten to a pulp.*"

"Not this particular time, maybe. Give him another year."

"—manifesting acute pneumothorax. I equalized the air pressure inside and outside the chest cavity, as any physician would. A dramatic but simple procedure."

"So what happens now?"

"What do you mean?"

"Do you sit around waiting for when he does get beat to a pulp?"

"That is a difficult question but outside the boundaries of my mission."

"He's your patient, aint he?"

"A patient whom I have cured." As she spoke she was edging away. "I cannot be responsible for the future. The terms of my contract are clear. I serve at the pleasure of the authorities who invited me. If they become dissatisfied for any reason, they need only notify the health service and my appointment will be terminated. If I lose my appointment, my visa will be rescinded and I must leave the country. It is unlikely that I would find another place—appointments for foreign doctors are filled a year and more in advance. The boy is the son of a police officer, the agent of the law. I have spoken with his mother, but she does not want me to speak to his superiors for fear that her husband may lose his job and from fear of her husband. Am I to violate her wishes? You see the difficulties. I have promised the boy's mother that I would do what I can, but if I lose my position I can do nothing."

"And so you do nothing. All right, well, whatever."

"Mr. Faye—"

"That's Mister Johnny Faye to you, Ms. Doctor Chatterjee, and you got nothing to fear in these woods so long as I'm around. Now you go back to your car and your *mission* and I will go back to watching my friend the redbird and I will keep my eyes strictly off of any and every blackbird, even if she does plunk her beautiful shiny self right down and all but yell *Look at me!* You have yourself a good afternoon."

He walked away, followed by his dog.

Sunday afternoon in high spring and Brother Flavian's main thought was to get away from the tourists who arrived at the monastery like so many grackles searching for spiritual food. The allée leading to the main gate was full of their buses, and a cloud of diesel smoke from their idling engines drifted over the enclosure walls. Flavian knew that if he stuck around the enclosure likely as not Cyril, who had desk duty, would corner him to explain how his arthritis was bothering him and would Flavian mind taking the job? Besides which there was that manila envelope still tucked under his mattress.

He set out for the copse of the sleeping apostles, brooding over why he had become a monk except out of what a lot of people would call cowardice and how devoutly he wished he were anything, anyone, anywhere but here. The problem was that a monk's life, every life, took on its own inertia. At one point, too young to understand that actions had consequences, he made decisions—he had decided that under no circumstances would he allow himself to be hauled off to an illegal war, he had decided to join a monastery. Now, years into the job and it had become mere employment instead of a way of life, a job in which the never-completed list of things to be done took on a life of its own, the mornings flew past and then it was the midday hour, then there was dinner, then a nap, then two hours of prayer and meditation that had become a daily indulgence in guilt and self-recrimination. Then the evening services, with their formulaic predictability—years into their chanting and he was over and done with the psalms, way over and done with the psalms. What was the point of all this ritual anyway?

At the fork to the statues his feet took him to the left, deeper into the forest. He let them take turns of their own devising until he found himself facing the wall of cedars through which he'd pushed to encounter Johnny Faye and his dog JC. Over the beating of his heart he could hear the chup and thunk of a hoe.

Flavian hesitated for a moment—nothing but trouble on the other side of those cedars. But he was here and Johnny Faye was here and this time he could find out where he lived and then he could return the envelope. The man was on monastery property and Flavian had a responsibility at least to see what he was up to, or so he told himself as he set about finding the parting in the cedars that opened onto the bend in the creek.

But now the trees were so dense that he was scratched and bleeding by the time he shoved through them to reach the lip of the bluff. From there he caught a glimpse of a straw hat and the familiar torn white singlet, but then his boot hit a patch of slick mud and he was down, sliding like a sled over the creek bank clay to land with his boots ankle-deep in water and the vegetable patch right in front of his eyes, the corn already sprouting its spring-green leaves and Johnny Faye nowhere to be seen. He had been there and now he wasn't, a conjuring trick if ever Flavian had seen one, so remarkable that Flavian shook his head and rubbed his eyes, and when he opened them there was Johnny Faye.

"I was shared skitless. I thought you was Officer Smith or the like coming to haul me off to the pen and the crop barely in the ground."

"Scared? What for?"

"Next time you sneak up on me, give me a little warning." Johnny Faye pursed his lips and cooed. "*Ooo-aahh, ooo, ooo, ooo.* Like a mourning dove."

"Well, whatever you say, but you don't often see doves down in a creek bed."

"You're a bright boy, Brother Tom, even if you are a dumbass. That's the point. *You* know that and *I* know that but most people wouldn't give it a second thought. So when I'm down here and I hear a dove calling I'll know it's you."

"Well, OK, but why all this cloak-and-dagger stuff over a patch of vegetables?"

Johnny Faye rolled his eyes and knelt to his task. He was weeding with a trowel. For a few minutes he worked in silence. Flavian located the white-and-tan sycamore throne and was about to take his seat when Johnny Faye straightened and stretched. "Against your religion to work on Sunday?"

"Well, yes, actually, except in cases of dire necessity."

Johnny Faye tossed Flavian the trowel and sure enough he caught it. "If I don't get these weeds out, the next time I'm down here they'll be choking my—*vegetables,* and I won't be able to pull up the weeds without taking the *vegetables* along with them. I'd call that dire necessity. Stay away from the seedlings—you can tell them easy enough—they're the ones lined up between the corn and with the little mound of dirt around their stems. Another week and they won't need a thing, but transplanting is hard on a plant and a person both, least until they get theirselves rooted."

Flavian knelt to the dirt and worked his way down the row—weeding the corn plants was no problem but he had to concentrate on working around the little feathery plants in between. The silence grew uncomfortable. He looked up to see that Johnny Faye had taken a seat in the sycamore throne and leaned back and turned his head, eyes half-closed, to the sky.

"So what kind of vegetables are these, anyway?"

Johnny Faye raised his head—one corner of his mouth twisted as if in pain. "You still believe in the Easter Bunny?"

"Well. The Easter Bunny. Well, no, at least not strictly speaking, but the Easter Bunny is a type, you know, of the risen Christ. Pre-Christian cultures saw the rabbit as a creature given to . . . fertility, and as a harbinger of spring. Then at some point Christians saw an opportunity to embody in a children's myth the principles of rebirth and renewal that are central to Christ's Resurrection."

Johnny Faye laid his head back against the trunk and sighed, a heave of exasperation. Flavian understood that he had failed to grasp some important point. "Well, I'm sorry."

"Tomatoes."

"Tomatoes?"

"I grow a shitload of tomatoes. My old lady cans 'em and gives 'em away at Christmas time. Let's talk about something else."

"Like what?"

"I thought you told me the only thing you know anything about is God."

"Something like that."

"Well, then, I guess then you'd better talk about God. It's Sunday. I hadn't been to church. You're on, preacher."

For a moment Flavian was at a loss for words, until he remembered that on Sundays he folded the sheet with the day's epistles and stuck it in his pocket for later reading. He pulled out the sheet and cleared his throat. "Well. This is from the Letter of Paul to the Hebrews. You know who Paul was."

"Sure, who don't."

"OK, then, let's look at the letter for today."

Flavian flattened the crumpled sheet of paper against his thigh and began to read. "'Some had to bear being pilloried'—Paul is talking about the Hebrew prophets and faithful in the centuries before Jesus arrived, some of whom were chained up and mocked in public for their beliefs.

Some had to bear being pilloried and flogged, or even chained up in prison. They were stoned, or sawn in half, or killed by the sword; they were homeless, and wore only the skins of the sheep and goats; they were in want and hardship, and mal-treated. They were too good for the world and they wandered in deserts and mountains and in caves and ravines. These all won acknowledgment through their faith, but they did not receive what was promised, since God had made provision for us to have something better, and they were not to reach perfection except through us.

With so many witnesses in a great cloud around us, then, we too should throw off everything that weighs us down and the sin that clings so closely, and with perseverance keep running in the race which lies ahead of us. Let us keep our eyes fixed on Jesus, who leads us in our faith and brings it to perfection. For the sake of the joy which lay ahead of him, he endured the cross, disregarding the shame of it, and has taken his seat at the right of God's throne.

Johnny Faye made a show of looking alert. "OK, you got your work cut out for you. Tell me what all that means."

"Well, what part of it stuck in your head?"

Johnny Faye considered. "I liked the part about sitting at the right of God's throne—I never seen a throne, of course, but I seen one in my mind, all gold and shiny and with clouds all around it, like those." He pointed up at the bright summer sky, piled with lazy, light-catching cumulus. "And I liked the part about the witnesses in a great cloud around us. That's the way the dead live on—through us, and them watching, I always felt like that was true. And I know people who are too good for the world, yeah, and who live in the mountains and caves because they caint go out in the world, it's too filled with meanness. If they're alive at all. The guys I served with in Nam—seem like it was always the guys that was too good for the world that got hurt or killed, because they had what you'd call principles—they had certain things they was just not able or willing to do and Nam was no place for a guy who had things he wasn't able or willing to do. And the best guys—least if you're asking me—were the guys that drew the line and said I aint a-going to do it at all. Which is why I'm sitting here listening to you because I wasn't one of those guys, I did pretty much everything they told me to do and then some. I'm hoping you or your Paul will give me to understand why it was that I went, why I killed all those people who never done nothing wrong except get in the way. My way."

A long silence, except for the chatter and gurgle of the creek over its bed of stones and a lone cardinal's sleepy midday call *purty-purty-purty-purty-purty.*

"You did your duty," Flavian said. "At a different point Jesus, who is our final authority, tells us to render unto Caesar that which is Caesar's and to God that which is God's."

"Meaning what?"

"Meaning that we should give our government its due—you know, pay taxes and even go to war if that's what it asks of us."

"Hellfire. Here you was a draft dodger—"

"Conscientious objector."

"—caint even recognize a compliment when you hear one and telling me to think for myself and then you go telling me Jesus wants me to bow down to the boot. I know that part about Caesar—I remember hearing that and the nuns told us the very same thing, that it was about giving the government its due, but then I gave the government its due and I came away with a whole different notion of what the man is giving us to understand."

"Oh?" Flavian was amused. "And what do *you* think Jesus is giving us to understand?"

"Well, you show me. What belongs to Caesar?" From his sycamore armchair Johnny Faye threw his arm in a sweeping gesture that took in the trees and the creek and the sky and Flavian, still on his knees in the dirt with the trowel in one hand and the sheet from the morning service in the other. "What do you see that belongs to Caesar? There aint nothing that belongs to Caesar. There aint nothing that belongs to the government, there aint even anything that belongs to the monastery. And so when you tell me Jesus says to render to God that which is God's and to Caesar that which is Caesar's, I think that makes a lot of sense. Give the guy credit for some smarts—hell, we're still talking about him, he must have had more on the ball than your average Joe. He was standing there talking in front of the Pharisees and he knew damn well what would happen if he said what he wanted to say, and he also knew that it was going to happen anyways but that he weren't ready for the action. So he says what he says in a way that the people in the know will get what he means and the Pharisees aint got a clue. Because what he wants to say is that not one damn bit belongs to Caesar, every bit of it belongs to God including you and me, your life and my life, and that our job is to treat everything and everybody like it don't belong to nobody but God and fuck the big corporations and the government."

"Now where did you learn all that."

"Didn't learn it nowheres, just thought it out on my own."

"Well, you can make Jesus out to say whatever you want, people do it all the time but that doesn't make it true. At least you have the story right. That's something. That's more than most people."

Johnny Faye grinned and pointed at his temple. "I might be shooting blanks upstairs but I always been good at remembering. You tell me something, a year later I can spit it back to you. I could talk Paul to you chapter and verse if it comes to that, just from the times I heard it read out loud when I was a kid. I had a uncle who was a preacher, he used to tell me I had the gift."

Flavian hoisted himself to his feet, refolded the day's epistle, and held it out. "Here. You'll make better use of this than I will."

Johnny Faye pushed his hand away. "I told you I don't got time to read. I like better hearing it spoke out loud." He looked up at the sun, now a green slant through the trees. "You got time for a swim?"

"Swim? Where would you go for a swim?"

"In one of the monastery lakes, where else? Nobody uses the closest one except for frogs and horseflies. You guys went on city water ten years ago."

"It'll be freezing."

"That's right. But it don't get any cleaner nor clearer than this time of year."

"I don't have a swimming suit."

Johnny Faye was gathering up his tools. "You aint wore out your birthday suit."

"I have to get back for Vespers."

"No, you don't. It's Sunday. Vespers is late on Sunday, you got a extra hour. Come on, live dangerous."

"The last time I lived dangerous I ended up with an envelope full of cash."

"You still got that money? Lordamercy, I hope you aint lying awake at night over that. It's honest money, honest come by, which is a lot more'n you can say about most of the money that ends up on the monastery collection plate. Use it to help some poor son of a bitch that's got hisself in trouble and then don't give it a second thought. Now get moving. We hit that lake after the sun's off it, you really will know what's cold."

And so they went for the first time to the lake that in those days they called Basil's, after the farmer who was the last to work with horses in the monastery fields and who had overseen the damming of the little creek to make the lake and who died of a broken heart, or so they said, when the monastery sold its last draft horse and took to using tractors.

Johnny Faye wrapped his tools in plastic and hid them in a crevice under a rock, then picked up his walking stick and poled himself up the creek bank. Flavian struggled behind, slipping and sliding on the slick clay. With his stick Johnny Faye held the vines aside and pulled forth a big bay horse. "Bittersweet. 'Sweet for short. 'Sweet, meet Brother Tom." Johnny Faye hoisted himself up on 'Sweet and ran his stick through a loop on the saddle. "Here, put your foot in the stirrup. No, not that foot, dummy, the other one." Johnny Faye reached down and seized his arm. In a moment Flavian went from idle standing to being hauled up like a sack of potatoes—his shoulder would be sore for a week—and then he was astraddle the horse.

Flavian was uncertain what he was supposed to do. He

couldn't imagine staying on a horse without being in the saddle—for that matter, he couldn't imagine staying on a horse while sitting *in* the saddle. There was no place for his arms except around Johnny Faye, and Flavian was too shy to put his arms around any human being, much less a man. He discreetly gripped the saddle's raised rear lip, trying to keep his fingers from touching Johnny Faye's buttocks—he could only gain a small hold but it would be enough to enable him to hang on, so long as they rode at an easy pace. "Good thing he's sweet," Flavian said with a smile. "Otherwise—"

"Yeeeee-hi!" Johnny Faye cried, and gave 'Sweet a smart smack on the haunch and they were off at a gallop, JC running and barking at their heels and overhead the great blue bowl of a perfect summer afternoon. For the length of a breath Flavian held onto his shyness but in that same instant the world became a blur of blue and green and he was bouncing up and down exactly out of sync with the horse's gallop and he was visited by a vision of himself trampled and broken under its hooves and he threw his arms around Johnny Faye and held on for dear life, a life that suddenly seemed dear indeed and absolutely worth the price of the ticket. They galloped away from the creek, over pastures that in seventeen years Flavian had never seen, didn't even know existed, crashed through brush, climbed up and hurtled down a hill, leapt a small ditch and galloped up to a lake. There Johnny Faye drew up short.

Flavian half-slid, half-fell from the horse, so grateful to be alive and unbroken that he almost knelt to kiss the earth. Then his wits returned and he turned on Johnny Faye in fury. "You—careless jerk. You could have gotten me killed."

"You're still alive, aint you? O ye of little faith." Johnny Faye was already half out of his clothes. "Last one in's a cocksucker! No kidding, no taking your time on this one, you hold back one second and you'll never jump."

And then Johnny Faye was flying through the air with a banshee's cry, landing in a cannonball intended to splash water on Flavian. And it worked—Flavian's pants were drenched and he almost turned and stalked away until he realized that standing on the bank or walking in wet pants was no colder than if he just shed his clothes and braved the lake. And then he was seized by some imp of perverse and tore off his shoes and jeans and blue work shirt and underwear and went cartwheeling through the soft air to land in a great, stinging belly flop in the arctic waters.

Johnny Faye called over his shoulder. "That'll shrink your balls, all right. Over and back and we're outta here, keep moving and stay to the left of that big hackberry, I set out a box on the back side a few years ago and there's a wood duck raises a brood, comes back ever year, keep a eye out and you might see her," and then Johnny Faye was crossing the lake in powerful strokes and Flavian chugging along behind and in between them JC, who every once in a while let out a gleeful yip.

Flavian was a swimming skeleton—the icy water sucked away his body heat so that he felt only his bones moving and he thrashed as hard as he could to keep his blood from slowing to a stop. Johnny Faye swam ahead and touched the base of the far cliff—this was some kind of ritual—but in mid-lake Flavian reversed course. One bright patch of sunlight remained. Overhead the rays pierced the dark crowns of the trees, and even though Flavian knew that this late in the day the light would carry no heat, all the same he held as a goal the bright sunlit bank on the water's edge where he could pull on his warm dry clothes—or at least partly dry, which was better than soaked. The dark line of the woods, the darker bowl of the clear lake that doubled the bright sky, the shattering ripples from their moving bodies, and then he was climbing from the water only to have his numbed fingers lose their grip and he fell back in and Johnny Faye was behind him and his hands on Flavian's thighs and giving him a boost *up!* He scraped his chest against the ragged rock but he was out and hopping around to stay warm while JC climbed out in some easy doggy way and was shaking himself in one smooth nose-to-tail shower, scattering a cloudburst of rain over their clothes and soaking whatever dryness remained. And then Johnny Faye was out and they were rubbing each others' arms and hopping up and down.

"You see the wood duck?"

"I can't see the nose on my face without my glasses."

"Oh, yeah, right, too bad. She's over there, all right."

Johnny Faye pulled from his jeans pocket a scarlet bandana and they toweled the droplets from each other's backs and then they were climbing into their clothes, the distant tolling of the bells signaling fifteen minutes to Benediction, no way they could get there on time except then they were back on 'Sweet and galloping toward the oxbow in the creek and then over the creek and through the wall of cedars where Johnny Faye knew the one place where a horse and two riders and a dog could penetrate and then they emerged on the gravel lane that led toward the abbey.

They arrived at the back gate to the enclosure—how and from whom had Johnny Faye learned the secret ins-and-outs of that complicated place? Later Flavian wondered this, but right now he was off the horse and slipping through the door into the enclosure. He pulled on his robes and made it into his prayer stall just as the last bell began its slow sweet toll. He had never been so grateful for the scratchy wool warmth of his robes, had never before been so awake and alive to Benediction, to the blessing of the Lord.

Still turbulent from her encounter with Johnny Faye, Meena was at her car when she decided to investigate the abbey church. Bells were ringing, an invitation of sorts, so she drove from the statues, parked and entered through the visitors' door. The cool high echoing space enforced silence—her blood calmed. She sat in the visitors' pews and bowed her head.

Time passed and she was joined by a scattering of men and women who knelt or stood. A railing separated the visitors' seats from the monks' rows of prayer stalls. In the nave a tall cross held a starburst of gold at the intersection of its arms. Centered in the starburst, a round pane of glass. A priest in golden robes entered and mounted the altar. An acolyte followed, carrying a smoking brazier hanging on a chain. He opened a small silver box, from which the priest spooned incense into the brazier. Her heart rose with the smoke. Meena sat through the elevation of the host, the closing hymn, and the monks' processing to the abbot, who sprinkled each bowed and tonsured head with water from a silver bucket.

When she left the sun was still bright in the trees. She walked down the long allée and was surprised to find Brother Flavian falling in step at her side. "A pleasure to see you sitting in the visitors' pews," he said. "We keep an eye out."

"But surely I am permitted. I saw the others and assumed—"

"Oh, yes, the visitors' gallery is open to all. Even Hindus. *Especially* Hindus."

She hesitated a moment. "You are a monk—surely I may share this with you, yes? When you call me a Hindu, this is something I find very difficult to hear. Before the British no such concept existed. For us religion is not a separate thing that we label and practice in church on Sundays. It is how we live—it is who we are. Then the British came and told us that all civilized people must have a religion and that a religion must have a central book and services held in a church and so forth. And we wanted to be good servants of the Empire and so we created something called Hinduism, so we could be what the British wanted us to be. And then I was forced to choose—the circumstances are not important, what is important is that I was forced to choose between the old superstitions and the new world of reason and progress. You see where I am, the choice I made, but I still know what it is to be drawn to the old way of knowing things, the spirits in the forest and the hills and especially the rivers. So now when you tell me that I am Hindu that is a very complicated thing for me to hear. Because even though yes, I am Hindu and yes, I am Indian, I am

Bengali first. Once that meant everything and now it means nothing. And Bengalis are known for holding ourselves a little—apart. *Above*, some would say."

"But now you're an American."

"As easy as that," she said softly. "One speaks the word and it comes to pass. How extraordinary, so strange to me, that these are things one *chooses*. And that my own country depends not on my history and culture and the call of the heart but on pieces of paper properly stamped and filed. I have chosen to become an American. I am learning how to become an American. I must learn to understand the world in this way."

They walked down the allée. "Your church uses the same incense that the priest used in the chapel of the Loretine sisters' school in Calcutta—I recognized the smell. Perhaps that scent brought out all those feelings—smell can be so powerful! These labels and definitions seem so important—they shape a life, and without them one cannot say one even exists. Or so one thinks, and then one moves halfway around the world to find that the labels mean nothing. I hear so often in the American news this phrase—*born again*. I never understood what that meant before coming here. Now I find that I must work to be exactly that—*born again*."

From the end of the drive Flavian pointed to the top of a nearby hill. "From the statue of Saint Joseph we can see the sunset. Shall we climb?"

"We'd be fools not to."

As they climbed, the broad sweep of the valley opened before them, the fluorescent green of early summer flecked with brown-and-white cows, their heads nuzzling the rich, knee-deep grass and in the distance the valley's dark wooded rim. They took their seats in the Adirondack chairs at Saint Joseph's feet.

"And so I am a bit—*amused*, here in America, to see men still worshipping a piece of bread. I could as well be with my grandmother by the fireside, where before every meal she set aside a bit of food for the gods."

Below them the cows began moving through the pastures toward the barn. "That piece of bread," Flavian sighed. "I used to see it as more than that, but seventeen years here and I've changed my mind. Now it's a just a metaphor—a symbol. It makes so much more sense that way."

Meena nodded. "So comforting, when everything makes sense. I believe in the power of reason to make sense of the world. That is why I became a doctor. Then I come to America to find myself among people barely less superstitious than the village women of my childhood. The stories the women tell me here I can hardly believe! We educate our women as well or better in Bengal. The women here have been kept ignorant, by whom and for what reasons I do not yet know, but their ignorance is serving someone's cause, of this we may be sure. They should consider becoming nuns." At this Flavian laughed out loud. "But no!" she said. "I am serious. A monk or a nun is making a real contribution. To choose to refrain from bringing more children into our over-crowded world—to choose instead to give yourself over to a noble ideal—this is a responsible choice. A *reasonable* choice."

"I'm not sure how much choosing was involved—to be honest, I was on the lam from the draft board." He waved his hand at the fields, the line of slowly moving cows, the abbey church. "I needed a place to hide out and this place offered it."

"Then you too are a war refugee. We have more in common than one might have thought." A moment of silence, then, "I have met this funny man. Another war refugee, you might say." A small laugh. "He is my patient, though I have met him at your statues. A farmer, he calls himself, though he spends his days watching birds."

"You mean Johnny Faye." Flavian picked a daisy and began plucking at its petals.

"Why, yes, you know him. Though I am hardly surprised. You and he share that quality of being a monk—not a monk in the particular way of your order but in some deeper way. I see it in the way you walk."

Flavian held up the daisy, shorn of all but its last petal. He plucked it and tossed the stem over his shoulder.

Below them a car with a broken muffler sputtered as it passed, the bitter smell of exhaust rising on the still evening air. Meena waved at the last of the cows passing through the gate. "I do so enjoy watching the cows!"

"Take a long look. They're not long for this world." Flavian told her about the abbot's plan to decommission the herd.

"You mean selling them for slaughter."

"Well, yes, I guess you could put it that way. The accounting books make their demands and even the most idealistic must comply. It's about labor. Which means it's about dollars and cents."

"As are most difficult decisions. Institutions must make difficult decisions. I love children but reason dictates that *someone* must refrain from bringing them into our overcrowded world. I have made that choice. And I love cows but I understand why they must go."

"God gave us reason so that we could prove His existence, the better to worship Him. Or so Thomas Aquinas would say."

"And the next thing you know we are saving lives with penicillin and contraception."

"And destroying them with bombs. And slaughtering the cows."

They fell silent, watching as the sun lowered itself into its nest of clouds, scarlet to red to orange to yellow fading to lavender and to the east the deep purple of encroaching night. The first lightning bugs of the season emerged, until the pastures crawled and blinked with their miniature semaphores: *I'm here, I'm here! Take me, love me!*

Meena stood. "Another visit, another time. I enjoyed the service."

Flavian led the way down the path. Halfway down he turned and spoke. "The boy—Matthew Mark. Can I ask how he's doing?"

"Of course you may ask. I suppose it is not a violation of confidentiality to acknowledge what we both saw. The boy had been beaten, presumably by his father. Whether that brought about the pneumothorax is impossible to say but it is difficult to imagine otherwise."

"I have kept him in my prayers. I wish I believed that makes a difference."

"Do you believe that God cares what happens to this little boy?"

Flavian studied the opalescent sky. "I used to believe that. Now I don't know what I believe."

"My life has been a flight from evil wrought in service to religions, each as bad as the other, Hindu, Christian, Muslim, Buddhist. Pray if that brings you comfort but know that prayer is no substitute for an adequate foster home."

"There has got to be something that can be done. The man nearly killed the boy. What if the next time he does?"

The great disk of an early summer moon was rising. At the monastery the mimosas were coming on, cascades of pink, umbrellas of roseate. Meena and Flavian were at the allée before she spoke. "How American you are!" she said softly. "You are the fish in the sea and what does the fish know of the sea? 'Something must be done,' 'something can be done.' It is why I longed to come here, to a place where people believe always and everywhere that something can be done. You have your electricity and your cars and your telephones, and what is astonishing is not only that you have these things but that you know that they will work, you take for granted the fact that they will work, here it is so easy to take everything for granted, good health and a long life and seeing the birth of one's grandchildren and great-grandchildren, all this you may take for granted. How dull and safe it all is! How I longed for this dullness, this safety! I came halfway around the world for it."

While she spoke the moon rose to silhouette St. Joseph, so that for one moment the statue seemed to bear a bright disk in its upraised arms. "You are a doctor and you have taken a vow," Flavian said gently. "Might that require you to put the boy's interests above all other considerations?"

"And you are a monk, and you have taken a vow. Might not that require you to be better stewards of your cows?"

Flavian halted in the darkness under the gum trees. "Let's be kind to each other, all right? I just can't—that evening. I can't get that boy out of my head. I can't bear to be in the presence of such suffering without, I don't know. Doing something." He gave a hollow laugh. "Which, of course, is why I chose the world's most useless profession." The first bells announced Compline. "I have to go," he said. "Please forgive me."

"If you will forgive me in turn. It is a terrible matter."

The sweet gums cast shadows so black she stumbled. Flavian took her arm again and kept her at his side until they stopped at her car, where she paused. She took his hand in a firm shake. "What is that funny thing you say? Oh, yes. Let us stay in touch." She climbed in her car and drove away.

Chapter 10

The abbot had requested that Flavian take notes during his meeting with Harry Vetch, who was brief and to the point. Now, some moments after Vetch's departure, Flavian sat in silence, waiting for the abbot to resume dictating a letter to corporate milk producers that had been the morning's first business. But the abbot had swiveled in his chair to study the rippling leaves of the ginkgo that reigned over the meditation garden. His back offered no conversational clues.

The abbot was a small dark-eyed man of delicate bones and a fine sense of diplomacy, who kept his heavy beard trimmed for the sake of visitors—when he returned from his annual retreats it was scraggly and unkempt. Finally Flavian cleared his throat. "Should we continue? Let's see. ' . . . deadline for bids to supply the abbey with sufficient milk . . . '"

The abbot did not turn around. "I hope you took good notes."

"As always." Flavian flipped forward through his memo pad. "Harry Vetch, county attorney, personal interview, June 16th, 10:45 A.M. 'Revised federal statutes place the burden of proof on the owner, meaning that if marijuana is found growing on abbey acreage the abbey must prove that it did not know of such activity. Law enforcement officials believe that criminal elements are moving operations to the farther reaches of the abbey properties so as to escape confiscation of their own properties in the event of prosecution. As a public servant and devout Catholic I am paying you this visit'—uh, I'll skip that part—'the revised procedures permit the state and/or the federal governments to seize any and all property that may be involved in such activities.'"

"Any suggestions about how to check three thousand acres for pot plants?"

"Hire a teenager?"

"I'm not sure how one proves to the satisfaction of a court of law that one does *not* know about a particular activity," the abbot said. "Review what he said about personal responsibility, please. I don't want to hear it, which usually means I need to hear it."

Flavian ran his finger down the pages. "'In the same way that you are the abbot of a monastery, I am the desk at which the county law enforcement buck stops'—that's him talking, not you—"

"I should hope so. If twenty-five years of administration have taught me anything, it's the art of being away from the desk when the buck stops in. Go on."

"'—and so as abbot you may be held personally responsible for any illegal activity found taking place on monastery lands.'"

The abbot sighed. "Better me than the community."

The deep-throated bell began its call to midday office. Flavian gathered his notebook and pen and stood. He paused at the door. "Brendan?"

"Yes?"

"Is growing marijuana a sin?"

The abbot laughed. "Well, it's against the law."

"I know that. What I'm asking is, is it a sin?"

The abbot considered this. "An interesting question. The fact of its being illegal does not necessarily make it sinful. The saying of mass has been illegal in a variety of times and places but that hardly makes it sinful. The question probably falls under the rubric of rendering unto Caesar that which is Caesar's. At various points the Bible stresses that we are to respect authority."

"If Jesus had respected authority we wouldn't be here today."

"A point well made, if usually ignored."

"Besides, what about this interpretation. Maybe Jesus wasn't telling us to obey Caesar. Maybe he was speaking ironically—he was a pretty smart guy, after all, and there he was standing right in front of the Pharisees, and he knew that they would interpret what he said one way while his followers, who knew where he was coming from, would hear it a different way. Maybe he was saying that since everything belongs to God, our job is to render everything to God, and if we do that well enough then what we owe to Caesar—who after all belongs to God like everything else—will take care of itself. Maybe he was saying that finally we owe everything to God and nothing, or at least nothing that matters, to Caesar."

"Now there's a thought," the abbot said. "I don't think it would hold much water in a court of law, canon or otherwise, but I once heard a theology professor offer more or less the same gloss on that passage. But if you're telling me you're growing pot behind the cow barn, I'm telling you to pull it up." He grinned and nodded at the door. "We'd better make tracks or we're not going to make Sext."

After the midday meal Flavian changed from his white robes into jeans and a work shirt and went for one of his afternoon wandering walks. Some high scuddy clouds blocked enough sun so that Flavian cast no shadow. His first thought was to visit the statues, but just as he opened the door a tour bus disgorged its load of chattery, camera-toting faithful, and while Flavian knew he should keep a generous heart toward these dear people whose purchases and donations brought them prosperity, in fact he fled. Visiting the statues was out of the question—one might as well seek solitude in a bus station—and so he crossed into the dairy pastures to visit the cows.

They had scattered themselves across one of the nearer pastures. As soon as he appeared several lumbered to their feet and came slowly walking his way—a few still carried him buried in their memories. Flavian was touched by their bovine devotion, or at least their capacity to associate a human being with feeding time. The brothers had given them cow names ("Tulip," "Honeybun") but Flavian had never troubled to learn these. Instead when he worked among them he had secretly named each cow after one of his fellow monks—the herd and the community being similar in numbers.

The first cow to arrive was paunchy Bede, who had resisted the new-fangled milking machines to the point of requiring what Brother Cyprian pointedly called a hand job. She nuzzled Flavian's outstretched palm. "Sorry, dear, I don't have a snack," he said, but her large, darkly iridescent eyes showed no sign of annoyance. Flavian sighed. "Oh, to have the faith of animals," he said aloud, then took a seat on a small rock outcrop. "Oh, to be as dumb as beef. Ignorant of our destiny."

If you're telling me you're growing pot behind the cow barn, I'm telling you to pull it up.

But he didn't have a patch of marijuana behind the cow barn. OK, so that was sophistry. Courtesy of Harry Vetch's visit, Flavian could no longer ignore the obvious: he *knew* about a patch of marijuana—what else could Johnny Faye be up to?—and in the eyes of the law that was no different from growing it. His duty was clear: Tell the abbot what was going on. Either that or tell Johnny Faye that he, Flavian, had a responsibility to his community to turn him in. "And then the next time I go back, the plants will be gone, and so will he," Flavian said aloud.

He stood and promptly fell down—his legs had fallen asleep. He lay flat on his back on the ground, looking up through the branching pines to the indifferent sky. "I *am* a common sinner," he said. "But I am not going to turn Johnny Faye in to the police. I *am* going to tell him that he's seen the last of me, and that the police are wise to the game, and that if they come looking for him, he's on his own." He closed his eyes and stilled his heart and opened his ears to any retort he might hear, but he heard only the high-pitched cry of a hawk and the sighing of the wind in the trees. *Yesssss. Yesssss.*

Yesss that he was a common sinner? Or *yesss* that he had struck an acceptable compromise between kindness and duty, between helping a poor man keep food on his mother's table and what the law required?

On this promise to himself he stood: He would stop visiting the oxbow bend. This coming Sunday he would bring this strange acquaintanceship to an end. He wasn't, after all, turning Johnny Faye in, he was just putting an end to his own involvement with a highly suspicious activity. A vision rose to mind of the abbot being carted off to the penitentiary in one of those orange jumpsuits inmates wore when they picked up highway litter. Flavian shook it from his head and set out for the enclosure.

Chapter 11

This is the time of year in this part of the world when the glorious days of early summer lengthen and no one can entertain the notion that summer will ever end, that anyone or anything will ever die. Every living thing reaches to the sun, which is nearing its solstice but has not yet reached its brutal midsummer strength. The days are long and warm but the earth has not yet taken the heat as its own and the nights are deliciously moist and cool. On such a warm bright Sunday afternoon Flavian found himself standing in front of the tight wall of cedars, dreading his mission but firm in his resolve—to announce his intention never to return in terms carrying a not-so-veiled warning.

He pursed his lips and hollowed his cheeks into a passable imitation of a mourning dove *Ooo-ah—ooo, ooo, ooo,* and immediately he heard a responding call. The cedars parted for his passage. He picked his way down the bank and arrived at the bottom upright to encounter Johnny Faye shirtless and in overalls, a hoe in one hand, mopping his forehead with a scarlet bandana.

"Good timing, preacher. I was just about to take a break." With the hoe he waved toward the fallen sycamore. "OK, climb up into your pulpit and make it Sunday."

"I'm not sure what you mean."

"I make time for this particular patch when I can but it's pretty well established by now and it could go a couple of weeks on its own. But I always make it here on Sundays because this here is monastery land and I figure there's something about setting foot on monastery land that makes it kind of like Sunday even if it's not. And then you show up and it's Sunday for sure."

"Actually, that's not what I came to talk about."

"Well, that's what I came to listen to. How 'bout if I take a break while you talk about what I want to listen to and then I'll lay back and listen to what you came to talk about."

Flavian felt in his pockets. "As a matter of fact, I have today's epistle."

"Well then there you have it. All I got is time and what's time to a hog?"

Something about this question struck Flavian as both ridiculous and inarguably true, but in the absence of being able to put a finger on either he took the printed epistle from his pocket and smoothed it against the trunk, then climbed to the hollowed out seat. He patted one of the armrests. "Here. You can sit on one of the limbs and read over my shoulder. We can take turns."

"Nothing doing. I'll sit down here. You're the preacher, you belong in the pulpit, you know the fancy words."

"But that's part of the point. This is a religion of the Word and it has to be spoken out loud. Something about getting your lips and tongue around what's being said—it makes it concrete, it makes it physical so the words stick in your head better, and when they stick in your head better that means they'll stick to your heart, which is where you want them to stick." He motioned Johnny Faye to the horizontal limb that formed one of the arms of the throne. "Sit here. I'll help you out with the big words."

Johnny Faye hesitated, then climbed into the crotch of the tree but stayed standing at Flavian's back.

"No, no, it'll work better if you sit here, in the crotch." Flavian leveraged himself onto one of the armrests of the throne and thrust the epistle at Johnny Faye. "That way you can read better. I'll sit up here and look over your shoulder." Flavian gave the epistle a shake and pointed at the sycamore seat. "Go on, sit down. Don't be such a mule."

Johnny Faye took the paper between thumb and forefinger as if Flavian had handed him a poisoned lily. He stood looking at it for a second, then wadded it into a ball and threw it down. "I caint read."

"Sure you can. I can help—"

"I told you I *caint* read. How many ways do I have to say it for you to figure it out? Jesus, you aint that big of a dumbass."

A long silence.

"I don't believe you."

"Well aint that a fine piece of shit. You want me to prove it to you? How do you prove to somebody you caint do something?"

With some discomfort Flavian recalled the abbot posing the same question, albeit with more decorum. "I mean, you spent two years in Vietnam. The Army doesn't take men who can't read."

Johnny Faye made a noise somewhere between disgust and contempt. "There you go with the Easter Bunny again. There was a war going on that nobody in his right mind would go fight. I knew how to point a gun and nine times out of ten, sometimes more on a good day, I hit what I was pointing at. They didn't give a flying fuck if I could read the writing on my tombstone. You caint have a war unless you got bodies willing to die and they'd already made sure their own kids was too smart to fall for that one. So they come for us good ol' boys and we, a bunch of dumb fucks if I ever seen one, jumped on board. Every time I was handed a piece of paper they made sure there was somebody close by to fill it out. Come to think of it, that was the last serious offer of help I got from Uncle Sam."

Another silence.

Flavian reached up and took Johnny Faye's hand. "Sit. I'll teach you how to read."

"You won't be the first to have tried that, nor the first to give up neither."

"It's not that hard. Look, if you can ride a horse and plant a crop you can read."

"Says you."

"You told me to teach you what I know. Well, this is what I know."

Another silence.

"Look, I been doing just fine without words on paper. I got myself through the military, I even got a honorable discharge, which considering what all trouble I got into is like a redneck Purple Heart. I never had much use for authority. I'm independent as a hog on ice, aint nobody going to change that. Uncle Sam tried and gave up, and if I stood down the big brass ass of the United States Army I can sure as hell stand down you."

"That I do not doubt. I'm not asking you to stand down. I'm asking you to *sit* down." Flavian tugged on Johnny Faye's hand, a gentle tug but he did not let go, did not allow himself the thought of letting go and after a long moment Johnny Faye sat down and Flavian began to teach what Johnny Faye had never learned.

And it was not easy, Johnny Faye got that much right. In that first moment when Flavian realized that Johnny Faye couldn't read he thought, *He'll sit down and I'll walk him through a sentence or two, and pretty fast he'll figure out that he really can read, he just thinks he can't read, he's just forgotten because he never picks up a book.* Flavian retrieved the wadded sheet from the ground and tried having Johnny Faye read a line from that morning's readings—*The stone the builders rejected has become the capstone.* Fast enough it became clear that Johnny Faye recognized nothing. Flavian might have taken Johnny Faye's hand and pulled him down to sit but Johnny Faye never took up the page, never once took the printed words between his fingers.

After a hopeless while Flavian folded the page and tucked it in his pocket. "OK, that's enough for today."

"See, I told you so."

"No, I didn't say I'm quitting, I said that's enough for today.

For one thing we can't work from this. We need something with bigger letters that are easier to read. And we need something to write on. The best way to learn your letters is to write them down."

"I caint write neither."

"I figured as much. I'm going to teach you how to read *and* to write. But I didn't bring a pen and unless you are in the habit of carrying a pen with you, which seems unlikely, then we don't have anything to write with. Though I guess we could use a stick and write in the mud—it was good enough for Jesus."

Flavian jumped down from the sycamore armrest and broke a branch off one of the tree's dead limbs and leaned down to write in the soft, wet clay. With the point of the stick he spelled out:

J-O-H-N-N-Y F-A-Y-E

"There. Is that how you spell it?"

"You're asking me?"

"I see your point. But you're telling me you don't recognize any of this?"

"Yeah, I recognize that, sort of. I seen it often enough."

"Well then, you can read! That's a start, anyway. *J*. Not the place I might have started but it will do. Come on down here." He handed the stick to Johnny Faye. "You make it. Go on. Make one just like that one."

"If it'll make you happy. I don't see no point in it myself. I got along fine for close to forty years just like I am and anyways in my life the only writing that ever come my way brought nothing but trouble."

And so it went. Right away Johnny Faye scratched out a legible imitation of the letter *J*, but when Flavian wiped away the letter with the toe of his boot and asked him to write it on his own he got nowhere. Johnny Faye remembered the "J" and the "O" but he stumbled on the "H" and that was that. After several frustrating minutes Flavian found himself thinking that Johnny Faye was just being ornery—he was not a dumb guy and how hard could it be to learn to write an "H"? After a quarter hour, he began to think something else was going on, that maybe his student lacked some necessary intelligence required to link a letter with its picture.

In any case—the thought came to Flavian of its own volition—there was no question of stopping his Sunday visits or turning Johnny Faye in. Now Flavian was on a mission—he would teach Johnny Faye to read and write, and with that skill he could get a real job and give up his life of perdition.

After too many tries—Johnny Faye smart-mouthing all the while but not giving up—Flavian took the stick from his student's hand. "That's enough for today. We don't want to set the woods on fire. Besides, we've got a job to finish with those tomatoes."

A long pause. Johnny Faye screwed up his mouth and twisted one eye up at the lowering sun, then bowed his head, then looked back up at the sun. "OK. You take a seat. Up there on the sycamore. Go on, we can get back to the garden in a second, those weeds aint going to grow that fast. I think you better be sitting down for this one."

Flavian climbed back into the sycamore and sat.

"They aint tomatoes."

Flavian sighed. "I know that."

"You do?"

"I know a tomato plant when I see one and those don't look like any I've ever seen."

"Then what do you think they are?"

"I have a pretty good hunch, but I'd just as soon not have to say it out loud. If you know what I mean."

"I know what you mean. A thing aint happened til it's been told."

"You could look at it that way."

For a while there was the silence of the woods on a warm Sunday afternoon in summer. They heard the distant cry of a rain crow, a breath of air stirring the trees, the burble of the creek over the stones. Flavian sighed. "I do so like the smell of water over rocks."

"You can smell that?"

"Sure, can't you?"

Johnny Faye sniffed. "All I smell is cowshit and that only when the wind is blowing from your herd."

"Smell it while you can. They're on their ways to the slaughterhouse."

"So I've heard."

"From whom?"

"I got my sources. Caint have no cows around the joint, no sir, their stink might keep the Virgin away, caint have that."

"It's more complicated than that."

"It always is, Brother, it always is—except for the cows, it's going to be pretty simple for them. Anyways. Come on out of that tree, to hell with the weeds, time for a swim."

And they were up and off on 'Sweet and this time Flavian threw his arms around Johnny Faye before they loped across the pastures and through the distant, unknown forest. As they charged through the fields the thought came to Flavian one word at a time, the sentence punctuated by the banging of his buttocks against the horse's haunches: *I'll. Go. To. Hell.*

Chapter 12

Before taking vows one of the monks had practiced architecture in the cities of the plains and in designing the chapter room had transplanted the long flat lines of the prairie to these lumpy forested hills. Flavian wondered if the contradiction between the room's flat lines and its undulant setting contributed to the contentious tone of the community discussions. The monks sat on long thin benches of oak beveled and polished to a buttery glow and so hard that Brother Aelred, who had trained as a nurse, claimed they were the cause of the community's ongoing hemorrhoid epidemic. At least once a year someone proposed investing in cushions but the abbot understood that in decision-making, uncomfortable seats favored management and he took care to pocket the suggestion.

On this particular Sunday morning the community gathered to consider the fate of the dairy herd. The abbot opened the meeting by explaining that they had very little to consider. Corporate producers could supply the milk required to make their cheese at a fraction of the cost and less risk of spoilage than the abbey could achieve. New government regulations governing cheese making required investments that only big, well-capitalized corporations could afford. "Keeping this particular herd amounts to a decision to keep seventy very expensive pets," the abbot said. "Either we hire local workers at considerable expense and commit ourselves to major capital expenditures to renovate our facilities, or we sell off the herd and contract with an outside supplier to deliver milk."

"Or we stop making cheese." This from Brother Columcille, who spent afternoons holed up in his hermitage—a shack built of materials recycled from the garbage heap—and who abhorred capitalism as nothing more than a sophisticated form of usury.

Aged Brother Crispus used his walker to hoist himself to his feet. "I am as fond of animals as anyone in this room but the time has come to face facts. Twenty years ago we had a hundred and fifty monks, average age maybe forty, some of whom had been brought up as farmers. Now we have seventy monks, average age pushing sixty-five, most of us choir monks. Who among us is capable of the job? None of our two postulants knows anything about cows and anyway they have their hands full taking care of *us*."

"A Cistercian monastery without animals is like a Benedictine monastery without books." Cyprian, who studied the literatures of Asia and preferred sleeping in the barns with the cows to sleeping in his monastery cell, spoke from the back of the room. "For a thousand years—*a thousand years*—Cistercian monks have made our livings by farming. Slaughter the cows—because don't fool yourself, that's what we're talking about, selling them for slaughter—and we won't have a single animal left."

"Don't forget about Origen," José spoke up. "That cat would starve if it weren't for me. Nobody around here so much as bothers to put water in his bowl. If he were a cow, now, it would be—"

Cyprian ignored him. "While we're at it, let's spray a little DDT around the place to get rid of the birds—every time I'm about to hear God, one of them starts chattering."

"We could donate them to the Benedictines." This from fat Brother Bede, who had no opinion one way or the other regarding the cows but who enjoyed the sound of his mellifluous voice echoing off the brick walls.

"Progress is progress," Crispus called out—this time he did not trouble to stand. "And even if it weren't, old age is old age and

I'm speaking as an expert. Twenty years ago four different dairies in this end of the county bottled and delivered milk. How many are left? Not one. What makes you think we can resist that change? Are the Benedictines still illuminating manuscripts?"

"No, and the world is a poorer place for it." Flavian, whose minutes tended toward what the abbot called "novelistic," wrote *angrily* after Cyprian's comment, then struck the word. "Have we stopped to ask why this outside milk comes so cheaply? Why and how is it that these companies can undercut even our operation, where labor is practically free? What kind of lives do these cows lead and what do they do to them to get them to produce that much milk?"

"You're just being a paranoid Luddite."

"That's the label the big corporations trot out whenever anybody challenges them," Cyprian said.

Now comments came from all corners of the room, so many and so fast that Flavian could not track who was speaking. He raised his hand, intending to ask for a moment to catch up, to hear himself say instead, "We've already had this discussion." He stopped, brought up short by his own voice. All faces turned in his direction.

"Yes, Flavian?" the abbot asked. "Go on, speak up."

"A couple of years ago. We had this same argument. Discussion. Except it was the poor people we got rid of. We couldn't stand the poor crowding into the gatehouse for alms. The people in the tour buses didn't like seeing them and we didn't like seeing them either. So we decided to give charity through the diocesan and county welfare agencies. And I was in favor of that move, it all made sense—we still benefit the poor but we don't have drunks fighting on our doorstep. And now everything is peaceful and the rich people can come out here and feel like they're coming to a national park and they like that and so they give us more money. But you know what? We don't have the poor to remind us why we're here in the first place. And now here we go again, except this time it's the cows. Why don't we just change our name while we're at it. The first Holiness National Park—I kind of like the sound of that."

The abbot held up his hand. "Not for the first time I remind you: A monastery is not a democracy. I have heard and appreciated your feedback and I will take it under the most serious consideration."

Flavian left the meeting dispirited. It was afternoon and the hours between None and Vespers passed slowly, offering perhaps the greatest challenge to his faith. These days he held on only for the sake of holding on—life seemed a matter of placing one foot before the other in a slow slog toward death, and all the cherubs on all the ceilings of all the churches of the world could not persuade him that a heaven of fluffy clouds and harp-plucking angels awaited.

About those cows. All right, so he didn't like the thought of them being turned into hamburger, but some version of that fate awaited every living being and better to be hamburger for creatures at the top of the great chain of being than hamburger for maggots, right? For Flavian the question of what to do with them was not at all academic. When the abbot had shifted him from the dairy herd to desk work his first thought had been *Praise the Lord, I get to go back to sleep between Vigils and Lauds.* In this he sided with Crispus: Eliminating the herd was a simple matter of facing facts. Even if they kept the dairy, the cows went to the slaughterhouse the moment they stopped yielding milk anyway. So what if the monastery shifted to buying industrially produced milk? Just as some hardy souls had continued blacksmithing long after the arrival of automobiles, Flavian was certain that somebody, somewhere would continue to keep milk cows. But for his part he would relish the extra hour of sleep.

And now he found himself speaking up in their defense and being a smart-aleck in the process.

A voice in his head spoke. *You never used to talk like that. First*

Holiness National Park. My Lord. Where do you suppose you came up with that kind of talk? Flavian gave his head a sharp shake. The voice continued. *Who taught you to talk back like that? I'll tell you who.*

"Leave me *alone!*" Flavian cried.

Hobbling by on his way to the infirmary, Brother Crispus gave him a broad wink. "Up to no good?" he asked, and though Crispus was making a joke, Flavian felt his duplicity written on his habit for all to read.

On Sunday afternoons Johnny Faye's crew gathered to compare crops and share information and, when that time came, coordinate harvesting and distribution. Johnny Faye's mother's house was too small so they rotated among the homes of the other men. All their houses were similar, partly because they shared their crops and their income evenly and partly because whenever one of them made an improvement (a finished basement, an outdoor deck) the others helped him and then added the same upgrade to their houses in turn. These were small houses with small bedrooms, two or three children to each room, with a common room not quite big enough to hold their big families. On the coldest, rainiest days of winter they sent the kids to the basement but in any other weather they set them loose to roam the woods. The women sat on the porch and shared in detail the particulars of their medical histories and complaints and picked apart and reassembled their stories and their children's stories. The men stood around the garage and talked about cars and guns and the deer they hoped to bag in the coming season or had just bagged the year before. When supper was finished the women washed the pots and pans and burned the paper plates. Then they adjourned to the porch and the conversation shifted from the living to the dead, to their characters and habits, public and private. The men returned to the garage, where they took up the subject of their crops and the law.

Squat, whose head scraped the lintel and whose skin hung

from his bony frame, signaled the subject by loading a pipe, which they passed around, a declaration of the fellowship of lawbreakers, though Martin Stead passed because he never smoked and only grew because it was the only way he could make payments on his farm and Johnny Faye passed because he was the brains of the outfit and it fell to him to think straight.

"I say we shift the whole operation up north, Iowa, Illinois, wherever." Club-footed Paddlefoot had his crop closest to the highway—like Johnny Faye he had been arrested more than once. "They're getting serious about cracking down—Squat here says he saw two suits come by the county attorney's office. Now, *suits*. We don't know where they're coming from but I aint never seen a suit that didn't mean trouble. Here we already got land leased up north, season's just starting up there. We did pretty good up there last year and we didn't so much as put a hoe to the crop once it was in."

"That's a hell of a lot of trouble to go through for something you caint eat." This from Jerry Bee. "I don't think we got no cause to worry. Harry Vetch just needs to have a few heads hanging over the courthouse door. Once he gets those, it's back to business as usual."

Little cleared his throat and hawked a gob into an empty paint can. "You guys are first of all playing Little League and second you're going to get caught and you're going to get screwed. Let me put it this way: How much do you get paid for a truckload of pot? And what do you have to go through to make it look like something other than a truckload of pot, so you can deliver it? Think about all that field work in the sweat and chiggers of the July sun and then you end up rolling down the U.S. highway in a dump truck asking to be busted. I know a guy in the city, plugged in with those rich people on the horse farms, he'll pay us in one night what we'd work a season to earn growing pot."

"And what is he asking from you for this great favor?"

"Clear a flat place in the woods and help them fly in a little plane under the radar. And the pilot of the plane hands us a few little bags and we stick those in our pockets and drive them up to the city and drop them off. One night's work. One year's pay."

Johnny Faye took the pipe and stuck it in his pocket. "You been smoking too much of your own crop. My mamma never had no problem with my growing pot. Her daddy did it and her grand-daddy did it and that was enough to make it all right with her. She's been known to take a puff when the damp gets to her joints. But she made me promise I'd have nothing to do with the hard stuff and I gave her that promise because I am in the habit of obeying my mamma and because it seemed to me a smart promise to make."

Martin Stead spoke up. "You start dealing in that stuff and you can count me out."

Little made a great show of rolling his eyes. "You tell me which is smarter, a hundred thousand dollars that'll fit in your pocket or ten thousand dollars that you need a dump truck to haul around."

"What are you talking about, a hundred thousand dollars? What would you do with all that money anyway? You caint put it in the bank, you try that and you might as well check yourself straight into the pen."

"I'd buy myself a new truck. And a brand-new .270 Marlin with a Redfield scope."

"OK, so you just got rid of maybe twenty thousand. You got eighty thousand to go."

"I'd figure out something. I aint in the habit of dealing with the problem of too much money under the mattress but I expect I could get used to it."

"They catch you with hard drugs in your pocket you really *will* be in trouble."

"Check it out—I did," Little said. "I had a nice long conversa-tion with my friend Officer Smith. You get the same sentence from growing a field of pot as you get for carrying those little bags off the plane. That didn't used to be true but the feds have made it true now. You get arrested growing ten pot plants, they take your farm, you go to jail for twenty years. You get arrested carrying crack cocaine, they take your farm, you go to jail for twenty years. So why not take the safe and easy way the feds have laid out?"

"You don't know from shit," Johnny Faye said. "I seen what the hard drugs do to people. I'm telling you, keep your nose clean. And since when has Officer Smith been your friend or any of ours?"

"What do we care what it does to people? They want to fuck themselves up, that's their problem. It's just capitalism at work. They're the demand, we're the supply."

Johnny Faye moved to the center of their circle. "Our brother Little aint satisfied with enough, he's got to have more. Here we have ourselves a little farming cooperative—each of us gets to do what he does best, which is hunt and fish and farm, and we aint getting rich but we're not doing so bad for ourselves, neither. Somebody's crop gets chewed up or busted, the rest of us make up the loss. Somebody needs a new furnace put in, we help pay for it and do the work. That's the code of the hills. Let me ask you this: Are you ashamed of growing good pot? No, you aint ashamed because you were raised to do it, it just happened to be tobacco that you learned on but same thing only different."

Little executed a little clog dance. "Nobody's going to end up in the pen. Not me, anyways. Not so long as I got powerful friends in the right places."

"And who might those friends be?"

Little smiled and made a show of twiddling his thumbs.

"I even so much as hear anybody dealing in that shit and count me out," Johnny Faye said. "So you make your choice but you understand that I am no party to the hard stuff."

The argument raged on, until Jerry Bee got the munchies and it was time for dessert. They called to the women, who brought in strawberry shortcake and Cool-Whip. The men and the kids took two helpings while the women took one and joked about their figures but after everybody was served they stood picking at the leftovers. Then they all took off into the warm summer night and Johnny Faye the last to leave in the big white Ford F150 with JC riding shotgun.

Now he allowed himself a smoke. He drove down the winding lane, onto the U.S. highway to stop across from the little log cabin his mother's father had built as a hunting blind. Across from the cabin two rounded knobs came together to form a cleavage, mist rose from the creek, and the field was a phosphorescent sea of lightning bugs. It was a peacemaking place and Johnny Faye often came here in search of peace.

This was his problem. He had seen the world and they had not, and one thing he had learned on returning from the world was that there was no way to convince them that what it had to offer was no better than what they already had at hand. This they had to learn for themselves—he'd had to learn it for himself and now when he got restless he turned back to those times and places on the other side of the world when the war had taught him how to pray because there was no other defense against the fear. It wasn't as if he thought, "I'd better say a prayer," or "Now's the time to pray." It was pray or die and though the former was no guarantee against the latter it was all there was to do and he personally knew of no man who had not done it.

And what Johnny Faye had prayed for, what arose every time in his heart, was this field, these hills, and all he had asked for was to come back here for good. And so when his men got out of hand or the police got out of hand or when the demons came too close, when they started showing up in the daytime as well as at night, this was where he came to remind himself of his answered prayers, of who he was and where he belonged and the importance of standing firm in the place where history had put him.

Chapter 13

For several days the weather had been sultry and the close air hummed with electricity. Meena walked the few hundred yards to the Knights of Columbus Hall to attend a party that had been organized to raise funds for equipment for her office and to formally introduce her to the town. As she approached the KC Hall the couples standing in the doorway fell silent and slipped away— "another drink," "little girls' room." Meena made her entrance alone.

The KC Hall was a plain, low-ceilinged room with jaundice-colored walls. The west-facing windows were caked with grime so that, though they were bright with the setting sun, the hall and its occupants were bathed in the glow of overhead fluorescent tubes. At the far end of the hall someone had set up a portable screen and a slide projector. An aged, hump-backed man in baggy brown slacks and a shirt that matched the walls was setting up metal folding chairs. Raucous laughter erupted from people lined up at an open door—this must be the bar.

A large florid woman in floral print pedal pushers seized Meena's hand. "The good doctor," she said, and Meena found herself grateful for the adjective.

"You are—?"

"Oh, beg your pardon, I'm so used to everybody knowing who I am. I'm Virginia Drummond, Judge Drummond's wife?

But everybody calls me Ginny Rae, at least to my face. And I'm so *pleased*, I can't tell you how pleased we are to have a doctor in our little town, the last doctor we had, old Doctor Mudd? Great-nephew of the doctor who treated the man who shot Abraham Lincoln and jailed for his trouble, he was ninety if he was a day, Doctor Mudd, that is, not Abraham Lincoln, ha, *ha*. You'd go back into that dark little cubbyhole of his office and you didn't want to ask what was in those bottles that had been on the shelf so long the spiders had abandoned their webs, nosirree, you just took your prescription and marched right out of there and drove forty miles if that's what it took to get it filled in some place with a flush toilet. When the judge was a little boy—he's over there, with the wide orange tie with the palm trees? I keep trying to throw that tie away, I sneak in his closet and every time he catches me and I let him know that nobody has worn a tie like that in twenty years but it's his Kiwanis tie, he got it at a Kiwanis convention and every time he sees it in my hands he lifts it gently as you please and says now honey, you know that's my Kiwanis tie and I just have to go along even if he does look like a fool when he puts it on. Anyway, when he was a little boy he had this ingrown toenail? And his mamma took him to old Doctor Mudd and Doctor Mudd said—I can hear him now, that big deep voice he took on when he had bad news— 'Son, that's going to have to come out,' and Glen saying, 'Yes, sir,' like the brave little boy he is and Doctor Mudd saying, 'You see that robin out the window?' and pointing, you know, and Glen not knowing any better than to look which is just as well since what did Doctor Mudd do but take up a pair of pliers and jerk out that toenail right there. No painkillers for him, no sir, he thought pain builds character. 'Pain builds character,' I can hear him saying that to me when I was in *labor* if you can imagine, which I guess you would have to beings as you've never had a baby, but better childless than out of wedlock like our Maria Goretti Shaklett, bless her heart. A little whiskey, that was the only painkiller he trusted. And I've already heard how you saved little Matthew Mark Smith's *life*, you here not much more than a month and already you've practically resurrected the dead, at least to hear Officer Smith's wife tell it, I'm sure it wasn't so dramatic, she likes to—*embellish,* shall we say, is there something I can get you to drink? Yo, Maria Goretti! Bring the doctor a, I'll bet you'd like a nice gin and tonic, I hear that's what they drink in your part of the world, keeps the malaria away, right?"

"You're very kind but I don't drink alcohol," Meena said, but the judge's wife was already gone and now it was the judge himself, bearing down on her like a lorry, hand extended. "Dr. Chatterjee, Glen Drummond, my apologies again for dropping you off with so little ceremony but the trash must be picked up, that's the glamour of being judge executive, somebody's trash doesn't get picked up and you-know-who gets called. And now if you'll forgive me I am always and in every time and place running for reelection, the American blessing and curse, even if nobody is running against me I still have to buy my constituents a drink, ha, *ha,*" and he was off, a fireplug of a man on small feet, just as someone thrust a drink into her hand. "Gin and tonic with a squirt of RealLime, just like you asked."

"You're very kind," she said. She stood with the sweating drink until enough time had passed, then set it behind a plaster statue of a saint in armor, piercing a dragon.

Flavian was climbing the stairs to his cell when he remembered that earlier on that warm, close day he'd used the monastery truck to run an errand. A tympani of distant thunder had underscored Compline's last reading—after Brother Bede extinguished the last candle and the high, echoing spaces had fallen into darkness, the windows continued to wink on, then off, from distant flashes of lightning.

He retraced his steps and stopped at the tall urn they used as a collective umbrella stand—it was as usual empty—*nobody puts them back, must remember to grouse about that at this Sunday's chapter meet-*

ing. Outside, the sun had set into gathering clouds and an all-but-impenetrable gloom and a stiffening wind tangled the gum trees' limbs. He crossed the prayer garden, went through the screeching gate and climbed the knoll to the milking barn and maintenance sheds. There he found that, sure enough, he'd left the truck's window rolled down. He gave himself a light smack to his temple as an incentive to *pay more attention*, then rolled up the window and turned back.

He had taken only a few steps when the first drops of rain, gravid with promise of more, struck his head. Before he could quicken his steps, no more than twenty yards distant a bolt of lightning split a great white oak, a century and more old, from its topmost limbs down through its massive trunk, close enough that Flavian was struck with flying twigs and leaves and his bones hummed in his body, or was that from the ear-splitting crack of thunder *ka-boom*? In his next conscious thought he was inside the cow barn, deafened by the pounding of his terror-stricken heart.

Ten thousand drumsticks on the barn's tin roof. Earlier that day the place had been alive with mooing and blatts, the clang of stanchions swinging shut, the hum of the milking machines, and always and throughout the permeating, penetrating, fecund smell of hay and milk and manure, the before and during and after of the life of a cow. A forest of black plastic tubes dangled from the rafters, each equipped with a teat cup, a machine-age imitation of a calf's mouth, and all the tubes connected to a great pulsing vacuum cleaner that imitated the joy of seventy calves sucking their mothers' teats. The milk emptied into steel vats, which the overseer pumped into a truck to be delivered across the road to the cheese room, where it began the conversion that led to immortality. Now with the cows returned to their barn, the black polyvinyl tubes hung in silence. No animal sounds broke the smooth roar of the rain on the roof except the murmur of human voices.

Flavian thought his imagination was playing tricks—the rain varied in intensity, close his eyes and he could hear it pounding now soft, now deafeningly insistent, and its rhythm might be taken as the chattering voices of the storm gods. But underneath the sound of the rain he heard a laugh, then a raucous shout. Light leaked from under a door at the room's far end—the source of the shout? In any case that light should not be on now, long after Compline. Flavian felt his way through the dangling tubes to open the door and shut off the switch.

Inside: Cassian, Bede, Cyril, José, Aelred, Denis, Cyprian. Cassian, skinny and long with bony hands to match; Bede, swarthy and soft as an odalisque; Cyril, with his great mule's ears and long face and thick black beard flecked with gray; José, whose bushy eyebrows met to form a startling arc over the bridge of his nose—he had a certain rakish air, and insisted that they pronounce the "J" in his name; Aelred, tall as a poplar and bald as a new potato, with a great bulbous nose and protruding eyes magnified by thick lenses; Denis, a flat face, featureless as a plain except for his pouting rosebud lips; and Cyprian, a dark-skinned orphan from a tropical place who spoke deeply accented English, for whom the animals were the brothers and sisters he'd never had. Each monk held a plastic cup, and in the center of the circle was a bucket of ice and a near-empty bottle of bourbon and no cap or mixers in sight. The dim light brought out the hollows in their cheeks and the deep lines in their foreheads, and Flavian realized how much younger he was than these men, all of whom were old enough to be his father.

Fixed by seven guilty stares, Flavian grasped that someone had cadged a bottle and that a party was under way, to which he had not been invited. "Uh—excuse me, I was just—"

"Not a word to the abbot!" This from Cyprian, with a laugh that meant business.

"Stick around, Brother Tom. Pour yourself a drink." This from the deep shadows at the corners of the room, and it was a moment before Flavian figured out that the voice came from Johnny Faye.

And then somewhere very near at hand a bolt of lightning

rent the air and a smack of thunder sewed it up, leaving their ears singing and the room pitch black.

Meena watched as two amiable drunks used their hands to concoct a shadow play in the square of light thrown by the slide projector. First two birds flew across the screen, then in one corner a hunter raised a rifle, but before the play reached its climax she was accosted by a slender man—the only man wearing a suit. "Harry Vetch," he said, holding out a gin-and-tonic. "You looked a little dry."

"You are very kind," she said, "but I have been served."

Vetch gave the drink a stricken look. "In these parts it's an offense against nature to turn down a drink." He took a sip from each glass. "Opportunity presents itself when we're looking in the wrong direction. The challenge is to turn around and say yes."

"I am somewhat stuck, I'm afraid, in steadfastly facing forward."

An awkward silence. He took a second sip, then set down the drink and extended his hand. "I'm the county attorney," he said. "The organizer of the party. The guy who's raising money to buy you an air conditioner. The guy who's charged with introducing you to your patients."

She laughed then and took his hand. "Then I owe you my thanks."

Some casual chat, in which the county attorney revealed that he also came from far away and that he was the first elected official of the county who hadn't been born to or married into the job. "Or married into anything, for that matter." He wiggled his ringless fingers. "That's a joke, sort of, but somebody once told me every joke contains a grain of truth." Meena asked after his parents—did he miss them? He screwed up his face and scratched his head. "Not really. My father was a corporate attorney, my mother was a nurse. They retired out West. Arizona, I think. I call them every so often. Is that what you mean?"

"My father taught English in our little town. It was what the men of the family had done for many generations. In this country, you are what you do. In my country, you do what you are. There was no escaping it, really. His father taught, so he taught."

"But *you're* not a teacher."

She smiled. "How that came to be is a long story."

"More interesting than most people's stories around here. Maybe you could tell it to me sometime over dinner. We could drive up to the city—there's no place around here to take a date."

She paused and the moment grew too long. "I beg your pardon," he said. "I have good intentions, believe me."

"Everyone is so kind," she said finally. "In my experience these matters are arranged by the families, in consultation with stars and bank accounts. I hardly know what to say."

"How about 'yes'?" Vetch emptied his glass and took up the drink he'd brought for her. "Well. I think you might benefit—I think you might be doing yourself and the county a favor—look. Nobody who wasn't born here knows this county like I do. Why not let me show you around? That might be more fun than dinner, and good for your practice."

"You are very kind indeed to think of my needs." She caught a glimpse of a familiar face and raised her hand in recognition. "You will not mind, I hope, if I take some time to respond—I am so busy with organizing my practice. A challenge I am happy to have."

Maria Goretti approached them, a glass of wine in one hand and a drink in the other. The county attorney took her by the arm, lifting the drink from her hand. "You're too late—our guest is fasting. Dr. Chatterjee, may I introduce Maria Goretti Shaklett, I think you guys know each other from the hospital? And now I think the time has come to badger the judge into kicking this thing off." Vetch directed Maria Goretti toward a pair of friends from her high school days. He steered the doctor toward Rosalee Smith, standing near the door. "You won't mind waiting here? I'll give you the nod when your introduction comes. Rosalee, be a good hostess and keep our newcomer occupied." He weaved through the crowd.

The county attorney and the judge mounted a stage fashioned from empty cases of beer and a slab of plywood. Harry Vetch took the microphone and greeted those present, thanking them for their past contributions. The room went dark, while they watched slides of the conversion of the old gas station into the office she now occupied. Then the lights came up. The county attorney introduced her—she mounted the stage, where in her nervousness she bowed, her hands coming together in a gesture from that other, older world. She busied them smoothing her skirt. Scattered applause and she stepped down. The county attorney made his pitch—he was eloquent on her behalf, extolling her sacrifice, urging generosity. Checkbooks were produced, checks written.

Outside the windows the darkness had thickened and the patter of the first drops of rain against the glass made it difficult to catch what Vetch was saying, but then someone fiddled with the amplifier and after a screech of feedback the volume improved. He was taking the opportunity to introduce his project—the new golf course subdivision.

From the shadows, a murmur from Rosalee Smith. "He sure sounds like he's running for something."

"Yes, I would say so."

"Mamma, let's *go*." This from Matthew Mark, pulling at his mother's hand.

"Just a minute longer, sugar. We have to wait for your daddy."

Meena crouched to whisper in the boy's ear. "Stand quietly and I promise I will tell you another story." Matthew Mark opened his eyes wide and pinched his lips shut.

"For more than a year I've been involved in the planning of a major housing development," Vetch was saying. "Ridgeview Pointe will be built around a golf course in the style that you may have seen in your travels to other, wealthier parts of the country. The building of the course and its houses will jump-start our economy, creating construction jobs that bring good salaries and good benefits. After Ridgeview Pointe is completed, its success will inspire imitations. And it'll have created permanent jobs for those who manage the golf course fairways and maintain the greens.

"And so I asked the project architect to create a few slides that will allow you to visualize the final project—to see rolling fairways and emerald greens where now you see only rocks and trees, to see houses where there are none, and to see how the unemployed of this county, now dependent on welfare, will have the opportunity to earn respect and decent wages in a pleasant work environment." Vetch picked up the control unit for the projector. "Our first slide shows the property as it currently exists." He clicked the button. Up flashed a slide of a horse's hindquarters. Suppressed titters. Vetch clicked the button again. A second slide—the hindquarters of a mule. An open guffaw from someone in the crowd. "Mamma, lift me up!" Matthew Mark cried. "I want to see too!" The judge raised his hand to cover his mouth. A third slide—a pig's haunches and curly tail.

"We have *got* to teach that man a lesson," Vetch muttered to no one in particular and, courtesy of the microphone, to the room at large.

And then a bright flash lit the windows and a peal of thunder shook the walls and the screen went dark.

For a long while the monks scrabbled in the darkness—"Murder in the dark!" someone cried, and "Belly of the whale!" Finally someone found a flashlight, then a kerosene lantern, and before long they were sitting again, drawn closer together by the lantern's small circle of light.

Johnny Faye took up the bottle. "Another round, boys, in honor of the storm." He refilled their cups, then emptied the bottle with the last and most generous drink for Flavian. "Go on, Cyprian, finish up your story."

"All right. Well. Old Mrs. Hawthorne came roaring in here, had to talk to her spiritual advisor—would somebody tell me who made up that title? Every time I hear it I think of Casper the

Ghost—on a matter of such importance that she could not wait, no, buildings must be moved so that she could speak to the abbot right here, right now, because, it turns out, she had wanted a diamond for her twenty-fifth anniversary and her husband gave her an emerald."

The rain on the roof was making a fearful racket but still Flavian, since childhood always the one to ask why, needed an explanation. "Why on earth," he asked, "would her husband give her an enema?"

A puzzled pause, then a roar of laughter louder than the rain on the roof. Johnny Faye doubled over, gasping, until he finally came up for air. Then he seized Flavian around the chest with one arm and pulled him up till he was half-standing and made a show of inspecting the back of his head. "Boy, you are really wet behind the ears."

Flavian struggled free, stood, and edged toward the door. "I was just asking a question. A pretty logical one, if you ask me."

Johnny Faye upended an empty milk crate, grabbed Flavian's shoulder, and plunked him down. "Come on, sit. Here, take your drink. First rule. You can never have too much ice. Second rule. Drink water on the side, helps your liver out, keeps the hangover in your bed. Third rule. Stay away from that frou-frou shit—you know, strawberry frozen sunrise banana rum mush. Unless hangovers bring you closer to God. Support the local product. Stick with bourbon."

Flavian had taken his seat well into the party, and the others were already far down the slope that leads to the valley of cheerful drunkenness and beyond to the dark wood of despond. The whiskey went quickly to his head, but where others grew loud and bright he grew introspective, a dufus grin on his face but with his soul's lips sealed shut. Sitting with his brother monks, he realized he had never sat with his brother monks. He had always been an outsider, the watcher in the tree limbs looking down as the world passed by. He saw how the men told stories—the ritual that they knew and practiced without it having been taught. The floor was a battleground and the storyteller's job was to defend his territory. The storyteller worked his way through the story, interrupting himself now and then to offer comment, pausing for breath long enough to allow the others to interject smart remarks but never yielding the high ground, always returning to the story before the upstart could take the floor. And so the story built to its climax, but as the teller neared its end one of the members of his audience would be designated his successor—whoever had made the most biting aside or had brought out the most laughter with a jibe. And when the story reached its climax, amid shouts and signs the storyteller would be dethroned and the story would begin again, now with the upstart as the new king to be challenged in his turn.

And so the evening wore on and all their stories became one long continuing story: how Father Peter lost his turkeys became how Johnny Faye rode Hoover DeWitt's dead body around town in an open jeep wearing a suit he'd eased out of the bank director's bedroom closet because Hoover had never in his lifetime known what it was to wear a tie, became how Freeman Frank shot the Yankee reporter and got off with manslaughter with time off for good behavior. Then the tone turned darker, as Cyril told how a local policeman's wife came to him time and again fleeing her violent husband and how she always went back to him for the sake of their child and Cyril had no idea what she did with the money he gave her so that she might take her child and leave.

And finally the storm wore itself out, the gods and goddesses retreated to the hills to lick their chops and the rain diminished from a fierce thrumming to a gentle pattering on the roof and they, all of them Cassian, Bede, Cyril, José, Aelred, Cyprian, Denis, and Johnny Faye, were slipping into the sweet nodding that is the fate of the cheerful drunk. A pause came that ought to have signaled the evening's end, but Flavian was not tuned into that nuance of late-stage cow barn society and so he began a story of his own. "This was in the days before I became a monk."

"*No! Never! You were born tonsured! Your mama never had to change your monkly diapers!*"

"I was driving—"

"*Go on. The boy is old enough to drive? Let me see the license.*"

"*Hush. You let him tell it.*"

"—I was driving, a big old black Chrysler New Yorker, I can feel the wheel under my hands—it was my father's car and he let me have it for my last year of college. The back seat was big enough—"

"*for you and two sheep*"

"—big enough to sleep in and I set out across the country, just driving, trying to figure out where I was going, what I was going to do when I graduated because if I did nothing I'd be in Uncle Sam's Army before I had my cap and gown returned to the professor I'd borrowed it from. And I was driving through the desert—the mountains, really, but it was New Mexico, no, Arizona, and there was no tree taller than a man and only those funny cactus that are taller than a man and look like they're waving hello. Or good-bye."

"*Saguaros.*"

"Thank you. And I'm cruising at seventy miles an hour—you can do that in the West, the road is straight and flat and comes to a point on the horizon—and on either side are cactus bigger than men and big purple mountains and not a tree in sight or memory when *Bam!* my windshield shatters. It must already have been replaced once because that old Chrysler would never have had safety glass, but this glass shattered but didn't break, you know, just had that spider-webbing effect that makes it go all opaque and I couldn't see a thing. And I slammed on the brakes—good thing nobody was behind me—and got out of the car in that hellish heat and sure enough there was a six-foot rattlesnake—"

"*No! No way! Not possible!*"

"—a six-foot rattlesnake that had managed to crawl from the windshield to the roof of the car and there it was. Dead, as in deceased."

"*Manna from heaven! Snake from the sky!*"

"So I looked around—nothing—you tell me, but my best theory is that a hawk or an eagle had caught it and either the snake had twisted free of its claws or maybe the bird meant to drop the snake as a way of killing it, you know, the bird saw the hard flat surface of the pavement as a target and let go, only I and my seventy-mile-an-hour windshield got in the way. And I looked at that dead snake and up at the clear hot blue sky with no sign of a bird, no sign of anything except the road shimmering in the heat, and I raised my hands to the sky and said: 'I guess I'll be a monk.'"

A long pause after this story and then fat Brother Bede rose and stood before Flavian and then he was down on one knee—he had to help himself down, placing one plump hand on Flavian's head to steady himself until he was low enough to drop one knee to the cement floor, then following with the other knee, and then he was touching his forehead to the floor in a salaam. "O Flavian, seer and prophet!"

And then Flavian was helping Bede to his feet and Bede threw his arm around Flavian's neck to haul up his bulk and then Johnny Faye had his arm around Bede's neck and Cyril around Johnny Faye's and on down the drunken line until they were all on their feet and dancing, slowly, gravely, to a shared but unheard beat, to their left and then their right in a circle, each with his arms over others' shoulders and this is what they sang:

> *Pange lingua, gloriosi*
> *Corporis mysterium,*
> *Sanguinisque pretiosi*
> *Quem in mundi pretium*
> *Fructus ventris generosi*
> *Rex effudit Gentium.*

At one point the KC Hall had been designated a bomb shelter, and the government had stockpiled barrels of drinking water and battery-powered lamps guaranteed to last for the several years the townspeople would require before they could emerge to inspect the radioactive ashes of their lives. Now Harry Vetch hauled the lanterns out but no one had checked the batteries in years and none worked. Then someone remembered that acts of God had preceded acts of man as the likely cause of such disruptions, and that tornado shelter supplies were stored in a different part of the basement, and before long everyone was carrying a candle. The KC Hall looked like the church at Easter midnight mass, with men's and women's faces lit from the candlelight cupped in their hands, the men trying to get their candles to stand upright in empty highball glasses and the women taking care to keep the dripping wax away from their dresses. Harry Vetch wandered through the crowd, apologizing for the storm and noting that the dead lanterns were one more indication, if any was needed, of the dire straits of the county infrastructure.

In the darkness Meena turned to the window, to look at the sheets of rain falling on pavement. "And so arrives the monsoon, *maha Bengal*," she murmured.

"What is Bingle?" Rosalee asked.

"Bengal was my homeland, the place where I came from. A country of more water than land. Now it is divided between India and a part that has become its own country called Bangladesh. I grew up in what is now Bangladesh but I came to the States from India—that part of Bengal that belongs to India. If you think of the world as an orange, then Bengal is precisely the opposite side from where we are standing now."

"You mean, you couldn't come from any further away."

"Any farther and the traveler begins to return home—that is, assuming that she has a home to which she may return."

"Bingle," Rosalee said, then corrected herself. "Ben-*gal*."

Gradually the rain slackened and the cries and shouts grew bolder. Now the crowd was seriously drunk—when the building lost power, the bartender had opened all the bottles and left them out for all to help themselves. In the dim light Meena could see Father Poppelreiter at the bar between two candles fixed in beer bottles—with their light flickering over his ruddy face, he might have been standing at an altar saying mass.

"You ladies OK?" Harry Vetch passed by, a candle clutched in his hand, its wavering light playing over his smooth features. "We have *got* to put a stop to that man," he muttered before moving into the crowd.

"What man is he referring to?" Meena asked.

A small laugh from Rosalee Smith. "Oh, Johnny Faye, for sure. This stunt has Johnny Faye written all over it. I mean the slide show. But I wouldn't put it past Johnny Faye to cut the power, too."

"I might have guessed. I believe I know the man. A farmer."

"You could say that." A rich silence. "You met Johnny Faye?"

"Yes, he came to my office shortly after I arrived."

"I have a hard time picturing Johnny Faye in a doctor's office, but I'll take your word for it."

"I recall the name. I would have thought it a woman's name."

"Sometimes it is, sometimes it aint." Rosalee lowered her voice. "But I aint pestering you to talk about Johnny Faye. I want to talk about my Matthew Mark. He's doing OK thanks to you. But that's what I want to talk about. I mean, it hadn't ever got this bad but I can see that with that boy growing older and his asthma getting worse—I've done all I know to do—give up smoking, keep the cat outside, whatever. I know you've done what you can but I'm hoping and praying that you can do more. I beg your pardon if I'm a pest but I knowed I had to ask. Knock and it shall be answered."

"Dear Mrs. Smith. Rosalee," Meena said gently. "Asthma surely complicated your son's situation but it was not the precipitating cause."

And then they were not alone. The doctor could not see who had joined them but she smelled his aftershave, more powerful than the scent of the early summer rain, its overwhelming cloyness a kind of threat. He was trying to light a cigarette—she heard the scratch of match against sandpaper once, twice, but the air was damp and his matches slow. Finally the match flared, and in its sudden light she saw that Rosalee had stilled her face and she understood that the man behind her back was her husband, the boy's father, Officer Smith.

In some fashion, in some way that he might not even be aware of but could accomplish easily enough, he possessed the power to send Meena back where she came from. With one telephone call or one word at one meeting with one person in one office he could undo her years of work.

Between this man and this woman, with the streets and the KC Hall dark, where they were surrounded by the laughter and cries of the partygoers' search for light, here in this place where everyone knew that this man beat his child and probably his wife and no one would act—Meena knew this place. This was the place where she had come from, a half a world removed and everything had changed and nothing had changed. She was still in the power of men, they were all in the power of anyone who saw the ends as more important than the means, who lived to seek power, and if anything could be known about the world it was that this man would use whatever power he had in whatever way he could. Meena was not likely to change this by drawing attention to what he had done.

But where would that leave the boy? There was always the boy or someone like him, grist for the mill of fate, the children and women and men, once her friends and neighbors and relatives, murdered or raped and left for dead. Meena felt all the massed and indifferent power of the law standing behind her, in the person of Officer Smith.

Meena took Rosalee's hand, hoping that a human touch might ease what she had to say. "I cannot offer extraordinary promises at this particular moment. I am a doctor of the flesh, not the spirit."

"That's right." The man was at Rosalee's side, his badge gleaming in the candlelight.

She held out her hand. "Doctor Chatterjee. And you are—"

"Officer Smith."

"Why, yes, of course. You are the father of the brave little boy whom your wife brought to my office."

A pause.

"Of course I saw him in the hospital," Meena said, "but then he recovered so quickly and he was gone before I knew it. I took my day off, and then I returned to find the floor doctor had discharged him—I came back and an elderly woman was occupying his room. Imagine my surprise. I am pleased to have the opportunity to meet."

He gave her hand a perfunctory shake and turned to his wife. "We got to go, now."

"Before you go," Meena said. "Perhaps we could make an appointment."

"Nothing wrong with me. I suggest you drum up your business somewhere else."

"I do not wish to speak about your health but the health of your son."

He stood back so that his face was in shadow. "I'll raise that boy as I see fit. Then maybe he'll find what he needs among his own people instead of going halfway around the world where he's not—"

Rosalee touched his arm. "Honey. Please."

At that moment the porch light and the building lights blinked on and Meena was grateful for the blinding moment of confusion to gather her wits. She turned to look Officer Smith in the face—his blank, chinless face with its prematurely sagging eyes. Though he was clean-shaven he had heavy stubble, and in this bright light it emphasized what lay beneath, the tension in the cords of his jaws and neck.

Meena laughed a bright laugh she had learned from her grandmother as a means of concealing what had to be hidden in what demanded to be said. "How pleasant to be living across the street! But I wouldn't think of causing you the trouble of entertaining me. Remember though that in my country to work near the jungle was to risk a leopard's attack, and so I learned as a child to walk with the eyes and ears of a leopard. It is my duty to use all my skills in service to my patients. And your son is my patient."

Suddenly the county attorney was at her side. "Glad I caught you before you left. I just wanted to finish up our conversation. You don't mind if I phone you up?"

Meena looked not at Vetch but at Officer Smith. "Of course you may ring me at any time. I shall look forward to improving our acquaintance."

And then Officer Smith left, pulling his wife and son after him.

"Sorry if I was interrupting your conversation," Vetch said. "But you looked like you needed—well, rescuing."

"You are so kind to be concerned. In fact your timing was very good."

"I'll be giving you a call," he said, but already she was at the door.

Seen from inside the KC Hall, the falling rain had recalled the warm monsoons of her childhood, but the short walk to her office reminded Meena that these were the rains of the north—chilly even in summer. By the time she reached her office she was shivering.

Bede snuffed out the kerosene lamp while Cyril used a flashlight to lead them through the stanchions and milking machine hoses. A weirdly animated light flickered at the barn windows, then Flavian heard a click and buzz. Through a window he watched a mercury vapor lamp stutter to life. The power had returned and with it the various proofs it offered that men, not nature, control the world.

Bringing up the rear of the crowd of snickering, whispering, cheerful, holy drunks, Flavian glanced back to realize that the light switch was still turned on—when they'd left the room, they'd had no light to remind them to flip it off. He turned back. Inside the office he found several plastic cups half-filled with whiskey, overlooked in their darkened departure. "Good thing somebody's paying attention," he muttered. He poured their contents down the sink, then let the water run for a few seconds to wash away the heady smell. A last check around the room, then he flipped the light switch off and guided himself out by the eerie glow from the windows.

Outside: A million brilliant stars overhead, though the eastern horizon still flashed and grumbled from the retreating storm. For a moment Flavian stood in the barn door, captivated by the source of the glow at the windows: the lightning-split oak that had driven Flavian into the cow barn and into the arms of his brothers in service to the Lord. The oak's limbs lay shattered on the wet earth, but the great trunk smoldered with smoke and flame. Flavian stood transfixed until he felt a presence at his side. "Thanks for the evening," Flavian said. "I doubt I'd have stuck around except that you roped me in."

"I have a reputation for that," Johnny Faye said. "They're good guys, this crowd anyway. Watch out for them priests, though. They got a hand in the honey pot, they're in it for the power and they'll rat on you in a heartbeat if they think it'll make them look good with the boss."

"Maybe some are like that, but these are lay monks. There was a time when I worked with them side by side and I hope they know I won't run tattling to the management. But I don't know that I could have gotten comfortable with them, or they with me, without your greasing the wheels."

"It's the whiskey that greased the wheels but I thank you kindly."

"They trust you and they figure that if you trust me, then I must be worth trusting. You know how that works."

"I do indeed."

"It takes somebody comfortable in his own skin to make that happen. You meet somebody who's comfortable in his own skin, it makes you comfortable in your skin."

"That's the whiskey talking, but I'm obliged all the same."

"No, I mean, sure it's the whiskey but there's something more too."

"Well. I am what I am."

They stood a minute longer in silence, watching the pillar of fire and smoke glowing against the clear starry spring night, the great living thing struck dead in its prime for the crime of having raised its head higher and lived more grandly than its neighbors. Then Johnny Faye strolled down the hill, humming a tune and interrupting himself with an occasional riff on a chorus.

And Flavian stumbled down the hill after him, heading toward the monastery, guided by the blue light of the mercury vapor lamp that hung over the enclosure gate. Halfway down the hill he turned back to the great burning oak and executed a little bow, and then—with a glance to make sure that no one was watching—he bent one knee to the ground and signed himself with the cross, while Johnny Faye went singing into the night.

Part Two

The Disobedient Member

Men will seek beauty, whether in life or in death.
—*Bhagavad Gita*

Chapter 14

Justice, in Johnny Faye's case, took the form of the state's oldest courthouse, a small brick temple built by men whose architectural talents ran to churches but who were acutely aware of the need for a clear distinction between church and state. Nature had taught them proportion, they had heard reports of Jefferson's Monticello, and they had on all sides a forest of chestnut and poplar and walnut and oak. And so their courthouse was symmetrical, with a pedimented porch whose columns reached as tall as those virgin trees. After all that looking up, the eye found its rest on an octagonal cupola sporting a red cock for a weathervane that in the hot summer breeze of the day of Johnny Faye's trial twisted and turned as readily as the day it had been mounted.

But those same builders were frugal men who understood in muscle and bone the relationship between the labor of cutting wood and the warmth of a room in winter, and so they would not build rooms with ceilings as tall as those columns. The courthouse so impressively entered held a courtroom whose low ceiling barely accommodated a spectator's gallery in which a short person might scrape his head and a tall person was out of luck. In the courtroom proper, an oak railing with octagonal posts echoing the cupola separated the judge's dais and the straight-backed chairs of the jury from the benches that filled the rest of the room. Curtains patterned in dahlias and passionflower prevented snoops from spying on the proceedings. A plaque commemorated an especially bloody Civil War day when boys—some in blue, some in gray, some in the work clothes they'd been wearing when they left their farms—lay on the courtroom floor side-by-side in the comradeship of dying and death, and on every anniversary of the battle even the educated people of the town had heard echoes of their cries.

The judge, a glossy tent in black that might have sheltered a revival in its folds, was a woman—widow of her predecessor to be sure, but all the same modern ways were making themselves known. On either side of the room: Officers Smith and Boone— round versus square, shapeless versus chiseled, plump versus plank. A jury had been assembled for Johnny Faye's trial, and they were called forth.

Johnny Faye represented himself. The judge did not advise against this choice because she knew the jury to be more susceptible to eloquence than to law and she was confident that in this Johnny Faye could hold his own.

Harry Vetch presented the state's case: At previous summer's end Johnny Faye had been apprehended in a half-acre of fully grown marijuana within sight of the state highway, carrying a sheaf of black plastic garbage bags and clippers. Brief testimony from Officers Smith and Boone. A map of the field, some photographs of the crop. The county attorney rested.

For the occasion Johnny Faye had tied back his hair with a rubber band and put on a white shirt cinched with a string tie of black leather with a silver cow's skull for a choker. He acknowledged that even though he was not conceding his particular guilt, the state police had got the lay of the land pretty much right and he was always one to admire close attention to a job even when it involved his arrest. Although he did want to mention that the county attorney had offered no evidence other than his own suspicions and the fact that Officers Smith and Boone happened to have caught him, Johnny Faye, walking through the field in question carrying clippers and black plastic bags. "I don't know about you folks but pretty much every time I go walking in the woods I take along a pair of clippers and a gathering bag, you never know what you're going to see out there that you want to bring home, and you caint get to those particular woods without crossing that particular field." In sum, though he acknowledged that the circumstances looked bad, he saw plenty of room for reasonable doubt and he hoped the jury would agree.

Harry Vetch kept cross-examination to a minimum, not wanting to draw attention to the fact that the evidence was circumstantial. The officers ought to have staked the field and caught Johnny Faye in the act of harvesting, but Boone had been scheduled to leave that afternoon on a fishing trip and Smith hated the mosquitoes that clustered in the creek bottoms and they had jumped the gun. In the end the county attorney had no choice but to fudge the cracks. Now Vetch rose to deliver his closing argument, drawing himself up and meeting the eyes of one juror after another.

"Your honor, ladies and gentlemen of the jury. I pause a moment because I know how difficult this must be for you, not because the facts are unclear but because you will be torn between competing loyalties. I know full well that some among you are related to the accused, however distantly, and that others have done him favors and have had favors done by him in return.

"In the past those connections have earned the accused the mercy of more than one jury. I understand that the roots of those acquittals lie in the most important connections any of us have, which are our ties to our kin and to our neighbors. These are ties that we threaten or break at the risk of our emotional, financial, and community well-being.

"Today, however, I suggest that those ties are being endangered by an enemy of the sort we have never encountered before. That enemy is drugs, brought into our world from elsewhere but here all the same. There can be no turning our backs on this enemy. There is literally no future in pretending it is not upon us. Drugs *are* upon us and they threaten the minds and hearts of our children in ways you and I, born in earlier generations, can barely conceive.

"What we have on trial here is no less than the criminal element of our society. And in voting to convict you have an opportunity to declare your faith in our community." Vetch began to pace. "Now those are strong words. But the presence in our midst of a habitual lawbreaker spoils our efforts to build prosperity. And that is what I wish to speak to by way of convincing you of the importance of this particular conviction.

"Thirty years ago life here was hard. A single orange was a treasure and you chopped wood in the summer's heat so as to stay warm through the winters. Now we're experiencing some of the conveniences of life and more are available to us every day. We've freed ourselves from the tyranny of nature so that we can live in ease and comfort, secure in the knowledge that tomorrow will bring no surprises—we're prepared for and sheltered against every possibility that nature may send. We have days of leisure, in which we have nothing more to worry about than what to do with our prosperity.

"That leisure time has come about because people agreed—we, you and I, agreed that making money was our first priority. That may sound blunt but in fact it is only common sense. The way to best serve the common good is for each of us to pursue our individual interests to the fullest. When you get richer, our nation gets richer, and vice versa. That philosophy is the foundation of our national prosperity.

"So you may ask, why shouldn't anyone be allowed to grow and sell as many drugs as he wishes? The answer to your question lies in the particular nature of this business. What Mr. Faye is growing—I beg your pardon, what he is *accused* of growing—is a substance whose use saps our children of their willingness to serve their self-interest. It is the foot in the door, the tip of the iceberg for drugs you have never heard of or imagined that will rob your children of their money, their judgment, and their connections to you, their families.

"Make no mistake about it—we are talking about a war here, and like all wars it will require sacrifice and a willingness to make hard decisions. That we are fighting it in our backyards only underscores its importance. We're at war with the most dangerous enemy that has faced mankind in his long climb from the swamp to the stars. If we lose that war we will lose this way of freedom of ours and if we lose those freedoms we have no place to escape to. This is the last stand on earth, and we are fighting a war on drugs in which the enemy has cleverly disguised himself as one of our own even though in fact he is a homegrown terrorist whose target is our children.

"As you know, I'm involved in bringing investments to this county which will enable our prosperity for the future. When I go around the state talking to potential investors they tell me they love my project but they don't want to invest in such a lawless place. Today you have a chance to change that reputation. You have a chance to declare yourselves and this community on the side of peace, prosperity, and the law.

"Now I know when I mention the law some people's first thought is, 'authority imposing itself on my rights.' No. The law allows you to be more free because it frees you from constant worry. It gives you a future you can depend on. In voting to convict you are voting for that future. You are voting for progress. You are voting for our incredible freedoms in this great land we call America.

"I propose to you that in this verdict you are choosing between committing this county to one of two crops, both green. But one is against the law and the other is within it. For make no mistake— you are not simply jurors for the trial of one man engaged—I beg your pardon, *accused* of being engaged—in the production and distribution of illegal drugs. You're not just witnessing the struggle for our children. You are being asked to render a verdict on the very legitimacy of the law. You're being asked to choose between hanging back and staying poor and moving forward and getting rich.

Fenton Johnson

"I ask you to keep these thoughts close to your minds and hearts as you deliberate and that they lead you to the logical, inescapable conclusion: the accused is the enemy of all that we hold dear—the enemy of the church, the state, and the people, and, finally but foremost, the enemy of your wallets and purses. A vote to convict is your best choice for serving yourself, your family, and your community.

"The state rests its case, your Honor, ladies, gentlemen."

Johnny Faye rose to address the jury. He greeted each with a cheerful nod and wordless grin, then cleared his throat and stared out the window for a moment as if gathering his thoughts from the open sky. "When I was growing up here," he said, "we had thievery from meat lockers, thievery from yards, thievery of cars and whatnot. And the thieves—we know who they were—stole because they were hungry. I listened careful to my friend's argument—"

"Objection, your Honor. In no way might I be construed as the defendant's friend."

"Sustained. Mr. Faye, please refrain from projecting personal judgments onto other parties to this proceeding."

"Yes, ma'am. Your Honor. But if you don't mind, Mr. *Johnny* Faye." The judge sighed. "Mr. *Johnny* Faye."

"Thank you, your Honor. I listened careful to the argument of the lawyer who got his education in some big city where you have never been and do not want to go and I found it enlightening as I expect you did too. Before answering his arguments I want to point out that at no place in his enlightening and educational presentation did the lawyer address the facts. I am still looking for evidence that I was the individual who planted and intended to sell the bounty of that particular field. I suggest that you should be looking for that same evidence because without it the state has no case.

"I would also like you to consider another uncomfortable fact, which is that whenever ambitious politicians like our county attorney—"

"Objection, your Honor. The accused is attempting to slander my character."

The judge shrugged her broad black shoulders. "As best I can tell the accused is summarizing a widely shared perception that impugns no one, since in your own arguments you set forth the presumed benefits of ambition. Mr. Johnny Faye, please proceed."

Johnny Faye nodded. "I suggest you consider that whenever ambitious politicians are out to serve theirselves they start talking about the interests of the children. This practice is so common that I suggest you duck and cover whenever you hear the word 'children' in a politician's mouth, being sure to take your children with you to save them from this particular form of corruption. But I expect the lawyer who got his degree in a big city has already tested your patience for hearing about children from people who don't have none, and so I will leave judgment on that particular argument to you all who *do* have children.

"I am brought before this court accused of the crime of being a small farmer—"

"Objection, your Honor. The accused is brought before this court for the very specific felony offense of growing Class I drugs in quantities intended for sale. None of Mr. Faye's comments are germane to the crime that is the subject of this trial."

The judge looked over her glasses at the county attorney. "I concede your point, Mr. Vetch, but Mr. Johnny Faye has a way, as we know, of telling a story. I am interested in where he is leading us with this train of thought."

"But precedent requires—"

"Mr. Vetch. I concern myself as much with justice as with legal precedent, an attitude I recommend to the jury if not always shared by my colleagues, but by my view I am well within the spirit if not the letter of the law. And I will offer a digression born in part, I admit it, of too much coffee and consequent indigestion. In this as in certain previous encounters you seem to assume that a fat woman who talks country and works for the government is by definition stupid. I suggest you reserve your testing of that theory for your private life." The judge directed her attention to Johnny Faye. "Mr. Johnny Faye. Please proceed, though in consideration of our collective desire to spend our golden years somewhere other than in this courtroom I ask you to make your point with some efficiency. Much as I know that to be a challenge."

"Thank you, ma'am. Your Honor. I am brought before this court for the crime of being a small farmer. The crop I am accused of growing was grown by our grandparents and their parents before them and used in everything from the weaving of burlap and rope up to and including a smoke to take care of the aches and pains of old age. They built roads, they carved paths through the wilderness to convey this selfsame crop to market.

"Then one year a large corporation figures out how to make a product that serves some of the same purposes except that it is inferior in every way. It frays faster and gives out sooner, it's weaker, you caint wear the clothes you make from it without burning up in your own skin. Smoking it is a poor way to meet your Maker. This new-fangled product is inferior in every way except this one: You and I caint make or grow it. It's made with oil brought from afar, extracted from deep inside the bowels of the earth. And in one of those great mysteries of what the lawyer educated in a big city you have never seen and do not want to visit calls civilization—in the very next year after this large corporation obtains a patent for this *in*-ferior product made from oil taken from below the sands of the A-rabs—a patent for nylon, to give it a name—in the very next year our government makes it a crime to produce the *su*-perior product that our grandparents could and did grow and harvest. I don't know what to make of this remarkable coincidence. I'm just pointing it out for your consideration.

"I would like to stay on the land. You know what happens to people like me when we go to the big city. We live on the streets because we caint hold down a city kind of job and we caint figure out how to live in a city-type house where your neighbors look

through your windows, if you got windows, and where the land-
lord is ever ready to put you out on the pavement. Enough living
on the streets and we start to getting a little crazy and pretty soon
we start doing drugs, hard drugs, and that makes us more crazy,
and pretty soon we are a danger to our neighbors and ourselves. To
send me to the city would be a bad idea all around—bad for the city
and definitely bad for me. But if I am to stay in this place I have
only one way to afford to be true to my nature and that is to be a
small, independent, ornery, son-of-a-bitch farmer. I do it good—
in the way that the hawk soars or a bee gathers honey, it is in my
nature to dig in the dirt.

"Now the lawyer educated in the big city proposes to bring
more envy and more wanting into your homes and hearts. He wants
us to go looking at those big houses he is building on his mowed
golf course and say: Why caint I have that? I work just as hard,
maybe harder than the folks who live in them big houses. And
next thing you know we're raising prices at the store or charging
more to look under the hood of your car because we have agreed
to bow down to the boot—we, you and me have agreed that making money is our first priority. Why help your neighbor put a roof
on his house when you can charge him money for your time? Why
take care of your old folks or your kids at home when you can pay
somebody to do it for you so's you can use that time to go out and
make more money, which you are going to have to make if you are
going to keep up that big brick house on the golf course and payments to the bank which is what really owns you and your house?

"The county attorney has argued that he is a practical man
and that putting me in jail is the practical solution to the problem that is me. The way I look at it he is the all-time dreamer in
his rosy-eyed argument that the rich getting richer is magically
going to make us poor get richer too. The rich get richer on the
backs of the poor and their main way of getting richer is to wring
more blood out of us turnips, and if we're stupid enough to go
along without a fight then we deserve to have our blood wrung.

The county attorney would have you believe that if each of us is as greedy as he wants then all of us are going to get rich. I ask you to think about what would happen among your family and friends if each of you set out to do your own thing and screw your brother and sister and father and mother and neighbor. And then I ask you to tell me just how the world is any different between strangers than it is between friends and family.

"What you are facing is a choice between what is legal and what is right. For most of human history slavery was legal, but that didn't make it right. If you say what's legal is what's right then you're allowing the legislature to make up your minds for you. And with apologies to the exceptions, the legislature is as big a bunch of nincompoops and sleazebags as anybody might assemble on the planet, almost all of them in my opinion in the pocket of big corporation types who are even bigger nincompoops and sleazebags. You might just as well look to the church.

"I want to suggest to you that you have a higher authority right at hand to consult to tell you what's right." Johnny Faye pointed to his heart. "Whose law is it that the county attorney is serving in asking you to put me in jail? Is it the law that binds mother and father to son and daughter, sister to sister, brother to brother, neighbor to neighbor, the law of love that binds us all to each other and to the stranger? Or is it the law that sets each of these against the other and makes us all slaves to rich people in the big city where the county attorney went to learn how to do just that? At one time that law forbid us to make whiskey, now it makes money from us doing that very thing. Now it forbids us from growing hemp and wants to throw us in jail until such time as it figures out how to make money off of that operation. As soon as it changes its mind on that point, it will figure out some other way to make criminals out of the poor.

"You all know I served this nation. I am not proud of what I did, but when duty called I gave my best. Now the lawyer calls me the enemy of the state and the people when all I want is to be left in peace. I tend to my garden and to my mother and my friends, and I would give the shirt off my back to a stranger who needed it, and that is about as much of life as I can handle.

"You can put me in jail if you want. But you won't be putting me in a room smaller than the one I already live in nor serving me food any plainer than what I already eat, and you caint make me poorer than I already am because my riches are not made of stuff. I appreciate your time and your service."

The jury deliberated for the remainder of the afternoon. The judge let Johnny Faye take some air after making him swear on the Bible that he would return for the verdict. He stood outside the courthouse with JC as company, talking tobacco with the farmers. He located a patch of grass amid the cement and asphalt for JC to do his business, then came back and talked more tobacco. Vetch retired to his offices.

Late that afternoon they were recalled to the courtroom for the verdict. The county attorney entered with a jaunty step occasioned by the length of the deliberations but in fact the jury handed down a verdict of not guilty. The gallery erupted in applause. One of the spectators upstairs produced a pint of whiskey. The judge banged her gavel. Before dismissing Johnny Faye, the judge offered the observation that though the jury had determined he was not guilty, if she were planting a peach tree from which she planned to harvest peaches she would take some trouble to conceal it from the neighbors' children, and would Mr. Johnny Faye please draw from that little story the simple lesson the judge wanted to convey?

The spectators poured down the tiny staircase from the gallery. Jerry Bee proposed a beer at the Miracle Inn but Johnny Faye said, "Thank you kindly but I got to step outside to check on JC," and then he disappeared from their midst, leaving Harry Vetch alone at his desk and winter gathering in his heart.

Chapter 15

Now Meena went to the blind many evenings. She sat on the fallen pine and scooted sideways until her feet dangled over the little hollow that had once writhed with snakes and remained there until she could barely distinguish the silhouette of the trees from the blue-black star-spangled sky. Then she drove back to her office in the old Electra.

One especially bright and perfect evening Johnny Faye stepped into her line of vision and stood still as the breathless trees. He stood in the green light watching and even so she gave no sign of noticing him but walked directly to her seat on the fallen pine. She stayed until the sun dropped below the horizon and the copse was lit only by the sky light that remained. On her way to her car she stopped at the statues.

She put her hand in her pocket and felt the small round stone, waiting since her visit to Rosalee Smith's house. Meena gathered some wildflowers and arranged them in a circle and placed the stone in their center. Then she slipped behind a tree.

Johnny Faye came to the clearing as a deer comes to water, careful and alert. He picked up the stone, inspected it, pressed its smooth cool self to his forehead and cheeks. "Talk to me, angel ball. Tell me where you been and what you been up to." He dropped it into his pocket. He searched through the bushes and scrub pines—for a long moment he disappeared, to return carrying a bird's elaborately woven nest. He placed this in the center of the ring of flowers.

Meena stepped into the clearing.

Johnny Faye jumped as if he had seen a ghost. "What the hell are you doing, sneaking up on a body like that."

"I might as easily ask the same of you. Only evidently you are more of a coward."

"You watch who you go calling a coward. Next thing I'll be calling your bluff."

"Then you will find no bluff to call."

"Well all right, then." He executed a complicated little leap. "Come with me for a walk. You might learn a thing or two."

"I'm afraid it is my turn to invoke my mother, who forbade me to walk in the jungle with strange boys. And I am—was in the habit of obeying my mother. In addition to which I have difficulty imagining what you might have to teach that I would have interest in learning."

"You're just afraid to learn, like most folks."

"So now who is calling whom a coward? When I was a child . . ."

"Go on, I'm interested."

"Never mind. That was a very long time ago, half a world distant."

"I'm glad to hear you were a kid, anyways, once upon a time. Nam made me into an old man but then I got back here and figured I'd try being a kid again. How about you?"

"Rubbish. My parents are long dead. And in my country you would be *harijan*, untouchable, though I thank your God, all the gods, for leaving all that behind."

He bowed his head and scuffed at the dirt with one toe. "I'm sorry to hear of your loss, ma'am. A pretty young girl like you should have her mother at hand or at least near enough by that she can call on her for advice."

"You may reserve your flattery for those genuinely young and pretty girls who will no doubt be susceptible to it. I *aint,* as you would say, young, pretty, or a girl. I thank you for your sentiments but I am accustomed to making my way alone."

"No brothers or sisters?"

"None."

"Well, the way I look at it you can go back to your office and cry into your beer—"

"I do not drink beer."

"Nor cry, neither, I have no doubt. Or we can have a nice little stroll in the beautiful woods that God in his wisdom has put here for us to enjoy."

"*Mister* Johnny Faye. Why are you persisting in this madness?"

On this he crouched to his haunches and took up a twig and drew lines and circles in the dirt. "Because you're smart. I like smart. And because you're pretty, though I'm thinking somebody gave you the idea otherwise." He was not looking at her but at his drawing, circles that went round and round. "And because for me you are all those people who died by my hand in a faraway place."

She was looking down on him, on his stringy dirty sun-bleached hair sparse at its crown. Of their own accord her hands reached out to touch his shoulder and nothing in her life had pre-pared her for the ripple of energy that rose from his shoulder through her hands to lodge in her throat. Her hand jerked back as if she had touched a burning brand.

He stood abruptly and walked down a little trail paved with pine needles, talking all the while. "I will show you something sweet, and then I will see you safe back to your car. JC, you stay here. Here, now, *here,* you sit. We won't be needing you on this little adventure." Johnny Faye waved his walking stick in front of them. "Web catcher."

Her feet led her after him, into the gloaming.

"You been married, I can tell."

"And how can you tell that?"

He turned around and studied her. "Because if you hadn't of been you'd of said so."

"Mr. Johnny Faye. If it is your plan—"

"I aint got no plan. I give up on plans somewheres between the first man I shot and climbing on the plane that brung me back from that crazy place. Now hush, both of us."

They stood still so long that only her determination to outlast him kept her standing. The emerald light dimmed, then grew brighter—dusk gave way to silver silence. A full moon was rising. No leaf stirred. Almost imperceptibly his arm rose—he might be one of the granite statues stirring to life. He was pointing at a tree limb close to the ground a few steps ahead. Nothing—then something. A mottled lump—the forest was too dark to discern color—stirred and ruffled. *Whip-poor-will! Whip-poor-will!* First hesitantly, then stronger and more decisive.

Time passed. The bird sang until they heard an answer from a distant ravine. The bird redoubled his call.

Finally Johnny Faye lowered his hand as slowly as he had raised it, a millimeter a moment. They turned to go.

Some steps down the path he spoke. "My grandma told me whippoorwills was a witch bird—that they would suck a goat or even a cow dry in the middle of the night. Funny thing is, they don't care for civilization but they're fine with particular people, which might be why I like 'em so much. People say they're shy, but the fact is that you treat 'em with respect and they will let you stand right on top of 'em, all but tame. You just got to make yourself known in the right way, I mean *their* way, not our way. You got to be still. You're good at being still. Aint too many people I can say that about. There's plenty that's heard a whippoorwill but I would guess no more'n two people in this county has ever laid eyes on one. Me and now you."

"You are an expert on birds."

"I like to think I'm a expert on something other than making trouble. You ever heard how the birds got their names?"

"No, I have not."

They walked on for a moment.

"You may tell me if you wish."

"I will tell you when *you* wish."

The path led them back, sometimes moonlit and silver and fast, sometimes in shadow so dark that her feet lost their sureness. At such times she allowed him to take her hand, though where the trees parted and the path brightened she took it back. Then they were in the clearing in front of the statues. She bent and took up the nest, centered in its ring of wilted flowers, and said, "Come here."

He stepped closer. She stuck her hand in his pocket. "Hey!"

She pulled the stone from his pocket and replaced it from where he had taken it up. "My father—who was a collector of stories, have I mentioned that?—and whom I was in the habit of obeying, would place a stone in memory of the god or goddess who once lived in this clearing. The statues are here because the place is sacred, or so he would have believed—not the other way around, as a Christian might think. In any case I hold with neither superstition. I place it here in memory of him."

"You found yourself a angel ball."

"I beg your pardon?"

He pointed at the stone she had placed at the center of the ring of flowers. "A angel ball. It's hollow, you crack it open and it's filled with crystals. One of those finds its way into your hands, you been singled out for something special. Not something easy—something hard, as a matter of fact. But special. Particular. Pay attention. Watch out. You done anything for that boy? Rosalee Smith's boy?"

"*Mister* Johnny Faye. I am committed to confidentiality regarding my patients."

"Well, at least he's still your patient. The question is what you do from here."

She hung the nest in the bushes and walked down the path.

Chapter 16

The clouds departed and the skies became hot and blue. The grass crackled underfoot and the river shrank. Attendance at the monastery services skyrocketed. Most of the farmers and many of the monks subscribed to an ancient understanding of the rituals: *We pray to You; You give us rain.* The abbot did not like to encourage this kind of tit-for-tat approach to prayer but eventually he yielded, raising his arms at Sunday mass and intoning, "Let us pray for rain." The congregation's collective response was a tangible thing, a swell of hope as tall and wide and deep as the abbey church . . . and still there was no rain.

"'The stone the builders rejected has become the capstone.'" Flavian was sitting in the sycamore throne, reading aloud from a children's Bible. Johnny Faye sat on the branch at his side. On this hot blue day the forest was airless and still, its silence underwritten by the gurgle of the creek and the breathing of JC, panting at their feet.

Earlier that afternoon Flavian had walked from the monastery and stood at the lip of the creek and pretended he was a mourning dove, *Ooo-ah, ooo, ooo, ooo,* all the while feeling like an idiot, a sentiment he found preferable to feeling like a criminal. On Johnny Faye's response the cedars parted and he climbed down the bank, to be put to work tying dental floss around the tops of the plants. Johnny Faye showed him how to knot the floss and then loop its other end around stakes that he had pounded into the dirt around the perimeter of the patch. Flavian made a lame joke about helping nature reduce cavities to which Johnny Faye responded with a patient explanation.

"People are always trying to make their lives easy, but the fact is that nothing good ever come of the silver spoon. This little bottom land is paradise for these plants—lots of sun, water even in a dry year, you and me to come and plump their pillows. They get lazy, they give us all leaf and no bud or maybe only a few buds here and there. And what we want is bud. So we tie 'em down—I have a friend that works for a dental supply company and we got a little exchange going, that's where the floss come from. We tie 'em down and then they got to work for the sun. The lower limbs think their top has been cut off and so they reach up and produce their own buds. So instead of having a single top with a few buds you have fifteen or twenty tops on one plant, all of 'em reaching for the sun and all of 'em budding out. Scrodding, 'swhat I call it. Also keeps the plants down in the corn where they caint be seen by some plane snooping overhead."

After an hour of scrodding no plant was visible above the cornstalks, even as floss ran like guy wires holding the patch from levitating into the sky. Johnny Faye hid his tools in the crevice. Flavian climbed to the sycamore throne and pointed to one of its arms.

"Climb up here." He opened the Bible. "'The stone the builders rejected . . .'"

Johnny Faye climbed up and laid back against the sycamore limb, shut his eyes, and made a show of snoring loudly—it was that kind of dozy afternoon—but Flavian took up the paper and pens he'd brought and thwacked Johnny Faye with them until he sat up. Flavian smoothed flat the pages of the illustrated Bible and pointed. "OK, let's start by writing out that sentence. *The stone the builders rejected has become the capstone.* Don't worry about how good it looks. Just write what you see—make the letters one by one."

"My mamma told me many times never write down nothing you don't want nobody to read. And I am—"

"—in the habit of obeying your mamma. Well, you write something down and then you can take it back to her to read."

Johnny Faye took up the pencil, wrapping his thick, dirt-lined fingers around it as if it were a cue stick. Flavian crouched in the hollow formed by the sycamore's three branches so that he could peer over Johnny Faye's shoulder. "Relax your hand. Loosen your fingers. The idea is to make fine gestures, not big broad ones. You need to hold the pencil so you can make small movements. Don't worry about making letters. The idea is to get your right hand in the habit of wrapping itself around a long, skinny, small object."

"My right hand is already in the habit of wrapping itself around a long skinny object. But it aint that small nor even that skinny."

A small silence, which they broke at the same moment.

"Sorry, Brother." "Oh, I get it, it's a joke."

Johnny Faye sighed. "No shit, Sherlock."

He set about making shaky imitations of the letters but what he wrote was not very good at all. If Flavian had not known the letters Johnny Faye was trying to form he could never have deciphered them. The capital "T" was acceptable, but after that the letters disintegrated into scribbles.

"It's no good, right?"

"No, no. It's my mistake. I've never tried to teach anybody how to write. I should have started with all capital letters."

"Capital letters? Oh, you mean the big ones."

"Yes, that's right."

"Don't treat me like a first grader. Teach me to write like a grownup or forget it."

And so it went. Months later Flavian would remember this day and others like it as a summer idyll: The student seated, the teacher crouched at his side in the mottled embrace of the old water-loving tree that filtered the hot summer sun into a green translucence, with JC's panting and the creek's trickle overwhelmed by the hot still silence of the midday woods, broken from time to time by the liquid warble of a red-winged blackbird seeking refuge from the heat of the open fields. Above them, at the lip of the little ravine 'Sweet waited in a copse of sumac and wild honeysuckle, making himself known only by an occasional snuffle or the stamp of a hoof as he shook off a horsefly.

Months later, in the sunless gorge of despair, that is how Flavian would remember these days and the remembering was a knife to the heart because it came paired with the knowledge of paradise lost, the inarguable reality that however beautiful the opera of memory, at the time, immersed in those particular moments, what he felt was not wonder at their beauty and his good fortune but frustration and something nigh on to anger. Looking over Johnny Faye's shoulder Flavian reminded himself silently, constantly, that his pupil was more frustrated than he, that Johnny Faye picked up and magnified his teacher's emotions, that the key was to keep it light and relaxed because tension fed on itself and only made their work harder. But Johnny Faye rang like a tuning fork with the vibration of Flavian's growing impatience, and though Flavian was impatient not with Johnny Faye but with his own inability to teach, the result was the same. Johnny Faye never said *I told you so* but Flavian felt the words hanging between them, an enclosure wall, high and blank and DO NOT ENTER.

But there was his warm summer-caramel flesh and blood and though Flavian had not yet learned the lessons of loss he knew enough of desire that he prolonged the agony of their lesson until long after it became clear that he was not getting through. And for all his smart-mouthing Johnny Faye stuck with it, stayed with the pen, listened and repeated and drew the letters as best he could, pausing between each letter to study the next as if it held all the secrets of a rune. THE STONE THE BUILDERS REJECTED . . .

Finally Flavian's knees could handle his half-crouch no longer and he stood and stretched. "You have your homework. Do you remember the alphabet?"

"A B C D E-F-G. H I J K L-M-N-O-P. Q-R-S and T-U-V, W, X and Y and Z. Now I know my A B Cs—"

"OK, enough, right. Take this primer with you, and between now and next Sunday I want you to print the capital letters of the alphabet until you can write them without looking at the book. And bring that notebook with you when you come back."

"Yes, *sir*." Johnny Faye snapped his hand in a soldier's salute so crisp and instinctive that it recalled a war-torn world very far removed from this small creek, this lingering summer sun, this peaceful place. Flavian regretted his impatience then but Johnny Faye had already set aside his notebook with the exhilaration of a child released from school—already he was down among his scrodded plants.

But he did not take up his hoe. Instead he climbed past Flavian to the lip of the bank. "Come on, Brother, we've got a lake to break!" Before he could think Flavian was out of his seat and up to the top of the bank and hoisted onto the haunches of 'Sweet and they were off like a rocket, JC nipping at their heels.

While they were at the oxbow bend Johnny Faye had worn his usual ratty white cotton singlet but somewhere between the creek bottom and mounting 'Sweet he had put on a long-sleeved tan shirt spun from some synthetic material that had not seen sunlight in a few million years and that when they dismounted showed not so much as a wrinkle. Johnny Faye unbuttoned it and hung it on his walking stick, propped against a rock outcrop.

"Nice shirt."

"Some threads, huh. Looks even better with the badge."

Johnny Faye pulled the shirt back on. From a pocket he pulled a silver badge and a nameplate, which he pinned to the shirt. Flavian leaned closer. "STATE POLICE. SMITH. Is that your real last name? What's so mysterious about that?"

Johnny Faye took off the shirt and hung it back on his walking stick. "Not my last name *now*. But will be when the right time comes."

"What's this business about STATE POLICE? And SMITH. Who is Smith? Do I want to know about this?"

"Officer Smith. He's the state policeman ragging my ass. But that's enough. Bad luck to tell a story before you get through to the other side. Don't worry, you'll hear about it quick enough from me or somebody else."

"I don't know. News reaches us pretty slowly inside the enclosure."

"Then you'll hear about it from me. If you hear about it from somebody else, just remember the hillbilly's famous last words."

"And what might those be?"

"Watch this!" Johnny Faye roared, even as he was out of his pants and into the lake and Flavian following and for yet another time Flavian missed an office for no good reason at all. He was lazing in the lake, now a warm summer-comfort bath, treading water to stay with the occasional cold spot where a spring welled up from the deep, when Johnny Faye called from the limestone ledge. "We better get a move on or you're going to miss Benediction."

And Flavian turned and swam farther from the shore, out to the middle of the lake where he lay on his back staring up at the deep blue sky of drought. Three turtles sunning themselves on a snag—their beaked heads swiveled as one as Flavian drifted by, then *plop! plop, plop!* they were gone, and he dawdled and doodled so that by the time Johnny Faye dropped him at the back entrance to the enclosure he could smell the incense and hear the hymns already underway. A shame-faced late entrance was out of the question— better to miss the service outright than draw attention to himself by showing up late—and so Flavian slipped through the vestibule and into the enclosure and up to his cell from whose open window he could hear his brothers in prayer. The thought came to him a second time, now with a different, lighter valence: *I'll go to hell.*

Chapter 17

Rosalee Smith's apron reached to Meena's knees. "You don't work with flour without an apron," she said, tying it behind Meena's back. Matthew Mark sat at the table nearby. "That boy does love to be in the kitchen but at home I caint let him help, my husband won't have no part of it."

By now Matthew Mark had redeemed Meena's promise of a story several times over, but on this particular evening mother and son arrived together, Rosalee lugging a basket of peaches. She disappeared and returned with another basket. "I do so love a ripe peach," she said, setting it down with a heave. "But a hundred ripe peaches is *work*."

Some discussion then, about how best to turn the ephemeral peach into something more enduring and the admission by Meena that though once she had prided herself on her cooking she had not been near a stove since leaving India. And so Rosalee went back across the road to return with sugar and flour and lard and butter and cinnamon and pie pans. "We'll make ourselves a pie, won't that be a good thing to do, we'll put it together here and then take it over to my oven—if we turned the oven on in this little bitty place of yours we'd be cooked before the pie. That'll use a handful of these peaches and the rest we'll cut up for preserves." She set about searching through the tiny kitchen's cabinets until she found a measuring cup. "Pie crust has got a temper that you

159

got to pay heed to," she said, sifting and measuring out the flour. "You got a day that's wet and sticky, you use less water because the flour's going to suck up some of that wet from the air and you got to be careful or the dough will turn gummy. You got a day that's dry—they make the best pie days—you can ride herd on the dough pretty easy."

She pinched off a chunk of lard and, using her fingers, mixed it with the flour until it grew crumbly, then pinched off another chunk and mixed some more. Then she sprinkled the dough with water, raked her fingers through the mix, and sprinkled a few drops more until she gathered it up into a neat round ball. This she stored in the refrigerator while they adjourned to the patio to peel and slice peaches.

Rosalee sat with a big brass kettle between her feet and gave a smaller bowl to Meena, with an old blue granite bucket between them for peelings and pits. "I pretty near grew up in a peach orchard," Rosalee said. "We had a hundred peach trees and a thousand white Leghorns, and believe me when peach time come on and the hens was laying you didn't have time to wipe your bottom. That was how we kept ourselves in shoes, though. This would have been your great-uncle's farm"—this as an aside to Matthew Mark—"he was your mamma's daddy's brother, we called him Uncle Peach."

"Better than Uncle Chicken."

"You said it exactly right. He pretty much took the place of my daddy, beings as mine was already dead."

"My parents died when I was young," Meena said.

"I'm sorry to hear that," Rosalee said. "Both of 'em at once?"

"Yes. At least I think so. I have never known what happened. There was a war, I was sent away to the house of *Thakurda*—the house of my father's father. I never heard from my parents again."

"Somebody that loses her mamma and daddy so young will always be looking for a home," Rosalee said softly. "What was they like? Do you have anything to remember them by? Seems like it would be hard, so very far from home, to remember who you come from, and I don't know how you could carry much in the way of a remembrance."

"I have very few things. My land was divided and I along with it. For many years I was not allowed to return. I returned to the village of my childhood only once. It was a difficult journey. I have tried to forget those times. I came here to leave all that behind. It has been a blessing to leave all that behind."

A long silence, broken by the plop of peach slices into the bowl. "My daddy died in Vietnam, same week that eight other boys from this little bitty county was killed," Rosalee said. "They sent us back dog tags and a coffin and they told us they knowed it was him but we would rest easier if we didn't trouble to look for ourselves because they was nothing in there we wanted to see. And I don't know that my mamma or his folks ever looked inside, I don't think so, I never had the nerve to ask. I know they didn't let me look, I was only a little girl 'bout the same age as Matthew Mark here and I know that not letting me look was the only thing to do, but I got to think sometimes that even the remembering of a bloody mess would be better than remembering nothing atall."

"I know what you mean. I have awakened in the night to precisely that same thought about my parents. It is always the *chotolok* who get caught up."

"What's that?"

"My people make a distinction between the *bhadralok*—the big people who choose and shape their lives—and the *chotolok*, the little people whose lives are a matter of yielding and accepting what is given to them. The *chotolok* suffer most."

"You pay attention to that, Matthew Mark," Rosalee said. "You be grateful you live someplace where they aint forced a mother's son to go to war in a long time."

"There's the war on drugs," Matthew Mark said. "Daddy talks about it all the time."

"Well, that aint the same. Here, you go dump these peelings in the compost heap, I expect that dough has chilled long enough."

Matthew Mark took the heaping bucket and ran across the road. "That child," Rosalee said, more to herself than aloud. "He's a skiff of a boy for certain, but he's got his daddy's smart mouth." She hauled herself to her feet. "Let's get ourselves inside."

Rosalee took the dough from the refrigerator. With her palm she fanned flour across the countertop and placed the dough in the middle. Matthew Mark brought the emptied peelings bucket inside, banging it with his hand. "Hush that racket, we're almost done. You sit and be quiet or you won't be sitting there atall." Rosalee rolled up her sleeves.

Meena stepped to her side to watch, to see a blue-black bruise on Rosalee's arm. "Rosalee—how did you injure yourself?"

Rosalee sprinkled flour over the ball of dough and cut it in uneven halves, setting the smaller half aside, then covering the larger half for a long minute with her hands. "You chill it so as to keep it smooth but it's easier to work with if you warm it up a little before you roll it out. You want to be gentle with it. Worst thing for pie dough is to handle it too much. Makes it tough. I just bumped myself on the kitchen counter, being stupid and clumsy as usual. You bruise easier when you get older but you know that. I hadn't expected it to begin so early, is all." She took up an empty whiskey bottle that she had brought from her house. "I caint keep a rolling pin in the house but these work just as good." She coated it in flour, then set about rolling the dough into an even circle.

"When did this happen—I mean, when did you strike your arm against the counter?"

"Oh, sometime today. Or yesterday, I don't pay attention to little things like that."

Matthew Mark sat still as a small creature caught far from shelter, watching and listening and making himself invisible so as to avoid being made to leave, and everything was washed in evening color and summer light.

Rosalee took up a dinner knife and with a flip of the wrist carved a circle from the rolled-out dough. She laid the dough in the pie pan and sprinkled it with flour, then gathered the scraps into a second ball and returned it to the refrigerator. "Here, Matthew Mark, you break those eggs, your daddy don't need to know you had your finger in the pie. You watch him now, he's good," and Matthew Mark jumped up. He took an egg in each hand and broke them one on each side of the bowl's brim. With a shy grin he held out both hands to Meena, a perfectly halved shell in each. "He taught hisself that trick," Rosalee said. "Lord knows I caint do it." She brushed the pie shell with egg white, then beat the eggs with sugar and a little flour. Then she filled the pie shell with sliced peaches, poured the thickener over them, dotted them with butter, and sprinkled the whole with cinnamon.

"Now for the hard part," she said. She took the second ball of dough and rolled it out. Taking up the knife she cut the dough into strips, then set about weaving them into a lattice. "I guess you got to figure that the world belongs to the big people," she said as her hands moved back and forth across the pie, "and those of us that never made much of ourselves got to sit back and keep our heads down and the best thing we can hope for is for nobody to notice. I do wonder sometimes, though, what it would be like to make something of yourself."

"You made something of yourself, Mamma. You made a pie."

"Oh, a pie. Any old fool can make a pie." Rosalee pieced the last strips of dough together into one long strip, which she attached to the pie rim with wetted fingers, crimping and fluting with her right hand as she turned the pie with her left. She sprinkled the finished lattice with sugar. "OK, now. I'll scoot this over to my house. Matthew Mark? Your job is tell me when it's been exactly one half hour, because that's when I'll need to start thinking about getting back over there to check on the pie."

Alone with Matthew Mark. He had pushed the four-wheeled oak chair from the office into the kitchen and was rolling it back and forth, back and forth as Meena wiped the counter and washed the bowls. After a moment he stopped his chair at her elbow. "She didn't bump her arm against the counter."

"I know that."

"Then you can make my daddy stop hurting her."

Meena dried her hands on a dish towel and crouched to face him. "I would like to do that, Matthew Mark. But your mother must have her reasons for telling us what she did. I have to respect those reasons even if I cannot understand them."

"You're all just afraid. You're all just afraid of my daddy."

She stood and turned back to the dishes. "You will grow up and then you will understand," she said, because it was the only thing she could think to say.

Rosalee returned and they sat outside in the twilight and finished peeling and slicing the peaches. Matthew Mark pulled his chair to sit beside Rosalee. First he laid his head on her arm, then, when she turned to dump sliced peaches from the pan into the kettle, he slipped his head into her lap. Rosalee placed her hand on Matthew Mark's towhead, shut her eyes, and sang in a low, tender voice.

Slumber, my darling, the birds are at rest,
Wandering dews by the flowers are caressed,
Slumber, my darling, I'll wrap thee up warm,
And pray that the angels will shield thee from harm.

"What a lovely lullaby," Meena said. "Once all I wanted was to have a child."

"I'll be darned. What makes you think you're too old to have one now?"

"The world has too many children. That is our greatest problem and challenge. And I have other priorities. To begin with I have no security in this country."

"I tell you what. I'll light a candle to the Virgin for you to get yourself a baby."

Meena smiled. "That is sweet of you but my reasons are not entirely political. I am unable to bear a child."

A pause. "Well, I swan, aint that a shame. You're certain about that? I guess you would be, being a doctor and all. All the more reason to light a candle."

"I suggest we place our faith in more *scientific* means. I am grateful that I am childless. If I had given birth to a child, I would still be in India. All the same, I thank you for your concern. You will light your candle and I will bear a child. A miracle child, like Krishna born of Devaki. And then you can teach me your lovely song."

Rosalee shifted Matthew Mark's head in her lap. "I aint never met anybody from another country, I don't think, except maybe the Mexicans who come to work tobacco."

Meena filled her bowl with peaches. "I love walking in the woods in the evening light. As a child I knew nothing like it. The sun rose, then it set—it was light, then it was dark. Here the light lasts and lasts and everything changing all the while."

"You been walking in the woods? Alone?"

Meena busied herself cutting away holes the birds had pecked. "I walk to the statues at the monastery, but not usually alone, no. Often I have Mr. Johnny Faye for company." She stole a glance at Rosalee's face—a blank page. "Oh, I can imagine what you are thinking but he's just—a *character*."

Rosalee kept her eyes on her quick-cutting knife. "He's more than a character, he's a, a—force of nature. Johnny Faye—he's like your Shivo. Dangerous, in a skinny lawbreaking kind of way. You watch out."

"Oh, Johnny Faye wouldn't hurt a fly. You should see him with the birds. He could talk one off its nest."

"It's not *him* I'm telling you to watch out for. I know what I'm talking about." A loud *burrrr* sounded in a nearby tree. "The first katydid of the summer. I hate that sound. You hear one of those, winter caint be far behind. I think a lot about that story you told about the woman who rides the lion. I liked that story—you don't hear stories like that around here, where the woman comes out on top. You got to ask yourself—why would a smart woman like Durga take up with a rounder like Shivo in the first place?"

"I've never thought about that. Durga marries Shiva, we take that for granted."

"Well, there aint nothing you can take for granted. I hope your Durga was in love with the man. I hope she had that much."

"Were you in love when you married?"

A shadow on Rosalee's face, a cloud drifting across a summer-blue sky. "No way. I knowed it was a mistake from the first but I went ahead, I was young and dumb and had got myself in a rough patch. Seemed like he would be my security, him with the police and all. That might have been when I learned about the little voice."

"What little voice?"

"The little voice that tells you what to do. Least, it does for me. It always tells me what I ought to do. Problem I have is paying attention. I can always find some reason not to pay attention. Johnny Faye—he's a summertime lake."

Meena smiled. "Yes, lovely. Though I might have said a river."

Rosalee tightened her lips and raised her eyes to Meena's. "You can drown in a river just as easy, maybe easier than in a lake. I know, I come close. If I'd had the money—" She turned back to her peaches. "That's enough of that."

Meena dumped her sliced peaches into the kettle and sat her bowl on the ground and leaned forward. "Would you mind if I shared a bit of news? I have no one else to tell and *a good story wants to be told*. Mr. Johnny Faye is just an—*amusement*. A companion for a forest walk. I have a real suitor. I have been asked for—a *date*. Thirty-three years old and I have never had a date. In my country this was not how we accomplished such matters—there the family arranges everything. I am so—nervous."

"And who might be your beau?"

Meena spoke in a conspiratorial whisper. "Mr. Vetch, the county attorney."

"Hunh. No surprise. What I'm wondering is what you see in him."

"Mr. Vetch organized the benefit to buy equipment for my office. He's well-connected and prosperous and he's an attorney." Meena smiled. "One cannot help but find some attraction in a law degree. Even a doctor can dream, yes? It makes so much sense."

They finished the peaches in silence. After the last peach Rosalee put her knife in her bowl and set it atop the kettleful of sliced peaches. "I really hate to go home. Peaceful here and safe. I expect that's why Matthew Mark comes over so much. Can't blame him. I'd do the same if I wasn't married."

"You may come over any time. Night or day."

"That's awful kind of you but I'm a married woman and I got my responsibilities. For better or worse I said it out loud with my hand on the Bible. And I wouldn't mind so much but I feel like I'm missing something important."

"You have Matthew Mark."

"Thanks be to you and I thank God for him. But that's not the same. You know that."

"I do know that."

Rosalee shook Matthew Mark's shoulder. "Come on, now, sugar, you're too heavy for your mamma to go lugging you around like she used to and we got to get that pie out of the oven before it burns up." She gave Meena an apologetic look. "I guess you'll have to wait til tomorrow morning for your pie. I'd ask you over but my husband will be home any time now and he's not much one for company."

"I shall look forward to my pie," Meena said. "And in any case I took my pleasure from watching you and Matthew Mark put it together."

After she left Meena sat alone on the darkening patio until the katydids fell silent.

And now he came to mind at times not of her choosing. She would be talking to a patient when in an instant Johnny Faye would be so present to her that she had to excuse herself to collect her thoughts so as to drive him as far from them as possible, as if she were a ruminant cow and he a pesky fly. Not a happy feeling, not at all, a disease in its own right, if only she knew a pill that could make it go away and give her back her calm and untroubled indifference to the world. In her native country wise women understood this. The family would take charge of a woman suffering from this disease and isolate her until she had recovered. She would be kept at home and fed well and tenderly ignored until enough time had passed and she had regained her good sense.

Once Meena had been a lake, now she was a restless river.

Enough of this and she resorted to reading novels, in whose pages she had always found solace, an entrance to a dreamland that was not *her* dreamland. She took up this book or that and every fabricated tree and table called forth his ropy veined arms, the moles across his *broad shoulders*. What was going on? She must be lonelier than she had ever been, in a life filled with times and journeys alone. This was nothing but obsession, a trick of the hormones, a flaw in the logic. And still he was there. Something sweet.

Chapter 18

Meena was following Johnny Faye from the statues to the Rock House.

"Careful of the poison ivy." He pointed with his stick. "I can knock down spider webs and scare away snakes but you got to watch out for poison ivy on your own."

"As a child I played in jungles inhabited by leopards and crocodiles. I am capable of watching out for myself, thank you."

"Suit yourself." They continued down the path. "If this was winter I could show you a sight. There's a holly tree on the edge of a creek, ever year loaded with berries and ever year this flock of cedar waxwings comes through and shows up right when the holly berries have froze and thawed and set to fermenting and then the day comes, they figure it out ever year, and you'll see that tree covered with those little guys duded up in their party clothes, ever limb with a cedar waxwing on it like they've come together for a big party and all sitting on that green tree with the bright red berries like they was posing for a Christmas card. And then what do they do but eat the berries for the buzz, you know, for the alcohol from the fermenting. They get so drunk I seen them fall to the ground and wobble around like they been swilling whiskey. There's a red fox come ever year and hangs out at the bottom of that tree waiting for Christmas dinner to fall into his lap. Prettiest drunks you'll ever see too, look like they put on a hat and coat just to go out on the town and get plastered. Not that they're the first to do that."

"You, for example, smoke *ganja* more than is good for your health, physical or mental."

"When I want advice about my health, physical or mental, I'll pay for it."

"This taking of drugs is a question of escape. Wanting to escape suffering instead of confronting and engaging it."

"But I aint suffering and I like a cold beer and a hit of pot as much as the next guy."

Meena stopped in mid-stride. "I have to ask myself why I am doing this."

"I been asking myself that selfsame question." Johnny Faye kept walking. "I expect we're both interested to find out the answer. Now just down this little creek we'll come to the Rock House, big overhang that's always dry underneath and with a little spring in the back. There's a red-tail hawk that shows up, there's a pasture left from an old farm just over the ridge, mousey heaven, he orders up his supper over there and then flies over here to chow down." He turned around then. "You coming along or what? See, you just got to ask the right questions. You got to put yourself in the place of the bird—you got to be the bird instead of yourself. You got to look for the little things that hardly nobody sees except for the birds. They don't miss a lick. All animals are curious. Except people."

"Mr. Johnny Faye. Why do you suppose I am interested in all this chatter?"

"You're here, aint you. If you ask me it has to do with getting closer to God."

"I beg your pardon?"

"Taking drugs." He pointed skyward. "We don't call it *getting high* for nothing. The problem is you get too close to God and you caint find your way back or you don't want to, amounts to pretty much the same thing. I seen a lot of people lose their ways. I come pretty close myself." He dropped his voice to a whisper. "Look. Turn around, slow."

She turned around and saw only the dark line of the water seep at the rear of the overhang. She turned to him. "You mean over there? Nothing. A waste of—"

A great flapping of wings so close to her head that she ducked. Johnny Faye placed his finger against her lips and then his hands over her ears and slowly turned her head toward the far end of the great overhang. "I don't see—" And then she did see, the slate-blue bird grasping a faintly struggling smaller bird.

His voice at her ear. "I'll be damn, it aint a redtail, no, this one's a sharp-shin, a female, I'd say, they're bigger. And she's caught herself a goldfinch."

The hawk began to pluck its prey, starting with the top of the head and working its way down to the breast. Turning its beak from one side to the other, the bird seized a mouthful of feathers, yanking them loose with a twist of the head. It devoured the smaller bird's head, neck, wings, legs, feet, leaving a small pile of feathers. Then it turned to cleansing its talons, splaying its claws to grasp each in its beak, plucking them clean as if here indeed was the greatest delicacy.

They watched in silence. The light failed.

"I am telling you, you caint just *see*, you got to *look*. And you got to look for what's there instead of what you want to find. *Especially* if what you want to find is nothing."

"Please. I would like to return to the car."

They turned to go. "You don't have much stomach for killing?"

"I am trained to heal—to help people recover and to stay well. That is my focus."

"You ever thought about healing yourself?"

"I have no idea what you are talking about."

"Neither do I but I like getting a rise out of you. That was the goal—that was the *objective*, like the U.S. Army taught me to say."

"I *aint* the U.S. Army."

"You could of fooled me."

They moved down the path.

"But you still got to have a objective. Knowing what you're looking for don't mean you'll find it but it sure improves the chances."

She quickened her step to catch up with him, touching his swinging arm so that he turned around. "And what are you looking for? What is your *objective?*"

She had been drawn to his dark eyes for their openness and transparency—now they grew narrowed and clouded with secrecy. "I don't rightly like to say. You?"

"I am looking to immigrate. Since my first day at the Medical College I have thought of and worked for nothing else. No, that is not correct. I have thought of it since the day I saw my first American movie when I was ten years old, alone in a Calcutta cinema."

He resumed the path. "You got to want something bigger than that. You got to want something that's yours, not theirs. You go wanting something that's theirs, that's a sure ticket to hell. You got to want something they caint take away from you."

Matthew Mark presented himself to her thoughts.

"My mother told me that we meditate at dusk or dawn because that is when good mixes with evil, light with dark. Everything is a part of the whole, including illness and death, that what we call good and evil are different sides of the same coin, dependent on each other. Night and day, life and death. And though we are to strive for the good we are also to know that our effort is part of a turning wheel too large to comprehend. Our job is to submit to the wheel. Submit and accept. But I could not submit and accept. Everything I have achieved, I have achieved by refusing to submit and accept."

"You seem pretty accepting of the deal with Officer Smith over that boy. Sorry, I caint let it go. I got my own share of bullheadedness."

Meena sighed. "The situation is not as simple as you believe."

"It never is. Maybe that boy is your fate, to put it your way. Maybe he's been put in your life to teach you something. I was mad as hell at the U.S. Army until I got old enough to see that maybe for a independent warthog like myself a few lessons in obeying orders wasn't such a bad idea. One person I learned to obey was myself. You might give that a try. There was this time, a priest was saying mass and he asked me to throw a camouflage tarp over a pile of mortar rounds to make a altar and it was no big deal except that I got to thinking about that altar, what we were going to use it for, and sure enough not a half hour later—"

"Please. Finish your story."

"Naw, I want to hear your story first. Here we are at the statues."

That night he came to her in her dreams.

Chapter 19

Dr. Chatterjee was making her first rounds of the monastery infirmary—the abbot had appointed her visiting physician. She accompanied Flavian as he listened, cajoled, and ministered to his aged brothers. She busied herself elsewhere when he sneaked a beer to Brother Zaccheus from a stash concealed in the medications refrigerator but insisted that he take one away from Brother Dismas who had diabetes and no business drinking. She listened as Brother Wilfred, lost to Alzheimer's, told the same anecdote three times. She stood by as he plumped pillows for Brother Eustache, who needed his bed cranked up so he could watch the changing light.

Their last patient was Brother Zaccheus, immobile and obese from multiple sclerosis. Flavian handed her the blood pressure cuff, which she looped around the great ham of Zaccheus's arm. She pumped and released the bulb—a pneumatic sigh.

"A priest, a rabbi, and a minister were walking down a street in San Francisco," Zaccheus said, "when they ran into a prostitute carrying one of those yellow plastic bananas that squeak when they're pumped."

Flavian put his finger to his lips. "Later with that one, Zack."

"Your pressure is marginal, the dipstick shows you spilling protein, we need to check that further. We'll do a blood test—I may need to change your medications."

Zaccheus placed the back of his hand on his forehead and rolled his eyes upward. "*She's* the reason my blood pressure is up. How about a sponge bath?"

Flavian tucked the cuff into his tote bag. "Sorry, for that I need a second pair of hands and Adrian's stuck with the cows."

"*She* could help." Zaccheus gave Meena a beseeching look. "Puh-*leeze*."

Meena patted his puffy hand. "I'm afraid that's not my job. But do save your joke for my next visit. I want to know what happens to that banana."

"No you don't," Flavian said. "Take my word for it."

Zaccheus cupped his hand at Meena's ear. "Adrian won't show up because the abbot brought in a woman doctor."

"Oh, so that is the story." Meena laid down her clipboard and pushed up her sleeves. "Perhaps I may lend a hand after all."

Flavian was already at the door. "Not to worry. Zack can wait on his bath."

Meena was poking in the closet, pulling out towels. "Brother Flavian. The abbot has appointed me physician in residence. That means *all* the monks are under my care, including those who may not *want* to be under my care. As attending physician, I shall require Brother Adrian to perform his assigned tasks. But for today I will take his place."

A thumbs up from Zaccheus. "The boss has spoken."

Meena looked at her watch. "The paperwork will require ten minutes. Enough time for you to draw water."

She returned to find Zaccheus shirtless and sitting on the edge of his bed. Together she and Flavian levered him from his bed and into the bathing chair. Flavian began sponging his great folds of flesh while Meena changed the linens. "Brother Zaccheus," she said, "what do *you* think the abbey should do with its cows?"

"Big Macs," he replied promptly. "With cheese. Good old American cheese, too, not that smelly French stuff we make around here."

Meena took a sponge and began soaping his back. "What if we understood that the cows and the trees and rivers are God's ways of making herself known to the world? Is it so hard to see each of these creatures as one of the infinite aspects of God? Consider how much they give us and how little they ask in return." She wrung out her sponge and soaked it in rinse water. "Must compassion always yield to efficiency?"

"Everywhere except in a monastery," Zack said. "Or so I'd like to think. By any standard of efficiency, the abbot would have parked my ass in some cheap nursing home ten years ago. Instead here I am being hand-washed by a gorgeous woman."

Meena squeezed her sponge over Zaccheus's back. "If the choice must be efficiency or compassion, then perhaps we should prefer compassion."

Flavian dropped the soap, splashing water into Zack's eyes. Consternation and confusion until Meena flushed Zack's eyes and Flavian regained his composure. "That's a new tack coming from you," Flavian said. "Last time we talked you were in the Big Mac camp. 'Institutions must make difficult and unpleasant decisions.' And so forth."

"That is correct."

"So what changed your mind?"

Meena considered. "A little bird."

"Women change their minds," Zaccheus said. "That's what they do. They're the river, we're the rocks. And we know who wins that war."

Meena tested the water with her elbow. "Too cool. More hot water, please."

"Yes, *ma'am*," Flavian said. He left to draw water—Meena was not unhappy to be left alone. "Close your eyes," she said to Zaccheus, then lifted the sponge over his head and squeezed. Warm water ran over his tonsured head, down his neck and over his shoulders, which seized up in an involuntary shiver of pleasure. "Do that again," he said. "These guys would never think of doing that."

Meena had not been this intimate with a patient since her first months in medical school, when as a newly-arrived student she had been assigned similar caretaking tasks. And yet was not caretaking the best medicine for someone beyond the help of drugs and machines? The healing touch of the hand in love. Had anyone touched her in this way? Only Johnny Faye—the memory came of its own accord: placing his hands on her temples and turning her to look at the hawk devouring the goldfinch.

"Oh, ma'am, I'm so sorry." Zack opened his eyes and looked down. "It's got a mind of its own, I swear I have nothing to do with it."

Meena draped a towel across his lap. "Your physician is happy to see that the nerves to your trunk and leg are still responsive."

Zack gave a bitter little laugh. "They can get that thing to stand up but can't be bothered with the rest of me."

Flavian returned then and set about sponging Zack with rinse water while Meena worked with his feet, testing them for sensation. "What comes to mind when I speak of India?" she asked. "Disease and poverty and filth? That is what most people say."

"That's not what I think of," Zack said. "I think of elephants. Tell me there are elephants. *Ow!*"

Meena smiled. "There are elephants." She moved her hands up his calves.

Zaccheus closed his eyes again. "And opium smokers, I guess. Don't know where—*ow!* that came from."

"Yes, very good. I am sorry to hurt you but I am establishing benchmarks for sensation."

"You're not a doctor, you're a theologian," Zack said. "Punishing me for enjoying myself too much. As for opium smokers, we have our own, right here in the hills. Calls himself Johnny Faye."

A long silence. Zaccheus cracked one eye. "Did somebody say plastic banana?"

Flavian busied himself toweling Zaccheus dry. "So how do you know Johnny Faye?"

"Flavian, if you'd lift your nose out of a book you might learn something. Everybody knows Johnny Faye. If it weren't for his philandering ways, the kitchen ladies would have to talk about, I don't know, something important and boring. Like God."

Now Meena busied herself with towels and talcum powder. "And what do they say about his philandering ways?"

"Sorry," Zack said. "The Rule of Benedict tells us: 'Above all, no murmuring.'" He drew a finger across his lips.

"He doesn't really smoke opium," Flavian said. "Pot, grass, weed—marijuana. There's a lot of it around here."

"Well, now, listen to the expert," Zaccheus said. "How do *you* know Johnny Faye?"

"Didn't you just say everybody knows Johnny Faye? *Everybody* includes me." Flavian directed Meena to Zack's other side. "Careful, now, this is the risky part. One, two, *three*," and they hoisted Zack into his bed and eased him back on his pillows.

Meena rolled down her sleeves. "In India people grow what we call *ganja*. When I was a girl, my father took me to the cinema to see American Westerns. I saw cowboys and outlaws and I decided that American men must be like *ganja* growers."

"This I got to hear," Zack said.

While Flavian cleared the basins and towels she told them about Queen Postomani, who had been born a mouse but could not be satisfied with her humble fate. "So her guru, a great holy man, transformed her, according to her wishes, into a cat, a dog, an ape, a boar, an elephant, and finally into a beautiful woman who married the great king. But then her ambition led her to fall into a pond and she drowned." Her hands grew animated as she spoke, two small fluttering birds. "The king was devastated with grief and so he sent for the guru and begged: *You who can do so much, bring her back!* But the guru said: *What is fixed by fate must come to pass. Let her body remain at the bottom of the pond and fill it with earth. Out of her flesh and bones will grow a tree that will be named the poppy tree, after Postomani. From this tree you will obtain a drug called opium, which will be celebrated through the ages as a powerful medicine. The opium smoker will have one quality of each of the animals into which Postomani was trans-formed. He will be mischievous like the mouse, quarrelsome like the dog, filthy like the ape, savage like the boar, intelligent like the elephant, regal like a queen."* Meena smiled. "That is how I thought of American men. *Ganja* smokers. Cowboys."

"That could be our Johnny Faye, all right, if you listen to the women in the kitchen," Zack said. "Imagine the woman it would take to handle a man like that. A wild woman."

By the time Flavian and Meena finished, Zaccheus was snoring. An hour remained before Vespers and so the monk and the doctor walked to the statues, to find them littered with pine needles and twigs. Flavian had tucked a broom behind a tree and now he took it out to sweep them clean. Meena bent to pick up the small round stone marking the center of the clearing. She returned to the bench, rolling the stone between her palms. "That bird we hear singing—I have heard it here before but I have never thought to look for it."

Flavian cocked his head sideways and watched. "Something's different about you. Something's changed."

Meena peered into the trees. "I have discussed the boy with Johnny Faye, as well as the fate of the cows."

"You sure seem to know that man awfully well."

"Oh, dear—it flew away." She sat back. "If only they would sit still!"

"Like a good patient." Flavian pointed to the plaque set into the base of the stone apostles. "Do you know the story of the man the grove honors? He was a seminarian—Episcopalian—who worked for civil rights. A white guy pulled a gun on a black woman registering voters. The seminarian threw himself in front of her and took the shot. Martyred. The ultimate *unreasonable* act."

Meena stood and walked to the engraved memorial and ran her fingers over its letters. "Thank you for telling me that. I have always been drawn to the stories of such people. When I was young I was told I had a special destiny."

"Like Queen Postomani."

"Indeed. Though I hope I may avoid her fate."

From across the fields the bells tolled Vespers. Flavian returned the broom to its hiding place. "And so you have had no success with finding a safe home for the boy."

"And you have not saved the cows." Meena returned the angel ball to the center of the clearing. "I am not the only one to have changed. Once you told me that keeping the cows was a simple matter of dollars and cents. Now you defend the seminarian's *unreasonable act*. To keep the cows—surely that would be *an unreasonable act*."

"That's is a whole different order of magnitude. They're just cows. The boy is a suffering human being."

She waved her hand, an angry flick. "What can you know of suffering? You are protected by your citizenship. You are protected by your whiteness. Even in your monastery, you are protected by your money."

"To refrain from acting can be as wrong as an evil act," Flavian said.

Meena stood, brushing pine needles from her skirt. "Brother Flavian. What you call evil I define as the consequences of our actions. You have said that you became a monk to avoid going to war."

"Not the reason people like to hear, but essentially yes."

"Very well. I became a doctor because it was one of the few careers available to a penniless, intelligent woman from the provinces that might enable me to come to America. Now you propose that I place those years of work in jeopardy.

"I think of Matthew Mark every day. I park my car where it cannot be seen from their house so that the father cannot know when I am at home and when I am away. I leave a light burning in my office so that both the father and the mother may see it. I hope that it serves as a warning for him and a comfort and invitation for her. And yet if I act more boldly, I may well lose my position, and who benefits from that? The question is not whether what we saw was evil, but what is the best course of action. Every day I think that if I put my wits and intelligence to the problem long enough, I will arrive at a solution. The problem is that there is no solution. We are living out the solution."

"So what do we do? Live with the evil we know, but can't do anything about? Or try to do something about it, knowing that anything we do has a chance of making the situation worse?"

"You are a monk. Your duty is to contemplate those questions."

"And you're a doctor, and your duty is to figure out their answers and make them happen."

On the drive back to her office, through hills verdant amid drought, the questions deviled her. Why had this boy come into her life? Could not one single thing that she desired arrive without complication and challenge?

Throughout Vespers Flavian was a confusion of emotions, so much so that he had to take up the book to read prayers that had long ago etched themselves in memory. What was this tightness in his chest, dogging his every step? In the midst of the responses Flavian thought, *Is this what they call being in love? But with whom? The doctor?* A strange but not unpleasant thought—appealing, even. Such things had happened to his brother monks—he had heard stories, *murmuring.* Maybe his time had come.

Flavian returned to his cell and lay on his bed. Across his years in the monastery he had come to rely on the voices and visions he had in that numinous place between waking and sleep, and on this particular evening this is what came to him: He would broach the subject with Johnny Faye, who at least in Flavian's life was the greatest expert on love.

Chapter 20

Harry Vetch sat nursing his whiskey on the ratty couch that Maria had covered with some kind of polyester throw that would give him a prickly rash if he weren't careful. "We need to talk, Maria, and not about the weather."

She took up her wine and rolled her eyes. "That's easy for you to say. You work in an air-conditioned office. But then so do I, as of today."

"I have central at home, but my courthouse office is an oven. We were supposed to get window units last week. According to the judge. I'm not holding my breath."

"Well, we beat you to it. Nineteen of them showed up on the loading dock the other morning. Nobody knows where they came from but the timing couldn't be better."

Vetch had been on the verge of standing to give himself a clean path to the door but something Maria Goretti said snagged in his brain. "Wait a second. The hospital just got nineteen brand-new air conditioners?"

"Well, yes, that's what I just told you."

"And you don't know where they came from."

"No, but that's not such a big deal. Rich Catholics are forever dumping stuff on us."

"But we're talking nineteen brand-new, completely service-able air conditioning units."

"That's right. We used them to replace some of the old ones in the patients' rooms."

"And they just materialized out of nowhere and nobody asked any questions."

"Never look a gift air conditioner in the mouth is what I say, especially when it arrives in the middle of the hottest summer in anybody's memory."

Vetch considered this with a growing suspicion, the specifics of which he did not care to face . . . but something about that odd number—*nineteen* air conditioners . . .

He called the judge, who had just come in from watering his cannas and was relaxed and jovial. Quickly enough they established that he had approved a work order for twenty air conditioning units from Sears and they were at least a week overdue and he had been planning to look into that—"Twenty, you say. Not nineteen." Vetch covered the mouthpiece with his hand and turned to Maria. "You don't happen to remember the brand name."

"Well, yes, as a matter of fact, my lab table is right next to the window so I watched the guy install it. It's that generic Sears brand. Kenwood, I think. No, Kenmore."

Vetch ran a finger around his collar. "If I were the sort of man who cursed . . ."

"Harry." She snuggled next to him.

He phoned the Sears in the city, where after throwing some weight he was connected to the loading dock, where the supervisor told him that twenty air conditioners had been signed over to a state policeman named, let me check the invoice, Officer Smith.

Vetch hung up. A moment's indecision, then he turned to Maria Goretti and said, "Maria, you know how much I respect you." On his words she stood and pulled him into the kitchen and shut the door. "Let's not make this harder than it has to be," Vetch said. He took her hand.

She took it back and folded her arms. "And exactly how hard does it have to be? Have you calculated damages with appropriate compensation charts? Here's what I'm wondering: Why now? Harry, you wouldn't lay down one fishing pole unless you had a fish on another line or at least saw a good twitch on the bobber."

"That is not correct," he said with conviction. "I was a happy workaholic bachelor when you insinuated yourself into my life."

"There's the doctor."

He turned away. "Whatever you need to believe."

"So it *is* the doctor."

Vetch paced the kitchen, flinging his hands about, his eyes fixed on the floor—pink and green linoleum. "Look, Maria. From the first—*from the first* I laid out the landscape. You remember that, yes? Yes. Short-term fling, company for the road—I made all that very clear, yes? Yes. But I just don't feel right, stringing you along while I'm keeping one eye on the rest of the room. And I've dedicated my life to doing the right thing. I have to do it here. You're an amazing lady. You deserve somebody who really loves you."

"Love," Maria said. "Harry. You want the doctor, you are *desperate* for the doctor for one reason, which is that she is *not* desperate for you. Everything—every*one* has come easy for you. Until now. I'm interested to see how it turns out, but not so interested that I'll just shut up and watch. Not my style. You know that."

He moved to the door. "Unless you have more to say—"

She blocked his way. "Yes, I suppose I do have one thing more to say."

A long pause. "Maria," he said, resting his hand on her arm, "don't—"

She stopped, started to speak, stopped herself, started again. "Harry. You're not a fraud. Really, you're not. You're a politician. It's in your nature. You're an actor—I don't know if politicians were ever any other way but that's what they are now and you've got a future.

"And you know, I like that about you or at least I've made my peace with it. *Love*—we're in our thirties, we're past love, soon enough we'll be past sex. Take my word for it—I work in a hospital, I know what's coming." She held out a stiff forefinger, then let it droop. "And every politician needs a wife. You need somebody who's going to scope out a roomful of people and whisper in your ear the names of the ones whose hands you need to pump *and* the names of their wives and children and pets. You don't need a lover, you need a wife. And I'm the perfect candidate. You need somebody to take care of you. I need somebody to take care of. I won't be your doormat—you know me better than that—but I'm happy to be your partner in crime. Which in politics, sooner or later is what it will come to. You're old enough to understand the difference between what you want and what you need. The question is— my question is, have you grown up enough to give up a little of the first for the sake of the second?"

"You do what you have to do. Just know that it's over."

"The answer to my question, evidently, is no."

He stepped around her and into the living room. He was at the door when she said, "You forgot something."

He patted his pants for his wallet and keys. "I don't think so."

"You forgot the part about being friends. 'This is as hard on me as it is on you but I hope the time comes when we can be friends.'"

"If that's what you want."

"What *I* want, as you know perfectly well, isn't worth a shit. But since you raised the subject, what I want is for you to come to your senses," but he was out the door and in his car and down the drive. Only when he had arrived at the judge's house did he surprise himself with a word of comment. "Gosh. She's *tough*."

The judge was sitting on his veranda in an avocado green metal glider that screaked when he shifted his bulk. He had a whiskey in one hand, a funeral home fan in the other. He pointed at a wicker chair. "Have a seat. I can't handle the air. Ginny Rae says it helps her arthritis so I had it put in, but nothing worse for your health than walking out of a freezing house on a hot day. But what do I know? They're her knees. What can I do you for.

How are things going with that Shaklett woman? You popped the question?"

"Do me a favor and don't mention Maria Goretti Shaklett to me again," Vetch said. "Who, for your information, I just broke up with, but keep that to yourself. It's none of your business and anyway it's not why I came. I'm not in the mood to sit. I'm too mad."

"Gotta get a handle on that. Bad for your health."

"I'll tell you what's bad for my health. Drug dealers are bad for my health. We have got to figure out a way—at least now I have the goods to make it stick."

The judge lifted his drink to his lips.

"Don't laugh at me. These are felonies. Impersonating a police officer. Theft of government property. *Your* property. *Our* property." Vetch was pacing now. He related his conversation with the loading dock supervisor. "Half of me is mad at Johnny Faye and the other half at the Sears supervisor for being so gullible. And another half at you."

"At *me?* Why me? What did I have to do with it? I suppose I authorized the purchase of the air conditioners. Are you going to name me as an accessory?"

"You put up with it. You think he's cute. You practically encourage him."

"Harry. Calm down. Have a seat. Please. Go on. Sit. Don't get so bent out of shape. Have a drink. Lord, I'm beginning to sound like a Catholic. Maybe it's rubbing off. Another ten years and I'll be calling for a rosary on my deathbed."

"You see? *You see? I'm* fighting the war on drugs and you sit around on your *fat ass* cracking jokes."

One moment the judge was carefully placing his drink on the glider's wide arm, the next he was in Harry Vetch's face. In bare feet he was a head shorter than Vetch but he stood close enough to use the bulk of his gut to back Vetch against the porch railing. "I am about to offer you another pearl of wisdom and I advise you to listen up. You are not out to recreate the *pax Romana*, look it up. You are out to get rich and get ahead in your so-called career and the courts are serving you nicely as a means to those ends. Now. Can you *prove* that Johnny Faye stole those units? All we know, unless you have information up your sleeve that you have not shared, is that someone disguised as Officer Smith presented himself at the Sears loading dock to take the order and that later that evening twenty units—"

"—nineteen. He probably kept one for himself."

"—probably the same units but we don't know that, showed up on the hospital loading dock, deposited by an unknown benefactor whom the hospital staff has wisely chosen to identify as Divine Providence." Here the judge placed a finger on the county attorney's chest. "And here we find the heart of my pearl of wisdom: Politics is the art of the possible. You are in service to your career, fine. I would have thought you'd do a better job as a real estate developer, given all your hoo-hah about Ridgeview Pointey—"

"Ridgeview *Pointe*. You don't say the 'e.' As you know perfectly well and I wish you would stop—"

"As I was saying. In my day we didn't have careers, we had professions. But those days are gone, *adios*, too bad, time marches on and we submit. May I remind you, though, that yours is an elective office which I assume you would like to retain and use as a stepping stone for the next way station in your glorious *career*. How may you best serve that ambition? You can forget about the air conditioners and focus your time, money, and attention on Ridgeview *Pwante*, if you want to get French about it. The county will report the air conditioners as stolen to its insurance company, which will conduct the most cursory of examinations to establish that they were stolen. Your investigation will ascertain what you and I already know: The supervisor at the loading dock will not be able to identify the culprit. Our thief is not dumb, and I *seriously* doubt he kept one for himself. With a few phone calls we should be able to get Sears to absorb the loss since it was their employee who improperly released the air conditioners. Everybody wins except

Sears or the insurance company, theirs or ours, and you show me a registered voter who gives a rat's ass about insurance companies and I'll *buy* you an air conditioner and personally install it.

"*Or,* you and your army of righteousness can take those air conditioners away from the sweet old innocent Sisters of Charity. The air conditioners will sit in some storage room for a year as state's evidence so we'll sweat out the summer in any case, but every overheated voter in this county will hear that twenty air conditioners were bought by the big bad politicians who took them away from the old and the infirm so as to cool our fat heads. Meanwhile you arrest Johnny Faye for a crime he may or may not have committed—my guess is that he sent somebody else to that loading dock, but who knows? So you launch another trial in which you *may* succeed convicting him. Or he may *yet again* make a fool of your puny, prematurely balding *fat ass.*"

Vetch pushed away the judge's hand. "And so you are advising me to act as an accomplice to a felony. Which the last time I checked is a felony in and of itself."

"Most explicitly I am *not* advising you to take any particular course of action, not at all. I am only pointing out the likely consequences of the choices with which our criminal, whatever his identity, has presented you. Based on my considerable experience as an elected official in this county. Which you may choose to ignore."

The judge turned away. After a moment Vetch saw his shoulders quiver. The judge dropped into the glider, which protested this insult with a salvo of squeakings and groans. "I'm sorry, Harry," he said. He took the paper towel from under his drink to dab at his eyes. "I can't help myself, I'm a sucker for genius," and the county attorney realized that the old fart was laughing, and that he, Harry Vetch, was the butt of the joke.

Chapter 21

"You haven't shown me your homework."

Johnny Faye was peering into the crowns of the surrounding trees. "Caint decide if that's a vireo or a Tennessee warbler. A little early for a warbler to be coming back through but maybe this one wants to beat the crowd."

"You were supposed to write letters until you had them memorized."

"Is that a fact. A warbler would be, I don't know. More lively, kind of."

"How can you learn to write if you don't do your homework?"

"What homework."

"Oh, come on. Next time I'll give you a quiz." Silence. "Johnny, that's a *joke*."

"I told you I *caint* write. How am I supposed to write something down if you aint taught me how. And the name's Johnny *Faye*, Professor Tom."

Flavian took up his clipboard and pens and paper and climbed into the sycamore throne. "Come up here." After a moment of sullen hesitation Johnny Faye climbed up. Flavian yielded his seat, sitting on the limb so that he looked over Johnny Faye's shoulder. He clipped a sheet of paper to the board. "Here. I'll draw an *A* and then you draw it." Flavian drew a large block letter *A* and next to it a small *a*, then handed the clipboard and the pen to Johnny Faye.

"Look them over. Got that? OK, now it's your turn." Flavian concealed his *A*s under a fresh sheet of paper.

"Let me look at the picture."

"No, there's not going to be somebody standing around to show you a picture, you have to write it from memory. Look, I rattle off nearly a page of the New Testament and you can say it back without missing a word, surely you can memorize a few letters."

A long pause.

"Can I look at it again?"

"Sure, take as long as you want."

Flavian lifted the top page. Johnny Faye squinted and stuck out his thick lip and pulled it back and chewed on it and then stuck his pen in his mouth and chewed on that. Flavian clipped the blank page to the clipboard and handed it over. "OK, give it a try."

Johnny Faye touched the pen's nib to the page. It stayed in that spot until it grew a little corona, the tip bleeding ink into the paper.

"I see." Another long pause. "Have you always had this problem?"

Johnny Faye threw down the pen and jumped to the ground. "I aint got a problem. Or anyways, I don't need to add more problems to the ones I already got."

He took up his clippers, moving from plant to plant and clipping the strings of floss that tied them to the surrounding stakes. The side stems of the scrodded plants had grown toward the sun so that in some cases they were as full and bushy as their original tops. Johnny Faye worked his way around his plot until he was underneath the tree.

Flavian cleared his throat. "I think—I think I might be in love." The sycamore cradled Flavian in its big arms. "I said—I think I'm in love."

"Shit."

"Please, Johnny. Johnny Faye. I'm serious."

"Sorry. I didn't mean you. I broke off a stem of primo bud. It's a risk you take in scrodding and it's worth it but it don't make me any happier about it." Johnny Faye waved stem crowded with palmate leaves about his head. "Yee-hi. Jesus welcomed to Jerusalem. I heard you the first time. What do you want me to do about it?"

Flavian shifted uneasily in the sycamore throne. "I don't know. I just thought since you have so much experience maybe you could give me some idea of whether that's what's going on. I mean, I have a vow, you know, we swear—well, not exactly to celibacy, that's an assumption that most people make that's not really true, but we swear to undertake to reform ourselves in Christ's image and as part of that we take a vow not to gratify the, the—promptings of the flesh. So."

"So what." Johnny Faye laid down his clippers and came to the sycamore's trunk. He held his hand up in a fist, then counted off. "First, if you need somebody to tell you if you're in love then you aint in love. Second, fuck this meeting of the minds shit, the question is what gets your dick hard. If Jesus gets your dick hard then I guess you're in love with Jesus though I never saw much future in being in love with a dead man. Third, who's the lucky stiff?"

"Well. I don't know that I'd call her by that—"

"Well, *her*. That eliminates half the human race."

Flavian jumped down from the tree. "If you think—"

"I don't think nothing, I just pay attention and don't take nothing for granted, I learned that in the Army. So who's the lucky lady?"

Confronted so directly Flavian wilted. He found he could not shape his mouth around the words but Johnny Faye was waiting. "The doctor. You know the doctor."

To Flavian's surprise Johnny Faye did not laugh or make a smart remark but dropped to a crouch and began gathering his tools. "When do you got time to see the doctor?"

"On Sundays. After I leave here. She comes to Benediction, then we walk together and talk about, oh, I don't know. Religion, and ideas, and India, where she grew up. And what's going to happen to the cows."

Johnny Faye hid his tools under the rock ledge. "That aint love, that's—talk."

"I guess I figured people have different ways of coming to love."

"You said a mouthful there. Where's JC."

"She told me *you've* been lecturing *her* on what *we* should do with *our* cows."

"It gets boring out here sometimes, you smoke a little pot, your mind can get a little weird. Anyways, they aint *your* cows."

"So whose cows are they? Oh, yeah, right. God's. Well, we claim the right of ownership on this patch of earth and so *we* get to decide what happens to the cows."

Johnny Faye hooked his fingers in his mouth and let out a piercing whistle. "Where is that damn dog. I caint leave him here."

"Look, it's not like I was chasing after her. Dr. Chatterjee, I mean. It's just—I don't know. I mean, I'm not sleeping very well, and I spend all my time thinking—"

"—about her?"

About you came to Flavian's lips.

"Close your mouth," Johnny Faye said, "the flies will get in."

JC came dripping out of the creek. He planted himself near Flavian and shook, spraying him with water.

Flavian wrinkled his nose. *"Pee-you!* That dog has tangled with a skunk."

Johnny Faye sniffed. "I don't smell anything. You smell skunk?"

"You can't smell that?"

"I swear you could smell a gnat fart." Johnny Faye put his nose to JC's fur. "Yeah, you're right but he aint tangled with one, maybe just got in the neighborhood." He pulled the remaining tools together and heaved his knapsack to his shoulder.

"But you haven't even written a single letter."

"That damn dog. Now he's gone and run away again. It's like he can read my mind. When I want to stay he's forever in my way and then I want to go and he disappears."

The cornstalks had leafed out, creating a dappled canopy through which Flavian could just discern the bushy plants. "Well, your plants are looking good, anyway." He regretted the "anyway" before it was out of his mouth but he was compelled to say it by some demon born of impatience and frustration and some other powerful force that gave voice to itself even as he would not give it a name.

"Anyways my ass. You aint seen a better grower than me and you won't, neither. Plants know when they're being taken care of by somebody who knows what he's doing."

"Right, absolutely. I'm impressed. I couldn't raise a weed."

Johnny Faye whistled again for JC. Flavian climbed down from the fork of the tree and listened to the silence grow. Minutes passed and the sun was sinking.

"If we're going to make the lake we'd better go. I have to get back for Benediction."

"I know when you have to get back."

More silence. Flavian dusted off the rear of his jeans. "Well, I'll be seeing you."

Flavian climbed the bank and crossed the small bottom and forced his way through the wall of cedars, now dense and unyielding. He walked back to the monastery, the sun hot on his shoulders. He resisted an impulse to turn back but his every cell strained to hear the sound of 'Sweet's hooves on the gravel. He heard only the stillness of the summer afternoon, broken by the high drone of a small plane somewhere overhead and then by the bells, a half an hour until Benediction. He would be early today and smelling of sweat instead of lake water and the plane's droning overhead was a wound to the heart. Maybe Doctor Chatterjee would be at Benediction. Probably Doctor Chatterjee would be at Benediction, but though he tried to dwell in anticipation instead he drifted back to memory—on this hot afternoon he wanted so many things, none of which had come to pass: He wanted Johnny Faye to show some small evidence of learning to write. He wanted their swim in the lake. He wanted . . . the only thing he knew for certain was his wanting, he was a convergence of desires and what was he to do with that?

Chapter 22

Harry Vetch arrived as the second hand crossed the hour of their date. He drove up in the dark blue Mustang and leapt out—concealed behind a curtain, Meena was watching. He wore jeans and sneakers and an open-collared polo shirt. For the occasion she had purchased a beige pantsuit with a long-sleeved white blouse.

"Hey, who knew such a lovely lady was concealed beneath that lab coat." He held the door for her as they left her office but then stood looking at the building, his features curiously twisted. "You've made improvements."

"I am not certain what—oh, the air conditioner! I returned one evening to find it installed in my absence. Do, please, convey my appreciation to your donors!"

"I suggest pinning a note on the air conditioner." He slammed her door shut.

He had decided they would go to the caves. He popped a beer and tucked it into an insulated cup holder. A half-hour down the road and she was relieved to see his good spirits restored. He held forth on the power of capitalism, the brilliance of the unseen hand that guided the marketplace, how nature's laws of supply and demand produce the best of worlds if only we will let them act. "The way to best serve the common good is for each of us to pursue our individual well-being. Like the great Darwin said, 'survival of the fittest.'"

"Indeed Darwin was a great man. But those are not his words."

"Excuse me?"

"Forgive me but I am a fan of Mr. Darwin. *Survival of the fittest.* Those words are commonly attributed to him but they were spoken by Herbert Spencer to justify the rule of the rich over the poor and the English over the dark-skinned world. Others took up the phrase but—"

"Ah, the inscrutable Orient." Vetch gave her arm a playful punch. "I love it when you talk like that."

She gave him her most dazzling smile. "Such a vast subject demands a long conversation."

"I like the sound of that," he said, raising his beer in a toast.

They drove through scrappy little towns, the road lined with small brick houses and an occasional farmhouse with its wraparound veranda, a relic of a time before air conditioning. *Veranda*— the word owed itself to Meena's liquid mother tongue. They passed churches of steepled brick featuring stained glass rose windows and bell towers topped with crosses. Then a billboard *Last Chance / Last Liquors / Beer / Whiskey,* and they stopped at the drive-up window, where Vetch bought sodas and a pint of bourbon, which he stored in a backseat cooler. They crossed a small river. Through cables and girders she caught a glimpse of a boy standing on a rock above the water, alabaster against jade, his wet white underwear showing forth his vitals, the heads of the other boys bobbing on the rippling stream. She heard their shrill cries *Jump! Jump!* and at that moment the boy leapt, but then they were across the river and driving past small white clapboard churches with windows of frosted glass, each skirted with a close-cropped lawn flecked with gravestones upright and toppled. They traveled through dusty green hills under a cloudless blue sky—the white hot midday glare bleached the landscape of color. "So many churches!"

He patted her knee. "Welcome to the South."

They stopped at a small store with gas pumps in front of a

decaying assemblage of cement tepees *BBQ / Burgoo Home Stile*. The air was redolent with tomatoes and onions and cooking meat. A small boy wandered into the store and stood in the doorway staring at Meena. She looked away, then looked back. He was still staring, transfixed. She closed her eyes. A paper bag was placed in her hand—she opened her eyes and peeked—Vetch had ordered bologna and cheese. The boy was gone.

Back on the road now, a bubble of cool moving through the glare, the pavement an unspooling shimmering black ribbon saying *strangers, more, better, somewhere else*, the asphalt littered with corpses of small animals, each attended by a cortege of vultures with shining black feathers and red raw meat heads. The heat stunned driver and passenger to silence.

Then they were driving past the sideshow, the 100 Life-sized Dinosaurs and JR's Redneck Miniature Golf, the haunted house and the fossil shops. The road wound up a hill to the caves. There were two cars—theirs and the guide's. A tour required five visitors. "Somehow I thought it would be more, I don't know. Professional," Vetch said. "Let me take you someplace else."

"No, no," she said. "Others will arrive. I have never been in a cave. A great adventure."

Not far from the cave entrance a massive tree shaded a picnic table. Meena brushed away leaves and spread a sheet of newspaper on the tabletop. While Vetch opened their drinks she took a plastic cup from his cooler and filled it with water and plucked daisies to make a bouquet for the table. She used a towel as a spread and arranged their sandwiches atop paper napkins.

Vetch poured half of the contents of his can out, then refilled it from the pint of whiskey. "Baptist highball," he said, raising the can in a toast. "A doctor *and* a homemaker. May she find herself a home."

"Indeed two can accomplish together more than each can accomplish alone. But I fear I have been given the path of the solitary wanderer."

"You and me both. But that's nothing that can't be addressed with a little help." He grinned. "In my vision there are kids playing in the yard. I'll need some help with that." He made a show of looking over his shoulder, then dropped his voice. "Can you keep a secret? Sure you can, you're a doctor. Just between you and me—I'm going to switch parties and run against the judge. Not a word to anybody, now. Timing is everything—that's another lesson I learned in law school. But anybody with a licked finger can see where this country's wind is blowing. And I like the direction. It's *my* direction."

"My vision—my *objective* is to obtain my green card and establish a private practice."

"That's a completely different question. That's a career."

"Of course. As you were saying."

"I was not saying. Or maybe you misunderstood."

"Or perhaps you misspoke," she said, smiling.

He did not return her smile. "I'm trained in the art of making myself clear. That's my job. I don't misspeak. I make others misspeak."

"But from time to time we all—"

"Take you, for example. You're an illustration of Darwin. Survival of the fittest. That's a compliment. You bailed from a bad deal. You took charge of your destiny."

"I would be arrogant to consider myself in charge of my destiny."

"So now you're calling me arrogant."

She turned to him, astonished. "No, indeed, and I beg your pardon if—"

"You said the word. Each of us is in charge of our destinies. If not us, then who? Does that make us arrogant? I'd say it makes us American."

"But I am not American."

Vetch pointed at the ground. "You're here. Time to get with the program. Maybe I can help. I'd like that."

The guide appeared in the doorway of the gift shop. "We got three more victims. Let's head down to where we're all going to end up anyway, like it or not." Vetch drained his soda and dropped the can in the garbage.

Their guide was a thin young man with black hair and a mouth that pulled into a rosebud when he was given to thought but widened to a toothy grin at his own jokes. An older couple and a young woman joined them. The guide led the group down a set of metal stairs into the cool damp until they were standing in a glittering room walled with folded, dripping stone drapery. The guide spoke of stalactites and stalagmites and pointed to a standing mass of stone. "We call this a column," he said. "We'd call it a pillar but in these parts a pillar is where you lay your head when you go to sleep."

He asked the tourists what they did in the upper world. The older couple (government bureaucrat, school teacher) had retired. Their granddaughter was studying to be a veterinarian. "You work with people?" the guide asked. "I mean, as part of your training—you cut up dead people? Because people are just animals if it comes to that."

The girl shook her head. "I wouldn't want to work with people. They'd give me back talk and then they'd sue."

"Not if they're dead, they wouldn't."

"You might show some respect," Vetch said. "We have a physician present. My companion. My date." He pointed to Meena. "And I'm an attorney."

The guide turned the flashlight on Meena, then turned to the girl. "Watch out now, when we're down there in the dark she'll steal your spleen. Doctors are like that."

He led them down more stairs and turned on a second set of lights. He pointed out formations in the glistening rocks—an eagle with a hooked beak, a dragon breathing fire, the world's largest nostril. "You all feel dripping on your backs? That might be something other than water."

The young woman giggled. "What did I do to deserve this?" Vetch muttered.

They followed a passageway, twisting and turning, the meanders of an ancient river frozen in stone, its walls cemented with small creatures' bones and shells. A touch of a finger could stop time—the smallest smear of oil from human flesh and this rock, thousands of years in its growing, would die. Meena allowed her hand to brush against a damp stalactite. She quickened her steps to catch the others.

"This was where the guy who discovered the cave found the skeletons," the guide was saying. "The Indians used it as a burial ground, then outlaws hung out here and then rebels during the Civil War and some say *they* left bones, maybe a Yankee lawyer or two they shot because they were parasites on the people. Now I'll turn off the lights so you can see what real dark looks like."

"You don't need to do that," Vetch said, but then the cave went black. Meena waited for her eyes to adjust to the dark until she realized that her eyes would never adjust to *this* dark. Before this moment she had not realized how the universe was filled with light, even its farthest darkest reaches were illuminated by the light of the stars. Few places were truly dark and they were standing in one of them—at the bottom of a cave.

She closed, opened, closed her eyes—no difference. The blind knew more light than this. She feared that Vetch would take her hand and found herself grateful that he could in no manner find it or distinguish between it and the hand of any other person. The thought came unbidden and unwanted: She did not want to be here with Harry Vetch. She did not want to be here with anyone. She wanted to be here alone, in this sunless sightless place. If she could not be alone, if she *must* have company, then let it be—Johnny Faye, the outlaw, the character, the *force of nature*. A revelation. A shock.

"If you stayed in this room for six months you'd go blind," their guide was saying. "A white film would form over your eyes and you wouldn't be able to see a thing. After a while you'd think that dripping was the voices of children, calling your name. You'd hear the cave breathing—yep, the earth breathes, in and out, every morning and around sunset, you don't believe me you come back at suppertime—you'd hear that breathing and you'd think it was the voices of all the dead the Indians buried here. You'd feel the dripping on your skin and you'd think it was the hands of the dead—"

"Stop it." Vetch's reedy voice out of the black. "Stop this nonsense and turn on the lights or I'll see to it that you and the owner of this place regret it."

"Well, sure, sir, gee." The lights came on. Now she was blind again, in a different way. "It was just a joke, all right?"

"Some joke. Get us out of here."

Up the stairs they climbed through folded, dripping crystal drapes, the cave's breath soft and cool on her skin, until they were back above in the bright steamy summer heat and Vetch was buying soft drinks from a machine. He put hers on the table, then poured half of his on the ground, his hand trembling. "Geez. You won't catch me down there again. And that clown of a guide. He wanted a tip, did you see that? He was hanging around with his hand practically held out. Fat chance." He tipped the pint into his can, then sat.

A bird's flutter drew her attention to the tree, with its large leaves and dangling clusters of green nuts. "Look, a pawlonia!" Meena exclaimed. "It grows in Bengal. How strange to see it here—like encountering an old friend halfway around the world."

"I don't see what's so strange about that. We live in a marketplace economy. I'll bet half of what you see came from someplace else."

"All the same. They are so beautiful when they bloom. So tropical, really."

"Hey, at first you said you couldn't wait to get out of your country, now you're talking about it like it was paradise."

She studied a file of ants, drawn by the soft drink's sugared spill. "I don't recall saying I could not wait to get out of my country but—"

"Didn't you say that you had never known anything but war and violence?"

"That's not precisely—"

"Yes or no, did you say that or not? Were you thrilled to leave there or not?"

"I felt so many emotions, Harry, I am scarcely able to name one apart from another. Coming to America—my first trip abroad and I was committing myself to living in another country. I could not possibly have understood what that meant."

Vetch groaned. "I ask a yes or no question and I get a lecture on human psychology. In the courtroom there's a winner and a loser, a right and a wrong, a conviction or an acquittal. That's the way the law works. And I know which side I aim to be on."

He stood and went to the car. He pulled a map from the back seat, spreading it on the car's roof. She sipped from a soda and a fiery sweetness filled her mouth—she had taken up his can, spiked with whiskey he'd bought at the *Last Chance.*

She followed him to the car, where she faced him head on. "Harry, you are speaking with the voice of the alcohol. The voice of your drinking."

His mouth made a small "o," then his face crumpled. On his face she saw warring impulses—to strike? Or to weep? She turned away.

A flock of birds rose from a nearby field. She watched as they flew, guided by an invisible, inaudible signal, turning and diving as one. "Swallows." She pointed. "No, starlings."

"My, aren't you the birdwatcher."

"I have had a teacher." A demon had got hold of her tongue. "A farmer named Johnny Faye."

"*Johnny Faye?* Where in the—how have you come to know Johnny Faye?"

A little spark of triumph in her heart, overwhelmed in an

instant by a wave of remorse—surely one did not speak this way on a *date*. "He came to me as a patient, but he has shared a bit of his knowledge of birds."

Vetch refolded the map and sat on the bench. "Look, I know you have less choice than I do about who walks through your door, but steer clear of that guy. He's a criminal." He narrowed his eyes into an uncomfortably direct stare. "Not the best acquaintance for someone whose future depends on the good will of the law."

"Harry, you are a very good attorney."

"Uh, Meena." Vetch took up his drink and rolled it between his palms. "I know I sometimes say things—well, I have a few drinks and then I speak the truth, *in vino veritas*, you know, but I can sometimes be a little blunt, maybe a little too direct."

"I have no difficulty with directness."

He leaned across the picnic table and pecked her cheek. "But if I may offer you some counsel, as we say in my trade. For your well-being. For the sake of the dreams you must carry, yes? You are an immigrant. In the part of the world where you come from people just live in history. It sweeps them along one way, then another. In this country you can seize history and make it your own. Immigration was only the first step. Listen to yourself sometime, telling those old stories—what it was like back there. Why are you fixated on that place? What did it offer you? You're here now. Let it go."

"Home is the well of suffering and of love." She had not known she possessed such words. She closed her eyes and turned away.

Vetch reached across the table and laid his hand over hers. "Meena, those aren't necessarily connected."

She withdrew her hand. "Now I know I am in America."

A shadow crossed Vetch's countenance. "Nobody here cares about your past. You're free from all that—that's what freedom means, don't you see?" His hands grew animated, beseeching. "Of course you can't see, you've never known it. America is the empire, we're where the power is, we want to hear about action. We want to know what you're doing *now*, not what trees you lived under twenty years ago. Isn't that why you came here?"

The starlings rose again as a mass. A hawk swooped and circled at the edges of the great fluid fluttering flock—whenever it tried to attack, the birds closed ranks. Finally it flew away. "The strong protecting the weak," Meena said.

"What's that?"

She pointed at the birds settling to earth. "A challenge to *survival of the fittest*. The flock flew as a group so as to protect themselves against their attacker. They concerned themselves not with any particular individual but with the whole. They prosper through cooperation, not competition." She turned to him again. "Let me tell you a shocking thing. Perhaps the most shocking thing an American attorney can hear? I am not legally alive. I have no birth certificate. When I went to obtain a passport I was told I needed sworn statements from witnesses to prove the time and place of my birth. But any witnesses there might have been were dead. They had been bombed by planes or shot with guns bought with American money. Or they were Muslims killed by Muslims. Or they were Hindus killed by Muslims. What difference did it make? After the hearing I sold the first of the rubies my mother had sewn into the hem of my school uniform when she sent me away from the war. Within the month I had my passport. But let us for the moment imagine my fate without those rubies." She took his hand and pinched it.

"*Ow!*"

"How remarkable! You feel my pinch, when according to the law I do not exist. Must you have a piece of paper to tell you who I am? Must I have a piece of paper to know?" She dropped his hand.

Vetch picked up a rock and tossed it into the midst of the flock. The birds rose as one, then moments later resettled to earth.

Then they were back on the road. The landscape grew wilder and more rugged, the houses more widely spaced. For an hour and more they rode in silence until the traffic thinned and the roads narrowed and they were almost back where they came from.

Vetch pulled to the side of the road and turned off the car. "Meena. May I take your hand? Please, I won't bite and I promise to give it back." He took her hand. "I feel like we've gotten off to a rocky start, which is too bad because I think we really like each other. When you came into the room on the day of that screwed-up slide show—the one good thing that came out of that, shall we say, disappointing evening is that you walked into the room and it was like I heard a voice in my head that said: This is it. There she is. Maybe I'm old enough, finally, to understand the difference between what I want and what I need. I just wanted you to know that from the first time I saw you I thought: This lady is special. This beautiful woman is worthy of my love. Tell me at least that you'll think over another date. What harm is there in a date? Think of your future in this community. Your future in this country. This is not a place that takes kindly to the presence of single women."

She took back her hand and folded her arms and looked out the window. "If there is a place in the world that takes kindly to the presence of single women, I have yet to encounter it."

He started the car and turned down a gravel road. "I want to show you something. The highlight of the day." They came to a stop in a rolling green field sliced open by a dusty red gash. "This is it," he said, waving his hand in a wide sweep. "Welcome to Ridgeview Pointe. Oh, I know it's not much to look at right now. But you have to see it like I see it. Standing here we're looking down the dogleg of the ninth hole fairway. My house"—he pointed at a hole carved into the woods—"will sit right there."

"How lovely."

He turned to her then and took her hand. "What's good for me or for you is or can be good for everybody, that's what you've got to get your head around. That's the American way." After a moment he put the car in gear and drove forward, bouncing across the rutted dirt.

They reached the site of his dream house and stepped from the car. He showed her where the great room would rise to its beam and where the windows would look out onto the fairway.

Meena murmured appreciative noises before turning back to the car, but before she could reach it the skies opened up—a brief, dense shower that came without warning, the kind of rain that precipitates itself after too many rainless humid days.

They jumped in the car and Vetch threw it into reverse, to hit a patch of mud—the summer's drought had crumbled the bulldozed earth to the finest dust and the briefest wetting turned it slick. The wheels spun. He shifted again. The wheels dug deeper. He shifted to reverse and gunned the accelerator. A blue cloud enveloped them and rose to tangle itself in the limbs of nearby trees. Vetch muttered to himself, then sat back. "Well. I'm going to have to find a rock or a limb and wedge it under the rear wheel."

He stepped from the car and into the nearby forest. The setting sun emerged from the clouds and the car grew warm. Meena climbed out and stepped through the mud to the rear of the car.

At her feet, a small orange flag, dug up by the spinning wheels—a pennant.

RID   VIEW PO T

She bent to pick it up but could not pull it free—it was attached to a thin white pole that led to something deeper.

Vetch returned carrying rocks. She drew his attention to the dirtied pennant. He crouched to look at it more closely. "What the heck—"

"I should say it looks like a pennant," she said. "Of the sort one sees on golf carts."

He wrapped his hand around it and pulled but it did not give. "Um, would you excuse me?" He walked to the rear of the car, turned his back to her and raised his hands. A cry of anger and frustration. Meena stifled a smile.

Vetch climbed in the car and gunned the accelerator—forward, then back. She was surrounded by blue smoke, so much that she took off her shoes and walked farther into the open muddy field . . . and then it began to rain again, another shower, a warm tropical rain, brief and intense, the monsoon rain of her childhood.

She threw her pumps to the sky and ran through the rain until she was far from the car's exhaust and there she stopped and stood with her head tilted back and the warm rain falling in her eyes and ears and open mouth.

Across the ruddy field the Mustang bucked and smoked and lurched from its ruts. It moved slowly across the horizon against the backdrop of the forest, dark with evening shadow. She gathered her shoes and plodded across the mud.

Vetch was leaning against the car, arms folded. "What was that about?"

"Only a moment of pleasure at the feel of rain in this dry summer," she said. "Mr.—Harry. In this country where I am in charge of my destiny I will ask for your help. As the physician responsible for Matthew Mark Smith, I am asking you to intervene to protect him and his mother from violence at the hands of Mr. Smith. Officer Smith."

A pained silence, then Vetch moved from his car and stood before her. "Look, Meena. Please don't misunderstand me. I'm thrilled to have a doctor in this county—I'm significantly responsible for your coming here, you know that, yes? But no good deed goes unpunished. Plenty of people are already saying, 'We got along fine without a doctor.' Some of them object to a—*foreigner* in our midst, a doctor who is first, a woman, and second—well, not like them. If you prove to be—*difficult,* you-know-who will get the blame. I have a vision for this place. I don't want to see it derailed by finger-pointing and gossip. I'm assuming I don't need to finish out that line of thinking."

"You do not need to finish out that line of thinking."

"Now. You understand that I'm not the bad news, I'm just the messenger, I'm describing things as they are, not as I might want them to be. You are the boy's physician, you can push me to take action against Officer Smith and I'll oblige. But consider what might come to pass. The boy gets placed in a foster home and that's no guarantee that his situation will improve, not in my experience. Or he doesn't get put in a foster home and you've waved a red flag in front of the bull. And *you* don't have to live with the bull. It's his wife and the boy who are living with the bull."

Meena turned away. "I understand what you are saying."

"On top of which Smith comes from a big family in a small county and they vote for their friends. Watch your tongue—for the sake of the Smith child but first and foremost for your own sake. So long as you are not a citizen or at least resident alien you are very vulnerable. You understand this, yes? Forget about protecting *him*. Think about protecting yourself. I will help in every way I can but I need your assistance." He met her eyes. "Or at least cooperation. Yes? Can I count at least on that?"

Then they were driving back to the town, around the central square with its symmetrical courthouse, past a large church with white pillars and a silver steeple. He stopped in front of her office. She opened the car door.

"Meena. Think about what I said."

"On that front you need not concern yourself. I think of little else." A gesture was wanted. She held out her hand. "Thank you for your concern."

Inside her office, alone with her thoughts. The air was a hot wet clutching hand—it might have been the last of the nights before the monsoon except that there would be no monsoon, only more drought. No man in her life had ever worked to earn her favors. Her father's voice in her head. *A hundred ways to do something and our Meena will choose the hardest.* Many years since she had laid eyes on her father and she would rephrase his observation: *A hundred ways to do something and the hardest will choose our Meena.* The room was a cinderblock oven.

She had not gone on this date for the sake of Matthew Mark. She had not gone even in hopes of marriage. She had gone in hopes of being saved from herself. Saved from her responsibilities to Matthew Mark. Saved from Johnny Faye. And Harry Vetch would be happy to save her. All that was required was submission—no. All that was required was the *appearance* of submission. And she was a Bengali woman, well-schooled in the art of the appearance of submission.

She knelt and turned on the air conditioner and basked in its stream of cool air.

For the past year Harry Vetch had found himself conscious of his hands. He had always admired them—small and fine-boned. As he aged their veins had grown more prominent in a way that gave them character. Lately he had taken to displaying them to his clients—splayed against the polished wood of his desk they conveyed authority.

Driving home from his date with Meena he felt them acutely—he waved his right hand in the space above the passenger seat where a few minutes before Meena had been sitting. He removed first the left, then the right from the steering wheel and flexed each open, then shut. His fist was not as compact as it had once been—swelling in the joints. In the gesture he understood his growing consciousness of his hands' breadth and length and bones, the tightness in their muscles and sinews, the prominence of their veins: Evidence, *prima facie*, inarguable, of his growing old—of his mortality.

The next day he sent her flowers.

Chapter 23

"Listen."

Meena tilted her head. A sweet bobbling, pure and cool—spring water.

"Carolina wren."

"When are you going to tell how the birds got their names?"

"Are you asking?"

"Yes, I am asking. Please."

"Well. Since you say please. Not long after settlers arrived in these parts the birds pretty much disappeared. I know all this because of a accident of the blood. My mamma is the youngest child of the oldest child of the youngest child in her particular family. And that meant that when she grew up the stories she heard every day were stories from way back because of the way remembering works. You see what I mean? Since her mamma was the oldest child she heard the stories of the oldest people alive and so her stories went way back. But since *her* mamma—my mamma's mamma, my grandmamma—was the youngest child, she lived a long time into my mamma's remembering and so my mamma heard all her stories over and over and she had plenty of chances to remember them.

"And she's the one that told me about the years when there weren't no birds. The birds was mad at white people for our guns and our selfish and thieving ways and they turned up their bills and went away, stayed north or south depending on their natures, and if they had to fly from one place to the other they did it at night so we couldn't have the pleasure of seeing them and they flew quiet so we wouldn't have their music in our ears.

"But then one day a little bird with a big voice found its way into a patch of woods in these parts and got lost. It was one scared little bird too, because it had heard all about how mean white people was. And so the little bird was lying in a dust hole hoping not to be seen and wondering what to do when a little girl comes along. A little girl who has come from a far and foreign land that feels lost and alone in this strange new country."

"That would be me."

"Like you say. And the girl takes up the little bird and at first the little bird is wondering if he has saved up enough money for a wooden coffin but after a while he relaxes and lets her make a fuss over him and shares her bread and cookies, and before long they are best friends.

"But the little bird notices one day that the little girl is sad and he says, 'Little girl, why are you so sad?' And she says, 'I am sad because where I came from there was lots of birds and my heart lifted when I looked up at them but there aint no birds here except for you and I know that you'll get lonely and that someday I'll come looking for you and you'll be gone back to the place where you're not the only bird.' And the little bird says, 'Don't cry, little girl, I can tell you how to bring back the birds.' And at first she don't believe him but then she figures what has she got to lose and so she says, 'You're on, little bird.' And the little bird says, 'Now just imagine you went to a party where nobody had a name. How could you talk to those people? The people that came before had names for all the birds. But then white people came and they was too busy making money to pay attention and give us names. But if you want the birds to come back all you got to do is give them names and call them out. They will come back if you just invite them back.'

"And the little girl said, 'Aw, stop pulling my leg,' and wouldn't believe him until finally he stomped his claw and said, 'OK, you call out a name for a bird and if that bird don't come back you can bake me in a pie and serve me to a king.' So she says, 'OK, all right, whatever. Sparrow,' and pretty soon there comes a great flapping and flittering and chirping and sure enough a flock of sparrows has taken up roost in the woods. And the little girl sets about right away calling out name after name and more and more birds come until the trees are filled with that particular chattery noise they make around sunset.

"And finally all the birds have come back, the old crow and the slate junco and all the ducks, horned larks and meadowlarks, the whippoorwill that you never see and the starling that you see too much, grackles and shrikes and chickadees, vireos and robins and thrushes and kites, orioles and herons and egrets and the warblers and the peewee so happy to be back that all it can say over and over is its name, *pee-wee!* And all the others, too many to name, and the little girl says, 'Have I forgotten any?' and the little bird bows its head and she takes it up tender in her hand and she says, 'and you I will call my friend.' And the little bird says, 'Beg pardon?' And the little girl says, 'My friend, my friend!' And the little bird rises into the sky, singing, 'My wren, my wren!'"

Meena turned to walk down the path.

"Where are you off to?"

"You have told me not merely to see but to *look*. I am going to *look*. There is always something to look for."

"Well, yes and no. You been lucky."

"In America people make their own luck. Or so I have been told. So *hush up* and walk behind and allow me to make my own luck."

They walked into the deepening green. She had exchanged her pumps for a pair of Keds and each step was a creation of silence. The path twisted and turned of its own accord until she had no faith that she could find her way back and still she pushed on. When she could no longer see the lines in the hand held in front of her face she turned to him. "On this particular evening luck seems to be elusive."

"For you, maybe. I feel lucky just being here."

"Then you may use your luck to lead us back."

He laughed, a little explosion of air. "It don't work that way. You been leading the way, I took a little vacation from paying attention. I aint never walked in this stretch of woods long enough to be walking 'em at night."

"You're not serious."

"'Fraid so. I'm serious but I aint terrified. It's warm, we aint going to freeze to death. Once the sun comes up we'll be fine, no problem."

"But I have to get back. We have to get back. I have paperwork, I have early appointments."

She heard his grin in his voice. "Welcome to the woods. They got a mind of their own. There's no moon, neither."

"You do know the way back. You are trying to make a point. You have made it."

He sighed deeply. "No, ma'am, I aint got a clue as to where we are but there's not much to trouble us except poison ivy and the foxholes that grab your ankle and give it a good twist. If you watch your step I'll see what I can do. Follow me. Close, now."

He set out in the opposite direction from that she would have chosen. Earlier that evening a breeze had stirred the leaves but with the approaching dark the forest fell still and closed around them.

"Your turn to tell a story," he said as they walked. "The price of the ticket of getting us found, though I kind of prefer lost. Any kind of story. A story from when you was a kid. Talk the way you talked when you was a kid—I just want to hear how you talked. Not in English, in your own language. I don't need to know what it means. I just want to hear what you heard in your head when you were young, the way your people talked. The way you talked."

"What kind of story do you want to hear?"

"Makes no difference. Whatever you want to tell. Maybe something about the first time you thought about coming to America."

Meena considered this a moment, then spoke.

আমি বড় হইসি আমগো দ্যাশের একখান ছোড গ্রামে, কিন্তু এক বছর আইলো যখন আমার বাবা ঠিক করলো যে আমারে চোখের ডাক্তার দ্যাখান লাগবো। বাবায় কইলো যে কলকাতায় ডাক্তার এর কাছে লইয়া যাইবো। আমি পুরা একখান সপ্তা ঘুমাইতে পারি নাই। কলকাতা! বাবা যেন আমারে চান্দের দ্যাশে লইয়া যাইতেসে।

আমরা ট্রেনে কইর‍্যা শিয়ালদহ ইস্টিশনে আইলাম আর ঐহানে এতো এতো মানুষ আছিলো যে আমি কখনো চিন্তায় করি নাই। দুনিয়াতে এতো মানুষ আছে! আর তারা কেউ আমার নামডাও জানতো না! আমরা চোখের ডাক্তারের কাছে গেলাম—অহনো চোখের সামনে ভাসে, ছোড্ড ছোড্ড বর্ণ লেখা আছিল আর যারা পড়তে জানে না তাগো লাইগ্যা আছিল ছবি।

His white singlet a beacon in the dusk. "I must be boring you. I have heard that Americans do not like to listen to tales from the past."

"Naw, I like hearing it, the way it runs up and down. Kind of like a river over a riffle."

ডাক্তারখানা খেইক্যা বাইর হইয়া বাবায় আমারে cinema hall–এ লইয়া গেসিল। বাবা আমারে ভিতরে লইয়া একখান বেঞ্চিতে বসাইলো আর আমার হাত ধইর‍্যা কইলো, "মাগো, আমার একখান জরুরি কামের কথা মনে পড়সে, একদম ভুইল্যা গেসিলাম। তুইও আমার লগে আইতে পারতি

কিন্তু তরে বৈঠকখানায় একলা থুইয়্যা রাখতে আমার মনে সায় দিতেসে না, তরও একলা ঐহানে ভালা লাগবো না। তুই তো জানস যে তর মায়ে যদি শুনে যে আমি তরে একলা cinema hall—এ রাইখা গেসি তাইলে খুব রাগ করবো! কিন্তু অহন তো তুই বড় হইছস, আমি জানি যে তুই সামলাইতে পারবি। আর cinema শ্যাস হউনের আগেই আমি তর কাছে আইয়্যা পরমু। কিন্তু তর যদি ডর লাগে তো আমারে ক, আমি তরে লগে লইয়্যা যামু।"

আর আমি cinema দ্যাখনের লাইগ্যা থাইক্যা গেলাম, আর বাবারে কথা দিলাম যে আমি মারে একটা বর্ণও কমু না। কারণ আমি জানতাম মারে কিছু কইলে মা আমারে আর কহনোই বাবার লগে কলকাতা আইতে দিব না। আমি এই কথা গোপন রাখনের কথা দিলাম, এমনকি ভগবান চাইলেও আমার পেট থেইক্যা কোন কথা বাইর করবার পারবো না।

"I got a little of that. I heard you say 'cinema'—you're talking about going to the movies. I wouldn't have thought you had movies but that goes to show how dumb I am. They had 'em in Nam, why not India? What kind of movies did you see?"

"Every few months my father took me to Calcutta for an eye examination. He left me alone at the movies while he took care of his business. Sometimes I saw Indian cinema but mostly I saw American movies—not at all like Indian movies. American movies make sense. Sometimes I think that is what made me want to come to America— I wanted to come to a place where the movies make sense."

আর ঐ cinema hall—এ একলা একলা বইয়্যা থাকতে থাকতে আমি বুঝলাম যে আমার কপালে বিশেষ কিছু লেখা আছে, আমি বুঝলাম যে আমি একদিন আমরিকা আমু।

They reached the clearing with the statues. "I fell in love with America at the cinema," she said. "My father left me there when he ran his errands in Calcutta. But one day he was late—the cinema hall had emptied and the usher told me I had to leave. And I went out into the street and I was alone.

"The theater was near a monastery where foreign guests stayed. That afternoon I saw my first American—I knew this man was an American because I had seen men like him in the cinema and because he was tall and white and walked like an American. He took space for granted. And he was wearing Levi's, like the cowboys in the movies.

"A little boy—I had seen him at other times when I came to the cinema, a street urchin, really, raised to beg, with his territory guaranteed by a protector who would beat him if he did not pay— this little boy was begging the American for money and the American walked on, until finally the little boy seized the American's hand and even so the American kept walking. The little boy followed him into the street—he ran in front of him and tried to block his way. A lorry was bearing down on them, and the man, who was walking forward, saw it first. The boy didn't see it because he was small and had his back turned and he was hungry—what was life to him? The American saw the lorry and stepped in front of it— he was protecting the boy with his body. All this happened so fast that the American and the boy were acting from who they were, from instinct—they had no time to think. The American seized the boy by his arm and dragged him out of the lorry's path. And then he stuck his hands in his pockets and kept walking.

"So this American who would not dig in his pocket for a rupee was willing to give his life to save the child." Meena turned to Johnny Faye. Her expression drew inward. "We are so many and yet I know you never give us a thought because you have no reason to think of us. You were the powerful, we were the weak. But we thought of you all the time because you were in our minds, you were in our cinema halls. You never imagined me but every day of my childhood I imagined someone—an American man whose broad shoulders carry no weight of history—someone like you." She placed her finger in the center of his breastbone. "As God is my witness, I'll never go hungry again." A small grimace. "I have always wanted something different, larger, greater, more. Like your Scarlett. That is what brought me to this country. But the gurus speak of a state—a way of being in the world they call *rasavadhana*, a place outside of desire, of pure consciousness and joy. When we saw the—what did you call it? The bird of the forest."

"Whippoorwill."

"That was for me an experience of *rasavadhana*. That is what I was looking for tonight—that is what I set out to *see*."

"Is that a fact. That's the kind of thing that you caint *set out* to see. That's the kind of thing that happens when you made yourself ready but you aint looking." He took her hand. She felt again that surge of electricity, of power, of desire. Life—she fought back as a swimmer fights the flood—she had never been so alive. She left her hand in his. She *the doctor of the flesh, not the spirit* had never known desire, she had never before been seized in its fist and dragged in its wake, never before this here and now.

And then she recognized their surroundings—they were back at the clearing. He led her past the statues and up the hill to the blind. JC trailed behind.

At the blind he pulled aside the hanging vines that formed the door and led her through. JC laid down outside with a heave and sigh.

Inside he fumbled in his pockets—the flare of a match, then the flame from the stub of a candle, at first timid, then bold. It was as much light as she could bear. He sat on the clean-swept earth and tugged at her hand. After a moment she sat next to him. Their shadows large and monstrous on the blind walls. He rested his hand atop hers. After a small while she turned hers over and linked their fingers.

He told her his stories then, stories of Vietnam, of desolation and terror and sorrow. She responded in kind—stories of Bengal, of planes flying over her grandparents' home, flying east to bomb her parents' village. While they spoke the insects' infernal buzz grew louder, grind and racket and saw, until as if by some invisible, inaudible signal they stopped. Now there was only the thin lone chirp of a cricket and the pounding of her pulse. The candle guttered. "That is what I know. That is what I remember," she said, but in telling these stories she understood for the first time why her father had taken her as a young country girl to Calcutta, why he took her for eye examinations for her nearly perfect eyes every month for three years, why he left her at the cinema alone—unheard of! a little girl, left alone in the great city—for those long afternoons of American films, why he exacted her promise, eagerly given, never to tell her mother where she had been. Her father, who read only poetry written earlier than Wordsworth—what monthly "business" could he have had in Calcutta? Sitting in the blind with Johnny Faye, she understood that her father had made these journeys because he had taken a lover.

She had never been so revealed, to herself or to another. Desire stripped her naked. She turned to him and pulled him to her and covered his mouth with hers.

After some time he leaned back. "You wait." His voice was thick. "You hold on."

He stood and knelt to his boots, ankle high and caked with dirt, and unlaced them and took them off and stood them one beside another, witnesses. He unzipped his jeans—they dropped to the floor . . . He fought his way out of his t-shirt, then stepped out of his underwear in slow motion, or so it seemed to her, she who wanted him all at once. He was slim-hipped, smooth above, hairy below—a satyr. She was clothed and he was not, and in his nakedness she understood many things—the power of clothes, the yielding of his nakedness, how much he had known and done to understand this.

She stood and seized his hand and held it behind him and

covered his lips with hers and seized him at the root and he raised her skirt with his free hand and worked her until she gave a great shout and he was shouting with her, both of them shouting in tongues.

He sank to the floor amid the littering twigs and leaves, his chest rising and falling. He unzipped and pulled down her skirt—how strange it seemed that she was still clothed. He pulled her down to him and raised himself on one elbow to unbutton her blouse and cup her breast and then she was unclothed in the warm summer night and they kissed, a long, proper embrace.

They lay in silence. He cleared his throat as if to speak and she placed a finger to his lips. Around them the high thin call of the tree frogs, an owl's *hoo-who-hoo-who?*

After some time she rose and took up her clothes. He lay watching until she was dressed—he of the sun-darkened arms and chest and shoulders and legs, a band of white flesh pale as moonlight between his waist and each thigh. For a while they watched each other—she clothed, he naked. Then he shook his head free of some thought from the other world. He pulled on his clothes and followed her outside.

The sky was clear now, the bowl of stars overhead, the white graveled path plain before their feet. In silence they walked to her car. The starlit night became a great mother heart, a silence more profound than any voice.

At the car they kissed—she felt again the clutch of desire from a place deeper than knowledge. Then Johnny Faye disappeared into the night forest.

Chapter 24

An indifferent Monday. What concatenation of chance and choice, destiny and free will, had brought Flavian to this place, where his morning's task was to enter addresses and telephone numbers from cheese and fruitcake orders into the newly acquired computer, pride of Brother Cassian? This was the work of the Lord? Why was he here? Why had he become a monk and, more to the point, why had he stayed?

The abbot entered, all hustle and bustle, a short good morning before he sequestered himself in his office to make calls from his very handsome white oak desk. Several times Flavian stood and walked to the abbot's door, seeking the courage to walk in and say—what? "I've been helping the local renegade grow pot and I'm falling in love with a woman from halfway around the world and I quit."

Abruptly he stood and entered the abbot's office and sat. The abbot looked up from his paperwork. "Flavian. You have lived in community long enough to know that a knock before entering—"

Flavian studied his hands in his lap during this gentle and appropriate reprimand. When the abbot finished he raised his head. "Brendan. Why do the innocent suffer?"

The abbot scrunched his lips and tilted his head sideways and frowned. "Flavian, something's bothering you. Something's been bothering you for a while."

"At any particular time of day a lot of things are bothering me, but what's bothering me right now is why innocent people suffer. You tell me. I want to hear the standard operating procedure argument because when you get right down to it, what is the point of religion if it can't answer that basic question? I mean, we have these smoke-and-bell services that make people feel all holy and good, and then they go back to their desks and sign orders to drop bombs. Or whatever their jobs' version is of dropping bombs. I mean, not everybody drops bombs but if you want to follow the chain of responsibility even we're dropping bombs because we're paying taxes and so we're supporting the guys who are dropping bombs."

"As a matter of fact we don't pay taxes."

"So much the worse then, because what we have here is a deal whereby the guys who *are* dropping the bombs or, in the case I'm thinking of, beating his kid to within an inch of his life, those guys are saying to us, 'OK, here's the deal, you make us feel good about screwing everybody else for our benefit and we'll let you dress up in costumes from the twelfth century and play at medieval theater tax-free.' Why aren't we *doing* something, anything? What is the point of all this navel-gazing?"

The abbot sneaked a glance at the wall clock.

"Brendan, I'm serious."

The abbot sighed. "I know you're serious. But I'm a better administrator than theologian. As you know."

"But you're the abbot."

"Right you are, for better or worse."

"We're practically rolling in dough and here we sit, making and selling cheese and chanting prayers while the world suffers. And—" he indicated the correspondence on the desk "—preparing to ship to the slaughterhouse our last connection to the real, beautiful, created, animal world."

"Better than dropping bombs," the abbot snapped.

A moment of silence in observance of this remarkable departure from equanimity.

The abbot swiveled in his chair to look out the window at the green canopy of the meditation garden's ancient gingko. "Um, look. I have to review last quarter's financials and get them off to the bean crunchers by the end of today. Your question is, I'm sorry to say, not going to go away, whereas if I don't review these financials in time for tomorrow morning's conference call, the community may well be reduced to stealing bread."

"Sure, fine, don't call me, I'll call you."

The abbot swiveled back. "Now, Flavian."

"Brendan. Hear me out, please. I'm not being naive. Seventeen years without red meat and I still dream of a good hamburger and it's not like I don't know where it comes from. I'm not saying we have to keep the herd. I get the picture. But I just don't think we've thought that one through nearly as much as we ought, considering what's at stake. These are creatures of God, after all, who give us so much in return for so little. Maybe that's why I really became a monk—not to dodge the draft but to be a man of faith. If the rains fail and the cows die or my back gives out when I'm unhooking the milking machines, that's a challenge to my faith that I can rise to, or so I hope, with my brothers at my side to lend a hand. But when the milk comes to us in big stainless steel tankers from who knows where I'm not working for God anymore. I've become just like everybody else—I'm a capitalist who's taken his faith away from God and placed it in a corporation shielded by an insurance policy and the government from whatever lives or places or animals it nukes along the way. And we're not everybody else— at least, we're not supposed to be. We're monks. So what do we say when people look to us to be models of faith? How can we ask them to have courage when we're being cowards?"

Here he paused for a silence that grew longer until finally the abbot spoke. "Flavian, I've noticed that you've been—distracted. You've missed offices—a *lot* of offices. You need a break. Go visit the foundations out West. The change of scenery will do you good. By the time you get back we'll have this business with the dairy herd settled."

Usually Flavian found the bells announcing midday service to be an annoyance but today they spared him a response to the abbot's suggestion. He gathered his notebook and pen and tote bag. "I don't want to be a monk," he said. "There. I quit. That's it, pure and simple," and so it seemed, though as he spoke the words he felt something willful in them, something to do with fear and a failure of heart, a loss of faith.

The abbot leaned back and passed his hand over his eyes. "Well within my time here, and not long before yours, we would have conducted this conversation with our hands. Often I think that might have been for the best. Words, so seductive in the mouth and to the ear, have a way of betraying the heart." Here he reached across his desk and touched Flavian's hand, an extraordinary gesture—it was the first time Flavian could recall any physical contact with another brother that was not work-related. "I will offer a few last words, speaking from my place as your abbot: A man who's never had a crisis of faith isn't to be trusted. A monk who's never had a crisis of faith isn't paying attention. You are being taught to pay attention. That's the good news. Now is the time. The way is dark but God has given you hands. Feel your way forward, in faith."

After the midday office, after dinner, after a nap, back in front of his blinking, beeping machine, Flavian groaned aloud. "You could find a moral dilemma in a baked potato," he said and at that moment the computer froze up. He tried all the tricks the salesman had shown him—CONTROL ALT DELETE, plug/unplug—and then threw in a few tricks of his own, including a gentle slap to the side of its vomit-colored casing (*o Queen of Computers, forgive me*). Nothing. Flavian sighed and turned to sorting the day's mail, which included an envelope from the office of the county attorney.

Only a few months before, he'd have opened it and placed the contents in the abbot's in-box. Now he furtively tucked the envelope into his tote bag. He had grown so jaded that his once-bedeviling conscience did not register a peep of protest.

In his indecision and anxiety he forgot about the filched letter until that night, when he was preparing for bed and pawing through his tote bag. He pulled out the envelope and, using his forefinger as a letter opener, ripped back its flap, which rewarded his impatience by slicing his skin, a nice paper cut that sprouted a drop of bright red blood. "Only what I deserve," Flavian said aloud. He sucked on his finger as he read through a press release paper-clipped with Harry Vetch's card *FYI*.

MEDIA RELEASE

FOR IMMEDIATE RELEASE   U.S. Department of Justice
June 16, 1989   For more information:
                                           502-628-7898

The Organized Crime Drug Enforcement Task Force, consisting of representatives from the Drug Enforcement Administration, State Police, Internal Revenue Service, and Federal Bureau of Investigation have entered an investigation of residents growing marijuana outside the state. To date marijuana has been seized from 29 sites, including 25 farms located outside the state. Law enforcement officials have seized a total of 182 tons of marijuana. Sixty-eight persons have faced federal or state charges concerning this marijuana.

Evidence collected by the Task Force has revealed that the marijuana seized was produced by an organized group of residents who pooled money, machinery, knowledge and workers to create the largest domestic marijuana producing organization in the history of the United States. The cooperative frequently obtains leads on farm land that is for sale through real estate firms. In many cases, one cooperative member will travel to a certain geographic area to observe and evaluate farm properties for lease or sale. A second cooperative member then travels to the area and purchases a pre-selected property, with a minimum down payment and a contract for payment of the balance due over a period of years. Deed to the property, therefore, does not transfer to the buyer until payment of the balance. Thus, many of the farms are not seizable under federal forfeiture statutes.

The cooperative generally plants marijuana in corn fields. The corn is planted late, which leads neighbors to believe the planters have little knowledge of farming. However, the later planted corn stays green longer, concealing marijuana for a longer period of time.

Once the marijuana is planted, one or two people move to the farm to monitor the crop. At harvest time, bands of workers, often consisting of the growers' wives and children, travel to the farms to harvest, process, and package the marijuana. Many workers have $300 to $500 on them at the time of their arrest, apparently for getaway money, should law enforcement disrupt their activities. Oddly, this money, as well as money used to make down payments on farms, is usually moldy, dirty, and has an unusual smell.

Flavian read this twice. After the second reading he knelt, lifted his mattress, reached to the far corner and pulled out the manila envelope stuffed with money that Johnny Faye had given him on that night not so long ago—not so very long ago at all. He pulled out some cash, held it to his nose and sniffed. Not that he had given much time over to smelling money but it smelled pretty much like—well, like he expected money to smell, kind of papery and green, though underneath this smell was a scent at the same time completely familiar and *unusual* . . . he put the money down, put his nose to the window screen, took a couple of deep breaths of fresh air, then smelled the money again—yes, there was that smell . . . he looked around his cluttered cell, at the basket he kept in the corner for his dirty underwear and—socks, yes. What he was smelling was the warm, human scent of his feet, parked every night near the envelope of money.

The summer nights were still short but at this latitude, even at their shortest, they were long enough for a body to seek out the bottom of the pit of despair and for the second time that strange summer Flavian felt himself falling. The mattress on his narrow bed managed to be at the same time thin and lumpy but before that night at the pool hall and that envelope of greenbacks Flavian had slept like a child, or so it now seemed. He had stored the envelope under the far corner of his bed, there was no logical way he could feel it, and yet he might as well be trying to sleep in a rocky field surrounded by wolves.

And it *was* a boulder-strewn field, the rocky pastures of desire. What, or whom, did he want? "Chosen by God." Why had he taken that left fork, ordered that beer, played those games of pool, the memory of which—the thought of his near victory—even now brought him to bask in the bright sun of vanity? Suppose he could turn the calendar back, erase that night and this stupid envelope and all that had led from it—would he take the right fork and head straight back to the abbey? He knew that he would not change a thing, which only went to prove that he was a common sinner, handmaiden of the devil, who like every son and daughter of Adam and Eve had freely made his choices and chosen sin over virtue. "What is fixed by fate must come to pass," the words from the doctor's story came to mind. Ridiculous. Left to its fate, the field produced only weeds and thistles. Anything more than that required the shaping hands of men and women.

But perhaps thistles were what we were meant to eat. After all, the first person to clear a patch of forest and dig a hole and plant a seed was the first to thumb her or his nose at the Almighty, and the history of the race since then was one long tale of woe.

And yet there was some great honor in choosing rebellion over submission, in refusing to bow to the inexorable laws.

Flavian found himself on his knees before the crucifix that hung on the wall of every cell—how had he come there? He had no memory of kneeling, but all these years and habit would have its way. Maybe that was all that we were, and are, and could be—creatures of habit. He considered the gory Christ in agony, the incarnation of God learning in a particularly brutal way the lessons of the flesh. He climbed stiffly to his feet—from whence that stiffness? How long had he been on his knees? He was thirty-eight—he was beginning to stiffen and harden until the only part of him that wasn't stiff was the part that he wanted to become so. Yes, he knew what awaited—the old monks talked about it. "Oh, God," Brother Cyprian joked, "when will this horniness cease?" And God gave an answer: "About fifteen minutes after you're dead." The desire never left—only the capacity to bring it to fruition. And here he was, ripe as Augustine's pear, dangling. Was that to be his fate? Unrepentant, unfulfilled? A creature of the flesh, a creature of habit, whose habits happened to be a white alb with a black scapular cinched at the waist with a broad leather belt; whose habit happened to be reading and writing?

He lay down and pulled up the sheet and studied the bloody Christ. *The Word made Flesh.* In that last liminal second before sleep the dull ache in his knees told him what he must do, the approach he must take to teach Johnny Faye how to write.

Chapter 25

Doctor Chatterjee had trained herself in the discipline of skeptical inquiry, or so she told herself when she scrutinized a patient's records or test results. And now her skepticism was unrelenting. What was she doing, taking up with this *character?* What future could he hold for her? She had accepted assignment to this town with every intention of completing her required service and then obtaining her green card and establishing a practice in a prosperous suburb. There was no imaginable circumstance under which Johnny Faye would accompany her. What had she been thinking? Sex with a *harijan,* he might as well be untouchable, no matter the continent. A lifetime of infertility and she did not fear pregnancy, the odds were in her favor but she knew they were only odds, what had she been thinking? She was a doctor, *his* doctor.

Each time she drove to the statues she promised herself that this time she would speak to Johnny Faye about the impossibility of what they were doing. From her conviction of the rightness of this path and to keep firm in her resolve she wore her drab dark suit and squat black pumps, all business she was, what had she been thinking? In the evening light she walked down the graveled path practicing speeches that she would deliver, making clear that she accepted her responsibility in setting this nonsense in motion but that she was breaking it off, this time was the last time, no, not even that, this time was good-bye.

And then he arrived, summer rain, the recovery of something lost, dawn after night. She said little and he said less. He took her hand and led her to the blind and his eyes were a sweet devouring as much as if she were dressed in the raiment of a goddess.

After that first night he brought blankets so that they made love now without the prick and grate of sticks and stones. His hands were on her and then his fingers inside her, this penetration, this fact of him inside her. He was the plow, she was the earth, it was so simple, how could she not have understood? Until now she had thought of sex as a process, a function like peristalsis or breathing, one of those things the body did to perpetrate itself into the world of *samsara*, the world of suffering, a means to an end of the endless world of life devouring life with no purpose other than to make more life. An instant's pleasure—no, not even that, how could she think of this wild loss of herself as pleasure, it was what it was, nothing else, all-consuming, no identity, no Meena, no Johnny Faye, but something new that was of the two of them but more than the two of them. His fingers were inside her, one then another, opening her up until some part of her yielded and she was open to him, every part of her was open to him. He entered, not fast, he had known too much suffering to enter fast, he supported himself with his arms while she wrapped her legs around his back and he entered one thread at a time, a tender thrust each barely deeper than the one before until she clutched his buttocks and pulled him into her in one swift thrust that brought him against her *entrails*, the word came to her from some delicate British medical journal because exactly so, precisely right. Now he was thrusting harder and she was rocking in time and they were one, one and one much greater than two. *And so this*, her last thought before losing thought, *is what we call love*.

In afterglow he asked again that she talk to him in her native language. She told him stories in Bangla, from the Mahabarata, Great India, tales of Krishna and Hanuman the monkey king and Arjuna the reluctant warrior and Sita his faithful wife. Once she told how Sita lived in exile with her king Arjuna and his brothers, deep in the forest in a hut exactly like the one in which they lay right here, right now. At the story's end, silence, in which she understood the spoken word, her mother tongue, as the key that had opened her to him, even if he did not understand what she was saying—better, perhaps, that he did not understand.

Then he spoke. "Mouth music."

"I beg your pardon?"

"It's like mouth music, hearing you talk on like that and the pretty little way you bob your head with the words when they go up and down, kind of like you're saying yes and no at the same time. That's all words are anyway. Mouth music. We're just like sparrows at sunrise, making all that racket just to say hello to another day and prove to ourselves and anybody that's listening that we're alive. It don't mean a thing excepting it means everything."

He was echoing her thoughts, she understood, because he was meant to say the right thing at the right moment. "I should break this off. I should stop seeing you."

"That is what you ought to do. But you aint never much done what you ought to do nor said what you ought to say else you wouldn't be here, aint that right."

"I have my whole life in this country at stake. Why am I doing this? I am Brahmin, you cannot know what that means but a Brahmin must marry someone worthy." A terrible thing to say but she made herself say it, whatever was needed to bring this to an end. "You might as well know. I have had *dates*, Harry Vetch is eager to see me again."

"Then maybe you should see him again." He kissed her breast. "Maybe he can help you out with Rosalee's boy."

"I have asked him as much."

Johnny Faye lifted his eyes to hers. "I knew you'd figure out something. You just got to take your time, like a lot of people. What did he say?"

"Precisely what I have already told you but with the authority of the law. I am to guard my tongue and keep my place."

"So do you listen to the law or do you listen to your heart?"

The little voice, Rosalee's words came of their own accord. She broke her gaze from his. "Matthew Mark Smith is my patient. He is no concern of yours."

His turn to look away. "How about letting me be the judge of that."

A sinkhole of silence.

"In my childhood I read novels and I thought, 'The stupid things people do. They must be making this up. How can they not know better? Who can believe this? Nobody could be so reckless.' And here I am, a Brahmin, creeping through the woods to meet with a *dacoit.*"

"Here we are." He took each nipple between thumb and fore-finger and put his mouth over hers and they did not speak for a long while.

He asked nothing more than her presence. Not once did he ask to meet her, he never came to her office, though after their love-making he always saw her to the edge of the woods. Her heart's deep spring, once desiccate, flowed anew. She loved him because he loved her as she was—a childless and once-married exile.

An evening came when she dressed in a pale blue *choli* and the single sari she had brought from India, a scrap of the evening sky star-bangled and edged with silver, wrapped around her waist and thrown over one shoulder. Though it was not a night on which he might expect her to appear she followed the path to the statues on nothing more than the hope that he would divine her longing and of course he was there waiting because he was her destiny.

In the clearing in front of the sleeping apostles she struck a pose her body remembered from the dancing classes required of all Bengali girls. She moved with the bearing of a woman wearing a garment held in place by presence and grace. Her hands assumed their poses, agile and independent, two actors on the stages of her wrists, Parvati hands that of their own accord know how to sleep, to rest for centuries at the edge of a lap, or else to lie palms up, invoking the stillness of eternity until in an instant they wake, her fingers forming complicated little temples that dissolve with a circular rotation of the wrist opening outward to reveal a flat palm with a blood red dot at its center, the thumb and forefinger a perfect circle and the remaining three fingers saying *up!* Released from its skewered bun her hair fell almost to her waist, gleaming as if brushed with oil. She wore gold bangles at her wrists and the hot breeze from the west carried their tinkling. In one nostril a chip of glister in the evening's last light—a diamond. She joined her hands palm to palm, then moved them left-to-right while her head moved right-to-left, even as her eyes followed her hands. Contradiction in union—the parts of her body discrete and independent even as the body was complete and whole—the tension between the movement of her body and the tranquility of her countenance, between time and eternity. She formed a complex knitting of the hands and fingers around a ball of air and in that moment the space her hands enclosed and contained became as real as a stone, a place that she shaped into a house that she inhabited and into which she invited Shiva, her consort. He was his father's son. She was her father's daughter. "For me you are this place, a place to call home. My own country." She took his hand and led him to the blind.

Chapter 26

Meena knelt on the floor of Rosalee's kitchen next to Matthew Mark, who lay with an array of colored pencils in front of a square of poster board. The aged nun teaching summer school had charged her students with illustrating some principle from their catechism, and after much deliberation he had chosen *Three Roads to Heaven*. "Everybody thinks you can only get to heaven by being a priest or a nun or a monk or getting married," he told Meena. "But the catechism says a single person can get there just like anybody and I thought about you and how you're not married and how I want to be single when I grow up because I want to be like you. So that's what I'm going to draw."

"Surely a very hard thing to draw," Meena said. "Might you choose an easier subject?"

"I always choose the hardest subject. It's more fun that way." He was drawing big puffy clouds with an azure pencil. "Heaven," he said, by way of explanation. "Where Jesus lives. Jesus was single."

"I see."

"Did you learn about Jesus when you were a kid?"

She smiled. "I prayed to Jesus, because he was the most handsome."

And so they worked together while Rosalee quartered tomatoes and dropped them into large kettles on each of the stovetop burners. "I used to wait for a cool day to make juice," she said, "but don't seem like we get cool days in the summer anymore."

While sharpening pencils the doctor explained to Matthew Mark that yes, she had learned about Jesus in the convent school but that at home her father had taught her about Lord Krishna, who was a bit like Jesus in that they were both the subjects of a lot of good stories. Matthew Mark asked for a story and the doctor said there are many but the most famous involved a great battle and Matthew Mark interrupted her to say, "Tell that one!"

And so while Matthew Mark drew his poster the doctor told of Lord Krishna and Arjuna at the great battlefield of Kurukṣetra. Arjuna had engaged Lord Krishna to drive his chariot but when the day of battle dawned Arjuna's courage failed him. Looking across the field he saw his opponents arrayed in their splendid armor and he knew that he should fan his hatred for them so that he could kill as many as possible, but all he could think about was how they were men just like him, some of them his cousins and friends and all of them men who just wanted to be happy in the same way that he wanted to be happy and how could he summon any pleasure for the task that awaited?

Matthew Mark held up his pencils. "Do music notes have to be black? I wore the black down and I don't like using it anyway."

Meena crouched at the boy's side. "Music notes?"

Matthew Mark turned the drawing so she could see. It showed a field of red tulips from which a road branched into three paths. The leftmost path led to a cloud that contained a cross and a miter hat and a scarlet heart pierced with seven swords. "That's the religious life," Matthew Mark said. The middle path led to a cloud that held two interlocking rings and a paper labeled "CONTRACT" and a baby bassinet labeled "Junior." "Married, I assume," the doctor said and Matthew Mark nodded. The rightmost cloud was blank. "I can't think of anything that stands for being single," Matthew Mark said, "so I thought maybe I could draw some music notes. But when I hear music notes they sound like all kinds of colors but in the music book at school they're always black. So should I draw them in black like they are in the book, or in colors like they are in my head?"

"Musical notes must be black," the doctor said. "But what do musical notes have to do with being single?"

"Single people get to be happy all the time," Matthew Mark said. "They don't yell at each other like my—anyway, they don't yell at each other and they don't look mad all the time like Father Poppelreiter. So I thought I'd draw a bunch of dancing notes on their cloud."

"I see," the doctor said. "Perhaps you should make them different colors after all."

And so he selected a rainbow of pencils while she told how Lord Krishna spoke to Arjuna about how each of us has his duty in life— how some have the duty to lead and others the duty to serve, some have the duty to be shoemakers and others the duty to be kings but each profession is just as important as the other in the great scheme of things, which is too vast for people to understand. And so Arjuna's duty that day was to be a soldier and as part of his duty as a soldier he had to kill other men. And even though it was not a pleasant part of his duty, his job was to perform it as well as he could because when each of us performed his duty as well as he could he helped keep the universe in harmony. "Like your three roads," Meena said. "Each person has a road to follow and his job is to follow the road as well as he can, and Lord Krishna is equally happy with all three roads, so long as we contribute to the harmony of the universe."

Rosalee handed her an apron. "Now's where I need some help. Matthew Mark, you climb up on that chair and get ready with the tomato mill. I'll pull the jars out of the hot water. Meena, you get the messy job—you bring the tomatoes to Matthew Mark and let him run them through the mill. Then you carry the juice— it'll be boiling hot now, you be careful—over to the sink and I'll ladle it into the jars."

They worked until the half-gallon jars were filled with bright red juice and the compost bucket a steaming pile of pulp. Then

Rosalee took some watermelon sticks from the freezer and they went outside.

They sat in aluminum lawn chairs, listening to the *pink* and *pock* of the juice jars sealing. Matthew Mark sat at the picnic table putting finishing touches on his poster. Next to their chairs was a crude structure of wooden slats and sheets of translucent plastic. "My greenhouse," Rosalee said. "Winter comes, it can be awful gray around here. I like to see something bloom."

"How lovely! May I look?"

"Oh, there's not much to look at now. I raise things that bloom in winter. Orchids and cactus. The cactus I scatter around the yard in the summertime, the orchids are just a bunch of green sticks right now. I like 'em because they look ordinary and no-count and then right when you need it most, out comes this beautiful flower."

"I had an orchid once, my favorite flower, that bloomed in *basanto*, our season for weddings," Meena said. She told how as a teenage girl, sent by her grandparents to bring in the family cow from its foraging, she found a bright yellow orchid in a damp hollow of a banyan tree. A stream of water trickled from a spring in a rock wall and followed a limb down to a mossy hollow in the trunk, where the orchid had rooted itself and lived on air and water and filtered light. "I visited it all the time after my parents sent me to my grandparents' village. On the day I was married, I cut one of the stalks and wove the blossoms into my hair."

A moment of silence. "I never knew you was married."

"A complicated and difficult story," Meena said. "I should never have mentioned it. If I could be so bold. Please—if you would—I would be so grateful if you would keep that knowledge to yourself."

"Well, of course, honey, you know you can count on me but little pitchers have big ears," Rosalee said, staring at Matthew Mark. He did not look up. "Matthew Mark."

"Yes, ma'am."

"You heard the doctor."

"Yes, ma'am."

"And what do you say."

"I promise."

"Cross your heart?"

"And hope to die."

"All right, then. I don't guess you ever worked this hard in Bengal," Rosalee said. "Nothing hotter than canning tomatoes in August. Though if you was a country girl I expect you had work of your own. For all I seen of the world you might have been canning tomatoes."

"Mrs. Smith—Rosalee. Might I ask your opinion on a private matter?"

"Why sure, honey, however I can help." A pause. "Matthew Mark, you take your poster inside and finish it up. We'll be along directly."

A small protest overruled, and then the women were alone. "I appreciate your sensitivity," Meena said, "though I am only curious, of course." She described Johnny Faye's pointing out the birds and Harry Vetch's vehement warning. She could hear her effort to keep her voice colorless and uninflected. "And so when people say Mr. Faye is a *character*, what do they mean?"

Rosalee twisted her wedding band. "Could mean a lot of things. Partly it's a compliment. Says you give people something to talk about. You could say he was a community asset, though I caint imagine my husband seeing it that way. It's not like he breaks the law—I mean he does, but he and his kind never lived by no law that come from anywheres but inside. Let's just say you won't ever have to worry about getting paid on time and probably a little extra. He's too ornery to pay attention to the ins and outs of the law. I wouldn't go trying to civilize him. He's too honest to be civilized."

Meena sucked on her watermelon stick. "What would you do, if you were given a choice between love and security?"

"I already told you. I'd listen to the little voice."

"But what if there's too much noise to hear the little voice?"

"Then I'd get myself to some quiet place, I guess. That's one thing church is good for. But you know better than me you're choosing between something that is and something that aint. There aint no such thing as security, not that I been able to see, anyway. I went chasing and I know. That's just a dream somebody come up with to get us to buy whatever they happen to be selling."

"I might as well tell you. Harry Vetch has asked me for a second date."

"I aint surprised. Harry Vetch can be a pain but he aint dumb, and you're the best thing that's happened to this little town in a long time."

"What would you say? Our first date was not especially successful."

Rosalee shrugged. "That can happen on a first date. Aint no harm in a date. Keep your legs crossed and make sure he pays your way, he can afford it. And don't be too eager. He's got a reputation for notching the gun, if you know what I mean."

"I know what you mean, but with Harry I don't feel the need to worry about keeping these legs crossed," she said, pointing to her legs. "Instead I have to keep *these* crossed," and she pointed to her lips. "That is considerably more difficult. I have been told before that I can be too—direct. That is what I like about Johnny—Mr. Faye. I can say anything with him, or nothing. Either way we have a lovely time."

Rosalee gave her a peculiar look. "How many times have you seen Johnny Faye?"

"Oh, a few. We encounter each other at the monastery—at the statues. He comes to watch birds and I come—I enjoy the peace and quiet."

"Peace and quiet's not the first thing I think of when I think of Johnny Faye. What is it about that man? Seems like everybody—every*thing* that moves has the hots for Johnny Faye. Something about that mix of rounder and saint, I guess. And the little boy, we all want to take care of the little boy. Sometimes I think it's women's fault that men are so messed up. We don't want 'em to grow up, we want to keep 'em kids forever. Our kids." Rosalee bent to tug a handful of crabgrass from the orchid planter. "I'd keep a tight rein on that if I was you."

"And what makes you say that?"

"You live with a police officer, you hear lots of things you best keep to yourself."

"The same is true of a doctor."

"Let me just say that I've heard talk—my husband and Little—Benny Joe—one of Johnny Faye's crew—guy that owns the auto parts store. Not the first person I'd want to get tangled up with. Talk."

"A doctor cannot concern herself with talk."

"You're right there, but this kind of talk—money talk—I don't know. I aint heard this kind of talk before. Drug talk. It's new to me. Anyways, you be careful." Rosalee knocked the dirt from the weeds and tossed them on the compost pile. "Your Arjuna always does his duty."

"Yes, the stories teach us to do our duty. When I was a child I thought that meant only one thing—to live as others would have me live, and so I always did what I was told. *A thing aint happened until it's been told,* according to Mr. Johnny Faye.

"And so I will tell you the unhappy story of my marriage. My grandparents married me to a rich man three times my age. How fortunate I was, a penniless young girl with only her wits for her dowry, to find such a husband! Or so I was told and so I told myself, but when I could not give him a son he took a second wife. She was pregnant within the year and my disgrace was complete. But in my disgrace I discovered a different duty—a duty to myself and to others, to people outside my clan and my village. That is when I left for medical school, for America. Perhaps you are discovering the same. Perhaps that is why I have been brought into your life."

"I wouldn't know much about that. I caint afford to think about that kind of thing." Rosalee stood. "I got to get inside now to see if that boy finished his drawing. Let me bring you a jar of juice—it ought to be cool enough to carry by now." She returned carrying a jar wrapped in a towel. "It's still a little warm, but this way you can carry it."

Meena crossed the road and sat outside for a long while with the jar of juice, still warm, wrapped in a towel and resting in her lap. If she were possessed of Matthew Mark's imagination, she could deceive herself into thinking she cradled a child.

Chapter 27

Flavian stood at the lip of the bluff above the oxbow bend, hands on his hips. These days the cedar thicket all but parted in welcome—he'd make his mourning dove's call and stroll right through. This particular Sunday he clutched in his right hand the Department of Justice press release. Below him Johnny Faye was clipping away the lower leaves of his plants. Flavian rattled the paper. "You listen to what they're saying about you."

In the creek bed Johnny Faye gathered a cluster of clipped stems in one hand and heaved them to one side. Flavian thought again of Palm Sunday—oh, for those days of innocence, before he'd met the Voice, before he'd brought the envelope of money back to the monastery, before he'd been born—but Johnny Faye's gesture drew his eyes to the stack of discarded stems and leaves. "Why on earth are you doing that?"

"Doing what."

"Cutting them down. After all the work we—you put into growing them."

"I aint cutting 'em *down*. I'm cutting 'em *back*."

"In August? I don't know a thing about raising plants but even I know you don't prune plants in August."

"I told you I know what I'm doing." But then Johnny Faye straightened from his task. His voice took on a patient tone, as if he were talking to a child. "You trim off the bottom leaves because they aint gotten enough light to be worth much of anything to any-body except maybe a compost pile. Then you cut off all the buds except those at the end because a plant aint like a human being. Well, it is and it aint. It is because no matter what anybody tells you, they got a sense of the world. They seek out what they need to grow and prosper, and they will do amazing things to get what they need. Especially this particular plant, which as plants go is somewhere well nigh a genius. But you cut your skin, at least up to a point it'll heal over. You nick a plant and it just dies. We got our power scattered throughout, different kinds of power in our heads and hands and feet. You cut off a guy's hand, the guy works at it hard enough and all that power shifts over to his other hand, I seen it happen to a guy who lost a hand in Nam, you'd see what he could do with the hand he had left and you'd hardly even notice he only had one. Not so with a plant. They send all their power to their tips. Once you know that you can shape them so that all the power goes where you want it to go. I want the power to go to a few buds at the end of each branch, I don't want it wasted by getting spread out over a lot of leaves and stems and puny little piss-ant bottom-feeding buds. So I cut off the lower leaves—they're just sucking the power away from the ones higher up—and I cut off all the buds except the ones at the tips of the branches. Don't you worry your-self, I don't waste so much as a twig. I'll dry this early cut and bake it in cookies. Then the buds left on the plant—I'll leave them on a few more days so the sun can finish 'em out and fill 'em with its power. That way all the power of this place"—he waved in a big arc at the sun overhead, the creek bed, the bluff on which Flavian stood, the great mottled three-armed sycamore—"gets into the buds I leave behind. And when the winter comes, you can put that in your pipe and smoke it." He grinned.

"Well. You've really thought this process through, I give you that much."

Johnny Faye turned back to his plants. He was shirtless and his back gleamed with sweat—from the bluff Flavian could count the knobs on his spine and see the workings of the muscles in the broad universe of his star-speckled back. Flavian looked for longer than he ought but not as long as he wanted. Then he unfolded the press release and read aloud.

```
The Organized Crime Drug Enforcement Task
Force, consisting of representatives from
the Drug Enforcement Administration, State
Police, Internal Revenue Service, and
Federal Bureau of Investigation, has
entered an investigation of residents
growing marijuana outside the state. To
date marijuana has been seized from 29
sites . . .
```

When Flavian finished reading he looked down to see Johnny Faye standing in rapt attention. Johnny Faye arched his neck and then doubled over from some kind of shaky feeling, then he raised his head to the sky and roared. *"Yeeeee-hi!"*

A flock of crows rose from a copse of water maples and circled three times, their raucous caws echoing Johnny Faye's shout. Johnny Faye scrambled up the clay bank and plucked the press release from Flavian's hand and studied it. "That's what this says about us, huh."

"You better believe it."

"Well if it aint true it ought to be. I'll have to see what I can do about that."

"I don't think you understand what this means. These guys are playing hardball."

Johnny Faye doubled over again, gasping with laughter. Flavian snatched at the press release and it tore down the middle. Flavian looked at his half and sighed. "Explain that to the abbot."

"What the abbot don't know don't hurt him. Why does the abbot need to see this."

"What the abbot don't know—what *you* don't know might get us all a long term in the penitentiary."

"I'll make sure I go alone, don't you worry your holy head. Look. I'm living my life in dog years. I do things different from what you might expect, you know that. Hell, if they don't talk about you, you aint no count."

"Then I guess you're the number one count."

"That is the objective. Although I truly acknowledge before the Virgin Mary that I never thought it would come to this. Those are United States government lawyers talking, right?"

"That's right."

"Holy shit. Good thing this crop is closing in to harvest." He took Flavian's hand and gave it a shake. "My brother, I thank you for the information. I got some guys in my crew sniffing after the hard stuff. They watch too much television, they aspire to be among the idle rich, caint stand prosperity, no, they got to make easy money. You remember Little. Big buck of a guy you almost beat playing pool with a little help from Lady Luck and yours truly? First night we met."

"Oh, yes, I remember. Big red-faced guy."

"That's right. He's itching to have stuff he don't even know he wants and he's ready to do whatever he has to do to get it." Johnny Faye stuffed his half of the press release into his rear pocket. "Maybe I can use this to talk some sense into him."

And then he was back down in the creek bed, back at his job, clipping and tossing aside, and Flavian allowed himself the guilty pleasure of watching his brown, gleaming, mottled back, the glistening ropy muscles of his arms, the excellent hollow in his lower back just above the waist of his jeans, where the sweat pooled before seeping into the denim to make a dark inverted pyramid of wet, the flip of his sun-streaked hair bound with a bright purple rubber band into the rattiest of pony tails, the half of the press release that Johnny Faye had stuffed in his rear pocket twitching with every waggle of his hips like some wildwood fan dancer's tease, switching back and forth as his body moved in the easy working rhythm that across these summer months Flavian had come to know and love.

The word presented itself to Flavian with the ease and inevitability of sunrise, and his very next thought was what could he do, what *must* he do to distract himself, to cut this desire from his mind and heart and some other deeper place, whatever it took to save him from himself.

But after a moment to gather his self-control Flavian was able to tell himself that love was a good and natural thing, especially the love of a teacher for his student. After all, if Johnny Faye could really learn to read and write he could free himself from the poverty that gave him no choice but to grow pot—that was the goal, that was Flavian's *objective*. And so he climbed down the bank and into the seat of the sycamore throne. He pulled his writing tablet from his tote bag. He did not permit himself to watch Johnny Faye but waited for a pause in the clip and swish of his pruning and when that moment came he cleared his throat. "Let's give writing one more try."

"I hadn't done my homework, if that's what you're asking. You're slipsliding down a pole covered with shit and nothing at the bottom but more where that come from."

"No, I had a bright idea about how to teach—how you can learn to write. I want to try something different. Just this once. If this doesn't work, fine. I will type out and sign a certificate suitable for framing that absolves you from ever having to try to learn to read and write and that you can show off to any idiot dumb enough to take you on as a challenge." Flavian studied his blank tablet, not allowing himself so much as a peep in Johnny Faye's direction, but he could hear him thinking it over.

"OK, teach, you're on. What do you want me to do."

Flavian patted the trunk of the sycamore throne. "Come up here. Settle in."

After a moment Johnny Faye was standing above him in the tree.

"OK, have a seat. Right here, next to me. I need to be able to wrap my arm around you."

Johnny Faye sat. The salty, fecund smell of sweat assaulted Flavian but now he was all teacher, all business. He settled Johnny Faye inside the crook of his right arm.

"OK. Here's my idea. Learn it in your body, not in your head. Forget about your head. Forget about everything anybody ever told you about how to write. Close your eyes. I want you to take up the pen and then I want you to let me wrap my hand around yours. That's right. Keep your eyes closed. I don't want you to look anywhere or at anything. Just let your hand go loose and follow where my hand goes. Learn it in your body, not in your head. Let your hand follow what it is I'm doing. That's it, let it go loose. Can you tell me what I'm doing, what letters we're making? Never mind, forget I asked that, just keep your eyes closed. Don't worry about thinking about what letters we're making, just do it from the same place where you are when you pick up a pool stick or a hoe. That's right. Take a breath, a deep breath—you remember telling me that? Well, you were right. And then let it out easy. The power comes natural, it's already there, it's always been there, you don't have to make it happen, what you have to do is learn how to use it."

And so for some timeless time they wrote, or rather Flavian wrote, his hand over Johnny Faye's, his fingers guiding the pen that Johnny Faye held

J-O-H-N-N-Y F-A-Y-E

J-O-H-N-N-Y F-A-Y-E

J-O-H-N-N-Y F-A-Y-E

until Flavian's hand grew tired and he laid down the pen. The length of his left arm, wrapped around Johnny Faye's shoulders, felt the rise and swell of Johnny Faye's chest.

Then Johnny Faye shrugged free and stood and stretched. "We got just enough time to go looking for ditch weed."

"Ditch weed?"

Johnny Faye was on the ground and scrabbling around among his tools. "See, they planted hemp all over this countryside until just before World War II—I'd be surprised if the monastery hadn't grown some—turned it into cloth and rope and even paper. And hemp is just another name for marijuana—same plant, same pollen that comes floating through the air in search of my babes.

"And that means this creek bottom is filled with pockets of ditch weed left over from the days when it jumped every fence and river and went wild. And in that ditch weed there are male plants dying to get their pot pollen jism into my big fat female buds, which I have kept innocent as the farmer's daughter because—exactly like the farmer's daughter—the longer they're unsullied as the driven snow, the harder they work to get the guys. By denying these girls what they want we have caused them hardship. And just like with people, hardship makes them work harder. They don't want the silver spoon neither, which in the female case of this particular plant means they make more of the gooey sap to catch whatever male pollen might be flying around. And the stuff that brings you closer to God or makes you believe you're closer to God for a little while anyways is the gooey sap, yee-hi. We have here a creek bed Playboy Club for the male marijuana plant, all those luscious babes longing for that pollen, yearning for that pollen, ready and eager to give up their power for that pollen. And our last job of the afternoon is to make sure my babes don't get what they want, that they stay as innocent of pollen as the Virgin Mary of Saint Joseph." Johnny Faye held out a tool, a long handle with a flat, toothed blade at its end. "It's for cutting down the ditch weed. I'll show you how to swing it."

Flavian climbed from the tree. "OK, whatever, lead the way, but see if you can pick up a pen sometime in the next week—or any kind of stick, doesn't have to be a pen, maybe it's better that it's not a pen, any kind of stick and write on some surface, any surface. I just want you to see if you can remember—I want your hand, not your head to see if it can remember how to write your name. Don't worry about whether or not you're writing. Just move your hand exactly like I moved your hand, over and over and see what happens. Will you promise me that? Promise?"

"OK, teacher. You got my word." Johnny Faye crossed his heart with the blade of his sickle. "I'm a man of my word. If I say it I'll do it." He pointed down the creek. "This won't take long. I spent the last few weeks cleaning out the half-mile or so upwind and now all we got to do is check a few hundred yards downwind to make sure I didn't miss out on some little scrawny guy that's waiting for the wind to blow in the wrong direction. Those are the ones you got to watch out for, the scrawny little guys, they look like they couldn't push over a cornstalk and then you get 'em in bed and they got all the juice. Same as with people. All it takes is one of those little guys and my whole crop goes to seed."

"Literally."

Johnny Faye cocked his head and twisted his mouth and then laughed. "What the hell—you *do* have a sense of humor. You been spending too much time down in this creek bed, watch out, you'll start sounding like me. Anyways you just come along with that sickle and chop away at anything you see that looks like it's the wild-ass version of the same plant—like it's hungry for my girls."

They rolled up their pants legs and made their ways down the creek. All the dense growth on the banks looked the same to Flavian, one big wall of green, but in one or two places Johnny Faye waded into the green and swung his sickle, and Flavian, feeling useless and dumb, followed his example.

Then the creek narrowed and grew deeper and they came to a water maple that had fallen across the water, bank to bank. Johnny Faye climbed to the bank and pulled off his jeans and underwear. "No way to get around this tree except climb up and over the bank and I could do that early in the season but I tried it last week and got a butt full of smartweed. The creek gets deep on the other side so you got to get your pants wet or take 'em off and swim across. Best thing is just to strip and duck under."

Flavian hesitated a moment, but what was the difference between stripping to swim in the lake and stripping to swim in the creek? By the time he had pulled off his clothes and placed them on the bank and ducked under the tree Johnny Faye was far downstream—only the whites of his untanned buttocks showed through the overhanging branches.

And Flavian followed after, flailing his sickle at random weeds that were probably innocent bystanders—after all, sharp-eyed Johnny Faye had already passed by—but doing something, anything made him feel less *stupid*, a naked middle-aged monk wading in knee-deep water and swinging a sickle.

They thrashed their ways down the creek. To Flavian every branch seemed adorned with poison ivy, every rock concealed a cottonmouth and so he anticipated the attack—maybe in some pheromonal way brought it on. All he knew was that in a single moment he went from a place where he was thrashing along in a fog of foolishness, to a place where Johnny Faye was splashing past him yelling *"Run! Run!"* and Flavian, ignorant but aware of something gone wrong, went splashing after him, scraping and cutting his bare feet on gravel and the razor-sharp shells of freshwater mussels. Spider webs filled his mouth and he had some dim worry of ticks amid the adrenalin rush, but Johnny Faye was crying *"To the hole! The hole!"* and Flavian realized he meant the deep pool where they'd first ducked under the fallen water maple, and then he felt a hot white brand of fire on one arm and he got the picture, he went double-time for the last twenty yards and dove into the pool of water even before Johnny Faye got there—though later it occurred to him that Johnny Faye hung back so as to present a diversionary target.

Unbelievably, the hornets followed them into the water—Flavian would stop thrashing to catch his breath and there they'd be, dive-bombing his head.

"*Duck!* and swim underwater! And head for the shade, they don't much like the shade."

And Flavian ducked into the cool green wet and did not emerge until he found a place under the trunk of the fallen water maple that was sheltered from the sun and with an underwater limestone ledge at the right height for him to sit, leaving only his face exposed from the lips up. And after a moment Johnny Faye's wet stringy head bobbed up beside him and last but not least JC. The dog climbed up the maple's trunk and shook, sending a little shower over their heads that could only help, or so Flavian hoped, drive away the hornets.

So they sat there for a while.

"You think they've gotten off for today?"

"You mean the hornets?"

"No, Sherlock, I mean the flying cows."

"Well, I don't see any more of them."

"Did they get you?"

"Only once. How about you."

"One on my arm, another on my back."

"Let me see."

They compared war wounds. Flavian had one, Johnny Faye had two bright little nips of flesh surrounded by scarlet aureoles. "Damn. Sorry. Must have swung into a nest." Johnny Faye took Flavian's arm and raised the wound to his mouth. "Hold steady—the spit does it good, neutralizes the poison."

"It's OK. I'll live."

"OK, your turn," and Johnny Faye held up his arm and Flavian wrapped his lips around the meaty hunk of Johnny Faye's biceps and he was very, very grateful that the water hid that part of his body with a mind of its own.

"Sit still. They come after anything that moves. We better hang out here for a little bit."

"Oh, sure, yes. Let's stay in the water. Absolutely."

A canopy of green arched overhead, enlivened by the grating

of cicadas and the panting of JC, now sprawled on a wet ledge on the bank.

"So what made you become a monk, anyway? I mean, there must have been something besides the war."

"Well, you're right. Not at first—at first I was just hiding out. But then I spent more time at the monastery and I came to like the place, you know, it just made so much sense, I don't have to tell you that. Living with the brothers and trying to make something as a community instead of this idiot notion that somehow magically a good world can come out of everybody being selfish. You drive along the highway and you can tell the second you come onto monastery land, there's something *sacred* about the place, it's like the land belongs to God. Which is who it belongs to anyway. And our job is to take care of it for Him. Her. It."

"Which is why you should keep the cows."

"All that God stuff comes out of people wanting—not to be so alone."

"I can see that."

"When we're not really alone in the first place."

"I can see that, too. That's what people are looking for and aint finding in sex."

"I wouldn't know about that. All I know is that people want to be one with the One. One with the Whole."

"You don't say. I have always said that sex was about being one with the hole."

Flavian leaned over to cuff him on the ear.

"Sorry. I got a smart mouth. In the Army they tried beating it out of me but might as well try to beat the kick out of a mule."

"It's OK. Maybe it's the same whole. For you, anyway."

"Wow. All those years I thought all I was doing was fucking when it turns out I was communing with God."

Flavian sighed. "It's not like that's the only kind of desire. There are lots of kinds of desire."

"Such as? I'm listening."

"Well, you know. Desire."

Johnny Faye made a circle with his thumb and forefinger, then poked his other forefinger in and out. Color rose to Flavian's cheeks. "Well, I don't mean that kind of desire. Or at least not only that kind."

"Oh? What other kind is there? There's only one kind I ever known and it drives me crazy and makes me alive at the same time. Caint do with it, that's for sure, but caint do without it, neither. Sex is this funny thing. You got to have it. You caint think of anything but it. It makes you toss and turn—it's like knowing that the next morning you're going to start a long trip to someplace you never seen. You think about it all the time. And then finally you get it and you go to that place for a few minutes. Maybe it's the place the animals live in all the time, I thought about that, a place where the only thing that matters in the world is what you're doing right here, right now."

"A monk would call that *perfect prayer.*"

Johnny Faye gave Brother Flavian a funny look. "Is that a fact. It don't start out that way, of course. Most people have to be warmed into it a little—even most guys, even if they won't admit it. And then you get hot, and then it takes over and you belong to it for a few minutes. And you're alive, nothing dead about you, everything says go, go, go, live, live, live. And then it's over and done with and all you want to do is smoke a joint. You're a stranger to yourself—you have to lie there a few minutes to find your way back to the person you left behind a few minutes before. And the other person, the person you're with, you want to be tangled up in them and away from them at the same time. Least, that's how it is with me. I heard a guy say once that people used to think that a man could only do it so many times in his life, could only—"

He stopped here to search for a word and the searching grew too long.

"Come."

He stretched his neck a little and dropped his shoulders.

"Like you say. And when I first heard that I thought, No, that caint be true and then another part of me, the smart part, said, But you know, I can see how you'd think that way if you didn't know no better. Because it takes something out of you, it surely does. Religion ought to be all about it, you know. It's not like the place I get to in church but it's where I'd like to go."

"You go to *church?*"

Johnny Faye's eyes narrowed and he gave a little laugh that came from some secret place. "You act like you're surprised."

"Well, I am surprised."

"I always like it when people trip theirselves up. They think they got somebody pegged and they aint got a clue. I'd never darken the door of that church in town, no way. Father Poppelreiter would have a cow, for one, and besides I don't want to go giving people the wrong impression."

"And what impression might that be."

"Oh, you know, like I was getting their kind of religion, all that kissy-padre's-ring-assed stuff. No, I go to mass at Calvary when the mood strikes. Good friends with the priest there. He's happy to see me, if you get my drift." Johnny Faye pinched his forefinger and thumb together and put them to his lips and made a sucking noise. "Don't ask much where I've been. Pretty little church. And that priest, he's been around, he served in Nam, he don't ask questions. Most of these priests, they don't know jack. The church is just like the Army—the more ignorant they are the higher up they rise. Hell, if you're dumb enough and willing to stab enough backs, you just might make general. Or pope, same thing, more or less. You take a guy twenty-plus years old, stick him in a room with a bunch of other guys for four or six years, tell him he caint even put his hands on his own dick. Then you send him out into the world, all a sudden everybody's calling him Father and kissing his ass and buying him supper at nice restaurants and he don't know a thing about sex and life except how to feel bad about having it. Now how in the hell can he help people be better than they are, when most of the time their problem is sex or something coming out of it. You tell me that."

"Because when I'm alone and in silence some things reveal themselves that otherwise I can't see or understand."

"Is that a fact."

"Like the birds. You can't order the Spirit to show up when you want it to. Instead you have to sit in patience and silence so that after a while, if she chooses, she might raise her bashful head and look around. You walk through the fields and the woods making noise, talking with somebody else or just shuffling through the leaves the way we do when we're with somebody else and you'd think the birds had all flown to Mexico. But then you go some place and sit alone and in silence and after a while they're all around you."

"Well, you got that right. Let me think about that one."

"Yeah, well, I'll think about it too. I never thought of being a monk like that until now."

For a while they sat still, until Flavian relaxed a little and his tongue got the better of him. "So why did you go for a soldier?"

"Because I wanted to be a monk but I caint stand religion."

"Oh, come on."

"I mean it. I wasn't so dumb as to believe all that shit about how we had to go save the world for democracy—I mean *follow the money* as some wise guy said, any idiot could see who stood to make money on this business and it was definitely not the guys in my platoon. But I wanted to join up with a—*brotherhood of men*, like you say. And they promised me they would teach me how to read and write and then I could find me a good job when I came back. So I made my mark because I thought if anybody could figure out how to teach me how to read and write it was the United States Army. And that was pretty much the last time it got mentioned."

"I'm sorry you had to go through that. I guess it's one reason to believe in paradise. Surely all those guys who died got more out of life than just those twenty years."

Johnny Faye spread his hands flat on the creek's cool mirror. "I don't believe in death."

"What do you mean, you don't believe in death?"

Johnny Faye grabbed Flavian's head and ducked him under—he came up sputtering. "Don't you get it?" Johnny Faye cried. "Aint you been paying attention to nothing? Dying is just a dream the devil cooked up to make us scared so then he could have his way. Get with the program, man! You're a monk—act like one!" Johnny Faye pointed around the creek bank. "You show me where there's death. You could climb all over the banks to find a dead bird or a turtle but you'd be a long time looking. Ever think about that? All that dying going on—least, if you see things your way—but we don't see a single dead thing. I look around and all I see is life, life turning into more life." He slapped the surface of the water. "And this is my paradise, right here, right now and hell is all those people that don't know theirselves. Like Little. Or Harry Vetch. Where are the damn wild places anymore, is what I wonder. Some place a misfit like me can call home."

Flavian touched his heart. "Maybe it's in here."

They sat for a moment in silence.

"I'll be damn. Something else to think about."

"For you and me both."

A long burr from a cicada stationed in the water maple over their heads. Johnny Faye looked up. "I think the hornets are gone."

"I think you're right."

They ducked under the water maple and retrieved their clothes from the bank and waded wordlessly up the creek. JC trotted after, tongue lolling. When they reached the oxbow bend they waded out of the creek. Their hands brushed. Flavian stiffened like a flagpole and turned away and worked his way up the bank in an awkward crabwise step, trying to conceal his privates. He pulled on his shirt and grabbed his jeans and tried to get one leg into them but in his haste he caught his foot in his pants leg and fell down, his cock pointing at the sky and then Johnny Faye had his mouth around the thing, that is what happened. Flavian opened his eyes wide and took it all in and for one second he tried to think of something to say but then some other part of him took hold and spoke in a deep, calm voice: *Suffer the consequences.*

Then Johnny Faye stood and took his hand. "Come on. Come here. I aint lived forty years for nothing. If you're going to do a thing you may as well do it right and it aint going to be paradise lying here in the mud."

He took Flavian's hand and led him to the great sycamore and climbed up first and pulled Flavian up after and all the while Flavian's mind saying *No, no, no* and every other cell in his body saying *Yes, yes, yes* until Johnny Faye sat him down in the sycamore throne and knelt in front of him. He tucked his hand behind Flavian's neck to pull him forward so that he could shrug the shirt off his shoulders and his arms. Then Johnny Faye took the shirt and folded it tenderly and used it to cover the tree's scaly trunk. He placed one hand in the small of Flavian's back and the other in the center of his chest and leaned him back until he was resting against the sycamore's cloth-covered arm. He tucked a hand under each of Flavian's knees and lifted them and propped his feet on the tree's other arms. Then he took Flavian's hands, one in each of his and raised and locked them over his head. He buried his mouth in Flavian's open armpit, then he covered Flavian's mouth with his mouth and for the first time in his life Flavian tasted that most familiar of smells, the smell of his own sweat. Then Johnny Faye took Flavian's root in his hands like it was some kind of scepter. A timeless while of this and then Johnny Faye took his mouth to the sweet nether places and the next thing Flavian could remember was a loud cry *Jee-sus!* that echoed in the pantheon of green. He would never have believed any human being capable of making such a sound except that when he finally opened his eyes—he kept them closed very long, because so long as they were closed he was in some other timeless universe, one where actions had no consequences—*maybe that was what they meant by paradise, a place where actions have no consequences*—and when he opened them he would be back in this ordinary world of telephones and mail orders and Benediction—*what about Benediction, my God!*—and then he opened his eyes to see Johnny Faye grinning his crazy chipped-tooth grin from ear to ear and he had been waiting, Flavian could read it in his eyes, for Flavian to open his eyes so that the first thing he saw was Johnny Faye lifting his arm and wiping his hand across his mouth like the lanky stringy-haired tempter that he was, and Flavian understood that he, Brother Flavian of the Order of Cistercians of the Strict Observance familiarly known as Trappists, had been the one to shout at the top of his lungs and on this sycamore throne the name of the Lord.

"Sssh." Johnny Faye pointed up. "Kingfisher."

But Flavian's glasses were cock-eyed and when he lifted his hand to straighten them the bird took off into the September sky.

"Now aint that something. He sits there through all that racket but then flaps away when you so much as make a move. Whatever. Now it's your turn. You don't have to swallow, that aint in the rules, but you got to at least give it a try and see how you like it, that *is* in the rules."

Johnny Faye stood in the tree's crotch and Flavian knelt before him and closed his eyes against the slipping sliding late summer light and felt Johnny Faye place his hands gentle as the setting sun on Flavian's head so that they guided him in an act for which he was amazed to find he needed no guidance because he loved this man, every part of him he loved. And when Johnny Faye said in a low humble voice, "Excuse me, Brother Tom, but I am about to come," Flavian raised his hands and guided Johnny Faye's hands back onto to his temples and kept his hands over Johnny Faye's hands until he heard a guttural moan and his mouth was filled with something like life and Flavian was seriously present to the cause, he had never not once in his life been so present to his own reality, *perfect prayer.* Then Johnny Faye gently tipped up Flavian's head and pressed his thick-lipped mouth over Flavian's.

For a very long while they stayed that way, Flavian kneeling in the sycamore throne, Johnny Faye bending to his mouth, and gradually the twitterings of the evening birds and the grinding of the cicadas coming back to consciousness until Johnny Faye stretched his hands to the sky and leaned back against the sycamore's branch.

And in that moment all of history, all the past and future, all of memory and responsibility and his vows to his brothers and to God came rushing back and Flavian opened his mouth to say *I'm sorry, I am so sorry* when Johnny Faye took his head in his hands and looked him in the eyes and did not let him turn his head to one side or look down and his eyes were deep brown and full of love. "Aint it glorious," he said, a three-dollar word he would have learned in church, and Flavian held his tongue and looked up through the dense canopy of leaves, the sycamore leaf so broad and shapely, all of a piece, whole unto itself, and for the first time the thought occurred to him that he too might become all of a piece, whole unto himself.

"Aint it glorious," Johnny Faye said a second time. "Now that is what I call a conversation with God. Or Beauty, if you got to be so high falutin about it and you do, I know that, it's part of what I like about you. You know why I got brown eyes?"

"No."

Johnny Faye held a hand flat at his forehead. "Because I'm full of shit up to here. And you, you with your barely blue eyes, you're a quart short. Which is why you take everything so serious and why you ever been, are now, and ever will be a monk."

And after he said this, for the space of a few seconds Flavian forgot everything he had promised, all the vows he had made, his place in the world, everything but right here, right now and the thought *I will follow this man wherever he goes. Only say the word and I shall be healed.*

Johnny Faye worked his way around Flavian and slid down the sycamore trunk to JC, who had been biding his doggy time. He picked up Flavian's shirt from where it had fallen from the tree.

"I am a liberal-minded man but I have to say that, when it comes right down to it, I'm better at hard and sharp than I am at soft and round."

Something in Johnny Faye's voice and in what he said lodged a little dagger in Flavian's side, somewhere just below his heart—maybe it lodged *in* his heart. He didn't want to put a name to the feeling—he'd never felt it before and he would have been hard-pressed to name it. But it was there, all right—not a sharp, quick pain like a pinprick but more like a splinter, hardly noticeable, the kind of injury that he was innocent enough to think would go away on its own instead of suppurating into poison.

Johnny Faye held up Flavian's shirt and jeans. Flavian jumped down from the tree and grabbed at them but Johnny Faye stepped out of reach. "Maybe I'll just disappear with these. Explain *that* to the abbot." But then he held up Flavian's shirt with the arms out while Flavian slipped it on.

Flavian pulled on his pants in silence. With every moment the weight of what he had done grew until he was nearly choking with remorse.

"See you next week, same time, same place."

"I won't—I can't promise that."

"I aint asking for promises. I aint much on promises, you know that. Just letting you know where I'm planning on being. Now let's get out of here before they send out that dumbass cop and a search party."

And then they were out of the creek bed and through the parted cedars and into the fields and onto 'Sweet, whom Johnny Faye sent cantering through the early September evening light, no sun by now, the sun had set but the world was still filled with light fading every moment but everywhere at once.

Chapter 28

The doctor pondered the evidence: Spots of blood in her underwear, three days running. Her period had never been dependable—sometimes she missed it altogether, other times it came as a painful flood. Medical school had taught her to understand this irregularity as one of many pieces of evidence of her infertility. These spots, however—a trail of scarlet tears—were something new.

And something else was afoot—something unmeasureable, unanswerable. Hundreds of miles from the nearest ocean, a sea change. The world had a sharper edge. She found herself inexplicably cheerful one morning, downcast the next. The blandest American foods turned her stomach, even as she longed for the mustards and cumins of her youth.

One night she dreamed of these knobby hills, these people, her patients. Speaking the tongues of her childhood, they gather to bury her living self but they cover her with only a few centimeters of earth so she can breathe. She is very calm, she feels no fear. As she is lying in the darkness with her eyes closed, flowers sprout from the earth, covering her body. She rises up whole and complete in herself and in that predawn moment she spoke out loud: "How the body remembers."

Meena met Maria Goretti at the end of a slow Friday shift when they would have the lab to themselves—Maria, who lived near the hospital and so at some remove from Meena's town. Maria chattered while she drew blood, and Meena took comfort in the ceaseless river of words from someone who'd performed this test many times, first with rabbits and frogs, now with all this high-tech equipment. She recorded pretty much the same rate of false positives no matter the method but Dr. Chatterjee had nothing to worry about, she had a perfect record—"I don't report out a positive unless I'm sure, and I haven't been wrong yet."

Meena had never given thought to lab techs as repositories of information—she had never given much thought to lab techs at all, a fact for which on the drive home she reproached herself bitterly. She could not keep herself from imagining that she had made a terrible mistake in coming here to this hospital, *her* hospital, and trusting Maria Goretti Shaklett, who until this moment struck her as entirely trustworthy, to run this test. Meena had settled on Maria exactly because she was an unmarried woman with a child *born out of wedlock,* as Ginny Rae Drummond said. On Meena's drive to the hospital this logic had made sense, but now with a Band-Aid on her arm and the road a green tunnel through the late summer heat Meena realized that the quality that led her to seek out Maria—the fact that she, the doctor, felt comfortable in asking her to keep a secret—could turn in another direction.

Meena shook her head to clear it of such thoughts. She was being too sensitive, an old problem. Besides which she needed to know and to know fast because if she *were* pregnant she would have to call her medical school colleagues and find someone, somewhere who would terminate as soon as possible, no questions asked, privacy inviolate. Most likely she was worrying about nothing.

And so the doctor set aside her fears, that hairline fracture in time, and concentrated instead on praying, yes, that was the right word for it, *praying,* for—whatever she was praying for. One moment she prayed for the test to be negative, the next she found herself praying for a child, *their* child, *her* child.

Chapter 29

"I have come by some information that I am certain you will find of great interest."

Harry Vetch was facing Maria Goretti across the glassy expanse of his desk. He had been tapping away at his computer keyboard—he kept his fingers on the keys. She wore a sober dark dress and held a canvas tote bag perched on her knees—she might have been the opening speaker in a high school debate. Vetch was touched. At the same time, a small reminder was in order. "Excuse me, but this is ridiculous. We have no claims on each other. I don't know why we're having this conversation."

"We're having this conversation because you know me well enough to know that we would not be having it unless what I know is important."

"On that front I see your point."

"And so, your Honor, may I continue?"

A flick of his hand.

"The doctor is pregnant."

"You don't say."

"I do say and I have proof. I personally processed her pregnancy test. No one is in possession of this knowledge except me. Not even the doctor. I've put her off a day but I'll have to tell her tomorrow."

"And why do you bring this pearl of gossip to me, assuming it to be true, which, by the way, I do not?"

Maria Goretti rolled her eyes. "I hadn't thought that I would have to explain politics to a county attorney, but life is full of surprises and a man's capacity to believe his own fairy tale is never to be underestimated. Nobody in this county cares if a lab tech fucks around—especially an unmarried lab tech who has a child as constant evidence of her questionable character. Nobody cares if a *middle-aged* man fucks around, even if he's the county attorney, so long as he keeps it on the sly. Men will be men, blah-de-blah. But when the dark-skinned unmarried lady doctor from halfway around the world fucks around, people sit up and pay attention."

"I see your point. I'll remind you of what you already know, which is that you are risking at least your job and maybe more in revealing this to anybody. Including me." Maria Goretti was studying him closely. "Maria. I'd prefer you not look at me like I was a specimen under a microscope." He returned to his computer monitor.

"Harry. Do you have any idea—no. Back to your question. Yes, I am well aware that I am risking my job, and no, I don't really know why I'm bringing this pearl—and it *is* a pearl—to you. I laid awake last night, asking myself this very question. And the best answer is the simplest answer. Some kind of commitment to you and, let's face it, the lack of alternatives brings me to your door.

"Dr. Chatterjee has been seen in the company of exactly one man who might conceivably be of interest to a woman of her education and social standing—"

Now he sat back and looked directly at her. "You're not suggesting—"

"'Suggesting' is the perfect word for what I am doing. Not stating. Only suggesting. I am a medical professional. I deal in facts, not gossip. And in this case the facts are that the doctor is pregnant, and that marriage to an American citizen brings benefits that the doctor is surely aware of. The last time I checked, pregnancy requires the presence of another party, the Virgin Mary notwithstanding. So. I thought about that a long time and it came down to this. I don't think you're the father. At first I thought, 'Oh, sure, obviously, Harry.' But having a kid under, let's call them 'unconventional circumstances,' has taught me—for that matter, my kid herself has taught me, that the most obvious explanation is not always the right explanation. Something about the doctor during that visit—I don't know, hard to put a finger to—let's call it an intuition. If *you'd* been the father she'd have been, I don't know. Excited. Or something. And she wasn't. She was—I don't know. Jumpy. Anyway, if you *are* the father, you'll find out soon enough. You must have some idea of what this will mean for your career."

"What do you mean, my career?"

"Jesus, Harry. I have my doubts that you'll ever get married but that's another subject. But why are you so indifferent to getting trapped into it? I am telling you this so that you might think about what it means for the good doctor's future. Even more to the point, for *your* future. And if you're *not* the father—well."

Outside, the silence of the warm afternoon, broken by a sparrow's chatter.

"That damned clock," Maria Goretti muttered. "I don't know—"

And at that moment he knew. *Birdwatching*. In that moment Harry Vetch became both present to and apart from himself. He turned his back to Maria Goretti. He saw himself reflected in the mirror that backed the pendulum clock. Disbelief, uncertainty, grief, rage, jealousy, hatred, betrayal were written on his face in a script that bore the signature of Johnny Faye.

Vetch composed his features. He circled in his seat, saved the document on his monitor, and stood. "If you don't mind. I appreciate your bringing this information to my attention. I will be in touch sooner rather than later, I promise you that. I need some time to think through the right course of action."

"Whatever you want. But I'm telling the doctor tomorrow." Maria Goretti rose and walked to the door and then turned and faced him head-on, crossing her arms. "Harry. Let's forget about facts for a second and think about the truth. You are terrified of love. You use your good looks and your power to lure women in, and then once we're within arm's reach you swing and knock us down—you have to punish yourself for being so weak as to have feelings and punish us for being so stupid as to fall for you. You turn to the bottle to give you the nerve to swing, and then once you've swung you go back to it so you can forget what you've said and done. You go back to it because it will always provide you with a story that makes the other person out to be the villain or at least the sucker. You're a storyteller all right, just as much as the rest of us. Making up stories where you're the hero, and where the other person is too needy, or too demanding, or too something, you fill in the blank, it doesn't matter so long as the problems are their problems and not your problems.

"This is a recipe for disaster, loving somebody who loves the bottle more than me or even himself, but the problem is it's too late, I love you and fuck me for it. I guess it's in my nature to take care of people, that is why I became a health professional and why I had a child.

"You're a facts kind of guy—OK, then here are the facts. You can marry the doctor, which is surely what she will work to make happen, it's what I would do if I was in her boat. And she has the kid seven months from now, tough to explain but I am sure you are capable of explaining it, no matter if it comes out looking like, I don't know. Chicken Little. I will not breathe another word to anybody, you know that.

"Or you can bail on the doctor and keep doing what you're doing until you've fucked every woman dumb enough to let herself get within reach or you're too old to get it up. Which point you're going to reach pretty soon. Do the math.

"You can do one of these things. Or you can choose *the right course of action*. You can quit drinking. You can join forces with the best partner you're likely to find in this life who is eager to help you make something of yourself, whatever that might be. I'd give up drinking in a heartbeat if you'd give it up. I don't even like the stuff and I'd lose a good ten pounds. You've got the ambition and I've got the will to support it. As for everybody else in this podunk corner of the world—ask yourself this question. Do you want to be liked? Or feared? Do you want to spend your life doing what other people want? Or getting what *you* want? You've heard the news about Martin Stead."

"No, I have not heard the news about Martin Stead."

"Another piece of evidence, as if we needed one, of how much more I know about this place than you. Shot himself. DOA in emergency this morning. Somebody turned him in for having pot on his farm and the feds served him with notice to take possession even before serving charges, which was probably the next step and probably would have happened today, as surely he anticipated. That farm had been in his family two hundred years. He had two sons. I guess he figured that if he was out of the way, he could save the farm for them."

"As a matter of fact, that's not at all clear," Vetch said. "His death doesn't change the fact of his breaking the law. They may yet encumber the property. That's what I'd do."

"There is that," Maria Goretti said. She opened the door and stood, hand on the knob, waiting. "There is that. Call me if you want. I won't be calling you." She eased herself out, closing the door with a quiet click.

Vetch opened his desk drawer, pulled out the bottle of whiskey, poured himself a tumbler full, and left the bottle sitting on his desk. He sat long into the evening. At one point he rose from his chair and went to the door and locked it, then shut off his computer. Then he lay on his office floor, his knees curled to his chest. For a long while he lay there, consumed by all the predictable emotions and their attendant fantasies—the confrontation with the doctor, the bitter and contemptuous words. He wanted to weep and shout with pain. He lay silent. In the lambent light of reason the path was as obvious as if some great hand had pointed the way.

He stood and tossed the tumbler of whiskey out the French doors into the garden. He poured the rest of the bottle in the toilet and flushed, then turned back to the French doors to watch the last light of summer fading into night.

Chapter 30

And so she was pregnant. With child. She could not be pregnant. She must not be pregnant. *I don't report out a positive unless I'm sure and I haven't been wrong yet.* There must be some mistake. There was no mistake. The test confirmed what she had already known. She would get an abortion. Someone from her medical retraining could provide a reference. Phoning someone and asking would be the greatest imaginable embarrassment but they all lived at some considerable distance and what did she care? No great problem. A weekend out of town. No one would notice. She would close the office on Saturday and with luck be back on Monday, though to be safe she had better close Tuesday as well and then the office was closed Wednesdays, a nice little vacation. She would get an abortion. She would not get an abortion. Shouldn't she consult the father? Fuck the father. You see, she was learning American English, small town, *jungli* American English. "Fuck the father." She spoke the words out loud. Such useful words, so satisfying on the tongue. "Fuck the father." I beg your pardon, Doctor Chatterjee, but that is the problem. You *did* fuck the father. The father fucked you. You're fucked, as the father might say, exactly so. What was she to do? She would lose her position, she would have to return to Bengal, pregnant. Disgrace on two continents, not so easily accomplished and she had accomplished it. No, in Calcutta worse than disgrace. She and the child would be without money, without relatives. And the father. Who is the father? The obvious question that no one would ask and everyone would ask. Disgrace. How could she burden a child, her child, with such a fate? How could she take this child back to that world? She longed to go to Johnny Faye. She longed to fuck him, as a matter of fact, and her desire was a horror and a boundless need. She could not bear the child. The duplicity of words: She could not *bear* returning to Bengal, where disgrace lay in her barrenness. She could not *bear* the child here, where disgrace lay in her fertility. But she would bear the child. If she had to return to Bengal, if she had to undo all she had done, she would bear the child. She could never return to Bengal. A single mother, no, not single, still married, she had never divorced but simply walked away, and now a child *born out of wedlock*, who is the father? Inconceivable. Not to be conceived. But the child had been conceived—she had conceived it. Her. Him. With help, of course. Should she not tell the father? She would not tell the father. She would let Harry Vetch fuck her and see where that led. After seven months, with luck maybe more, first babies often took their time, the child would be born. By then Harry Vetch might be her husband, a marriage her grandparents might have arranged except that she had arranged it by herself as she had done so much, most everything by herself—except conceive this child. She would marry the county attorney and she would not tell anyone her secret, not even the child. And if the marriage ended in divorce, in this country that was of no great consequence and she would still possess the papers and their magic seals, she would be legal, she would be American. It made so much sense. No, a better plan: abortion, then marriage. No need to take risks. What if she never conceived again? With an attorney as her husband, so much the better. She did not need a child. Had she not made her way this far alone? She did not need anyone, except as a means to the end of the piece of paper that would allow her to make her way in this new world where she had come to be herself. She was a wanderer, a foreigner. She had no home but herself and her work.

She went to the statues at midday. He was not there. Suffocating heat. She might as well be in Bengal. The sun a hot white presence in a cloudless sky. No rain. Why had there been no rain? If there had been rain she would not have come to the statues, she would not have been fucked. When would it rain? The statues were no help. Jesus in agony, littered with pine needles and resin. She sat on the fallen pine and dangled her feet over the hollow that had once writhed with snakes. Nothing now but an empty hole. She was not barren. She had conceived. A miracle. She had conceived a miracle. Unto her a child. The Lord has taken away the disgrace I have endured among my people. All generations will call me blessed. Thanks be to the Loretines for teaching me the words. An abortion, easily enough accomplished, problem solved. Later, much later, perhaps another child by another father. A respectable father. A father worthy of a Brahmin. An attorney, perhaps the county attorney. Not now. I cannot bear the child. This, my child. She placed her hand on her womb. You, our child. I am so sorry. A few days' holiday, a quick journey north, the problem solved, all problems solved. I cannot bear this child. Meena wept. I will not bear this child. I will not bear this child and I will marry Harry Vetch. It makes so much sense. I am so sorry.

Chapter 31

Officer Smith stood before Harry Vetch, smoking a cigarette. The sun was a fist on their bare heads. At the far end of Ridgeview Pointe a lone backhoe roared and farted and puttered about. With each pass at the dry earth a cloud of red dust rose and drifted the length of the project to settle on their shoulders.

"Do you have any idea," Vetch asked, "why I have asked you to meet me here?" He loosened his tie.

Smith took his cigarette between thumb and forefinger and sucked hard before exhaling a cloud of smoke. "No, sir."

"Or why I asked you to wear your uniform on your day off."

"No, sir."

"Look about you. This is a public place—we have nothing to hide." He waved the length of the development at the backhoe operator. "Go on, give him a wave, you know him, Dakin Thompson's son." The officer lifted his hand. "Now." Vetch began to pace. "Let's start with the obvious and say that I have asked you to come here because I am concerned about vandalism. I would like you to make your presence known out here from time to time, maybe even leave your patrol car parked here overnight. You got that? Secure the perimeters, that sort of thing. Good. I want you to exercise a little imagination. You know what imagination is?"

"Yes, sir, I guess so."

"For our purposes imagination is the talent to perceive trouble before it happens and then act to defuse it or, if that's not possible, then to deflect it onto somebody else. Now, if I were to ask you what you think about the people who are growing marijuana in this county, what would you say?"

"Well, sir, I'd say they are breaking the law and that it is my responsibility to see that they are arrested and prosecuted."

"That's right, that's good. But what if you arrest them and they're prosecuted but their friends and family see that they go free? What would you say to that?"

"I'd do my best to arrest them again."

"Thereby wasting the taxpayers' money. Unless you count the spectacle of their coming before the court and you hauled in to testify and me losing the case as entertainment worth the public expense."

Smith sucked again at his cigarette. Vetch pulled a handkerchief from his pocket and mopped at his forehead but the sweat came as fast as he could wipe it away. His handkerchief was a smudge of orange. "Now, if I were to ask you if you smoke or have ever smoked marijuana, what would you say to that?"

"No, sir, I do not smoke marijuana."

"And you have never smoked it."

"Sir, I'm not sure where you're going with these questions—"

"What if I asked if you had any idea as to the whereabouts of a considerable amount of marijuana that disappeared from the inventory of the crop taken from the farm of Martin Stead? What if I asked about the precise nature of your relationship with, to select a name at random, Benny Joe, the guy they call Little?"

Officer Smith's expression changed from a squint against the sun to a sullen scowl. "I'd tell you I have to protect my sources. Sir."

"I can well imagine that you do. Have to protect your sources. Don't worry, it's a rhetorical question. By that I mean I don't want you to answer it. Don't answer it."

The officer took out sunglasses but before he could put them on Vetch lifted them from his hand. "Not just yet. I have a few more questions." He resumed his pacing. "Have you ever killed a man?"

"No, sir. Well. There was once when a guy had me cornered in a stairwell and he raised a Louisville Slugger over his head and I said, 'Drop it or you're a dead man,' and I had my gun on him faster than he could swing and sure enough he dropped it."

"But you would have killed him."

"Yes, sir. It was him or me and I knew which one I wanted to come out of that building feet first."

Harry Vetch halted in his pacing in front of the officer's sweat-soaked chest. "What if it wasn't you or him? I mean, what if the questions weren't so clear-cut? Let me give you an example. What if somebody was threatening you and your home or maybe your community or even your country—that's a good example. The president of your country calls you to war and you go, and after a few months you find yourself with a gun in your hand, firing across a field at some man who has never done you the slightest harm, that if you met him in the Miracle Inn you might buy him a beer and shoot a game of pool. Would you kill that man?"

"Yes, sir, I would."

"And why would you kill him, when he's done you no harm?"

"Because it was my duty. If I was a soldier and he's the enemy and we're at war."

Vetch clapped him on the shoulder. "Now you're talking. Long story short, Smith, we *are* at war, President Reagan has told us so. We're fighting the war on drugs and you're a front-line soldier in one of the hot spots, one of the main battlegrounds, and you've got a chance to make a difference for your kids."

"She only has one boy, sir, and he's a runt if I have to say so myself."

"We are, as you know, one of the nation's hotbeds of marijuana production. And you know who is the mastermind of that. You know who brought it into our lives, made it happen almost singlehandedly. The same man who impersonated you—who used *your* good name—in stealing a truckload of air conditioners."

Officer Smith was silent.

An especially big cloud of dust rose from the backhoe. The county attorney's tongue stuck to the roof of his mouth. "If you should find yourself in a difficult situation—and you understand, I hope, the nature of the situation to which I refer—I want you to know that I will be behind you to the fullest extent. Beyond the fullest extent, if that becomes necessary. Do you understand?"

The officer nodded.

"I'd like to hear you say it aloud."

"Yes, sir. I understand that in any difficult situations you are behind me up to and beyond the fullest extent of the law."

"I want you to know that I understand that you are the first interface between the law and the criminal, and that I further understand that in the course of your duties you encounter situations that require on-the-spot reaction. If in the course of the pursuit of your duties circumstances should put you in a difficult position, I want you to know both that I trust your judgment in acting on the spot, and that I want you to use discretion in contacting the appropriate authorities. Let me be clear on this point. In any genuinely difficult situation, I want to be the first person whom you call. Even before the sheriff. He may be your boss but I am charged with protecting you from any parties who might question your judgment. And as I hope I have made clear, I do not question your judgment. So far as I am concerned, your judgment *is* the law." The backhoe revved up for a last assault. Vetch raised his voice to a near shout. "What I am saying"—here Vetch drew in very close to the policeman and gave him a hard and direct look—"what I am saying is that you may be sure that I will not ask you for information that I do not need. I will not ask you—"

Dakin Thompson's son killed the backhoe engine, which died with a rattle and cough. The roar tangled itself in the branches of the forest before fading to silence. Vetch lowered his voice with each word until he was near a whisper.

"—for more information than you care to volunteer. Should you decide that illegal behavior that frustrates the channels of the law might require a more direct approach."

"Yes, sir. I understand that. And I can be plenty direct if the situation calls for it."

"I'm glad to hear it. Courage carves its own path and, I assure you, will receive its appropriate reward."

Dakin Thompson's son jumped from the backhoe and beckoned them over. The two men crossed the field to inspect the hole. "How do, Mr. Vetch. Hot enough for you?"

"It's getting there," Vetch said.

In the hole they could see a green-striped upholstery spotted with dirt but otherwise none the worse for its time in the earth. "You're lucky we had such a dry summer," the driver said. "If we'd had a lot of rain this baby would be toast. I might have it out of there by the end of the day, if you want to ride back out here and check."

"I might be back," Vetch said. "Depends on how mad I am at the end of the day and how much madder I want to get." He handed Smith his sunglasses, then took him by the elbow and steered him toward the car. "The situation we are facing in this county calls for action. In the course of that action you might find it necessary to go to the dark side. You take that away and think about it and then you do what you think best when and where the opportunity presents. And if it doesn't present, then you think about how a successful man makes his own opportunities and how you are the front line of the law and how the law will back you up." Vetch handed the officer his sunglasses. "Go ahead, put them on. Now. About that missing marijuana. Whoever took it took the best buds, not the leaf, so he had some idea of what he was doing. And since you just told me you've never smoked marijuana—that is what you told me, correct?—you don't know your pot, so obviously you have no knowledge of this incident. You might mention it, however, among your *friends* and *contacts*"—here he paused a moment—"just so the message gets around. And you might think very carefully about what I've said to you and the possibilities it offers for advancing yourself in the eyes of the authorities to whom you are ultimately responsible."

And then the county attorney climbed into his Mustang and was gone, leaving Smith to his small battered truck with only a windshield and a roof between him and the blazing late summer sun.

Chapter 32

September. A lazy Sunday afternoon, the planet turning its other cheek to the sun. Leaves were still green but the forest had exhausted itself and with every shortening day a little more of its life drained back into the earth's dark heart. Here and there amid the dusty green a staghorn sumac showed forth autumn's bright scarlet. The showiest flowers of late summer—the black-eyed Susans and the bright purple ironweed—were mostly gone, though the fields were still lively with sky-blue asters and nodding goldenrod and tall wands of mullein now past their bloom. In his childhood Johnny Faye's mother had cut and soaked their dried blossoms in lard so as to use them as torches to light her way about her winter chores. She still called them "Our Lady's candles" and gathered their basal leaves for tea and poultices. Johnny Faye would gather some this evening, after he checked his crop for the last time. The next time he returned, he would bring clippers and sacks and harvest in a day what the earth and sun and their shaping hands had taken a season to grow. He could have harvested today—a fine day to bring in the crop, the bright cloudless September sky and all around him the knowledge of the long sleep shortly to come—but though Flavian's company and help had been excellent he was after all a monk, and Johnny Faye thought it would be bad manners to harvest in the presence of a monk. Besides which, Johnny Faye was planning a little surprise and he didn't want the day cluttered with too many projects.

And so he arrived and stripped to his waist—such pleasure to feel the sun as a beneficent caress instead of high summer's hammer. He climbed down the bluff and into the creek bed, where he clipped a few leaves that were shading the buds from their last, finishing bath of light. The thumb-length buds all but dripped resin—from the lip of the bluff, on the breathless still-leafed air Johnny Faye could smell their sweet cloy, and down in the creek the smell was overwhelming and that was good. All the power of this perfect place, this perfect summer, was contained in these perfect buds. Four or five months hence he would lift a burning brand from an open hearth and use it to light his pipe and in a single puff release every moment of this hot, dry summer, all those hours and days when he had not been at hand but the plants had understood that theirs was a good life and had made the most of it. Time would cease to be, and for some brief while he would understand time as the conjurer's trick that it is.

He laid aside his clippers and retrieved his walking stick and squatted in front of the bank of clay. JC stirred himself from his shaded bed of leaves to come and watch this curious human act.

"Hey, JC. Watch this."

He crouched and dug the tip of his walking stick into the glistening gray clay and closed his eyes and allowed his hand to carve what his body remembered:

J-O-H-N-N-Y F-A-Y-E

and when his body remembered nothing more he stood up and stood back and looked at what he had written, the marks he had made, the writing on the wall. He couldn't exactly say that he *read* them— he knew what he was doing bore no relation to real reading, he had seen people read, sucking their teeth, the flutter of pages under their fingers like flying autumn leaves, one hand held to the throat, their eyes cast down and fixed in single-pointed concentration, lost to time and space as surely as if they were dreaming or making love, and when they looked up the dream still in their eyes, magnified and obscured by spectacles. Forty years old and Johnny Faye could spot and name a warbler in heavy brush at fifty yards and still he envied them those spectacles, key to the lock on a door to a world he would never know—magic, mystery, *reading*. All the same, he surveyed the marks he had made and knew they were close enough, that anybody who came across them would read his name and know that he had been here. He had made his mark in time.

He laid his walking stick on the grassy ledge above the printed words and climbed up into the sycamore throne to study what he had wrought. He glanced up at the sun—it was past noon, Flavian might be along any minute. Johnny Faye leaned his head against the trunk and closed his eyes and gave himself over to imagining how Flavian would climb down the cliff. At first he would not see the writing—however smart he was, Flavian was not keen at seeing what was right beneath his nose. He probably wouldn't even notice until he, Johnny Faye, scrambled down from his sycamore seat and took Flavian's hand and pointed it out. Flavian would admire what he had written—crouched to the clay he would trace each letter with his forefinger and he would spell them out loud for Johnny Faye and all their babes to hear.

J-O-H-N-N-Y F-A-Y-E

And then they would make love properly, like two friends each of whom wanted to see what the other looked like with his clothes off and by the way is it OK if I put my hand here? And here? And if I use the scrub brush of my tongue to clean out the pit of your arm, that well of olfactory wonders? And what about this, yes, the rosebud of the lips around the stiff prick of love?

A sleepless night. Meena rose early. Sunday, the office closed. She did not feel well, though it was impossible to say whether it was her pregnancy or her agony or both. To abort the child, impossible, but she would make possible the impossible. She had done so many times. To marry the county attorney and endure, what. Two years? Five years? She had done it before. It was what women did. How interesting, if she rose above herself and looked down from the perspective of the goddess, how utterly inescapably the way things will always be that even as a doctor, even in America she was a woman in a woman's place. She had set out to change and shape her destiny, and here she was.

The blind drew Meena back.

As a child the stars had been the roof of her world as the earth beneath her bare feet had been its floor. The women in their patterned saris of azure and emerald and copper winding through the paddies to the day's work, the vendors of yellow-green bananas and coconuts, the policemen in their starched whites, the men driving cattle through the shady lanes, the beggars in their despair, real and faked, the misshapen bodies of the deformed, each living as she could. Food vendors' plates of recycled cardboard and banana leaf. The smell of cooking in the streets; the smell of tuberoses and defecation and diesel exhaust in the streets. The pressing crowds of dark-skinned people, her people, Durga Puja and the village priests have chosen her as the reincarnation of Durga, her people have dressed her in scarlet silk and crowd around the puja as a priest in white muslin sprinkles them with Ganges water using a stem of basil, placing handfuls of marigold and hibiscus petals into their outstretched hands, as incense burns and the drummers beat a wild rhythm against the backdrop of Durga indifferently piercing a blue-complected Azul with her trident. The Devi has chosen her for a special destiny.

Then the war. First the Army, then the collaborators, then the greedy neighbors sweep into their village to steal, rape, rob. Women are special targets. Those who are able flee to Calcutta. Her father stays because of the land, to save the land for her, his only child. Her mother stays because her father stays. They have no experience of an army, how fast it can move, how far it can reach. Who could have thought that in the remote villages there would be such carnage? This is the work of the collaborators.

Her father delivers her across the border to her mother's parents. She becomes a stranger from her home until many years pass and—married now—she is allowed to return. She takes a train to Calcutta, from there a bus and then a hired moto to the village of her parents. A young Muslim couple lives in the home she once called hers. Someone has replaced the roof—it had been thatched, now it is tile. They tell her they bought the house from a man who has left the village. They do not know who owned the house and the land before him, he had not spoken of her parents, no, so very sorry. Meena believes and does not believe. She returns to Bengal. Within the month she is gone from her husband's house. She takes only her dowry jewels, sewed into the hem of her sari.

Arriving at Howrah Station, an endless interrogation into the mystery of suffering. The monsoons have prolonged themselves, the tracks are flooded, the train is late, the station a vast space teeming with life and death, the refuge of those who have no refuge, in a sea of faces they are living and dying. Her second time in Calcutta since her childhood visits with her father. She enters the great station, past extended hands and pleading eyes, the blind, the lame, the starving. She walks out into the streets, where the sky threatens, dense clouds, no rain, when rain might have opened her way, cleared her a path through all this life, all this suffering. On the plaza jackdaws move among the dying, ready to thieve—if the dying devote a moment's attention to their pain the jackdaws swoop in and steal what little they have. Meena picks her way through the healthy and the dead, the dying and the sick whom in a few days she will see again, yes, that is why she is here, sitting with the dead but on her way to medical school, she has broken with all that has come before, she has rent the fabric of time. She will become a doctor, Dr. Chatterjee. She will devote her life to saving those she loves. She will break from all she has known and flee to the antiseptic and enlightened West. She will apply her mind to the task and she will save them all, all those she loves. She will seize and shape her destiny.

Her first examining room at the Medical College—her first patient, a bicycle rickshaw driver. A simple enough problem—an open sore on the sole of his foot, the wound so deep the bone is visible through the ooze, but he must pedal his rickshaw if his wife and children are to eat, what is to be done? He walks barefoot across a tile floor encrusted with mold and the dried mucus and phlegm and pus of a thousand illnesses, ten thousand lives, ten thousand deaths. A simple matter of antibiotics and antiseptic and bandages and time but there are no antibiotics, no antiseptics, no bandages, there is only time. He sits on the examination table, present to all the infections of today and days before. He displays his wound and grins, a gap-toothed smile full of life. He has found his savior and she can do nothing. Everyone she once loved is dead.

Then the stars vanish from her life, she lives in cities until she finds herself an exile in this dark countryside amid these temperate jungles. For years she had protected herself—filled out forms, shouldered her way to the front of lines, studied, planned, pleaded, maneuvered. What strange confluence of events, what configuration of these northern stars had brought her to be carrying a lawless man's child?

She drove to the monastery and parked at the graveled pullout for the statues. She understood that Johnny Faye might be at the statues at any time but she was resolute—though she knew that were she to encounter him all would be lost. After she parked she composed a note. *I am so sorry. With time I hope you may forgive. Meena.*

She walked to the statues and turned left to climb to the blind. How cleverly he had concealed it—not even a sharp-eyed hawk could discern it among the bushes and briars. She must not dawdle. Outside the blind she found a honey locust. She plucked one of its thorns. She parted the vine curtain of the blind and stepped inside and in that moment she is swimming in a great river of life, the crocodile- and snake-infested waters of her childhood, she is swimming upstream, always upstream. As she swims the dead of her life drift past—her mother (had she known of her husband's infidelity? The question occurs as Meena swims against the strengthening current), her father dressed in a Western suit and tie and radiant with the same anticipation that had governed her own life these past few weeks. Johnny Faye drifts by—he wears a dhoti and has arranged himself across a floating log and as he passes he turns to her with his chipped-tooth grin and holds out his hand. She *the doctor of the flesh, not the spirit* wants to stop swimming and drift downstream at his side, she who has never known desire now seized in its fist and dragged in its wake, but the river that is carrying him to the great sea is the river in which she may drown and she is carrying their child and so she continues to swim upstream. She fights the flood—she has never been so alive, swimming upstream. On each bank the trees drop their leaves and bare their branches. The water turns cold, she has swum that far north.

She found herself lying on the earthen floor of the blind. In her limbs she felt the first chill of winter. In her womb she felt life. She stood and pinned her note to the door of the blind where surely he would see it, though she knew that on this front she need not concern herself. Nothing was lost on him who was always paying attention.

Flavian was an agony of guilt and desire. For a week now his loins had burned. At first he balked at thinking of himself in that melodramatic way, so much a product of that side of Saint Paul that he detested. But two and three days passed and every night he bolted awake for no reason other than from the pure heat of his longing. In the solitude of his bed he gave himself over to it—how else could he get through the next day?—but the harder he punished his cock, the more it sprang back unfazed, eager for more. It knew what it wanted—it knew what *he* wanted, which was Johnny Faye's plank-hard body next to him, on top of him, under and yes, inside him. There. He had said it, or at least allowed himself to think it and by God it was no more or less than what he had read some years back in Saint Theresa, Doctor of the Church, in a passage so steamy that it made him blush and shut the book, never to pick it up again even as he had taken care to dog-ear the page and in a library book, no less. Snatches from it came to him of their own accord, bolts of lightning illuminating his dark night . . . *an angel in bodily form, bearing a great golden spear tipped with fire, that he plunged and plunged again into her heart and beyond until it penetrated her very entrails,* a word engraved in Flavian's memory because so uncommon and so true. And what lay in those entrails but her great love of God, the great sweet love of God that Flavian had been seeking all along. In that union with another soul he would find that which he sought, he would find ecstasy, he would find faith, he would find God.

And following these thoughts came the thunder of accusation: *Blasphemy!*

His whole being latched onto these images for long day-dreaming minutes at a time until the voice of his reason asserted itself and wrenched him back to the job at hand. Was not wisdom defined as control of the passions? And this desire for an illiterate criminal, of all passions! My God, what had he sunk to? Alone in his bed, fumbling at his privates he sought to call to mind the image of Jesus crucified, but the moment he lost himself to what he was doing lanky Johnny Faye came to mind, with his smart mouth and thick lips and chipped white horse's teeth and loud laugh and stringy sun-streaked hair and big hard dick, my God.

This went on for the week and then it was Sunday and he knew that Johnny Faye would be at the creek with JC and 'Sweet.

And so the mass. Flavian pulled on the snowy white alb, then the black hooded scapular, then cinched them with the wide brown leather belt. He took his place in his stall and went through the motions. The readings and the sermon washed over his head. He felt his desire was branded on his alb for all to see and that the abbot would surely say something that everyone would know was intended expressly for him and he silently welcomed public embarrassment. Nothing. And then the liturgy of the sacrifice, the ancient blood rites disguised as theater but still fraught with visceral power for anyone who was paying attention. The bread becomes flesh, the wine becomes blood, we eat the flesh and drink the blood. Compared to this, the central ritual of his religion, sex seemed like horseplay. Even sex with Johnny Faye. Here Flavian was at the focal point of all he believed, the elevation of the host and chalice, and what was he but a flaming pillar of desire, the tool of, no, the devil himself, incarnate.

Then the abbot raised the host and Flavian understood that it was not a symbol of anything. It was what it was, as real as dreams or love, a living breathing presence in their midst, daily resurrected. He was naked, stripped bare. The body had brought him to the abyss.

He fell to the floor and cried out. The abbot stopped the service; his brothers rushed to his side. Brother Flavian looked up—he had never seen the church in this way. The thought occurred that he is where he is supposed to be. A barn swallow peered through a crack in the stained glass—she hopped through and fluttered to her nest, clinging to the highest rafter. Lying on the floor, looking up, Flavian saw. Because of Johnny Faye, he saw.

The noonday meal came and went. Flavian ate nothing. He climbed to his cell and lay down. He was aflame with desire. He looked at the little windup clock, a hand-me-down from some traveling Catholic matron. He watched its second hand tick by. He stood and paced. He lay down. This was unbearable. Every cell of his body, every cell of the living loving world was a summons to his foolish heart *Go, go!* And still he fought back, and still he said no.

He lifted his mattress and retrieved the stuffed manila envelope, with its block printing DONATION TO THE DESERVING. Not troubling to change from his formal robes he descended the stairs—

the place was still as death, the monks all napping. He entered the pure bright blue light of late summer and crossed the state highway, through the gate. At the fork he summoned his will, he called to it in prayer, and he turned his feet not toward the forest and its cedar thicket and the oxbow bend in the creek but toward the statues.

Flavian walked past the sleeping brothers, straight to Jesus in agony. He fell to his knees at Jesus' side.

"Help me do the right thing."

Silence.

"Save me in my time of trial." He laid the envelope at Jesus's feet.

Nothing.

And meanwhile all he wanted, all he wanted, was to lie in his vagabond lover's arms.

And he didn't go, and he didn't go. The sun disappeared behind a scud of gray clouds and still he remained on his knees. At one point he wrapped his arms around the statue, half expecting that it would come to life and he would be saved by the miracle of stone into flesh, by the life- and love-giving touch of Jesus, come to life to rescue him from himself. But the statue was only cold stone that left his hands feeling greasy and chilled.

The sun slipped lower, below the spreading crown of sycamore leaves until a gray high cast of clouds covered it, and still Johnny Faye slept on. Only JC's bark roused him upright. The filtered green autumnal light, the creek's gurgle and slurp, the heady smell of the marijuana buds, but something was wrong—JC never barked, not down here. Flavian was coming—late, but he was here—except that by now JC knew Flavian like a brother and wouldn't bark at him. Johnny Faye sat up, cleared his head, and understood what was wrong. Flavian had not come, Flavian was not coming. On the still sweet air he heard the bells for Benediction. He did not want to stand and slide down the trunk to the fertile creek bottom dirt because once his feet were on the ground there would be no escaping the fact of the matter. Flavian had not come; Flavian would not come.

Johnny Faye let himself down from the tree. JC was up on all fours, a poised bundle of nervous energy with one ear cocked and his nose in the air, but Johnny Faye called him down "*JC!*" in a tone of voice that meant business and after a moment of canine doubt he trotted to Johnny Faye's feet and Johnny Faye squatted and took his head between his hands. "He's not coming, JC, and it's OK."

His heart was a trash-filled sinkhole and JC's eyes were two dark wells of doubt. Johnny Faye gathered his tools and pulled on his white cotton singlet and an old flannel shirt—summer's end and the surest sign was the cool wet dark that during July's high heat hid out under fallen tree trunks and in the mouths of the muskrat dens but now filled the creek bottom, the sun hidden by clouds. Still Johnny Faye dawdled, waiting, even as he told himself that he was only taking his time, but finally the facts of the matter were plain. Johnny Faye climbed from the creek bed and untied 'Sweet's bridle, mounted, tied his stick to the pommel, and rode into the forest.

But instead of returning home he rode to the statues. He would go to wait at the blind he had built for the night she had entered it and made it the temple that it was, plump and sweet as an autumn quail, all curves and flesh, this summer-ripe peach cupped in his hand, his fingers tracing the line of her love. Oh, he was a lucky man, and if this could not last, let it be what it was for as long as it was given to him to love. He had hunted enough deer to know that this moment drew power from its uncertainty, from his knowledge that most likely nothing would happen, most likely she would not come but then again she had come before at times of her choosing, miracles had been known to happen, they wrote about them in books.

Sunday afternoon and Smith stood at an entrance to the woods, shotgun in hand, .357 in his belt. Squirrel and dove season was not yet officially open but since he was low in seniority he was stuck with a weekend shift and he would end up working almost two weeks without a break, and so he felt entitled to stretch the rules in his favor. In any case when you got right down to it, *he* was the law, Harry Vetch had told him so and nobody was likely to give him any trouble.

The day was warm and blue and though autumn was just around the corner he saw no evidence of it except in a certain quality of light that gave the feeling of decline and slippage. Smith entered the woods via a familiar path that led through a gravelly flat that in his childhood had been scattered with flint arrowheads. These had long been picked over by children—no one had found an arrowhead in years. This saddened him—as a child he had ventured into these woods often, sometimes by way of escaping his father's drunken hand, and though he had never found an arrowhead, he had been sustained by the hope that one fine day he might come upon this remnant of a time when a man had no measure other than his skill at returning home from the hunt with his hands full of game. Charged by the fantasy of finding an arrowhead he returned home to dream of using a pliable strand of wild grape to lash his imaginary pointed flint to an imaginary shaft formed from an imaginary straight twig of ash. In his heart he fletched it with found feathers and proved his woodsman's skills by shooting the finished arrow into his father's neck.

As if in response to Smith's thoughts the buck materialized. A magnificent buck, too many points to count, the kind of animal one did not see in these woods or in any forest outside the verdant forest of every hunter's imagination. A brisk breeze stirred the leaves and carried away both the policeman's scent and any noise he might have made—otherwise he could never have come within shooting range of this beautiful creature, who could not have attained his age and stature without some understanding of the ways of men in general and of hunters in particular. His appearance was luck of the kind that Officer Smith had known little of in his life and he was not about to let it slip. He was indifferent to the meat. He wanted that rack. He raised his handgun and fired.

The deer's hindquarters buckled. Officer Smith darted forward, gun drawn, but the buck was off into the forest, leaving a trail of broken twigs and green leaves spotted with bright red blood. Officer Smith followed him deeper into the forest—so deep that he lost track of his surroundings and still he pressed on. Through the dusty hot September green he could hear the animal's thrashings—it was wounded badly enough that if Smith could sustain the stamina required to struggle up and down gullies, through briars, over creeks, sooner or later he would catch his prey.

And he kept going, following the buck through the most rugged terrain until finally he arrived at a clearing in the forest with no buck to be seen or heard. He tried to still his pounding heart so as to listen. Nothing. He saw blood at his feet—the deer had passed this way only to disappear.

He faced a dense stand of blue-berried cedars overgrown with honeysuckle, wild grape, cat brier. He had trouble imagining threading a needle through growth so dense but he saw no other possible route for his quarry. Several times he tried to force his way through the wall of green, only to be driven back by the scratchy cedars and the thorns of blackberry canes mingled with cat brier. Finally he raised his arms to the sky and cursed his luck out loud.

During his dash through the woods a dense cloud cover had moved in, so dense that the sun was useless in helping him determine east from west—on top of his misfortune he stood every chance of getting soaked. He kicked savagely at the unyielding limbs and then took his buck knife and began hacking one branch at a time until he cleared a large enough hole to push through, slapped and scratched by cedars and briars, but after several moments he emerged from their tight-fisted hostility to find himself overlooking an oxbow bend in a creek he had never before seen, he who knew this forest like the innards of his guns.

He walked to the lip of the creek's deep smile. Below him, thrusting through rows of cornstalks, as astonishing a sight as the buck—the most luxuriant patch of marijuana he had ever encountered.

He dropped to the ground. He lay there for a heart-pounding moment, then edged forward until he was peering through the broom sage that lined the lip of the steep bank. For several minutes he lay listening—still as ice; it might have been a frozen January afternoon instead of the overcast warmth of September with thunder distantly intermittent. Time passed until finally he summoned the nerve to scramble down the bank and justify his eyes. It was marijuana all right, cleverly concealed from any low-flying plane by rows of now-yellowing corn and soon to be harvested. The buds were longer than his thumb and so pungent that he could smell their thick narcotic scent on the warm still dog-day air. The policeman reached into the densest part of the patch—where even the most careful grower would not notice—and pinched off a few buds and tucked them in his pocket.

Elated, he turned to go. He had set out in pursuit of big prey but this was bigger, this could make his career—a promotion, a regular schedule, weekends off to hunt like a civilized man. And then he was facing the creek's clay wall and etched into its shiny blue-gray self was

J-O-H-N-N-Y F-A-Y-E

Smith read it three times, then he stirred himself from where he had gone, the dream of a new life catalyzing in his mind.

His first thought was to drive immediately to the county attorney's office, but then he calmed himself and took satisfaction in his new-found maturity. *No. This discovery could be of great service to me and Johnny Faye is not going anywhere, not until he brings in this crop.*

And then he heard someone coming through the cedar copse and he leapt behind the three-branched sycamore.

Eventide and Flavian climbed stiffly from where for some timeless while he had been kneeling next to Jesus in agony. His knees were in agony, though not enough to take his mind off his desire. Stand-ing, he felt the sharp corner of something prick his leg—he fished in his pocket and pulled out the day's reading.

Early in the morning Jesus came again to the temple. All the people came to him and he sat down and began to teach them. The scribes and the Pharisees brought a woman who had been caught in adultery; and making her stand before all of them, they said to him, "Teacher, this woman was caught in the very act of committing adultery. Now in the law Moses commanded us to stone such women. What do you say?" They said this to test him, so that they might have some charge to bring against him. Jesus bent down and wrote with his finger in the sand. When they kept on questioning him, he straightened up and said to them, "Let anyone among you who is without sin be the first to throw a stone at her." And once again he bent down and wrote on the ground. When they heard it, they went away one by one, beginning with the elders; and Jesus was left alone with the woman standing before him. Jesus straightened up and said to her, "Woman, where are they? Has no one condemned you?" She said, "No one, sir." And Jesus said, "Neither do I condemn you. Go your way, and from now on do not sin again."

On reading these words Flavian rejoiced—they seemed placed by the Spirit in his pocket to convey the message that even a sin so great as his might be forgiven. For the first time that week, his desire lifted from him and he felt some kind of peace. He was lost in an avalanche of feelings and thoughts but he tried simply to be present to his deliverance, to be grateful even for his tempta-tion, without which he would never have known the dimensions of his weakness. Johnny Faye had been his instrument of grace, sent to teach him the breadth and depth and height of his sin.

Meena stepped outside the blind to see Flavian kneeling by the statues. No moment so private as a moment of prayer, more private even than lovemaking, and she remained motionless against the blind. Then he stood and brushed the leaves from his robe and took a paper from his pocket and began to read. How plain and perfect was his robe! How handsome in ivory and black, the very expression in cloth of submission to the beauty of all that is.

When he finished his reading and had folded and tucked the paper in his pocket she walked down the slope. A little cough so as not to startle.

"My Lord. How long have you been here?"

She pointed up the hill. "I sit there sometimes to watch for birds—you cannot see it, but there is a blind built for that purpose. What are you doing here?"

"It's Sunday. I come here sometimes on Sunday. You know that."

"Of course. To pray."

Silence, broken by familiar bird song, a pure and bouncing melody.

"I guess I should be going or I'll be late for Benediction. It sneaks up on me—the sun sets so much earlier these days. And these clouds—it will be dark early tonight."

"Yes."

"Would you like someone to accompany you back to your car?"

"No, no, I'm quite fine, thank you. I enjoy this time of day. A good time to see birds, you know."

"Yes, so I have been given to understand. Well, you take care of yourself. Don't get wet."

"Yes, thank you."

He bent to retrieve the fat manila envelope, leaning against the statue of Jesus. He paused for a moment, considering, then thrust it at her. "This is for you," he said. "From Johnny Faye. A gift. Please. It's honest money, honest come by. At least, that's what he told me. I meant to give it to you a long time ago. Better late than never. Use it according to your judgment. You'll be doing me a favor to take it."

For a long moment she studied it. She made no protest. "I understand," she said. "I will see that it gets to those who deserve it."

Flavian walked rapidly away.

She sat on the bench and watched until he was out of sight, then she rose and returned to her car.

At the fork in the path Flavian's feet turned not toward the monastery but toward the cedar copse and the oxbow bend. He kept walking. Johnny Faye had surely gone home by now but Flavian could offer him a sign that he had stayed away not from anger but because the equinox was upon them, time to leave behind his summer foolishness and return to God. To vanish without some kind of sign would have been the height of bad manners, or so Flavian argued to himself, and though his gesture had about it an element of the alcoholic swearing *this drink will be my last,* nonetheless he pressed on in the failing light.

By the time he arrived the creek bed was lit only by the sunset light that remained in the overcast sky. The moon was just shy of full but it was no more than an occasional dull brightness through the clouds. The cedars that for the summer's length had been so kind were now knitted in some kind of autumn resistance and only his determination and his knowledge of what lay on the other side enabled him to push through. Now he stood at the lip of the bluff—no evidence of Johnny Faye.

Flavian climbed into the great three-armed throne and closed his eyes. The burble of the creek, the cool moist air that rose from it, the smooth round solid sycamore. This was the place. How could love be a sin? How could it be that sin—a word, an act so small and mean—could have any relation to this looping, benevolent place on God's earth, where he had tried his best to teach and Johnny Faye had tried his best to learn? Maybe the evil lay elsewhere—not in this place but in the recesses of his own heart, which demanded that Johnny Faye be someone other than who he was. What did it matter, finally, if he could read and write, or even if he broke the laws of man, when he knew and honored the law that mattered—the law of love—love of the Lord thy God, and of thy neighbor as thyself? Indeed the two of them, the monk and the soldier, were teacher and student, but considered in this light had not Johnny Faye, the student, taught Flavian, his teacher, the more valuable lesson?

Flavian decended from the tree. At the edge of the oxbow bend he paused, then plucked a bud from the nearest of Johnny Faye's babes and held it to his nose. Involuntarily he pulled back—the smell was that intense, the essence of some other reality. He dropped the bud and turned to tool up the steep bank, and there he saw the crude block letters J-O-H-N-N-Y F-A-Y-E and something fragile in him shattered into splinters and shards as surely as if dropped. He studied the letters, crude and tentative but legible. He took up a stick and drew a circle, surrounding and enclosing the name, Johnny Faye's name—a sign of something—a sign of love.

Flavian climbed the creek bank. Away from the crop, the still evening air brought him a different, cloying, manufactured odor that did not belong in these dry September woods. The smell grew stronger and Flavian stopped to sniff. Maybe Johnny Faye had sprayed more wolf piss? Although this smelled nothing like the wolf piss that he had used at the summer's beginning. Flavian recognized the smell from someplace—an old, familiar smell that in a different context he could have identified in an instant. But then the breeze picked up, the sheet lightning flickered, and Flavian passed through the cedar thicket.

Some measured moments after Flavian left, Officer Smith emerged from hiding.

Johnny Faye rode to the blind and sequestered 'Sweet in the bushes. No sign of the doctor's old Buick at the usual parking place. Why would it matter—how had he let the two of them, both of them, either of them come to matter so much? Why would these people who possessed the key to all mysteries—who could read and write—be interested in him except as a curiosity, a diversion, a toy? After all he had seen and done, nothing mattered or could matter, but he had allowed his heart to get careless, he had invited them in.

Pinned to the door of his blind, a note. He opened it and smoothed it flat and held it to the light of the moon, just shy of full and rising, to inspect its mystery. *The only writing that ever come my way brought nothing but bad news.* He tucked the note in his pocket. He waited in the blind, JC at his feet. The night forest was alive with cicadas and then it was not, the graveled path was dull white in the overcast moonlight and then it was in shadow. Johnny Faye lay on the floor of the blind and looked through the door into the balm of a late summer night.

Chapter 33

On this particular September day Brother José, impulsive as always, decided that the cow barn's infestation of rats demanded action and that firearms were superior to poison or traps, either of which might endanger Origen the cat. But José had never fired a gun and so he called in Flavian to execute the task. Flavian protested that the cows were scheduled to be shipped to slaughter in a few days and that they had no ammunition on hand and that once there was no feed and manure in the barn the rats would disappear on their own, but once José had decided on a course of action he was not to be dissuaded. Passive aggression being something of a monastic specialty, Flavian did not set out to buy ammunition until late afternoon, barely enough time to get to town and back for Vespers. And then as he was heading out the door, gabby old Brother Dismas buttonholed him to tell him the story of somebody telephoning the reception desk to ask for Brother Tom, Brother Thomas Aquinas to be exact, would those jokers never give it up, he thought he'd heard them all and then some guy comes along asking for a man who's been dead seven hundred years, who'd have thought anybody in these parts would even know the name?

Flavian was unnerved. The caller must be Johnny Faye—only he and the man they called Little had witnessed Flavian's little lie, and Flavian could imagine no circumstance under which

Little would call the monastery. But why would Johnny Faye tele-phone? Flavian shook the question from his head.

Now he found himself standing in line at the Saint Fran-cis Gun Depot with a box of .22 cartridges in one hand and a candy bar in the other—if he was to be saddled with such an unsa-vory mission he might as well get a little pleasure from the job. In front of him, a man in uniform—a state policeman. Butterflies in Flavian's stomach. Ever since his long-ago flight from the draft board, Flavian cringed in the presence of any gun-toting author-ity—the sight of a uniform was enough to bring a flush of guilt to his cheeks. And now he had given over a summer to helping a criminal grow pot and ended it by choosing desire over duty. He was nothing but a creature driven and derided by desire, unable to restrain his simplest wants—at this very moment he was longing to unwrap the candy bar and eat it on the spot. But someone was wearing aftershave lotion—the policeman, Flavian guessed. There were only three men in the store, and the cashier sported a thick, unkempt beard. The scent was both familiar and overwhelming. *So much for the candy bar,* Flavian thought sadly, which if he ate it standing anywhere near the policeman would only taste like Old Spice. Yes, Old Spice, that was it. Unmistakable.

And then Flavian, ever slow on the draw, put the smell together with where he'd so recently encountered it—yesterday evening on the bank of the oxbow bend.

Flavian stepped away from the cash register and busied him-self behind a magazine rack. *Guns & Ammo, Firearms and Hunt-ing.* Why, when, how had the policeman found the oxbow bend? In his head, the voice of reason: *Coincidence. Lots of men wear after-shave lotion.* In his heart, the little voice: *In God's universe there is no coincidence.*

The bearded cashier rang up the policeman's purchase. "I thought they supplied you guys with ammo."

"Give me a receipt and I'll get reimbursed. I got vermin to kill and the early bird gets the rat."

The cashier took his cash. "You hit a rat with one of these and all you're going to have left is a few whiskers and a bloody mess."

"The rat I'm after walks on his hind legs and has been a pain in the ass to the people of this county for forty years," the policeman said.

"Better buy two boxes." The cashier dropped the ammunition into a brown paper bag and gave it a little twist and handed it over. "You be careful, Smith. I hear a lot standing at this machine and what I hear these days is talk about trip wires and booby traps and what not. And you aint the only person in the county buying bullets for a .357."

Officer Smith laughed. "I'm not shaking in my boots. I got the enforcement officer's number one weapon, which is surprise," and then he was out the door and into his cruiser and Flavian was handing over the cash for his shotgun shells and candy bar, which he was still longing to eat but not in a cloud of human exhaust fumes. He took his shells and went out into the hot dusty late summer air and thought *here, surely here I can eat my candy bar.* Flavian unwrapped the candy but his first bite tasted of Old Spice and carbon monoxide. He tossed the candy into the trash.

Flavian climbed into the monastery minivan and started for home but the knot of unease grew, a poisonous tumor of dread and guilt. *Silly,* he thought. This was America, the law didn't just go out and hunt people down, but anyway if Officer Smith was on his way to arrest Johnny Faye—well, what was Flavian to do about that? *A pain in the ass to the people of this county for forty years.* Johnny Faye had broken the law and it was high time he learned the consequences, and it would get him out of Flavian's life for good and solve a lot of problems for everybody including himself, just as the policeman had said. *Render unto Caesar what is Caesar's* and what was about to be rendered unto Johnny Faye was a few years of cooling his heels in the penitentiary.

At the thought Flavian was instantly physically sick. He recalled the county attorney saying something to the abbot about mandatory twenty-year sentences but surely that was hot air, puffing and blowing for the sake of scaring people into submission. But this much must be said: a criminal would be put away. Flavian struck himself on the side of the head. He had given Johnny Faye proper warning, and it was one thing to stand by passively while someone grew a crop and another to interfere with the execution of the law. But there was that telephone call to Brother Tom, *Thomas Aquinas, to be exact.* Flavian's first lie, his original sin. Thank God Johnny Faye didn't know his proper name. Flavian struck his temple again. He drove through town. The word *vermin* replayed itself in his head. He drove past the Miracle Inn, past the doctor's cinderblock office, past Father Poppelreiter's church. By the time Flavian had reached the outskirts of town, his dread had grown into a certainty that something ugly was underway and that he had been intended to overhear the conversation in the ammo store so as to bring him face to face with his own weakness, the heart of his darkness. *The rat I'm after walks on his hind legs.* What if something was really afoot? What could he do about it? Nothing. Hide out in the enclosure. He had four-footed vermin to attend to.

And over all and under all was the knowledge that by any reasonable standard he was himself a criminal, and he was thinking not only about Johnny Faye's pot but about the vow he had made before his community and before God, that he had willfully broken.

—*Willfully?*

—*Yes, willfully. Why do you suppose you were so eager to get over there every Sunday? Why didn't you ever tell him your real name? You knew what you were up to from the beginning. And you sinned with your mouth, the very instrument of the Word. How can you even speak the name of Jesus with a mouth so befouled.*

—*But he is a man, a living, breathing soul, and—*

Flavian's chest tightened. He pulled to the side of the road and leaned his head on the wheel. He would not allow himself to put words to the voice in his heart. For some time he sat, uncounted minutes until he raised his head, made a U-turn, and headed back into town.

Flavian had only a dim idea of the structure of local government but he had met Harry Vetch and while Vetch had no reason to be well disposed toward Flavian all the same he was the desk at which the buck stopped—he had said exactly those words, sitting in the abbot's office with Flavian taking notes. He climbed the steps of the county attorney's office and summoned his nerve and pressed the doorbell. Somewhere deep in the house a gong sounded and after a moment the door swung back and there was Harry Vetch, looking slightly rumpled. Some perfunctory chat. Flavian was invited to seat himself in the big chair that faced the county attorney's desk. A pause. Flavian plunged in.

"I mean I know this sounds really crazy but um, you know this guy, a sort of a wild man, actually, Johnny Faye—"

Vetch turned to peer at a document on his computer screen. "Brother Flavian. If you are disturbing my quiet evening to bring me a message from Johnny Faye, I have to ask you to spare me the pleasure."

"No, this is not a message, no, sir. I should tell you though that he's been visiting the monastery and I took a liking to him because as it turns out he can't read or write, that's why he's always been such an outsider and so forth."

Vetch turned back to Flavian and rested his chin on his thumbs and concealed his mouth with his knitted fingers, the tips of his forefingers touching to form a steeple.

"So and I thought I might teach him enough reading skills that he could at least hold down a job, I mean, if he could read and write mailing labels, if he could manage even that much we could hire him on at the monastery. So I've been working with him and I realized, let's see, how to put this—well, I figured out that he was growing a crop of marijuana in the back acreage of the monastery and I was—I had gone there to his plot to see it for myself because

I was going to threaten to turn him in unless he plowed it under right away, you know, I remembered what you said about marijuana growers on monastery land and I have to say I didn't believe you then but I guess you were right."

"Of course I was right. Did you think I'd waste the abbot's time on a social call? Why didn't you come to me right away? Law enforcement is my job, not yours."

Flavian flushed with guilt. "I know, I guess I was just—I thought I'd give him one more chance, you know, warn him away. Like Jesus with the adulteress. Whoever has not sinned let him throw the first stone. And I thought if I could just teach him some basic literacy skills, you know, he could get a real job and get out of growing pot. He even wanted to do that at one point in his life, that's why he joined the army, he told me as much." Flavian paused for some sign of acquiescence with this simple truth. Harry Vetch was a blank slate. "Anyway, while I was at his plot, at least the plot that I think is his since I didn't see any sign of him so I'm making assumptions but I have a pretty good idea. Anyway. I have this really sensitive nose and while I was there I smelled this aftershave. Old Spice, you know the kind I mean. And it was a really strong smell, I'm very sure of it. And then today I went to the gun store to buy some shells because Brother José wants me to shoot the rats in the cow barn, doesn't matter that they'll all disappear as soon as we get rid of the cows, no, he had to have this done today, so I went to buy some shotgun shells and while I was in the store I stood behind the state policeman, you know, Officer Smith, and I was just overwhelmed by the smell of Old Spice. And you know he was, he is the father of the little boy who was beaten so savagely at the beginning of the summer. And standing in line I couldn't help but overhear Officer Smith bragging about buying bullets and about how he was going after two-legged vermin and you know that this is the kind of gun you only use for one reason, well, there's target practice, I guess, but it was pretty clear from what the officer was saying that he was intending to do some human target practice. And I know this sounds crazy but I just got this feeling—I thought I should come to you and let you know because I felt—I just had a bad feeling and I'm really afraid that Officer Smith is—well, you get what I'm trying to say."

The light was draining from the room.

"I mean, I know it's crazy but I figured better to do my duty and let you sort it out."

A growing weight of silence.

"Maybe you could telephone Officer Smith and just get some assurance as to where he is and what he's up to."

Vetch swiveled his chair so that he was looking out the French doors to a view of the garden, where yellow and lavender chrysanthemums were coming into their own. The yard was intensely green in the dying late summer evening light. A few scarlet leaves drifted down from a dogwood planted at its center. "And what are you proposing that I do in response to this, I have to say it, cock-and-bull story?"

"Well, gee. I don't know. I figured you'd know the answer to that. Check in with Officer Smith, I guess."

Vetch turned back around. "Brother Flavian. Your story is riddled with holes through which I could drive a Mack truck."

"Well, yes, I can see that but—"

"All the same I'm ultimately in charge of enforcing the law in this county and you're correct in assuming that it's my duty to respond to concerns and complaints of its citizens. No matter how crackpot."

"Well. Crackpot."

"*Crackpot.* I might begin by inquiring why you feel so responsible to your duty at this particular moment when by your own admission and evidently for some time you have been abetting a drug dealer and a lawbreaker. Respect for your position enables me to set aside that question but just barely and only for the moment. Now. I can pick up the phone and call the dispatcher and have him locate those officers in this county. You're correct—I can do that and I have sufficient respect for your judgment and your position as a man of the church that I would do that for you.

"But let's suppose your story is true. Let's suppose Officer Smith is on his way to arrest a man whom you yourself have acknowledged is engaged in criminal activity. Isn't this his job? And if violence should ensue—well, violence begets violence, and I submit to you that those who willfully break the law are guilty of committing the first act of violence, whether or not they are using a weapon, and that the law is entirely justified in responding in kind. It would be highly inappropriate for me to interfere with an officer who is enforcing the law. Even more inappropriate to interfere on the basis of a rumor. Unless I knew the officer to be in violation of the law. But that's no more than the responsibility of any citizen."

"Such as me."

"Well, yes, I guess you could say that."

"So you're leaving any action up to me."

"I don't believe any action is warranted. If I felt otherwise then I'd act."

"Well, then, would it be OK for me to use your telephone to call the dispatcher?"

a silence in which the darkness of the universe distilled itself into this moment, here and now in this ornately furnished room looking out onto a view of a garden where chrysanthemums were coming into their own

"Mr. Vetch."

Vetch stood and turned his back and spoke with a low tense fury. "Brother Flavian. I would ask that you have some sense except that you have no sense. I guess that's why you became a monk. Of course you can use my phone, but what are you going to say to the dispatcher? Some crackpot story involving aftershave lotion and a conversation overheard at the gun store?"

"I'd just like to register my suspicions with someone who may or may not sympathize but at least they'll be on the record."

At the phrase "on the record" the county attorney sat and

swiveled to face the garden. After a moment he swiveled back, a soundless semicircle. He rested his hands on the glass top of his desk. His face was a mask. The space between them hardened into something tangible, a wall.

"Brother Flavian. Allow me to explain some nuances of the law of which I'm sure you're aware but you will allow me to refresh your memory. For all I know you have been an innocent and well-intentioned bystander, used as a foil in a way common among hardened criminals, but intentions count for very little in my book, especially when I know you to be aware of the consequences of your decisions since I personally educated you along these lines. I must say that only a few years back I'd have found your actions incredible but this job has taught me that very little on God's earth is truly incredible. You may pick up that phone and call the dispatcher, yes. But I should make clear that I don't share your tender heart for drug runners and that I'll interpret any effort on your part at what I consider to be interference with the law to be another fact in a mounting pile of evidence that incriminates you in this matter." He lifted his hands from his desk—a slight sucking sound broke the silence. He folded them as if in prayer. "I recall to you our first meeting. At that point I indicated very clearly that if marijuana was found growing on monastery property, I would prosecute to the fullest extent of the law. I recall to you, you may check your *notes*, you are a good note taker, yes?—that I offered to provide the abbey with personnel to search its acreage. No one followed up on my offer.

"Now you sit in my office in a strikingly analogous situation. You may cooperate with the law or you may be an obstacle to its enforcement. I'm offering you a choice. You are aware of your complicity and by extension that of the abbot and abbey in a felony, with all the consequences such a decision entails—confiscation of property, prison sentences, public disgrace, financial ruin. If you'd like to contact the dispatcher by all means do so but know that your doing so will—*complicate*, is a good word, I think—my efforts to help extricate you, your abbot, and your community from a difficult situation of your choice and making. I believe I've made your alternatives clear but I'm happy to entertain questions."

Flavian wanted to stop time, to have some time, make some time, he needed more time but if what he suspected was correct he had no time, there was no time.

The silence deepened to darkness. What was this mass that pressed on his heart? *When it comes right down to it I'm better at hard and sharp than I am at soft and round.* Flavian could not breathe. How was it possible that he, a healthy man, could not will himself to breathe? He contracted his chest but the air stopped somewhere in his throat. The telephone sat between them. The clock chimed the half-hour. All time passed and no time passed.

The phone rang. Vetch took it up and turned away from Flavian. "I see," he said into the mouthpiece. A pause. "That is not true," the county attorney said. "I never authorized—" He swiveled in his chair and glanced at Flavian, then covered the mouthpiece with one hand and waved at Flavian with the other. "Excuse me. I need to take this call in private. Please. The front room. Close the door."

Alone in the front room. From behind the door the murmur of Harry Vetch's voice. A fly buzzed Flavian's ear. He struck at it savagely and there it was, smashed in his palm.

Vetch appeared in the doorway. "I think, Brother, that it's always right to side with the law. This is after all the teaching of our church, yours and mine. After many centuries we may discover that, for example, the earth is not at the center of the universe. But she is our Mother Church and our first duty is loyalty to her judgment, leaving to history the workings out of right and wrong.

"As it turns out there's been an incident involving the use of force to subdue a suspect who resisted. I'm not free to divulge more details but I have to let you go. As I'm sure you can understand, I have business to attend to."

Flavian half-rose from his seat, then sank back. The county

attorney wanted him to leave but once he left where was he to go? The phone rang again. Vetch took up the waiting room extension. A form greeting, then a low but audible "Shit." Vetch pushed a button and replaced the phone and turned back to Flavian. "My patience has run out. I have important matters that must be arranged in confidence. I thank you for your concern. I'll inform you if you may be of service. Now you have to go."

Flavian spread his hands. "I want justice."

The county attorney rolled his eyes. "You come to me speaking of justice when what I have to offer is the law. Allow me to realign your thinking. Now and always the question to ask is not, *What is just?* The question to ask is, *Who has power?* Now leave. That is a command, not a request."

Flavian rose on unsteady legs, searching for something to say—stalling, he knew it, because once outside the door he would be alone with the magnitude of whatever it was that he had done or not done . . . and then he could stall no longer, he was outside, the door shut behind him, he was alone.

In the basement of the funeral parlor, the body. The coroner out of town. In his absence, the only local person empowered to sign the death certificate: Dr. Chatterjee, summoned by Harry Vetch and presented with paperwork.

"I cannot do this. I must—summon the proper authorities."

"I am the proper authority."

The body lay face down on a stainless steel gurney, covered with a bloody sheet. The room held no air.

"I will need to examine the body."

"You don't have to examine the body. You can take my word for the events as described as well as the word of Officer Smith who was present at the scene. The coroner would, if he were in town. I wish that he were here. I am sure you wish the same. But he is not here and the responsibility falls to you."

"But I am not the coroner and I must examine the body."

A long moment. Vetch closed his eyes and pinched his thin lips together. No one spoke. Finally he opened his eyes and nodded.

Officer Smith pulled back the sheet. Johnny Faye's shirt had been cut away. The broad mottled shoulders and the skinny waist. The undertaker had wiped the blood from his back—two dark clotted gaping wounds. "You see? Enough."

"I will need not merely to look at but to examine the body, starting from the front. Please turn him over."

"I'm sorry, Dr. Chatterjee, but those bullets do a lot of damage along the way and he was shot at close range. The mortician hasn't had the time—he was waiting until we arrived. Now we're here, you've seen what you need to see, let him finish his job."

"Shot at close range while attempting to flee."

"Yes, ma'am." This from Officer Smith.

"I would like to examine him from the front."

"Doctor Chatterjee." Vetch passed a hand over his thinning hair. "Officer Smith may have acted without authorization—"

"Excuse me, sir, but you said—"

"—without authorization but he was well within the bounds of appropriate response. We need only your signature."

"Mr. Vetch. As you are surely aware, professionalism assuages a guilty conscience. One may find solace in the knowledge of a bad business thoroughly done. I have no desire to compound evil with cowardice."

"I will have none of that kind of talk here," Vetch said, but before he could interfere she stepped to the gurney and lifted Johnny Faye's dead weight. "Hold on," Vetch said, "you can't do that—" Meena leaned in with all her strength but the body was falling back and then Brother Flavian was at her side. He stepped in and placed his hands under Johnny Faye's body and helped her turn him over. Johnny Faye's chest presented two small bloodied holes. Their hands were covered in his blood.

"Brother Flavian. Leave immediately or Officer Smith will remove you by force."

"Officer Smith. It is your contention that Mr. Johnny Faye fell on his gun? Shot himself in the chest, perhaps, while running away?"

"Bullets act in unpredictable and confusing ways," Vetch said.

"A confusion an autopsy would resolve."

"How could you know that crop was his?" Flavian cried. "How could you justify murder?"

"He made it easy," Smith said. "He wrote his name in the mud. Like advertising. We got pictures but if you don't believe me, go see for yourself. It's still there."

"Officer Smith. Enough. You're not on trial. Keep your mouth shut." Vetch turned to the doctor. "The law allows me to bypass an inquest in circumstances where I feel none is warranted. We have before us such circumstances. A chronic lawbreaker caught in the act of committing a felony tries to escape. An officer who's done his best to resolve the situation is forced to resort to violence. The result is regrettable—I regret it—but that doesn't absolve Mr. Faye of his crime nor render Officer Smith's response anything but appropriate." Vetch produced and unfolded a piece of paper, which he displayed to Meena. "This note was found in the pocket of the deceased. A very interesting note and, if I'm not mistaken, under your signature." He refolded the note and replaced it in his pocket. He held out a file folder and a pen. "Given that you spread your signature so easily about, you can surely sign once more. That's all we require for all of us to go home except the mortician who can then get about his work. With the signed death certificate in hand I may forget Brother Flavian's explicitly illegal complicity in felony drug trafficking as well as the curious fact of a note under your signature in the possession of a drug dealer. Lacking your signature, all of our lives become much more complicated. Yours, Dr. Chatterjee, most complicated of all, if I am to believe what I hear from Miss Shaklett and I am given to believing what I hear from Miss Shaklett. She is, as you know, eminently reliable."

Flavian reached out, then dropped his hand. He spoke in a

low voice. "Dr. Chatterjee. Meena. You don't have to do this. This is America. You have choices."

The doctor bent to the bloody corpse, to be brought up short by the strangest of sensations, so unfamiliar that she paused and straightened. She looked down to find her hand on her stomach. Before she could name the feeling it was gone, leaving behind not absence but presence and in that presence she understood: a stirring in her womb. Impossible this early, she knew that, but all the same there it was. The little voice. *I am.*

Every day of Meena's childhood, a street vendor brought coconuts to her parents' house. He had survived a childhood famine with his arms and legs grotesquely deformed but he lived in her memory not mangled and broken but as the peddler who set aside his smallest coconut for her, small enough that she could hold it in her little girl's hands. He split the coconut with one chop of his machete and offered it to her with a straw. *With time I hope you may forgive.* But there was to be no time. What is time? Creator and Destroyer. She turned back to the body. Those bullet holes— the two small holes in front turning to gaping holes in back, then the single small hole in the back. She had chosen well. She had no choice. He is dead. She is alive. Their child is alive. She took up the papers and signed.

Flavian was inside his head and then he was outside his head. He had been outside the funeral home and then he was inside it. He saw the bloody corpse. He looked away. He looked back. He looked, he made himself open his eyes and see. He saw the doctor struggling with the body. He crossed the room to her side. Together they turned it over.

this was, how much, how long?

And the dog—where was the dog? What happened to the dog? *Where he goes I go and vice-a versa.* "What did you do with JC?" Flavian was shouting in Officer Smith's face. "What did you do with the *dog?*"

"I advise you not to answer that question."

"I didn't see any dog."

"I don't believe you."

Officer Smith shrugged. "If that's what you need to think."

Where was JC? Flavian would find JC. He would find JC and they would go live with the cows that were on their ways to slaughter. Somehow he would pray his way into the place where the cows lived all the time, the place where they knew death as surely as they knew the cycling of day and night and they paid it no attention. Somehow he would forget that he was mortal man.

Shotgun wore a mask and Little drove and where the road turned right to go to town Little turned left toward the monastery, and though Johnny Faye knew what was coming down, that was when the fact rose from his gut to his gorge and he started to sweat.

And so what did the man think about as the law was taking him to his death? *A death he had freely chosen.* Johnny Faye's mind went to the cloven hills, to his peacemaking place and below it the field, at least that was what he and anybody he had ever known except Brother Flavian would have called it, and probably it was just a plain old field. Flavian might have called it a *meadow* but the fact is that the creek running along one side had eroded its banks, exposing raw red clay, and the soil, though as good as it got in this part of the world, was stony and thin and gave forth equal parts of hay and thistles. But above the field a cleft between two rounded forested knobs held a clear-running spring where birds and deer went to drink, and each year between those two hills on one particular summer evening the full moon rose. Mist rose from the creek and hung above thistle and hay, thrush and doe and the mist was shot through with lightning bugs like starlight through angel hair and above the mist the clear mild light, soft as a lover's hand and the hills dark breasts against the moonlit night. Johnny Faye thought of his longing to be anywhere else but here in the back seat of this police car, about to go to his rest in the place where history had put him. For a man from Kentucky home is no other place. He had seen many men die and he was a singing bundle of fear. He thought of Meena, draping the sky around her earth-dark body only then to come walking through the fields to him, for him, for them. He thought of Flavian, what kind of big-worded answer he would give to these questions and how much he, Johnny Faye, loved his big words and mind and heart and clumsy hands. He thought of Rosalee, loyal to her duty, loyal to the law. He thought of Matthew Mark. He was muttering something over and over. "Jesus, Mary, Joseph," until Little who was driving said without turning around, "Shut the fuck up," and Shotgun who was wearing a ski mask said, "Let him talk."

Then Shotgun undid his seatbelt and turned around. He shoved his gun under Johnny Faye's nose and naturally that was the first thing he noticed but just about as fast he smelled his aftershave, volatilized by fear and anger.

"You don't have to do this," Johnny Faye said. He kept talking. He kept talking. He kept talking and the words were a balm on the wound, the ever-blossoming snakebite knowledge that Smith was surely a lousy shot and that it would not be a clean deal. What could he do? What can I do? What could he say? "Jesus, Mary, Joseph." You will know what to do when the time comes. You will know what to say when the gun speaks. That was his gift. He'd been practicing all his life.

The car stopped at the gravel road that led into the monastery fields.

"Walk. Keep your back to us. You run, you're dead."

And so they walked a mile and more into the deepening September dusk, a serenade of screech owls, great horned owls, barred owls, chuck-will's widows and whippoorwills, until they reached the cedar copse where the trees parted like the sea before Moses' staff and Johnny Faye appreciated their kindness. Then they were at the bluff above the creek and then they were down among his babes, his marijuana plants, and the full moon shining on his name circled with an unbroken circle, the circle only Flavian could have drawn because only Flavian knew of this time and place.

Johnny Faye took this in. He turned to face his captors head-on.

"Turn around." The man in the mask talking. "I want to see your back—"

Johnny Faye smiled and clasped his hands not in supplication but in prayer—

"—turn around, you motherfucking son of a bitch, I said *turn around.*"

The masked policeman and Little were silhouettes, shadow puppets against the disk of the rising moon, one big shining piece of gold. *Shine on, shine on harvest moon, up in the sky, I aint had no lovin' since January, February, June or July.* "You must not be getting any, Smith."

"What the hell does that mean."

"When I was a kid I said 'fuck' all the time. Fuck this. Fuck that. Motherfucking son of a bitch."

Johnny Faye knew he should *shut the fuck up* but he couldn't help himself, he was soon to be dead and he might as well give them a story to tell, something to remember him by.

"And then I got older and I knew what I was talking about, you know, I'd done the deed enough that I stopped treating it so common. These days when I hear a guy that says *fuckin' this, fuckin' that,* you know what I think? I think he must not be getting any. Because anybody who's getting any pretty soon figures out some respect for the word, because there's nothing to make you humble like your dick."

Smith fired quick, *one, two.* Johnny Faye looked down at his chest where a red rose of blood blossomed, all the promise of summer in its petals. He raised his hands higher. "Why did you have to do that?" he said, and with blood pouring from his mouth, he fell to the ground.

Johnny Faye has some few seconds before Smith walks to his fallen self and turns him over—Johnny Faye is skinny but broad-shouldered and at first the policeman tries to accomplish this using only his foot but that fails and so he bends and takes Johnny Faye's bloody shirt in both hands and flips him so that his face is pressed to his mother earth and then shoots him in the back and that completes the journey, Johnny Faye crosses over. In those few moments of transition between here and there the world is white hot pain and Johnny Faye's only and all-encompassing thought is *This aint happening. This aint happening to me.*

But there is a place above and beyond and behind and before thought and this is some part of what lives there: He is looking up at the night stars and he returns to the wide porch with the ladder-back chairs and the cane woven seats that look across the chattering creek to the low rounded breasts of the knobs, springtime and they are dusted with pink and white and unfurling green, redbud and dogwood, he is sitting with his mother and she is smoking her pipe and humming a tune known to him from before time, and on the thin hum of her voice and the sweet smoke come the faces and voices and bodies of all the women and men he has known in the intimate way. He has loved every one of them. He regrets only those he let slip away or those whom he refused, almost always because of a failure of courage or his own stupid arrogance, how dumb, what a mistake. The lovely breasts of the women in all their variety, some round and full in the hand like melons, others small and sweet like peaches. And the men with the beautiful shallow "S" that runs from under the nipple into the biceps of the raised arm and their heady rich smell. He is supremely happy at the memory of himself in their arms, of them in his arms, witnesses in a great cloud around him. There had been nothing on earth worth doing but searching for love and allowing it to have its way. The secrets of the cave. The forthrightness of the pillar. In death he loves them all.

Afterword

Those familiar with central Kentucky may recognize in this book certain features of its geography, history, and culture, but these characters and their stories are fabrications of my imagination. This is a work of fiction inspired by real-life events, researched in the course of writing a feature-length article for the *New York Times Magazine* ("High in the Hollows," December 17, 1989).

On September 9, 1971, the Kentucky State Police staked out a cornfield in Spencer County, Kentucky, where they killed a renegade storyteller and petty criminal named Charlie Stiles. Detective Marion Campbell, who shot Stiles, was later promoted to become a Kentucky State Police Commissioner. In 1986 Campbell was suspended with pay pending an internal investigation resulting from his indictment in federal court for his role in cocaine smuggling.

The press release reproduced on pages 224–225 describing the "Cornbread Mafia" was issued by the Western Kentucky office of the District Attorney of the United States Department of Justice on June 16, 1989. As of this writing several of the men who were convicted of growing marijuana and whose farms were confiscated remain in federal prison, serving mandatory sentences without possibility of parole.

In composing the speeches of County Attorney Harry Vetch I have borrowed phrases from the speeches of President Ronald

Reagan, Vice President Richard Cheney, and President George W.
Bush.

Song lyrics are drawn from the following sources:

"Shine On, Harvest Moon," 1908, Jack Norworth and
    Nora Bayes
"Slumber, My Darling," 1838[?], words and lyrics by
    Stephen Foster

Acknowledgments

The following individuals have lent their intelligence and support to the writing of this novel. Most of what is good I owe to them; the faults I claim as my own.

Dr. June McDaniel, Dr. Gerry Forbes, Bharati Mukherjee, Clark Blaise, Dr. Darril Hudson, Sandip Roy, my kind and endlessly hospitable hosts in Calcutta (especially Manas Ray, Sharmila Ray, Tanusree Shankar & Company, Tapas Mondal, Somnath Banerjee Bandhopadhayay), Dr. David Heiden, Margaret Jenkins, Molly Sutphen, Haney Armstrong, Shirley Abbott, Alfred McCartney, O.C.S.O., John Brennan, Cathy Cravens Snell, Pam Houston, Katherine Seligman, Shirley Abbott, the courageous and remarkable J.K.Vickers, diva in exile, Dr. Sanjukta Dasgupta, Dr. Krishna Sen, Dr. Aparna Viswas, Nabaneeta Dev Sen, Dr. Richard Eaton, Dr. Rajarshi Dutta, Dr. Swati Dutta, Dr. Anjanlal Dutta. Pawan Dhall, my friends at Swikriti, Calcutta's brave LGBT rights organization, and Rae Douglass.

A special thanks to the Camargo Foundation and its staff, especially Jean-Pierre and Mary Dautricourt, who provided me four months for writing and research overlooking the serene Mediterranean. The Creative Writing Program at the University of Arizona has been generous and forgiving in allowing me several leaves without pay.

Acknowledgments

A fellowship from the John Simon Guggenheim Foundation supported my final revision.

English-to-Bengali translations were provided by Ms. Supurna Datta, Dr. Shompaballi Datta, and Ms. Shantanu Das, former Bengali lecturer, Stanford University Language Center.

A special bow to the staff of the University Press of Kentucky, most especially my editor, Ashley Runyon, and my copyeditors, Julie Wrinn and David Cobb.

Kentucky Voices

Miss America Kissed Caleb: Stories
Billy C. Clark

New Covenant Bound
T. Crunk

Next Door to the Dead: Poems
Kathleen Driskell

The Total Light Process: New and Selected Poems
James Baker Hall

Driving with the Dead: Poems
Jane Hicks

Upheaval: Stories
Chris Holbrook

Appalachian Elegy: Poetry and Place
bell hooks

Crossing the River: A Novel
Fenton Johnson

The Man Who Loved Birds: A Novel
Fenton Johnson

Scissors, Paper, Rock: A Novel
Fenton Johnson

Many-Storied House: Poems
George Ella Lyon

With a Hammer for My Heart: A Novel
George Ella Lyon

Famous People I Have Known
Ed McClanahan

The Land We Dreamed: Poems
Joe Survant

Sue Mundy: A Novel of the Civil War
Richard Taylor

At The Breakers: A Novel
Mary Ann Taylor-Hall

Come and Go, Molly Snow: A Novel
Mary Ann Taylor-Hall

Nothing Like an Ocean: Stories
Jim Tomlinson

Buffalo Dance: The Journey of York
Frank X Walker

When Winter Come: The Ascension of York
Frank X Walker

The Cave
Robert Penn Warren

The Birds of Opulence
Crystal Wilkinson